Within the Hollow Hills

In memory of John James for the insight and wisdom that he shared with so many.

Within the Hollow Hills

An anthology of new Celtic writing

Selected and introduced
by John Matthews

With a foreword
by George Mackay Brown

Floris Books

First published in 1994 by Floris Books.

British Library CIP data available.

ISBN 0-86315-525-1

Printed in Great Britain
by Biddles Ltd, Guildford

Contents

Acknowledgments

Whilst every effort has been made to trace the copyright holders of certain texts, this has not always proved successful. Any omissions will be corrected in future editions, wherever possible.

I cannot go hunting tomorrow, by Henry Treece, originally published in *I Cannot Go Hunting Tomorrow,* Gray Walls Press, 1946.

Flowering Dagger, by Rosemary Sutcliff, from *The Real Thing,* ed. Peggy Woodford, Bodley Head, 1977, by kind permission of Murray Pollinger and Anthony Lawton for the Estate of Rosemary Sutcliff.

The Dark Tower, by Peter Vansittart, from *The Dark Tower: Tales from the Past,* Macdonald, 1965, by permission of Sheil Land Assocs.

The Story of Kigva, by Sian Hayton, from *Hidden Daughters,* Polygon, Edinburgh 1992, by permission of Edinburgh University Press.

Lapis ex Caelis, by Anne Cameron, originally published in *Tales of the Cairds,* Harbour Publishing, British Columbia, 1989.

The Music from behind the Moon, by J.B. Cabell, originally published in *The Witch Woman,* Farrar, Strauss & Giroux, 1948.

The Three Gwenhwyfars: A story about Guinevere, by Caitlín Matthews, first published in this volume.

Five Denials on Merlin's Grave, by Robin Williamson, originally published in *Five Denials on Merlin's Grave,* Pig's Whisker Music, Los Angeles 1979.

Within the Brugh, by John Matthews, first published in this volume.

An Adventure of the Grail, by David Spangler, first published in this volume.

My Lady of Hy-Brasil, by Peter Tremayne, from *My Lady of Hy-Brasil & Other Stories,* Donald M. Grant, Rhode Island 1987, by permission of A.M. Heath.

Finvarra, by Ann Moray, from *A Fair Stream of Silver,* Longmans, Green & Co., 1966, by permission of Lawrence Pollinger.

The Cold Well, by Margaret Elphinstone, from *An Apple from a Tree,* 1991, by permission of The Women's Press, Ltd., London.

Charliwill, a cautionary faery tale, by R J Stewart, first published in this volume.

The Rainslug and *The Waterhorse,* two stories by Dwina Murphy-Gibb, first published in this volume.

On Macha's Mound, by Diana Paxson, first published in this volume.

Foreword

There is more to a story than a narrative, with dialogue, about a group of people: though that is the kind of story that makes a "best-seller" or that can be adapted for television.

This is the kind of story that has been in vogue for the past century. Lately it has gotten so boring that liberal doses of sex and sadism have had to be added to the bland mixture.

I think the prose story, at its best, yearns towards the condition of the folk-tale or the border-ballads, where there is fuller ampler air to breathe, and there is mystery in everything, and people are seen in the double aspect of time and eternity, and destiny and freedom contend in every soul.

Any competent hack can write a story to fill a few pages in a magazine, or a fifteen minute radio slot (though there is always a remote chance that a good story might emerge from the ruck).

But a story to hold children from their play, and to enchant old men in the chimney corner: it is always invested with mystery, and with the certitude that there is more to life than the here and now, getting and spending, a dreary trek from the cradle to the grave.

The good story is always touched with wonder and delight. It makes us aware of ourselves as (in Wordsworth's phrase) "living souls."

George MacKay Brown

Introduction
The Lordly Ones

The beginning was so long ago
That it can join with tomorrow
Through an endless ring of seasons ...
(from *Taliesin Sees* by John Fairfax)

In 1992 I worked on a collection entitled *From the Isles of Dream* (Floris Books, 1993) which set out to chronicle what has been termed "The Celtic Revival" through the writings produced by such writers as W.B. Yeats, Fiona Macleod and George Russell (AE). Much of this writing was published in the nineteenth century, and reflects a certain dream-like quality germane to the writers concerned and their avowed endeavour to "re-create" something of the forgotten glory of the Celtic past.

After I had finished work on the collection I felt that it was a pity to stop there. The flames of Celtic vision did not end with these writers. It continued in the works of Arthur Machen, James Branch Cabell and John Cowper Powys, and it lives on today in the work of contemporary authors like Robin Williamson, Anne Cameron, and Rosemary Sutcliff.

I was therefore particularly delighted to be asked to assemble a further collection, bringing the story of Celtic visionary literature up to date, and to commission several new stories which appear here for the first time.

Each of the writers whose work is represented here is, in one way or another, an inheritor of the Celtic Revival. Though some of them might disagree with this statement all, I believe, would agree that they are part of the spirit of Celtic visionary writing.

But how has the Celtic vision changed? Or has it changed at all? Ultimately, I think not. There is, to be sure, a far greater awareness of the values of the outer world, though this is often perceived with a sardonic understanding of the loss we have succumbed to in severing many of the ties of tradition, which once gave us all a much closer communion with the past. This is perhaps best illustrated in R.J. Stewart's "Charliwill," an innocent seeming tale which shows what happens when the values of modern consumerism infect the realm of Faery.

The varying directions taken by this group of modern authors is reflected in the organization of the book. Thus Part One "The Darkening Vision" reflects the tougher, less romantic view of its authors, while Part Two "The Tangled Dream" looks both backward to the tangled woods and dark mounds of the past and forward to the brightening promise of a new time — a time most fully reflected in the third part "The Opening Door" which points to a re-establishing of ancient ties between this world and the other, and to a closer awareness of the needs and wishes of human and faery.

It seems appropriate to begin with a story by Henry Treece, a key literary bridge figure between the more romantic writers of the Thirties and Forties and the harder, more gritty style favoured by many contemporary inheritors of the Celtic visionary spirit.

"I Cannot Go Hunting Tomorrow" is from Treece's only collection of stories, published in 1946. It is an early work, written when its author was only thirty-five, but already it displays all the fire and insight into the minds and souls of the ancient people of Britain which was to illuminate his mature fiction in works such as *The Great Captains* (1956), *The Golden Strangers* (1956), and his electrifying trilogy set in the myth-haunted world of Ancient Greece, comprising *Jason* (1961), *Electra* (1963) and *Oedipus* (1964). We can see embodied in this work the trend which was to carry the Celtic vision firmly into the twentieth century. The sometimes vague, always lyrical prose of MacLeod and Yeats, gives way to a sparer, more sinewy style. There is more violence and a greater perception of character.

Thus in Rosemary Sutcliff's moving love-story the players are far more "real" than, say the druid girl and her lover in Edward

Burne-Jones' story "The Druid and the Maiden" included in *From the Isles of Dream;* nor is the outcome predictable. Darkness and light are mingled in equal measure throughout these tales.

There is certainly no lessening of the visionary power of their forebears among these more modern writers, though one sometimes has to look further to find them. One of the richest fields for the mining of this kind of story is children's literature, and it was there I found the story by Peter Vansittart.

Vansittart is one of the finest living prose stylists, with a number of adult novels to his credit. Most of these could be labelled as "historical," but are in fact much more than this. The trilogy of *Lancelot* (1978), *The Death of Robin Hood* (1981) and *Parsifal* (1988) are among the most subtle studies of the heroic archetype ever written. The story included here, "The Dark Tower," which comes from a collection of the same name, was written for children and is a re-telling of a British folk-tale immortalized by the Victorian poet Robert Browning in his "Childe Roland to the Dark Tower Came." Vansittart, in re-telling it, has added references from the whole of folklore and legendary, making it part of that vast inner world with a few deft strokes. Here, as in many other writings specifically targeted at the younger reader, there is a kind of innocence and freshness which is very much a part of the Celtic vision. One might even go as far as to say that one has to recover something of this sense of wonder to truly appreciate many of the works published here and in the companion volume. Without this we will hopefully enjoy, but it will be an enjoyment less fully tempered than it might, without a true perception of the magic and wonder at the heart of these "youthful" tales.

Peter Vansittart's tightly-woven version of the old folk-tale captures all the laconic understatement of the old Bardic tales, while the extraordinary poem by Robin Williamson, "The Five Denials on Merlin's Grave," bears witness to the strength of his personal commitment to the way of the Bard. As a performer of many years standing, initially with the Sixties rock-group, The Incredible String Band, and more recently with his own group and as a solo artist, Williamson has chosen to follow this path with single-minded dedication. To be present at one of his performances is to step back in time to the age of the Celts, to enter a land where the Lordly Ones, the ancient gods and goddesses, and the ancestral spirits of these islands, still hold sway.

It is thus that the memory of the ancient wisdom and knowledge has lived on in the works of the Celtic revival, and those who, like the writers featured here, have pledged themselves to keep that past alive. Thus, in stories such as "Finvarra" by Ann Moray, one of a collection of tales published as *A Fair Stream of Silver* (1966), we see pictured the bright colours and darkly passionate desires of real human beings (though touched by Faery), while David Spangler's wonderful Grail story shows just how close and real and even ordinary the mystical can be, and how the actions of an innocent youth can bring about changes in the world which have far reaching consequences.

Other writers, such as the late John James, whose untimely death prevented him from contributing to the present collection, bear witness to an age that many would dismiss as having little to say to us today. James' quartet of books, *Votan* (1966), *Not For All the Gold in Ireland* (1968), *Men Went to Cattraeth* (1969) and *Bridge of Sand* (1976) recapture the ancient world in all its myth-haunted power, and show it to have been inhabited by very real people.

It is the age-old values of these people — heroism, comradeship, devotion to the tribe, unconditional love — which permeate many of the works presented here, from Caitlín Matthews' powerful new telling of the story of Arthur's Queen in "The Three Gwenhwyfars," to Sian Hayton's deeply felt rendition of the story of Kigva, originally found within the pages of the *Mabinogion,* the premier collection of Welsh myth-tales. This story comes from the second of Hayton's trilogy of Celtic novels *Cells of Knowledge* (1989), *Hidden Daughters* (1992) and *The Last Flight* (1994) which evoke the complex world of a tribal people brought into contact with Christianity. The characters of her books inhabit a vanished world, as do the characters evoked by Dwina Murphy-Gibb in her linked stories of an Ireland virtually gone forever.

These tales, "The Rainslug" and "The Waterhorse" both grew out of stories told at the fire-side and remembered from childhood. They are, like the stories collected and told by W.B. Yeats, the very stuff of that vision which is a part of Ireland. These two gentle tales, captured with all the subtle nuances of a happily remembered world, appear here as a reminder of a past very far from dead, and still growing.

The Celts have always been a people whose past reaches out to their present. One has only to read Diana Paxson's extraordinary new story to understand this. The battles of the troubled land of Ireland are still those of tribal, rather than sectarian factions. "In Macha's Mound" shows that a contemporary political situation can lend itself to a powerful visionary awareness of the debt owed to the past. But these are qualities of perception to be found in virtually all of this author's work to date, especially in *The White Raven* (1988) a retelling of the story of Tristan and Isolt, which is one of the best evocations of the ancient Celtic world I have ever read.

In "Lapis ex Caelis" by the Canadian writer Anne Cameron, an ancient account of the origins of the Celtic peoples is made the foundation of a darkly satirical, moving tale, extending through all of time to the present, of the attempt to subdue those who would speak the truth about human dealing with creation, who tell stories destined to subvert the serious, deadly world of those who seek to organize everyone into submission. But the voices of those who sing songs of creation, and the glory of manhood and womanhood and the nature of animals, birds and fish, will be heard; and the past is present in the future as the quotation by the poet John Fairfax, which preceded this introduction, so aptly puts it:

> The beginning was so long ago
> That it can join with tomorrow.

We cannot ignore or forget, either, the subtle tug of satirical humour which runs like a silver thread through some of the darkest of these tales. This too has power, as we see both in

Anne Cameron's story and in Margaret Elphinstone's "The Cold Well" in which we learn that the old folk of the Otherworld are still close at hand, close enough to be called upon, and that they suffer every bit as much as the other wild things we hurt in our rush to possess the resources of the natural world. In this tale, joy and tears are but a breath away from each other, perils of accepting the gifts of the Otherworld without due care and forethought.

Again, in James Branch Cabell's "The Music From Behind the Moon," and in the stories by Caitlín Matthews, David Spangler and R.J. Stewart, we see how the interaction of the mundane world with that of the inner universe of gods, elves and faeries, can be painful to both sides. My own linked stories "Within the Brugh" are about the experience of moving inward to meet the gods, and about the beginnings of the gods themselves.

In essence then, these tales continue the direction begun by the nineteenth century writers of the Celtic Revival, looking back to the roots of Celtic tradition and forward to our own time, when that tradition is becoming more and more widely acknowledged. The love of life and the awareness of other realities, just beneath the surface, are just as much a part of these modern visionary tales as the old myth-lore of the *Mabinogion,* or the cycle of Cuchulainn, or for that matter the stories of Fiona Macleod and John Cowper Powys.

The contemporary fascination with fantasy literature which began with the writings of William Morris in his *Well at the World's End* (1888) and E.R. Eddison in his *Zimiavia* books (1935-58), and continued triumphantly in those of George Macdonald, J.R.R. Tolkien and C.S. Lewis, has itself given rise to a number of remarkable "Celtic" fantasies. Stephen Lawhead's trilogy of novels "The Song of Albion"— *The Paradise War, The Silver Hand, The Endless Knot* (1989-93) — takes us deeply into the otherworld; while in the writings of John Crowley, whose *Little, Big* (1981) is perhaps the best modern account of the Faery realm ever written, or in the fast paced "urban faery tales" of the Canadian writer, Charles de Lint — *Moonheart* (1989), *Greenmantle* (1989) — we can see the ancient themes given a new form.

The same urges drive the writers represented here as drove their fellows in the previous seventy years. There may no longer be a "revivalist" movement — if, indeed, there ever was — but these underlying themes and beliefs still bind them into a loose-knit confederacy, a shared background and a shared set of beliefs which, though manifesting in a number of widely different styles and approaches, nonetheless reflect the same age-old verities as those of MacLeod, AE and Yeats.

As with the previous volume, it has been an often moving and enlightening experience to work with the writers featured here. I am especially grateful to those who provided new stories for the collection: Diana Paxson, Caitlín Matthews, David Spangler, R.J. Stewart and Dwina Murphy-Gibb. Both the living and the dead have reached out with their dreaming minds and offered rare and extraordinary perceptions. It is my hope that those of you who read and enjoy this collection may feel moved to read more of the same kind of writings and that some of you will write stories and poems which will keep alight the flame of the Celtic spirit.

The Hollow Hills of this collection's title are the hidden abode of the gods, faeries and ancestors, the place to which they retired when later beliefs came along. There, they are said to live yet, enjoying the joys of companionship and the riches of story and song for all ages. The song of the Lordly Ones can still be heard, issuing from within the Hollow Hills, by benighted travellers on the road. Some even seek entrance to these Faery halls, to learn new songs and stories and emerge with inspirations that will re-enchant a world that has lost so much of its innate creative integrity. I hope that you, who read these stories, will also hear and be inspired.

John Matthews
Seattle, Spring 1994

PART I

The Darkening Vision

I cannot go hunting tomorrow

by Henry Treece

At sunset the young Roman captain galloped his black horse through the stockade, and made towards a cluster of beehive huts near the edge of the wood. He could not have been more than twenty-five, yet he already looked like a veteran. The thick curly black hair was grey over the temples and the dark aquiline face was lined. Although as any citizen knew, the British wars were over, the peace was infinitely harder to bear: and as Caius rode on, it came into his mind to apply to headquarters tomorrow for a transfer to a home-based Legion, even if that meant some loss of rank. While the fighting was on, one forgot the poor food and the shocking living conditions: but now one thought of little else. And there was always the stupid strife between the tribes, or between the secret societies, the Otters or the Wolves, the Bears or the Badgers. These Britons were a strange people, Goidels, Brythons, Belgians, red-haired, brown-haired; smiling at you today and hamstringing your horse as you rode past tomorrow.

Sometimes, as he sat in his tent, thinking before lights out, Caius got very depressed about the whole occupation. The Gauls had been a fairly simple military proposition; in spite of poor old Vercingetorix, who had had an unfair deal anyway. Yes, leave them their coloured clothes and their wine, give them the chance to boast and sing once in a while, and for the rest of the time they would shoulder their responsibilities as Romans and come to heel nicely with their rates and taxes. With their exquisite metalwork and their good wine, they were certainly an acquisition to the Empire. But the Britons, they were a difficult lot. They would adopt Roman ways, have baths built, dress in

Empire-style garments, talk Latin tolerably well, even make a show of respecting the Roman gods. Then, when everything seemed to be going well, houses would be burnt down, a garrison massacred out at a country station, the toga would be discarded and the tartan put on, and the woad-pot that had been hidden for months would be fetched out, and the tribesmen would forget their Roman names and go back to their unpronounceable gibberish and their meetings in the woods.

Less than a month ago Caius and his Company had surprised a party of fifty or more Brythons, armed and wearing warpaint, carrying out a human sacrifice in the forest above Vricon. It was too late to save the victim, who had already been pinned to the ground with a wooden stake, but Caius had apprehended the officiating Druid. Even so, the final victory was not his: the local chief had sent up to the garrison Colonel a few days later, to say that the priest was his nephew and was curing him of a very painful affliction of the bladder. And that if he were not released forthwith, he would take the Roman action as a personal affront and ask to be relieved of his citizenship. The result was that Caius had been given the job of escorting the smiling Druid back to his village; and, although he was as always courteously treated by the Chief's household, a certain loss of pride was involved which might make his job as an administrator difficult in the future. It was not an easy life, especially when one got such little support from home. It would do the Senate a world of good to ship them out, every one of them, to do six months' service in Britain. They would understand then why one asked for reinforcements and equipment, and why one couldn't always dispatch revenues by the correct date ...

At last Caius reined in his horse outside the central hut, the biggest of the group. An otter gnawed at the stout bars of his cage, suspended at the side of the door. This was the house of Gwyndoc, the Otter, chieftain for a radius of thirty miles, citizen of the Roman Empire, and an old friend of Caius. As the Roman approached the door, two shaggy-haired sheepdogs rushed out at him, baring their fangs. Caius was taking no chances; the native dogs were as uncertain as their masters, and one of his own sergeants had had to be invalided home only a few weeks before as the result of trying to stop a fight between two dogs in the village. He smacked his short sword on its brass scabbard loudly and threateningly, and the two dogs withdrew to a safe distance and began to bark at him, sitting between him and the hut door. The otter stopped biting at his bars, and ran round his cage in a paroxysm of terror. Caius felt annoyed at his reception. He had known these dogs since they were puppies and did not expect to be forgotten so soon.

"Ho, Gwyndoc," he called, "are you in? Call these wall-eyed brutes inside, if you please, and let me have a look at you!"

The answer was a sharp high whistle. The dogs stopped barking and immediately turned towards the door, rubbing and jostling each other playfully as they pushed inside.

Then, bending to pass outside, Gwyndoc appeared: a massive man, whose yellow hair and moustaches hung in the manner of a Gallic chieftain, and whose blue eyes twinkled as they saw the young Roman.

"But, Caius," said the chief, "how good it is to see you again, my boy. We had news that you were posted over to Mai Dun, to keep an eye on the rebels there!"

"Hail, Gwyndoc," said the soldier, giving a military salute, "It's good to see you too, and I can assure you I'll never garrison Mai Dun while I have breath in my body to protest!"

"Good for you, lad," replied the Briton, "but come inside, we shall both catch our deaths of chill standing out here. You must come in and meet my new son. We haven't thought of a name for him yet, and perhaps you can help us. He's going to be a real Roman, I guarantee!" He stood back to let his visitor see. At first it was hard to see inside the great wattle hut: then, by the light of the rush-lamps, and the fire in the centre of the floor, Caius made out the rough oaken table, the weapons stacked against the wall, the floor covered with rushes and a profusion of sheepskins. As he strode in, two red-haired slaves shrank into the shadow and whispered to each other, and a tall slim girl, whose long hair was the colour of the gold torque round her throat, rose from a heap of skins to greet him. She was dressed in native cloth cut in the Roman style, her arms glistened with golden rings as she held her baby to her breast.

"Greetings, Ygerne," said the young Roman, taking her hand. "It is very good to see you once more."

"Greetings to you, Caius," replied the girl in her slow Latin. "We have often talked of you, but didn't expect you so soon." She smiled at him softly, admiring his straight body, and his shining breastplate. Then she turned to the whispering slaves and her voice became harsh. "Bring meat for the Lord, dogs! Don't squat there like heathens making spells." One of the slaves rose and made his way out. Caius had a curious feeling that the red-headed man put out his tongue at Ygerne as he passed. But he only saw this from the corner of his eye — and in the dim light he couldn't be sure.

Gwyndoc towered over them. "Take off your belt and things, Caius," he rumbled, "and make yourself at home. Sit on the skins by the fire and warm that thin Roman blood of yours! And tell me what we shall call our son."

The young soldier unbuckled his swordbelt and sat by the fire. "Don't forget you're a Roman too, Gwyndoc — or should I call you by your Roman name, Gunducius — and so is your son! But let me have a good look at the lad."

Ygerne came across the room and handed the child to the young soldier.

"By Claudius, but what a man he will be!" he said. "You must send him to Rome later and let us make him into a lawyer or a soldier. He'd have the pick of our girls with that yellow hair and those big blue eyes of his!"

As he spoke he felt that his tongue had played him false. He had said the wrong thing. These islanders were touchy about going to Rome, not like the Gauls.

Ygerne, with her gentle native manner, relieved the situation. She came forward with a horn of mead. "Drink this, Caius," she said, smiling, "your tongue must be hanging out after your long ride."

Caius handed back the child and drank. One of the slaves picked up a native harp and strummed softly at the other side of the great fire. As he listened, Caius became aware of a face peering round the open door. Gwyndoc rose swiftly, excusing himself, and passed out through the door.

The slave played on quietly, looking at the ground, and then Ygerne began to sing: it was a lovely tune, melancholy and barbaric, but very sweet. Caius listened to the hypnotic rhythms of the sad cadences, and thought of the strange tales he had heard of the far Northern islands, of Ultima Thule, where the seals danced on the shore like princesses in the Northern Lights, and the wild geese carried away the souls of the dead warriors, to the Heaven of Ice ... The baby was sleeping peacefully now and the song stopped. Ygerne smiled sadly at him. She laid the child down softly on a bed of sheepskins and heather.

"Lug, Tan, come here and guard your master," she called into the shadows. The two sheepdogs bustled out swiftly and lay, nose on great paws, one on either side of the cradle.

"Well, that beats everything!" laughed the Roman. "Only half an hour ago those two were ready to tear my throat out, and now they are lying down like lambs!"

Ygerne smiled. "They were only teasing you," she said. "They hold you as a friend and knew you were coming long before we did. I think you hurt their feelings when you took out your sword to them!"

"Well, one must be careful in Britain," said Caius, smiling. But he saw the smile die on Ygerne's lips, and he knew he had said the wrong thing again. Oh, damn these folk, he thought. Why must they be so sensitive. Why can't they laugh at themselves like soldiers? What they need is enforced residence in a Roman town: they'd have to have a sense of humour then, or they wouldn't get very far.

Gwyndoc broke the silence by entering the hut. He walked to the mead bowl and poured out two horns, for Caius and himself. Then he sat back and stared into the fire, fingering the knife that hung from his gold-studded girdle. His brow was wrinkled.

"You look worried," said Caius, "what is it? And tell me, why was your visitor wearing woad? Surely your people have given up that custom. Only savages wear warpaint now."

Gwyndoc looked at him calmly and the young soldier's eyes fell away from their blue stare.

"Caius, my boy," said the Briton, "I am not able to answer your questions now. But I will perhaps another day. I must ask you to excuse me this time. And so that you shan't be troubled, I've arranged for you to eat and sleep tonight in the guest-house at the other side of the village. I have a man outside ready to escort you there when you are ready to go."

The soldier looked up at the chieftain, his expression changed now to one of determination. He allowed himself to smile. "My dear friend Gwyndoc," he said evenly, "this is not like you. I am your guest, almost one of your household. I am godfather to your daughter and I have always come and gone as your friend. You cannot treat me as an unwanted visitor or a child."

Gwyndoc frowned at the words and seemed about to make a sharp retort. Then he restrained himself and said quietly, "Yes, Caius, you are our friend and our brother. But I am master in my house and chief in my village, and tonight I say you shall not stay here."

Caius jumped to his feet and began to buckle on his sword-belt.

"Very well, Gwyndoc, and I will say to you that I am a Roman, and I am responsible no less for your safety than for your good behaviour."

Gwyndoc was already towering over him, his hand on his knife. The two dogs had risen to their feet and were waiting for the first blow to be struck. The child whimpered in his sleep — and Ygerne moved across to it. "Be quiet, you two," she cried. "You talk like a pair of stupid boys instead of like grown men and soldiers. How do you think the child can sleep with this brawling going on around him?"

Gwyndoc touched the Roman on the shoulder. "I'm sorry, Caius," he said, "I am a little overwrought." He sat down again suddenly.

"I'm sorry too, Gwyndoc," said the young man. "I am perhaps tired. But I must know."

The Briton spoke once more, "I beg of you, Caius, by all your Gods and mine, do not question me further, but do as I say." There was something in the soldier's face that made Ygerne cross the room. She stood behind her husband, with her hand on his shoulder. "You must tell Caius," she said. "He is our friend."

"Be silent, woman," said the Chief. "You are speaking out of your turn. Go back to your child. That is your business." The young girl looked at him, astonished at his sharp tone. Then she turned to the young Roman, "Very well, Caius," she said, "I will tell you since you must know some time."

The Chief flung off the girl's hand and rose to his feet. "That you shall not," he said. "If he must know, he shall know from me and not from the foolish chatter of a meddling girl."

The slaves nudged each other and coughed, and for a moment the young soldier half wished he had not pressed the question.

"You can trust me, Gwyndoc," he said, "but as your military commissioner, I must know. After all, it is I who write the reports on your district for the Senate."

The Briton spat, "Reports! Senate! Nonsense!" he said. "What I have to tell you is of death and blood, not of pen and paper and old women sitting round a council table."

The Roman smiled grimly. "Speak on," he said quietly. Gwyndoc coughed and stared into the flames, then he rose and poured out mead into the horn cups. "I am in trouble," he said. "Bleddyn, one of my Otter men, has spoken of our rituals in another village. It is against the rules to mention such things outside."

The young man smiled. "Very well," he said. "You must report him to your Druids and have him fined. That is a small administrative matter, isn't it?"

Gwyndoc sighed deeply, as though he were called on to explain a simple story to a very backward child. "No, it is not a small matter," he replied gravely and slowly. "It is a matter of death. Bleddyn must be killed as his punishment. If I, his chief, allow him to go on living, I shall be punished myself. The Druids will take my first-born son to be burnt in the wicker-cage. In any case, I shall be fined for avoiding sacrifice by killing him myself. He should go before the court of Druids: but if he does, I shall be accused of negligence in disciplining him and shall lose all next year's crops."

The young Roman smiled grimly. "Always the same thing, month in, month out: So-and-so must be killed, such-and-such must be sacrificed, he must be blinded, he must be fined ... Why? Because the Druids say so."

Gwyndoc leapt to his feet. "You forget yourself, Roman," he shouted. "You shall not speak lightly of the Druids in this village." His face suddenly turned crimson with rage.

"I offer them my apologies," the young man answered quietly. "I am very sorry if I have offended them and their Gods and you. I will get my slave to sacrifice a black cock to them when I get back to camp."

"Very well, and I will sacrifice three white cocks," said Gwyndoc, sitting down again. "It may turn out all right then. Though one can never tell; the Gods have long memories." He poked the embers thoughtfully with a spear-shaft.

There was silence for a few moments. Then Caius spoke again. "Gwyndoc," he said, "all this is a matter of grave concern to me. For ever in this island there are feuds, divisions, murders and treachery. You are a disunited people, a family warring within itself, and that largely because of the separatist effects of your religious system or your secret societies. Where a family is fighting amongst itself, the thief may slip in unobserved; and that is what will happen to Britain one of these days. The Romans have brought you freedom from the enemy over the Eastern seas, they have given you roads and cities and security against want: and all at little profit to themselves. But one day, all that will end, and Britain must then look to her problems herself. How will she stand with the sea-raiders then, do you think?"

The Chief answered gravely, with a touch of pompousness in his voice, "The British will defend themselves. In the hour of need, they will band together and forget their rivalries. Who knows but that a great leader will rise amongst us and lead us to turn back any invader, even to conquer the world. It might be my very own little son there, sleeping on the sheepskins ... Yes, even he may one day carry the banner of the red dragon and set our people free."

Caius smiled quietly at the Briton's words. "Yes," he said, "that may be so, but in the meantime you are forced to rely on the thousands of Roman soldiery that the good folk of my country subsidize. We are responsible for your safety: and it is only natural that, in return, we should ask you to follow our law occasionally. And to kill Bleddyn tonight, or any other night, merely because he has opened his mouth, when in drink, and divulged a secret of what is, after all, an illegal society, is against that law. For all the great friendship I owe you, I, as soldier and lawmaker, cannot be by and allow this deed to be done."

"How may it be avoided then? What alternative can you offer me?" asked the Briton.

Caius rejoiced at his friend's change of tone, at his own powers of persuasion. He felt very proud of his Roman citizenship as he spoke: "Gwyndoc, the answer is simple. Bleddyn goes with me tomorrow to Vricon. I will have him absorbed in the army and posted North to the Wall. I have no doubt that he will be willing to change his name and do this as an alternative to the fate which he expects."

"But the Druids? What shall I tell them? Surely they will find out?" said the Chief.

Caius answered confidently, "How can they find out? Bleddyn will lose his identity, he will cease to exist. So far as the Druids are concerned, he will have disappeared without trace. Even the Druids will understand that they cannot punish a man that does not exist!"

Gwyndoc slapped his thigh and rocked in his stool. He laughed in sudden good humour, "Caius, my good friend, you have eased my mind. I am an impetuous man, quicker to use the knife than the reason, but you must forgive me that. I shall learn in no time with a friend like you to guide me. Let us drink to our long friendship, to the success of our scheme, and to my son whom you have reprieved. And whatever may be his first name, his British name, his second shall certainly be Caius, and he shall be in your charge when he goes to Rome to study. Ygerne, my wife, you must drink too."

The sleepy girl got up from her couch beside the child and filled up three horn cups. One of the red-haired slaves flung logs on to the fire so that the flames crackled and leapt towards the roof. The tension of the situation was relaxed and the three friends smiled at each other as they drank.

"Caius," said the Briton, "we must celebrate your visit. Let us go out tomorrow and hunt the boar in the woods above Lis Pengwern, and I will send a runner on ahead to my friend Gradog, whose land we shall cross on the way, so that he may prepare food and drink for us in the evening. What do you say?"

"Yes, we will do that, Gwyndoc, if it is a fine day. But you will have to lend me suitable clothes. I cannot hunt in this armour. But I shall need a light boar spear: my wrist has hardly healed yet since that affair in Gwent, and I cannot use a heavy weapon."

The Briton grinned. "You shall have anything you wish, Caius, all except Ygerne — and after another cup of this mead, I have no doubt I shall be giving her to you too!"

Caius seemed embarrassed for a moment, but looking across the hut he saw the girl's mouth twitch good-humouredly, and he smiled too. These natives were like children, he thought, wilful, spiteful, even very dangerous children: but children nevertheless. They laughed, wept, fought and loved, all in the space of five minutes. In battle they were individuals, each fighting bravely and recklessly, often, like their Gallic brothers, tearing off their armour and clothes and rushing naked into the thick of the battle. Like the Armoricans, too, their mead-prompted boast was, "We fear but one thing — that the sky should fall on us! And even if that did happen we would push it back again with our spears!" Yet, despite their courage and their good-tempered boasting, despite their exquisite metalwork and their love of beautifully woven clothes, they were savage children; afraid of the dark, afraid of the moon, of the mistletoe, of the river; and, above all, afraid of the tree-men, the Druids. Destroy the power of the Druids, Caius thought, and the country will start to become unified. But until that could be done, the straight Roman roads, the garrisons, the medical services, the improved methods of agriculture, were all the merest shams.

He looked out of the open doorway into the growing dusk and saw the foxgloves and hellebore growing at the wood's edge; he heard the owl call and the badger sniffing among the bracken. The delicate scent of wood smoke from a neighbouring hut came to his nostrils, and he knew that he would never want to leave this island, even when his military service was finished. If only the interminable vendettas between village and village, tribe and tribe, province and province, could be ended ...

The young Roman was interrupted in his dreams by a sudden scuffling outside the hut, and then two woad-painted tribesmen entered, dragging a third man. Caius didn't need to be told that their prisoner was Bleddyn; his dark eyes stared in terror out of a shock of black hair, his red tunic was torn from neck to waist, and the leather lacings of his breeches dragged after him as he limped along. He had obviously put up a fight before being taken, for a great gash showed, black in the firelight, from temple to chin, where the axe had bitten in.

His terror on seeing Gwyndoc was pitiful. He flung himself from the hands of his escort to his chief's feet and babbled incoherently. Caius watched his friend closely: he saw the full lips grow thin and the blue eyes become hard and cruel. He saw the two tribesmen watching like hawks, their nervous hands twitching on their long swords. For a moment Caius expected Gwyndoc to take the grovelling prisoner by the throat and murder him there, before his own fire and in the presence of his household.

Suddenly the child whimpered in his sleep, and Gwyndoc's face relaxed. He spoke first to Caius. "My friend," he said, "this fool must be washed and clothed decently before I can allow you to take him among your civilized colleagues."

Bleddyn looked up, like a trapped wood creature, amazement in his wild eyes.

"Am I not to die, Lord?" he asked incredulously.

"No, my gap-mouthed barbarian," said Gwyndoc grimly, "unfortunately, you are not. In spite of your criminal stupidity, you are going to be allowed to live. In fact you are going to live much better than you ever have before. You are going to become Bledinius, put on a breastplate and become a Roman soldier, in fact. You are going to forget who you are, what you have done, everything of your past life; and you are going to live with the Romans a long way from here."

Bleddyn began to weep with relief: he knelt and kissed his Chieftain's shoes, until Gwyndoc bent and raised him to his feet.

"Have the goodness to act like a Roman, since you are so soon to be one," he said. "Let us celebrate your renaming now."

One of the slaves came forward with horn cups and everyone in the hut stood round the overjoyed Bleddyn.

Gwyndoc raised his horn in toast: "Hail, Bledinius," he said, "and may he be a better Roman than he has been a Briton!"

"Hail," shouted everyone, even Caius.

Then Gwyndoc in the highest spirits, flung the remainder of his mead over the still shivering prisoner. All except Caius did the same, laughing uproariously.

"That's an improvement on holy water, fool!" laughed Gwyndoc, and Bleddyn, dripping wet and shuddering, joined hysterically in the laughter, flinging the remainder of his drink over his own head.

Caius was amused. This was just like the barbarians, either one extreme or the other, sheer grovelling terror or wild horseplay. Then Gwyndoc became serious again, as he spoke to his guards: "Escort Bledinius to the guest-house, having regard to his forthcoming Roman citizenship, and see that he sleeps well."

The guards looked at each other, and smiled.

Gwyndoc went on, "And tomorrow, while I am at the hunt, see that he is washed and clothed decently, as befits his new status. I shall expect him to be ready to travel to Vricon by sunrise the following day."

Bleddyn stepped forward and bowed his head in homage to his Chief. "Thank you, master," he said, "I shall never forget your kindness. I shall sacrifice a white calf for our God when my first army pay comes through!"

Gwyndoc laughed, "I bet you will! More likely you'll sacrifice your manhood to the first camp-follower who has wit enough to wheedle a bottle of wine from you! Get on now, and mind your tongue in the future!"

Caius looked at Gwyndoc with a new admiration and his heart warmed to his friend. While there were men like this in power there was still hope for a great and strong Britain.

Bleddyn stood straight, looked his Chief in the eye and gave him the Roman salute. Then he turned smartly and went from the hut, followed by the two guards, walking like a proud man again, in spite of his sopping clothes and the dangling laces.

Caius watched him across the clearing into the dusk, and was about to sit down by the fire again, when his heart thumped in horror. A cloud moved away from the moon, and in the sudden white light, the Roman saw the two guards close in behind their charge, he saw two swords glisten in the dark and heard them fall. Bleddyn half-turned, screaming, as though to run back to the hut, then fell to the ground and lay writhing as the swords struck again and again.

Caius swung round to Gwyndoc and his tongue failed him. The Chieftain was sitting, his chin on his hand, looking at him through half-closed lids and smiling grimly.

Neither man spoke for a time, then at last Gwyndoc said, "Let us go to our beds, Caius. We must be fresh for our ride tomorrow."

Caius stared at him in horror. Then he forced himself to speak. "No, Gwyndoc. I cannot go hunting tomorrow."

"But my dear friend," the Briton began. Caius pushed past him and buckled on his belt. He could not stay an hour longer in this house of treachery and death. Better the long ride back through the hills than a warm couch in this village where men said one thing and did another.

As the young Roman flung his cloak about him and climbed into the saddle, the moon was again obscured and a light rain began to fall.

Flowering Dagger

by Rosemary Sutcliff

Below the Royal Village the stream broke up into a chain of alder-fringed pools; and it was there, just above the cattle ford, that the women brought their washing. Soon it would be a place of thick shadows, and sunspots dancing through the alder leaves to freckle the dark water, and maybe a hovering dragonfly to light the shadows. That was still to come; all the good days of summer still to come. Now the leaves were only a green smoke, too thin to keep out the young sunshine, and the cuckoo calling across the valley was a new and shining sound.

Saba, the High Chief's younger daughter cocked her head to it in delight, calling back softly, "Cuck-oo — Cuck-oo." And her heart lifted to the wide green springtime smell of the world after the enclosed smoky darkness of the house-place through the winter moons.

"Cuck-oo! Cuck-oo!" It was only the fourteenth spring that she had greeted.

She pulled her brother Garim's best tunic from the pile beside her, and plunged it into the shallows, then flung it wide over the bank, heavy with water, its blue and brown chequer darkened almost to black, and began to pound and squeeze it this way and that, beating it with the small round stone in the hollow of her hand.

Close beside her, Cordaella her sister was scrubbing an old but still serviceable kilt of her man's, and smiling at it as she scrubbed. Cordaella had been married all but a moon now, to Maelgun Swift-Spear, chosen for her by their father and the Priest Kind because he was strong among the young warriors, and of the right degree of kinship to mate with the Royal

Daughter of the Tribe. Cordaella seemed to like him well enough; and these days she had the bloom on her, the warm secret look that Saba had seen before in girls who had been making the man-and-woman magic, and found it good. Nevertheless, glancing aside at her, Saba was glad that she was only the younger daughter, and within limits and the custom of the Tribe, might choose and be chosen for herself, when the time came.

The girls and women laughed and chattered together as they worked. Someone began to sing, softly, for herself and anyone else who cared to listen; a man-child clad in a coral bead on a thong round his fat little middle, too young to be left at home, too young to swim, walked into the pool and was pulled out and soundly slapped by his mother, and for a while after drowned all other sounds with his bull-calf bellowings.

Presently, when the shadows of the alder branches had moved over towards evening on the clean washing that was now spread to dry along the bank, a knot of young men came down the green track that dipped to the ford. Hunters returned from a day's hunting, two of them carrying the spear-slung carcass of a roe doe, their hounds padding at their heels. They splashed across the ford, the hounds checking to shake themselves on the near bank, and went on up the track towards the village. All save one of the hounds. A young brindled bitch, full of the friendliest intentions, had broken away from the rest, and was heading straight up the streamside towards where the women were gathered. Two of the hunting party came after her, since it seemed that whistling was no use; but by the time Garim, the foremost in pursuit, had caught up with her and hauled her off, by a hand twisted in her rawhide collar, more than one of the drying garments bore the wet and woodland traces of hound's paws and human feet.

Amid the protests of the other women, Cordaella snatched up an armful of the nearest, glaring. "Garim! Can you not master your own hounds? All these will have to be washed again!"

No man likes the suggestion that he cannot control his own dog, especially if it be true. Garim flushed crimson. "Kea is little more than a puppy. She meant no harm. If your washing-ground is sacred, you should plant a fence of spears round it!"

Cordaella stood confronting him, the spoiled washing clutched to her breast, and about her an air of high tragedy. "With such heedless fools as you running loose, it is in my mind that we should indeed! It is not even your own cloak that you have fouled! — But you have always thought that because you are the High Chief's son — "

Garim, his hand still through the collar of the young bitch, stood leaning on his spear, and watched his raging sister with an air of detached interest. "I will tell you a thing, Royal Daughter," he said, when she seemed to have finished. "There are times when you grow shrill as a shrew mouse."

"Oh! You — you — " Cordaella threw the washing at him.

Saba was scarcely aware of them. All her sudden awareness had gone to the tall boy standing a little behind Garim, and seemingly as remote from the quarrel as she. Brychan, one of the hostages in her father's Hall.

In the old days there had been a constant ragged warfare of slave and cattle-raiding along the borders between her people and the people farther towards the Sunrise. It had been on one such raid that old Marrag, who was young then, had been captured, old Marrag who had been her own nurse and Cordaella's and their mother's before them. There was peace between the two Tribes now; but a somewhat fragile peace; and to give it strength, every seven years there was an exchange of hostages, three young warriors sent by each Tribe to spend their next seven years among the young warriors of the other. They were treated as equals in every way; sometimes friendships were formed, and brotherhoods sworn that lasted for life. But nonetheless, they were hostages, and if their own Tribe broke the peace, their lives would be the first to pay for it. Brychan had been with Saba's Tribe for more than a year, and she had seen him often among the New Spears, the young warriors. She had even poured the barley beer for him in her father's Hall when the women went round with the narrow-necked drink-jars. But she had never really looked at him before. With his mane of mouse-fair hair, his bony freckled face, and thin shoulders that had not yet broadened into a man's, there had not seemed anything special to look at. But she was looking now, a little puzzled by her own looking. And a breath of wind was flickering the alder leaves, and the cuckoo was still calling from somewhere across the valley; and Brychan was looking at her, as though that, too, was for the first time.

Suddenly, joyously, and in the same instant, they smiled at each other, as though in first greeting, as though they had known each other all their lives.

The quarrel, it seemed, was over. The quarrels between Garim and Cordaella generally ended as quickly as they began. And Garim, the hound bitch at his heel, was on his way up the bank, calling over his shoulder to Brychan, "Hai! Come then, or they will be claiming our share of the kill!"

Brychan turned and went after him, and Saba joined Cordaella and the rest in gathering up the scattered washing. The muddied garments that must be washed again would have to wait till tomorrow. Too late in the day to start again now.

She thought no more of Brychan through the rest of that day. But at night, lying on the fern-piled bed-place in the little hut in the Women's Quarters, that she had to herself now that Cordaella was married, suddenly in the drifting moment between waking and sleeping, she saw him again. Saw everything about him; things she had not been aware of seeing at all, among the stream-side alders. Not just his face, the shape of his eyes set level under thick fair brows, the mouth that seemed too wide for his bony jawline, the freckles that gave him a boy's look still, but everything, the way he stood, the way he held his spear; even the white scar, narrow as a leaf vein, on the brown of his spear hand, just above the thumb. Still on the edge of sleep, she wondered what it would be like to be touched by him. And the thought startled her awake, because it was so new and strange. She lay sharply wakeful for a while after that, filled with an odd excitement and a sense of waiting, she did not know for what, and listening to the quiet breathing of Den, the little slave her father had given her, who slept across the doorway. Den was not like Old Nurse, captured in war, she was one of the little Dark People, here before the coming of the Tribe who were now their lords and masters. They were not quite of the daylight, the Dark People, they Knew Things. If ever she had a secret to keep, she thought, she must be careful of Den. And that too, was a strange new thought ... But sleep took her at last; and when she woke in the morning the strangeness had fallen away behind her on the other side of sleep, and the world had returned, almost, to its everyday self.

In the days that followed, she saw Brychan from time to time, just as she had done before. But the magic seemed to have passed with the moment, swift as the blue flash of a diving kingfisher. Perhaps also there was in both of them a sense of warning against trying to catch it back. Among Saba's people, it was forbidden to mate outside the Tribe. No good could come of looking each other's way again, though the wind still flickered the alder leaves, and the cuckoo called from across the valley.

And then the cuckoo changed his note, and it was the eve of Midsummer. And at sunrise the girls were off and away, along the streamside and up the wooded combes of the High Chalk, seeking flowers to braid with the magic vervain into their hair, for the dancing that would come at nightfall with the waking of the Fire.

Saba soon left the group of girls with whom she had set out, and drifted off by herself, making for a place she knew of, a sheltered tangle of hazel and elder and wayfaring trees, where the dark blue dove-flowers grew. She found and gathered three stalks of the winged blossoms, with a small thrill of delight, because this was the first Midsummer that she had been old enough to garland her hair and dance among the women's side. Then she went searching elsewhere. Lower down, the thickets were starred with wild white roses, but she knew that those, gathered in the morning, would be limp and sad as dead moths by dusk, and left them to their growing. She found a strand of early honeysuckle, creamy clover-heads, scabious and freckled orchis of the open Chalk; and pulled the green linen web from her hair to carry them in; they would travel better so. In a patch of low-growing scrub murmurous with bees, she checked to break off a milky curd of elder blossom. She did not need it; she had more than enough flowers for three garlands already; she gathered it simply for the prodigal joy of gathering; and still carrying it in her hand, stepped out onto the faint sheep-track that skirted the thicket — and came face to face with Brychan following it up from the farther valley.

Startled, she said the first and most obvious thing that came into her head. "Brychan! There's no hunting in these runs; what brings you up here into shepherd country?"

"I might knock over a hare." He checked, leaning on his spear. "No, I have been over to Grey Stones to ask Drustic to sell me one of Fleet-foot's pups. But I have left it too late, they are all spoken for."

"I am sorry."

He shrugged. "There will be other pups."

"I have been flower-hunting, for my Midsummer garland," Saba said a little breathlessly; as though, having demanded what brought him there, she owed him a like explanation.

He said suddenly and softly, "And so we are come to the same place at the same time."

She was not sure whether he was laughing at her or not, and so left him unanswered, while, with exaggerated care, she added the scented curd of elder blossom she still carried to the rest of her gathering. The next thing happened very suddenly. An amber-furred bee had settled among the flowers without her noticing it, and disturbed by their rearrangement, blundered up into her face. Instinctively she made to brush it aside, and as she did so, felt a small fiery dart of pain below her right eye.

She dropped her flowers with a little cry: "A bee! It has stung me — "

"Let me look," the boy said. He laid down his spear, and taking her by the shoulders, turned her to the sunlight. The small fiery pain was spreading along her cheek.

"That is a bad place for a sting! And the barb still there. Wait now, I will get it out for you and there will be small harm done."

He pulled a little dagger from his belt, and tipped her face, with his fingers under her chin. "Look up. So — now hold still, I will not hurt you."

"I do not mind if you hurt me," Saba said, faintly scornful. "Only get it out. I am not wishing to look as if I had been in an ale-fight before the dancing starts."

She felt a small prick; a bright clear fleck of pain, white amid the red of the bee burning. And then the burning ceased to spread, seemed to grow less.

"Is it out?"

"It is out. Soon the smarting will ease. Look — "

He held the tiny black sting out to her on the point of his dagger. His fingers were no longer under her chin, but she seemed still to feel them there, more vividly, more frighteningly, with more of delight than she had ever felt anything before. She knew now, what it was like to be touched by him. She looked at the sting, then at the dagger in his hand. It seemed better not to look at Brychan himself, not just now. "Show me."

"I am showing you."

"No, not the sting, your dagger. I have not seen its like before."

He flicked off the sting, and held it out to her. "Take it, and look." And something in the way he did so told her that it was a treasure, and that it was not everyone he would let handle it. She took it from him in the same way, and stood turning it over. It was a small dagger, but deadly; sharp as the bee's sting. Nothing special about the hilt, except that it was of a kind she did not know. It was the blade that held the magic. A blade of the rare and precious metal that men called Iron, inlaid with three silver flowers, the largest just below the hilt, each one below it growing smaller with the taper of the blade. They too were of a kind that she did not know; a little like bell flowers, but not quite; more like the slender green-and-white star lilies she had found sometimes in the woods. Beautiful.

"What are the flowers?" she asked.

"I do not know. The dagger came from far away. Maybe the flowers are from far away, too."

"It is beautiful," she said, and gave it back into the hand he held out for it.

"It is the only thing that is truly mine," he said. And then quickly, as though afraid she might ask more, "Does the smarting grow less?"

"It is almost gone."

"Still, you should go home, and put some cooling thing on it."

But they stood motionless, knowing, both of them, that she should gather up her scattered flowers and he his spear, and they should be on their way. Saba brought up her eyes at last to his face, and they stood and looked at each other. Then they did an odd thing, in the same instant they each put up a hand to the other, and fitted them together; not holding, just touching, palm to palm, finger-tips to finger-tips, like the two halves of something that had been parted coming lightly and surely together again. "I must go," she said. It seemed to her that something, some living part of herself, was flowing out to him through their touching hands, some part of him flowing in to her.

"I must go," she said again, desperately.

"And get that sting-place salved." For an instant his thumb moved outward and curled round hers. Then they parted hands.

"My old nurse is wise in the way of herbs." Saba knelt and gathered up her fallen flowers, gently shaking off the dying bee that lay among them. She wished that she had not brushed it away. If she had stood quite still, it might have worked the sting out for itself and flown off unharmed. She did not want anything in the world to be hurt or dying. Yesterday, that would have seemed a foolish thought; but yesterday was gone ...

"I wish I had not killed it," she said.

*

Now that Old Nurse was growing old indeed, and had the pains in her joints that often came to old people, she had a small living hut of her own on the edge of the village. Saba had once asked her if she never wanted to go back to her own people. But she had said, "What would I be wanting that for? It is all so long ago. There would be no one left who remembers me. Here,

I have the children that I have reared, and the world that I have grown used to. I do well enough where I am."

And certainly she looked contented enough that morning, squatting on her painted stool outside the door-hole of her little turf-roofed bothie, nodding over a torn cloak that she was patching, while her big half-wild cat dozed on the edge of the turf roof just over her head, blinking amber eyes in the sunlight.

She roused at Saba's coming, and looked sideways up at her. "You have been gathering your Midsummer garland? — Well then, let you show me."

Saba opened her bundle to show. "There was a bee with the flowers. It stung me here — under my eye."

"Aiee! That is a bad place to be stung!" said old Marrag, much as Brychan had done. "Let me look." She got up, letting the patched cloak fall in a tangle to her feet; and also as Brychan had done, put her hand under the girl's chin, turning her face to the light. The sour smell of old flesh came from her; but all at once Saba saw that she had been beautiful when she was young — under the sagging and withered skin, her bones were beautiful still.

"You are flushed, and your eyes are very bright," the old woman said. "Little bird, have you a fever?"

"No, it is only the sting, and that I have come running."

"Well, the sting is cleanly out."

"Brychan got it out for me."

"Brychan?"

"One of the hostages."

"And what were you doing, up and away with one of the hostages?"

"Nothing. A bee stung me, and he came by, and got it out with his dagger. He did it so carefully that I scarcely felt it." But she had felt other things, his touch on her face, the strange current that had been like life itself passing between them through their joined palms. Suddenly her heart began to race; and once again there was the sense of warning in her; and as she followed Marrag into the warm shadows of the bothie, she began to babble of the thing that could not matter, to cover the deeper silence over the things that did. "It is the most beautiful dagger I have ever seen — not like ours at all — an iron blade, it has; so small, but sharp, and beautiful — and silver flowers on the blade — "

Old Nurse, reaching up for a little jar among several standing on the cross-beam, started violently and knocked it over. "Tch! Tch! I grow clumsy in my old age," she scolded; and then stopped groaningly to gather up the small wreckage. "Silver flowers on the blade? A strange kind of dagger that sounds to be."

"It is not like any dagger that ever I saw before." Saba knelt to help her. "He said it came from very far away."

"And what are they like, these flowers?"

"A little like star-lilies. Three of them — just a silver pattern inlaid into the blade." Saba began to wish that she had not mentioned the dagger either. But it seemed that Old Nurse had lost interest. She was reaching down some more salve.

"Now, turn your face to the door. There, is that not cool and soothing? Now there will be no swelling, and all the finest of the New Spears will be wanting you to leap with them through the embers, when the Fire dies down tonight on the Dancing Hill."

And then in the last moment, she took Saba's face between her old twisted hands, and stood looking down into it — she was a tall old woman still — as though she was looking for the answer to a question. "But let you have no more to do with this Brychan. I have seen — I have heard of such daggers before. They do indeed come from far off, and are not of mortal making; and those who carry them must serve them; and bring black sorrow upon all who come too near."

For the moment a little shadow seemed to fall across the shine of Saba's morning. But she left it behind her with the crowding shadows in the bothie. "Old Nurse is trying to frighten me. Maybe she is jealous because I have been all hers. Or maybe she thinks I am still too young to — " She left the thought unfinished. It seemed better not to finish it. Not just yet ...

She began to run, the flower-filled net swinging in her hand, down towards the stream, where the other girls would be already making their garlands.

*

At dusk, throughout the Royal Village, throughout all the villages of the Tribe, the fires were quenched on every hearth. And with the dying of the last fire, the Festival of Midsummer was begun, and it was time to raise the New Fire, the Need Fire, the Living Fire that must be born afresh each year.

Then a strangeness came over the world, as it came every year between the fires. And in silence, and something that had in it both expectancy and fear, the people wound their way up the steep shoulder of the downs above the village, past the ancient strong place that could hold the whole Clan in time of danger, to the Dancing Hill beyond. They thronged the level hill crest, crowding shadows brushed with the light of a lopsided honeysuckle moon. No sound among them save the soughing of a little wind through the thorn scrub. And in their midst the dark fire-stack waiting, as the whole night waited, for the wonder of the reborn fire. The first team of warriors took up the trailing rawhide ropes of the fire drill, and began the swift rhythmic pull and release, pull and release, the long step forward and the long swing back that set the sharp-nosed spindle whirling in its socket. Team followed team, one taking over as another tired, while the moon rose higher and whiter; and the people waited, watching, half-fearful as they were half-fearful every year, that this year the wonder would not come.

But at last it came. A smell of charring, a thread of smoke fronding up into the moonlight, a single spark that fell on the dried moss, to be followed by another, and another, a licking yellow petal of flame. A soft long breath of relief and exultation broke from the crowd, as Cuthlin, Chief of the Oak Priests, bent and caught the flame on his torch of plaited straw, and whirled it into a blaze, a spinning sun-wheel of light, then turned to the darkly waiting fire-stack.

Fire was born again, the life of the Tribe was born again for another year. And as the threads of brightness spread through the brushwood, and the bigger branches caught and crackled into ragged tongues of flame, and the light reached out to leap and flutter on the faces of those nearest among the crowd, Saba looked for Brychan, and could not find him. Maybe he was there, somewhere farther back in the throng, in the moon-brushed dark where the firelight could not reach. Maybe he had not troubled to come up from the village. This was not his Tribe, not his Need Fire on the Hill of Dancing. And so he would not see her with her Midsummer garland round her head, and she need not have taken such trouble with it after all.

Later, when the chanting was done, and the dancing over, the long snaking sun dance, and the young warriors whirling and stamping to the rhythm of the wolfskin drums; when the flames that had leapt skyward, casting their fierce and fitful glare all across the Dancing Hill, were sinking low, the warriors and their women who wished for sons in the coming year linked hands and leapt through the sinking fire. And then the young warriors who had no wives of their own as yet began to catch the girls of their choice out of the women's side, to leap with them.

Govan, who she had always thought among the fairest and fiercest of the young warriors, came and tried to catch Saba's hand, but she thrust him off, and he shrugged and went elsewhere. She could have had her choice of three, that night, the first night that ever she had worn the magic vervain in her hair. But she wanted none of them.

And now, before the flames sank too low, it was time to be taking the New Fire, the Need Fire, to quicken the hearths of the Clan for another year. And the youngest men of each household began to come forward, those who lived in the Royal Village merely dipping a branch in the flames, and running, with it streaming out in smoking mares'-tails behind them, while those whose homes were the outland farms, and the shepherd's and herdsman's bothies among the folds of the High Chalk, took carefully chosen embers and stowed them in fire pots. Now, men were stamping out the last dragon-red gleeds on the blackened fire-scars; and all around, the crowd was crumbling away, melting into the moony night that would soon turn towards morning.

A hand closed on Saba's, drawing her backwards into the

anonymous darkness. She did not start, or even look round to see who it was. She turned and ran with Brychan down the hill slope away from the village.

In the midst of a little hollow filled with elder and wayfaring trees, they flung themselves down, arms round each other, breathless and half-laughing, straining close.

"I wanted to jump through the fire with you," Brychan said, muffled, into the hollow of her neck. He was pulling off her Midsummer garland, and her hair tumbled loose across them both.

"I wanted it, too." It was strange, they had never even touched before this morning. Now they were so much a part of each other that there was nothing she could not say to him, nothing that must be held back. "Oh, I wanted it till the want ached in my belly."

"Was that why you pushed Govan away?"

"I could not," she said, "I could not bear Govan's sons!" And then she heard what she had said, and a great stillness took them both. No sound but the little night wind hushing through the elder branches. The white curds of blossom swayed in the dark leaf-mass above them, and a shower of moon-flecks scattered through. "I did not say that," Saba said. "If I did, I have forgotten."

"You did say it, and you have not forgotten." Brychan's arms tightened round her.

"You are holding me too hard — I cannot breathe — "

"And it is forbidden to marry outside the Tribe. Oh, I know that." But he did not loose his hold.

"It is against the Law, and the Custom which is stronger than the Law. We are too far apart ..." How smooth and cool the skin of his back was; just the faint raised lines of the warrior tattooing across his shoulders.

"I will think of a way," he said. "There must *be* a way. Saba, listen, the gods wouldn't make us feel like this together, as though — as though we were part of each other, if we weren't — if there wasn't a way to find — "

He was half on top of her. He began to kiss her; hard,

inexpert kisses that pushed her lips against her teeth until she opened them to him. His mouth was warm in hers, much warmer than the skin of his back. Little ripples of sensation began to run through her, a strange shimmering that rose and rose in her body as though in answer to something, and was like nothing that she had ever known before. She must strain against him, closer and closer, until they blended together and became the same thing. One hand was round the back of his neck now; she felt the dry springy strength of his hair between her fingers — and something else.

"There's a thing on the back of your neck — I'll get it off." She dug in a sharp thumbnail.

He yelped, and twisted away from her. "Wah! That's me!"

"It is a leech — "

"It's not, it's a bit of me. I was born with it!" He rubbed the back of his neck. "You have drawn blood, little she-cat!"

They began to laugh, lying loose to each other now, and the moment passed and went leaf-light down the wind. The green plover were calling over the Chalk. Brychan sat up, then scrambled to his feet, reaching to pull her up after him. "Soon the light will be coming. It is time that you were back in your father's Hall."

*

On the day after the Midsummer Fires, the High Chieftain rode out as he did every year, to circle the boundaries of the Tribal Lands; his hearth companions and certain of the young warriors with him. And among them, this year, rode Brychan.

They were gone close on half a moon, for it was a matter of feasting at the hearth of every lesser chieftain; the exchange of gifts; long sittings beside Council Fires. And for Saba, left behind in the Royal Village, the waiting days were strange ones, following a surface-pattern of activity that was like the pattern of all the familiar days that had gone before. And beneath the familiar surface, not like any day that she had ever known. Empty, for lack of Brychan, yet full of him because he was in everything; in the way the light fell through a leaf, in the sound of rain dripping from the thatch, in the taste of barley bannock, in the crimson wool that she was weaving on the loom — all colour seemed more brilliant in those days — in the softness of her own skin when she touched it where his hands had been. She was aware of all things, of life itself, as she had been when she was a child; only when you were a child, she thought, you did not know you had the mystery, and when you grew older and lost the shining awareness, you forgot ... She felt very close to the heart of things; and very kind. She had a great sense of kindness towards all life in those waiting days, and surely the kindness of all life towards herself in return. And soon Brychan would be back. She did not look beyond the moment of his coming. Something deep within her turned her away from that. Enough to hold the shining, fragile happiness in her cupped hands, and know that in a little while, he would come back.

And then one evening, the High Chieftain and his following rode home. And next morning, with the summer mist scarfing the course of the stream, and the shining midge-clouds already dancing in the clear air above it, Saba went down with the other girls as usual to fetch water from the stream, and made an excuse to linger behind. Brychan, who knew the pattern of the village's day, would guess where to find her.

Now they sat together between the roots of an ancient willow tree that spread its shelter down the bank.

"Have you missed me?" they had asked and answered, for the joy of asking and answering; and "Do you love me still?" They had kissed. And now the future that Saba had been so careful not to look at too closely was upon them.

"You said you would think of a way," Saba told him, her face against his shoulder. "You said the gods would not make us feel like this, if there wasn't a way."

"I know. But it's hard to find."

"If we were to go away together, and build our hearth far, far off, where no one knew the name of my father's Tribe — where there were no people at all — "

"I am a hostage," Brychan said heavily. "If we did that, there would be black trouble between your Tribe and mine."

A willow-wren was singing somewhere in the low-hanging branches.

"In five years, you will not be a hostage. I would wait five years. I would wait all my life, if I might be with you in the end."

"Even if they tried to make you go to Govan or another among your father's warriors?"

"Yes," said Saba.

And the willow-wren sang on. And in a little, she added, almost weeping, "But in five years, I shall still be of my Tribe, and you of yours."

Brychan put his arms round her and began with clumsy gentleness to rock her to and fro. Over the top of her head he was staring out along the valley. His face, when she looked up at him, was very white, unless that was the morning mist and the green shade of the willow leaves; and there was a deepcut frown-line between his thick fair brows. "As to that — " he began at last, and checked.

She made a small questioning sound.

"As to that — " Suddenly he seemed to make up his mind, and the words came out in an almost painful rush. "I've thought and thought, all these days and nights, until my head and my heart are sore with thinking, but — Saba, I was not born in the Women's Place behind my father's — my foster father's Hall. I was found lying on his threshold, none knowing how I came there. And beside me, my dagger with the silver flowers. Did I not tell you it was the only thing that was truly my own? He reared me as a son at his hearth; but when the time came for exchanging hostages — he sent me in place of his own. I swore silence, with my hands on his thigh, and now I am an oath-breaker for your sake, Saba — Saba — "

She ignored that part of it, leaping with a sudden unreasoning hope to the implication of his story. "So you are likely not of — of your own Tribe at all, and if not that, you might even be of mine."

"What use if I was?" Brychan said in a small miserable burst of fury. "We could not stand in the daylight and claim it. I have broken my oath to no purpose."

But even then, he did not try to bind the oath-silence upon her. And she was glad of that; that he should know there was no need. "We should know in our own hearts," she said, clinging to him. "In five summers' time — we should know ... I must go back, or they will miss me in the women's quarters."

And she tore herself free, and scrambled to her feet and ran.

But still with her was the feeling that because she wanted to be kind to all life, life must want to be kind to her. And as she ran, she was remembering something that she had not thought of since the Eve of Midsummer. She had had no reason to remember it. Now, suddenly, all that was changed. She did not go to join the other women, but to Marrag's bothie. Old Marrag was sitting on her painted stool beside the hearth, for the early sunshine was still thin for old bones outside; and she went and squatted beside her, with her hair shaken forward so that her face was shadowed.

"So you come again. You have not been, these past days," the old woman said.

And that was true. Old Nurse saw too much, and Saba had too much to hide.

"Old Nurse, when I came to you with a bee-sting for salving, at Midsummer, and told you that Brychan had got out the barb — and about his dagger, why did you start, and knock over the pot of salve? You are very wise. Do you know something that other people do not know?" She was holding the old woman's knees, and she felt them grow rigid.

"What should I know, Little Bird?"

"Something about that dagger with the silver flowers?"

The old woman jerked forward, and thrusting back the heavy curtain of hair, peered deep into the girl's face. Then, at what she saw there, gave a low moaning cry. "Aiee! Fool and worse than fool that I was! But I thought you still a child. Too young — too young ..."

"The dagger, Old Nurse."

"I will tell you. I will tell. But first, let you tell me — have you made the man-and-woman magic with this Brychan?"

Saba shook her head. "Almost, after the Midsummer Fire was sunk." Laughter ached in her throat. "But he has a mole on the back of his neck, and I thought it was a leech and tried to pull it off; and he cried out that I had drawn blood — "

"The Great Mother be thanked for that at least. But — a mole on his neck, you say? That, too?"

"Have I not said?" Saba gripped Old Nurse's knees and began to shake them. "Tell me! You *shall* tell me!"

Marrag was rocking to and fro like someone hunched over an intolerable pain. A little whimpering moan broke from her. "It is so long ago. So long — and your mother not yet wed. The harvest failed three years running, and the cattle dropped their young untimely; and so there was famine in the land. Then the Priest Kind said the gods were angry, and Lugh of the Shining Spear had turned his face from us, and it was time for the Royal Daughter to hang up her girdle for a sacrifice. So the thing was done, according to the ancient Custom, and a branch-woven bothie made for her beside where the trade road crosses the frontier ford from the South; and her crimson girdle hung from the branch of an alder tree for a sign. And she was left there for the first man who came that way."

Her voice trailed into silence. And after a few moments, Saba asked in a small dry whisper, "Who came?"

"A merchant from lands across the Great Water — far and far and far to the South. And when he had played his part, and moved on in the morning, he left her his dagger with silver star-lilies on the blade. She showed it to me. I was the only one, I think, she ever showed it to. A strange morning-gift, but it was his own, and he had told her, more beautiful than anything in his merchant bales. I have thought, whiles and whiles, that there might have been love between those two, given time for flowering and fruiting ... He left her something else, too. It was not long before we knew it, she and I, that she was carrying a child. Then there was great rejoicing for all men know that the birth of such a child is a sign of favour from the gods. 'Lugh's face shines upon us once again!' they said. But your mother did not rejoice, knowing that when it was born, the Priest Kind would take it and pour out its blood to quicken the furrows, according to the Custom."

A great stillness, and a great cold was creeping over Saba.

"The child was born, as such children must be, in a hut made sacred, away from all others — only myself with her — a fine man-child with no mark on him save a rose-mole on the back of his neck."

The cold reached Saba's heart and tightened round it. "But the Priest Kind took him and shed his life into the furrows."

"It was not him that I showed to the priests, but another, born dead — at least, I suppose it was born dead. There are always children being born among the slave-girls and the Dark People, and no one troubles greatly what becomes of them."

"And then?" Saba whispered. Even her lips felt stiff with cold.

"We had nine days. A woman who bears a dead child is Taboo for nine days in the birth hut, only one woman staying to tend her, who is Taboo also. That you know. So I took the babe, as she bade me, and the dagger — his father's dagger — and a skin of milk. And that night I stole away."

"But she was alone."

"Aye, alone. I left her the herbs that she must use. The food that was laid before the threshold she had to fetch for herself when none was by. And I set out for the runs of my own people. I came back to my own village like a beggar-woman, keeping my cloak over my face, lest any should know me again. And I came away under the wing of the dark, leaving the babe behind me, lying on the Chieftain's threshold, and the dagger beside him. And truly I did not think that he would live, taken at birth from his mother, and carried for days through the wild, and not thriving on the ewe milk ... But I could not wait; I had to be back with your mother before the nine days were up ..." She was still rocking herself to and fro, to and fro. It was as though if she stopped, she must stop also in the thing that she was forcing herself to tell. "Always, I counted him for dead, though I never told *her* so. And even when you came, with this story of Brychan, and a dagger with three silver flowers on the blade, I thought, 'He will have died, and they will not have let a beautiful dagger the like of that one go to waste.' And I thought, 'They will never have sent a hostage who is not the Chief's true son; they will not have dared!' And I thought, 'She is too young; no harm will come of it.' Aiee! Ochone! Ochone!"

There was a long silence. And then Saba said in that same dreadful little frozen whisper, "And so we are sib to each other, Brychan and I."

"You have the same mother."

"It is true, isn't it? You would not tell me if it was not true?"

"It is true. Why should I tell you a lie that — if you tell it again, I shall die an ugly death. I who am old and wish to die gently beside my own hearth; and the Priest Kind will take Brychan and do with him as they would have done seventeen summers ago; and there will be blood-flow again between your Tribe and mine. Why should I tell you what could let all this loose, if it were not that it is true and that I — must tell. Now I have told, and you must never look towards Brychan again."

She must never look towards Brychan again; nor Brychan towards her.

Saba crept out from Old Nurse's bothie like a little grey ghost; and managed to gain her own sleeping hut unseen.

Den was squatting just within the entrance hole, waiting for her. And when she sat down on the edge of the bed-place, the little slave crept to her, long dark eyes fixed on her face. "What is it? Let you tell Den."

"I have eaten bad berries, and there is a sickness in my belly," Saba said.

"I will go to Old Marrag."

"I have been to her, and she has given me a thing to drink. Leave me alone, Den. Bide in the doorway, and see that nobody comes near." All day she sat on the side of the bed-place, her knees drawn up to her chin, staring before her. Once, she heard Cordaella's voice outside, and Den's. But what they said, she did not know. And then Cordaella went away again.

When the dusk deepened beyond the door-hole, and the

sounds from her father's Hall told her that the evening meal was over, and the breaking up and shifting that always followed it would have begun, she sent the child to find Brychan, and bid him come to her behind the stable sheds. Better to send the child than go seeking him herself; the little Dark People made good messengers, for they could come and go like a draught through a wall-chink.

And when Den was gone, she gathered herself together and went out into the dusk, to the appointed meeting place. He was there almost as soon as she was, and would have caught her close; but she pushed him away.

"What is it? The child said you wanted me, and now you will not let me hold you."

She gave him his answer in a broken rush, "Do you mind, on the night of the New Fires, I said we were too far apart? The gods must have laughed, if they were listening. — We are too close. — We are sib to each other, you and I."

"Sib? You have been sleeping in the moonlight and talk madness!"

"There's no moon." Standing with her hands on his breast to hold him off, she told him all there was to tell.

He heard her out in silence; only she felt him begin to shiver under her hands, as though the night had turned cold. And when she had finished, he said in the voice of one trying not to retch, "I wish that old woman had died on her journey, or that my mother — our mother, had borne a dead child indeed."

"I wish that she had borne two," Saba said. And then, "What will we do, Brychan? What will we do?" knowing the answer even while she asked it.

This was a thing they could never escape. No waiting five years, no going away together. It would go with them. It was within them.

Brychan wiped the back of his hand across his mouth. "There is only one way that we can be together," he said, after a long silence; answering her unspoken thought.

She reached out in the dark and felt for the little dagger in his belt. It was cool to her fingers. "This?"

"Yes."

"Do it now," she whispered. "Let us hold very close together, and do it now."

"Not now. We must wait through tonight, to be quite sure."

"I am sure now. I am afraid. But I am sure."

"If you are still sure in the morning, come down to the willow above the ford. I will be waiting for you there."

*

That night in her sleeping hut, careful not to wake Den, Saba wept a little, for the children that she and Brychan would never have, for the winter nights that they would never lie warm under one rug, for all the things that they would never share together, and that she could never now share with anyone else; a little, too, for familiar and beloved things that she must leave behind, even for an old hound bitch of her father's, who nobody would give bits of honeycake to, when she was gone.

But when the first light began to water the darkness, she got up, and moving very quietly because of Den, coiled up her hair and put on her silver bracelets that she only wore for best, then stepped out over the little slave lying in the doorway. She hoped that Cordaella would take Den and be good to her, and checked an instant, looking down, and saw that the child was awake and watching her. Den knew. But she would do nothing, tell nothing. They were a strange kind, the little Dark People.

She went on, out into the green dusk of the morning. She stole a barley loaf from the bake-hut, and slipped out through a weak place that she knew of in the thorn hedge, and down towards the stream, and the willow tree above the ford.

Brychan was waiting for her. He did not ask if she was still sure. If she had not been, she would not have come. They took hands, and turned up the streamside. "I brought a loaf," Saba said. They had never eaten together. "At least we can share that. There might be wild strawberries."

It was a very gentle day; a sky watered between skim-milk blue and pale sweeps of cloud; a soft south wind blowing in from the sea, cool with the salt tang of it mingled with the sweetness of warm grass and thyme and the last of the elder blossom. They found their strawberries, and gathered them into a lap-fold of Saba's skirt as they went along. Some of the berries, ripe, and crushed a little in the picking, stained the blue wool with flecks of purple. But that would not matter.

Presently they ate, among the hazel scrub where a little spring broke from the chalk, halving the loaf to the last crumb, and dividing the strawberries between them with meticulous care; and afterwards drinking the cold hard water of the little spring from each other's cupped hands. Scarcely aware of what they did, they were making a small potent joining-ceremony, out of the sharing of food and drink in the dapple-shade under the alder branches.

Later, they wandered on again, still hand in hand like a pair of children. For a while they lay among the warm mouse-brown of seeding grasses that the south wind swayed all one way. If you lifted your head, you could see the wind coming, laying the grass over in long silvery swathes. "When I was very young, I had a tame grass-snake," Brychan said. "He went everywhere with me, hanging round my neck. He felt warm and dry, and he never made his bad white smell unless he was frightened; and he was never frightened when he was with me."

And Saba said, "The first thing that ever I can remember is lying in a soft rug beside the fire and watching my mother comb her hair. When she combed hard, it crackled and clung to the comb. I cannot have been more than two, because she died when I was two." And then she added, "Our mother."

And they were silent a while, and then began again, wandering on once more and telling each other things as they went; exchanging thoughts and memories, as though they sought to share their whole lives and blend them into one, in the single day that was all they had.

Once they found themselves in the midst of a whole cloud of blue downland butterflies; once the shadow of a hawk fled over them. And at last, with the shadows beginning to lengthen, they turned downhill towards the woods.

"It has been a good day," Saba said.

"It has been a good day."

And now it was over. "Brychan, is it because we are sib, that we seem to be part of each other? Is it no more than that?" She cried it out suddenly frightened on the edge of the dark.

"You are sib to Garim, and to Cordaella. Full sib. This is another thing."

And she was reassured.

On the fringe of the woods, in a little hollow where hazel and elder crowded close as though to make them a sheltered resting place, they stopped, and sat down. There was bracken to shield them, and a shadow-flush of willow-herb among the trees, and somewhere a chiff-chaff was calling as it flitted from branch to branch.

"Soon, they will come looking for us," Brychan said. "It is time to be on our way."

Saba nodded. "Show me the dagger again, first." And then, at something she saw in his eyes, "No, it is not that I am afraid."

"You need not be," he said. "We will be together, and I will not hurt you. No more than I hurt you when I got the bee-sting out." And he pulled the dagger from his belt, and held it to her, laid across his palm. In the greenish shade, the three silver star-lilies seemed to shine with a light of their own, as pale flowers do at twilight.

"It is beautiful," Saba said, as she had done before. "I am glad that it is beautiful."

They lay down together in each other's arms, and the bracken fronds closed over them.

The Dark Tower

by Peter Vansittart

Roland lived with his two brothers and his sister Helen, in the West, amongst small green hills. Their mother looked after them, their father having died. Very happy were they all together, with their life of thatching and sowing, hunting and hedging and harvesting, the summer's tasks. On winter nights they told tales by the fire, tales learnt from their mother or the old people in the cottages below. Of Wild Edric and Godda his wife who hunt in green on the Shropshire hills: of the fish-god who lies in a Shrewsbury pool girt with Edric's shield while a Roman ghost rows above: and of Llew Law whose strength was in his long hair and who was betrayed by his loveless wife. They told of the giant wolf who terrorized the old gods, but who was trapped by a chain made of the breath of a fish, the purr of a cat and the roots of a mountain.

One hot midsummer day Roland was tossing a ball with his brothers and by mischance threw it over the grey tower of the church that had been newly built near their home. "I will fetch it," Helen cried, running off, glad of this chance of touching the ball which her brothers said was not to be played with by girls. Was the ball magical that she should have no part in it?

The three brothers saw her run gaily past the church, going by the left, against the tall sun whose beams slanted down towards her through the broad motionless trees, like spears to drive her back. After waiting some moments one brother became impatient. "Burd Helen, we have not finished our game. What are you about? If you are hiding we have no time to seek you. But if the ball is lost, call out, so that we can come and help you."

But there was no answer: the church stood still and mysterious before them, sunlight streamed through the trees which stayed as if holding their breath. Finally, the youths went off to fetch her, grumbling that she was teasing them and spoiling the game. But amongst the bright grass and heavy unmoving leaves no Helen was to be found. For an hour the brothers ranged woods and fields crying aloud. "Helen, Burd Helen, call and we will hear you. It is time to go home for our mother waits. Helen! Helen!"

No Helen, however, made reply and at last, sorrowfully, for they loved their sister, and fearfully, because the church was new and its powers and Lord not yet wholly understood, they returned to their mother, whose face went grave, then anguished, when they told her what had occurred. All that night they waited, allowing themselves no sleep. But not a tap sounded at the door, not a footstep echoed on their stones. By the end of the week neighbours were saying that she must have been stolen by Herne, the forest-god, or Robin the Wanderer, both jealous of Christian souls and allowed no rest until the Last Days.

The mother wept and said, "We will never see her again, except perhaps as a poor ghost haunting Martinmas Night. Whom have we offended that this should be done to us? What sin have we committed, what rite have we left undone, that our dear Helen should be thus stolen from us?"

A year passed, and no word came of the lost girl. Villagers from many miles were without report of her. Then, on Midsummer Day, John, the eldest brother, rose early and began preparing himself. His mother, woken by the sound, found him. "My son, the red is scarcely in the sky and we do not go to the fields today. Why then have you risen so early, and what are these preparations that you are making?"

He smiled as he looked back at her. "Mother, for a year we have lost our sister. Now it is fitting that I, our father's eldest son, should go and search for her. Indeed, it is ill that I should have tarried so long. In the underworld father's shade is rebuking me and calling me 'Nought' on account of my faintheartedness. Embrace me, Mother, for I am off to seek Merlin, the wise old man who knows all things under sea and sky, sun and moon. Ancient Merlin, who advised Arthur the Raven-Lover in the days of long ago. He will tell me what to do. I am sure that our sister lives, for I have had no fatal dream of her. But she will not be content until she is back here, at our table and by our peat-pile, rose-cheeked and laughing as she always was."

The mother sighed but her heart was glad, and she thought of her husband biding in the life beyond, with his spirit wasted and his strength gone, and she knew that his son's endeavour would give him heart. So, plucking a shield from the wall, she said, "My son, I beg you take this, your father's good shield. Who knows what dangers you may pass through and whether God can protect you?"

After many days John found Merlin seated on a dark stone, and he was indeed very old, ancient as years, his beard white as a frothing hill-stream, his eyes, one blue, one green, cold as rain. A cloak of curious greens and greys lay over his shoulders and on his clawed hands dull rings caught little light from the sun. A pot of bull's blood was by his side, by which he divined secrets.

John halted and made him suitable flatteries to which the magician listened with satisfaction. Slowly he nodded his white, thin head.

"It is true that I am Merlin and am accounted wise. I have known gods die and come again. I have seen the giants overthrown. I have known trolls and the green men of the woods. I have seen the king disguised as a wren. I have seen the hero draw the sword from the stone, and the Spring Goddess captured by the Hag. I have shared bread with Mordred the Traitor. I understand numbers and vices and the Secret of Seven and Nine. I can see the New Times that have come, and how a new heaven will make a new earth. I can see too, my own ruin and hear my own grief. Now, tell me how it is with you, and for what you are seeking, for you have the appearance of Wanderers, and them too I have known."

John then told him about his lost sister: how she had run off after the ball and never been seen again.

Merlin's aged voice was still clear. "And was the sun shining, my young man? Was there sun alight in the sky?"

"It was Midsummer, and the sun was high and bright."

"Now listen with care. Did your sister run with the sun at her back or with the sun in her face? Mark well before you reply."

John considered, as he had been bid, then replied that the sun had been in her face.

Not without some strange, antique satisfaction Merlin nodded. His voice sounded younger as he stirred the bull's sharp blood. "Because she ran against the sun it is likely that the Green King must have seen her, caught her by her shadow and borne her off into his twilit realm. Go and seek Elfland. Past these stones, over these hills, on and on. Demand from whom you will the road to the Dark Tower. Take with you a sword and, when you reach the borders, cut off the head of any living being, be he high, be he low, who approaches to speak with you, or whom you yourself accost. And a warning: neither eat nor drink in Elfland, for if you but moisten your lips with a drop of wine or touch them with a morsel of bread, the consequences will be evil."

Thanking him, John hastened away towards the warm hills. Looking back, he saw Merlin, all blue and grey, and already seeming to merge with the stone on which he sat. Then, with the sun now only just above the steep hilltops, he set himself resolutely to ascend, telling himself that he must remember the wise creature's words.

A year passed but no John returned to the cottage. "Alas," the mother wept on Midsummer Day, "once I had a husband and four fine children. God has not saved them and now they are gone, who should be with me to comfort my old age, and who knows what dangers are already threatening my last two. My prayers are not returned and what now is left me?"

Her second son took her hand. "All your children live, Mother. See, I myself am this very day departing to find and help John my brother. We will come back together bringing our sister with us, and all things will be as before, only better, for those who have been lost are doubly welcome when they are found."

His mother tried to dissuade him but he would have it so, and, seeing that her pleading was without avail, she sighed and, drawing down a gold-hilted dagger from the wall, gave it him, explaining that it had been his father's and had never struck an unworthy blow. And, after his tall figure had vanished into the heat and dust, she wept, telling herself how barren a fortune the shield had brought his brother John.

And another year went by, but no news came from either son. It was then that Roland, the youngest, knowing what must be, begged his mother's leave to follow them. "For," he said, "notwithstanding my duty and love for you, my brothers have need for me wherever they may be, and as for Burd Helen she awaits her deliverance."

His mother grasped his arms and attempted to pull him back.

"You are the last of my children, all that is left to me. Will you too leave your mother to go down to the grave like a beggar-woman who stands all alone by the roadside, a contempt to the world and a sickness to herself? Stay with me, my son, for your brothers and sister are dead, and this present world will know them no more, and our Lord God in his anger will do with them what he will. Unless He too be overcome by what we cannot know."

Gently he pulled himself away. "I must go, Mother, for am I not my father's son? But give me, I pray you, that fine sword that has always hung there above the hearth, since I played with my brothers long ago, and which used to frighten me because you always kept it so polished and keen, and I saw dark faces on its bright blade. If you love me and wish me well, let me have it, for a good sword wielded in an honourable cause renews its strength two-fold. And my father's spirit will be with me, for the dead forget not the weapons that served them well."

So the mother, with many griefs, kissed his brow and gave him the sword and he set off. He too met Merlin and learnt that his two brothers had passed that way before him, and he gained the same advice, and left, and made for the hills, wondering. On and on he went, amongst rocks and high places. Gradually the air brightened and as at last he began to descend, the grass became a deeper green. And on the ninth day he encountered a drover, a man very much smaller than himself, guarding ponies of a size scarcely larger than that of rams. Of him, speaking courteously, he demanded the way to the Dark Tower.

"Go on, fine sir, on and on, until you meet the cattle of the Green King."

Roland was about to proceed when he saw malice and wily triumph glinting in the fellow's eye and, suddenly recollecting the injunctions of Merlin, he swiftly, with one stroke, beheaded the drover, who at once stooped, picked up his own head and continued his work with it under his arm. One eye was closed tight, the other staring. This made Roland realize that he had indeed reached a province of Elfland, and he moved on faster than ever and soon saw a dwarfish cow-herd guarding a field of small green cattle.

When asked the way to the Dark Tower the cow-herd made a surly shrug and said in a grumbling manner that he did not know. Roland persisted, however, and showed a threatening disposition, so the other reluctantly advised him to question the hen-wife whom he would discover along the road. Then he too was beheaded, the bright blood flowed, he picked up his head and vanished.

In a tiny thatched cottage that stood all alone in a weird and hostile light, both bright and dull, both clear and dim, stood the hen-wife, small, with little eyes hostile and demeanour unwelcoming. But Roland saluted her respectfully enough and prayed that she would show him the way to the Dark Tower. Smiling evilly, she thereupon pointed her sharp hand towards a hill, darker than the others, near but yet far, high but yet low. So eager was he to start immediately that but for the woman's low laughter he would again have forgotten Merlin's words. But her, too, he beheaded and then rushed outside without waiting to see whether or not she picked up her head.

Within a very short time he had climbed the hill and the Dark Tower rose up before him, old as Troy, four-cornered, straight and gaunt and menacing. Heavy sunlight lay over it yet did not light it, and in the sky could no sun be seen. All was silent: no sentinel stood on the walls, no beggar crouched at the gate, no bird flew. Three times he crossed himself, three times he marched round the Tower, against the sunlight, then three times he stamped, shouting for the gate to open. At his third shout a bright light streamed through the gateway, beyond which in the great Hall stood the outline of his sister Helen, bidding him welcome.

Without hesitation he darted forward to embrace her and only at the very last moment was he able to halt himself, draw back and, with a deep, troubled breath, flash their father's sword against her white neck. Her head tumbled, the entire Tower trembled and raged, but he stayed firm under the shadow vaults of the Hall and, as the agitation diminished, above the broken counterfeit body, there was standing his real sister, Burd Helen, of the bright hair and hyssop-blue eyes.

They embraced, they wept, they rejoiced together and she told him all that had been until at last Roland gently pushed her from him and seated himself to await the Green King, his sword on the round stone table before him. Worn from travel he requested Helen to bring him food and drink: at his words, however, all speech left her and her eyes filled with tears. But he asked her again, perplexed by her manner, and she turned away, weeping. In a short space she had covered the table with handsome dishes: silver bowls of sage and borage and valerian: platters of roasted calf and deer: cakes soaked in wine and cream: flat golden cheeses: wine flashing in jewel-crusted goblets. He was about to eat when he saw her eyes, mute and despairing and, at last remembering, flung the great table from him and leapt forward, grasping his sword as a vast voice thundered harshly throughout the Tower:

"Fee Fi Fo Fum
I smell the blood of a Christian man,
With this brand be he live or dead
I will dash the brains from out his head."

Up and down the Tower of Death and up the winding staircase Roland fought the Green King. His foe was stalwart and agile, with a pitted face, green and wrinkled and filled with pain, and his strength seemed unending and his resolution undismayed. Their swords clashed till the sparks flew and the damp stone walls echoed with the clamour. Yet, however savagely the Green King fought, Roland pressed him up and up the twisting stairs: his breath finally came in starts and, on the seventh floor of the Dark Tower, Roland caught him at the seventh corner, flailed him to the ground, smashed his sword and was instantaneously crouched over him, sword at his throat.

"King or no king, disclose me my two brothers living and sound, and restore my Helen's speech, or you die, and the stairs shall drip your blood and dogs drink it."

Faintly, soundlessly the Green King pointed, and there, in a shadowy recess lay the two brothers, stiff and cold, like stone statues fallen from a crumbling wall. With fennel and balm soaked in the Green King's blood Roland and Helen anointed their eyelids, their nostrils, their lips, hands and feet, and in turn they revived, stood slowly up, then were caught in the arms of their brother and sister.

Happily the four set off home and, as she went, the wind at her back and the grass dancing before her, Helen vowed that never again would she run to the left of the church against the Midsummer sun.

The Story of Kigva

by Sian Hayton

The girl-child woke suddenly. There was a light in the tent when there should not be one. Reluctantly, for there was an early frost that night, she sat up and looked over the edge of her bedding. The grandfather had lit a small fire and was huddled over it swaying back and forth and singing quietly. She realized with a shock that he was wearing the cape of office which should have been left for her alone. Then, horrified, she realized that he was taking omens, for on the ground in front of him lay a flat stone, a piece of horn, a length of bark and a roll of skin. He picked them up one by one and scraped a sooty twig over them, then ceremonially spat on each and rubbed it with his thumb. She was terrified and burrowed back into the heaped skins. The firelight threw shifting shadows on the walls and the husky, droning voice of the old man threatened to overpower her with the unfamiliar. In their clan women were the ones to talk to the spirits, but here was a man, of her own family, meddling in the forbidden. His winged shadow that now covered most of the walls showed her an aspect of him she had never seen before. It could only mean disaster.

She tried to hide in the skins so that whatever was nearby would not see her. Before she could seal her mouth a whimper escaped her and she lay rigid with fear. The old women who were training her had told her that when powers were loose it was most important to let nothing in or out of your body. She had been practising for weeks without success and now she failed once again when it mattered most. Something lifted her from the bed with supernatural speed and she closed her eyes so tight a tear was squeezed out. In despair she sobbed aloud and opened her eyes. Her grandfather was looking at her with concern. He put her down beside the fire and she sat up trembling.

"You were not intended to see this," he said, indicating the tablets at his feet. She did not reply.

"We live in desperate times," he went on, "and we need desperate measures. The High-King has set us down here, but the soil is too thin to grow crops. Most of our hunters have been taken away to foreign wars; there are no skins to buy silver; there is no silver to buy spears for hunting; the grazing is worn out since our sheep cannot wander. We will not live through another winter. Since your mother died three winters ago, no woman has appeared with the power to travel in the spirit world and you are still too young for the task. It seemed to me that one of our family might have the power even if he is a man. I am the only one of our blood left but for you. I have to try." She managed to keep her mouth closed on a groan.

"I am beginning to see something," he said, "perhaps if you sit with me you will help."

He paused for a moment, then draped the Cloak over her, covering her completely. Then he began to sing again. Hidden from his sight she closed her eyes and covered her ears but swayed in rhythm with his voice. Her body might be present, but if she did not know what was said or see what was done she might be spared punishment for this horrible blasphemy. The night wore on and she kept up ceaseless prayers for forgiveness.

*

She awoke again well into the drizzly morning. The fire was a little heap of ashes and her grandfather was gone. This was not new, for he often went off to hunt in the early morning and left her, but after the events of the night before she felt alarm churning in her stomach. Nevertheless she said nothing to the old woman who came to take her to the caves for training and when she returned she sealed the tent behind her as fast as she could. If they were to discover his absence what could she say?

She could never admit the shameful fact that she had been witness to his sins and had done nothing to stop him. What she could have done she did not know, but she knew she should have done something. Their food was left outside the tent as usual. After she had eaten she lay down and waited, her heart knocking against her ribs and her ears straining for every sound. He did not come. Another day passed in the same way and she thanked the spirits that they had not betrayed her secret. On the morning of the third day the old woman who came to fetch her said she was not clean enough and asked what had come over the old man that he had let her get into that state. He knew how important it was for her to be pure, she said, and he had never let her down before. At that the child had coloured and the old woman became suspicious.

"Kigva!"

The child flinched at the sound of her own name. She would have to answer now and she would have to tell the truth.

"Kigva, what has happened to your mother's father?"

"I do not know. He left two nights ago and did not say where he was going. It seemed to me he was going hunting."

"He went hunting and did not tell you?"

"No. I do not know what he went to do. Perhaps he went hunting."

Fortunately the old one did not press her further. The child could see that she was not pleased for she pressed her lips together and shook her head. Then, seizing her hand, she took her to the old women's tent where only adults went, and then only when they had broken the law. The child's heart sank further as they walked into the strange-smelling darkness. The three old women who shared this tent were the only ones allowed to keep a fire burning at all times. Flickering shadows surrounded her as they had two nights before and she was sure they must know what her grandfather had done. She peered into the darkness to see if there were any sign of him. Apart from the loom that stood in any woman's house and bunches of herbs which she herself had helped to gather there was nothing to be seen. She was disappointed that the tent where the terrible ones lived should be so commonplace. The caves where they did magic were full of mystery. Magic water dripped from the roof and none knew where it came from. The spirits spoke in strange voices and their breath blew your hair as they passed near you. The likenesses of animals appeared on the walls as the firelight shifted and the great hunting magic made the hair on your back crawl. Here all that could be seen in the firelight was skins.

Ignoring her, the three old ones whispered to each other. Then one of them said angrily,

"There has been too much of this," and she turned to the child.

"Kigva, come here." She approached the three and waited for the questions to start. They were bound to find out the truth, for they were the wise ones of the clan to whom everyone came for knowledge. All they said was,

"When your grandfather comes home you are to come and tell us at once. Do you understand?"

She nodded. The terrible one nodded back. This was worse — they must know already what had happened that night.

"Go on up to the cave now," said the old one, "and attend to your duties."

She felt as if her legs were made of stone as she made her way up the hill to the dripping cave. That day, as an offering to the ancestors, she worked very hard and made hardly any mistakes in her reciting, but as she returned to her tent she began to feel the fear again. What if he came home and swore her to silence once again? Whom should she obey — her teachers or her family? All her life she had been told that these were the people to respect, but none had told her who was more important. As it fell out she was spared the agony of this decision, for when her grandfather returned in the pale light of dawn he collapsed on to his bed and lay without moving. He did not even answer her when she spoke his name, so she had no choice but to fetch the old women.

They tended the old man with herbs and chanting until he recovered some days later, then they questioned him. He would not tell them where he had been — not even when they cursed him in the name of every spirit they could name. He lay on his back and stared at the roof of the tent where the smoke escaped, his lips moving silently, and say what they would, he did not budge. At last, saying that there was not much a mere man could do to upset the balance it was their duty to maintain, they left him alone. They did not think to question his granddaughter, for she was just a child, and an unpromising one at that.

Whatever he had done, it was for the good of the tribe. Some days later men came from the other world and brought them flour and salt, and would take nothing in return. Then a smith brought them metal spear-heads and in return took only two sheep-skins. The day he came all the tribe hid in their huts, but grandfather was brave and went to do the bargaining for them. The next spring the smith brought a metal plough and took only a wolf's skin from the men who had used his spears to kill it. The men of the clan began to speak to the old man with respect and asked for his help in finding game and using the new plough. The old women heard nothing of this.

The little girl saw it all and was sure the night her grandfather had put on her Cloak had brought it about, but she did not know how. Months had passed and the fogs of winter had come and gone before she saw that she had better find out the truth. She had got away with silence with the old women, yet there were Others, she knew, who would know what had passed, and they would be expecting her to act. For Them, and in her position as queen of the tribe, she ought to find out where he had gone. She laid her plans carefully, however, for she was in her tenth year and beginning to know wisdom.

The old man continued to go off on his own from time to time. The old women told her to watch him for them, so she continued to pretend that she knew nothing. After a while they lost interest, but she did not. Some mornings when he was gone, he left a heap of ash in the tent. She began to watch for these times and realized that this happened at the time of the full moon. Even now she was cautious and stuck to her plan.

The hunters of the clan found that they had a new apprentice. The queen's daughter had taken to following them around and pestering them with a stream of questions. They were not even good questions. She was not interested in the varieties of footprint or the texture of dung which told the hunters about the size and age of an animal. Her only interest was in following spoor, the quality of terrain and how long a trail would last. Since she was who she was they could not send her home, nor could they ignore her questions, for custom said that a child's questions were sacred, but it was tiresome to have her constantly at their side. To her credit she was light on her feet and as time went by she could move as silently as the best of them. In fact she often scared them badly by appearing on the trail ahead of them without warning, and sometimes made them angry by laying a false trail which deceived the most cunning. After a while she left them alone.

One dawn, before the stags went into rut and falling leaves could make tracking him too hard, the girl-child followed her grandfather into the forest. At first a heavy dew made her task easier than she could ever have wished, but as the sun dried it up she had to look harder for the broken twigs and dented ground that marked his route. Some time after the middle of the day she saw the silvery trunks of many fallen trees leaning on each other like stalks of sickled barley. As she approached she found that the lower branches of these trees were tangled tightly together so that they barred her passage. She started to skirt them but found the barrier wider than she had thought. If she went too far down the hill she might never find her grandfather's trail again. It would be better to see which path her grandfather had taken at the barrier.

She had to cast about for some time to find his trail. Once found it was very difficult to follow, for whereas before the old man had taken a direct route from point to point, now the path twisted like a serpent. Furthermore on the earlier part, as was to be expected from a man of his age, the footprints were deep and even, but now they were shallow and irregular as if he were creeping up on a quarry. She struggled on as the sun sank towards the tree-tops and realized only after some time that the trail was leading, not round the fallen trees, but through them.

Then, suddenly, she was standing exposed on the edge of a clearing.

Hastily she drew back into the trees and looked about her. The clearing was very wide and pleasing to the eye, with tall foxgloves and fennel growing abundantly. Below them were poppy, vervain, valerian, nettle and dozens of the other plants for healing and harming which the old ones had showed her. Birds and insects flew in the glade in great numbers and the sun-warmed air was filled with the sound of their voices. In the centre of this busy and colourful glade was her grandfather. He was lying on his back and at first she thought that he was sleeping, or worse. Then his head moved and she realized that he was watching a buzzard as it circled overhead. He looked very calm and cheerful and not at all like a man betraying the customs of his clan. The child was about to hail him when she thought better of it. There might be more to learn by keeping still, so she nestled down in the branches and watched.

The sun dropped below the tree-tops and the clearing grew dark. All at once the old man sat up and looked attentive, as if he had heard an expected sound. Then to her rage he opened his pack, pulled out her Cloak, put it round his shoulders, and walked gravely to a tree-stump on the far side of the glade. The light was changing so that for the first time she could make out a large stone building just inside the forest ahead of him. Grandfather sat on the stump and stared, waiting, into the forest. Twilight fell rapidly, and as the sky flared red with the sunset a light appeared in the building.

With her heart beating in her throat, the girl crept across the clearing towards her grandfather. He had begun to speak loudly into the trees and she wondered if he had lost his senses. Then she heard a voice answer him from the forest. It was a harsh, echoing sound, like the voices of the spirits in the cave and it reminded her also of the sound of the augury stones being tumbled in their metal bowl. The hair on her neck stood up and it took all her hardihood not to leap away through the trees like a hare. Clinging to a clump of grass to keep herself still, terror washed through her time and again. At last she had to lie down, partly for concealment and partly because her legs were too weak to hold her, but once she was on the ground she regained possession of herself and could take in what was happening.

Her grandfather and the other were talking like two old friends — discussing the crops. She would have expected her grandfather to abase himself and cover himself with protecting talismans, but he was as calm and unconcerned as if he had known this spirit all his life. Though she strained her ears mightily for a long time she could not make out a word that was spoken by either. All she got was the impression that the talk was easy and cheerful. Once she even heard her grandfather laugh.

As she lay on the ground a creature, probably an owl, flew overhead. A pause, then it passed her again. She felt uneasy at this attention and watched some time for the bird to come again. When it did not she tried to worm her way through the grass to get nearer and hear what was said, but just as she was getting near enough her grandfather bade the spirit farewell and stood up. She froze like a rabbit and turned her face into the grass, for the hunters had told her that a face would attract notice sooner than any other part of the body. The sound of his footsteps passed, going back to the forest, and to her dismay when she raised her head she could not see where he had gone. She had assumed that he would stay in the clearing for the night which was now drawing on fast. Following him would be impossible and she did not know the way back home.

In panic she scrambled to her feet, ran across the clearing and shouted into the forest.

"Grandfather!"

A chuckle answered her from the blue shadows.

"Grandfather, it's me — I need your help."

The chuckle came again and with it the rushing sound she had heard before.

"Grandfather," she cried, "don't leave me! PLEASE! I don't know the way back. I'm frightened."

Something tangled in her hair, tugging it painfully. She

screamed and fell to the ground. She felt a hand on her arm and she screamed again, squeezing her eyes shut.

"Well now," said a voice, "is this the one who will dream the dream for her clan — screeching in terror at a wood-demon?" The hand was hot, hotter than any hand she had ever felt before. She tried to pull away, but the grip was unshakeable. Suddenly it let go and she curled into as small a space as possible.

"It is not that," came another voice, "it is a hedgehog."

She felt a hand on her other arm, but this one was cool and dry. And the voice was familiar. Squinting round she saw that she was right. Her grandfather was stooping over her and he was smiling at her fear.

"Stand up," he said, "there is nothing to be afraid of. I will take care of you."

She got to her feet slowly and looked around. There was no one else.

"Where is the wood-demon?" she asked.

"He has gone back to his home. He knew you were spying on us, but he would not harm you, not as long as I am here."

"Who is he?" she gasped.

"I may not tell you his name. I only discovered it that night when we sat by the fire. He is very powerful and has great wealth and he lives in the forest. That is all you need to know."

"Did you ask him for his help? Is that why we got the plough and the spears? From him?"

"He helped me to change the tribe's fortune. He told me where to find some people — powerful people."

"Then why have you come here today? The tribe is doing much better. The hunting is good and we have enough to eat. Next year we will have trade goods. You did not need to talk to him."

"It is better to make sure such as he remembers you."

"But it is dangerous. The terrible ones may follow you, or send someone to follow you."

"Are you telling me they have not?"

"What do you mean?"

"I was wondering how you came to be here. It is a hard place to find. You must have had help. Admit it, now, the old ones sent you, didn't they?"

"Indeed they did not. I found you my own self. I did not need help. I asked the hunters how to follow spoor and they showed me. I have told the old ones nothing."

He pulled the Cloak out of his pack and thrust it at her.

"This garment is very old and has much power. If you lie it will hear you, you can be sure."

"I do not lie. The old ones asked me about you — where you went — what you did — but I have never told them anything — not even about the night you wore the Cloak and looked for the name."

The old man smiled at her.

"You are a good child and clever. You learned all about trailing from the hunters?"

"Not all. They tried to tell me about hoof-marks and droppings, but I did not want that."

"When we get home you will go and ask them about animal spoor. You must never miss a chance to learn anything."

He gave her some dried deer meat and they set off up the long trail home.

Once they stopped to rest and she returned to her question.

"If the tribe's fortunes are mended, why did you come to speak to the wood-demon?"

"You will understand one day."

"Tell me and I may understand now."

"You are still a child and in our clan children are spoken to. At any time they may speak to an adult and hear the truth. This is necessary for the children to learn everything they need. When the child becomes an adult he does not talk. He may talk to his fellows about work, or join in the chanting at the feasts. But if the talk is not essential it is frowned on. It is very hard."

"I know that. It is the way we live. It is not so very hard."

"For members of our family it is hard. We are forbidden to speak to anyone below our station, except the terrible ones, in case we say a word wrong and the world is put out of place. It was said that your mother died only because your father had talked to the High-King about her. We must watch our mouths for the good of the clan. But it is hard. You will find out yourself in time."

"That is why you come to the wood-demon? So that you can talk?"

"That is why. It is safe to talk to him — he is as powerful as we are, perhaps more so, and the balance is not disturbed when we talk."

"Will I talk to him when I am an adult?"

"I cannot say. It is more a question of whether he will talk to you. Now come on or we will not be home before moonset."

Summers passed and she became a woman. Then it was time for her to take her place as the queen of the tribe. The old ones washed her and led her to the biggest cave where she was to fast for nine days and nights. Her course was about to start again and it heightened the sense of doom bearing down on her. They led her far down the cave to the back where she was surprised to find a narrow tunnel she had never known was there. The old ones indicated that she should kneel and crawl through it. Fighting off a choking sensation, she did as she was told and found the tunnel soon widened again into a cave not quite high enough for her to stand up in. No word was spoken as a lamp was pushed through to her then, to her horror, she was left alone.

It was cold and damp in the cave. She was glad she had her skin Cloak to lie on for the chill would have struck her to the bone without it. As the day wore on she kept clutching at this tiny light of comfort — at least she had her Cloak to keep her warm. The old ones had told her water would be supplied and, already thirsty, she heard a dripping in the darkness behind her. On investigating with the uncertain lamp she found a small stone dish on the floor where it caught a runnel of water — a few mouthfuls a day for her. That was her other comfort.

She sat down and looked about her. The walls and roof of the cave were painted red. On the red background were painted the animals who would help her through her vigil as they had helped queens before her. The salmon, the hare and the goose had been described to her as particularly powerful, since they moved swiftly and strongly in all the different elements. She did not like the way they had been depicted here and wished she had been given materials so that she could paint them in the glowing colours their power demanded. In her mind she asked their forgiveness for this crude drawing with the eyes too large and the legs too thin, and begged them to continue friendliness towards her in her hour of need. After a while the lamp went out.

The rest of her time of trial passed in a nightmare. At first, since she knew her task was to dream, she lay down and recited the words she had learned over the long years of training. The old women had taught her to calm herself by repeating the words and thinking very carefully about the images that went with them. She soon found her way into the incantations.

"Lying here in the womb of the earth, I await the time of my renewal. Grant, oh mothers, peaceful heart and clear vision as I bind myself to creation. To the fox as he silently hunts to feed his family; to the seal as he traverses the wide minch; to the owl as she flies in darkness; to the wolf as he runs with his brothers; to the sow as she lies in the forest with her litter: to the crow as she searches for the dying; to the trout in the peat-stained water ..."

And so through the whole animal kingdom. Once they had all been greeted she went on to the vegetable world and to the rocks and minerals, to the sun and moon, to the earth herself and to the dead. After some hours she felt the ground under her begin to sway and consciousness left her. In her dreams she wandered the forest and the moors rejoicing. Every creature in every kingdom was her friend, and all of them returned her greeting from the pebbles on the shore to the maggots in a carcase. For a long time happiness ran through her in the same way a hive runs with honey. Then she woke up.

She opened her eyes into total darkness. The dark was so

strong it pushed down on her eyeballs. She closed her eyes again and there were tiny flashes of light yet when she tried to see again the lights still flashed. She sat up, gasping, and struggled to breathe evenly. With her hands she re-discovered the shape of her body and the cave she sat in. She found the water bowl and refreshed herself. It did not seem very full. How long had she been here? If there was so little water then she must not have been there long. What if she had only been there a few hours? There were still days to go — days in this darkness. Panic swept through her and she found she was gasping once again. She lay down and began her incantations again. She sat up again, choking. In spite of her training and her fast she needed to make water and did so in agony of mind. Her teeth were clattering together uncontrollably and the shaking travelled all through her body. Almost overcome, she moaned aloud, lay down on her Cloak and drew it round her. All around her in the shifting darkness she felt the walls of the cave begin to move rhythmically, closing on her little by little until something pressed on her face. She heard her own long scream of terror. And then she was not alone.

She felt a hand on her arm — hot, hotter than human — and steady, comforting her in her despair. The strongest one of all was there, as he had been in the forest and he promised, silently, that he would stay with her for the rest of her vigil. With tears she thanked him and felt herself gathered up in his arms. Together, from then on, they wandered the universe. He showed her things which only he knew. With him she touched the cold, hard moon and walked on the black rind of the sky. She found that stars felt like the taste of blaeberries and the north wind was truly a great river whose source was the mountains of the sun. He gave her jewelled collars and crowns and broke open an oak-tree so that she could feast on the honey. There was no one equal to him.

After nine days and nights the old women had to crawl into the cave and drag out her filthy, wasted body. They thought for a terrible moment that she had died and left her family without issue, but her eyelids quivered and with relief they began slapping her legs to revive her. In a little while she looked out at them and started to weep. This did not trouble them, for people often did strange things after their ordeal. Some never returned to their bodies at all so the signs of Kigva's awareness were all to the good. They washed her hair and her body and she began to talk to them. She told them only what they would expect to hear.

After her inauguration as queen she stopped speaking to anyone in public except the old ones and to them only when necessary. She could not speak to her grandfather while they were in the tent for fear that someone might overhear them. He had taken over the use of the Cloak altogether and she waited in vain for the old women to protest on her behalf. Perhaps they had not seen how much he wore it, or perhaps they no longer felt that far-seeing was important to them. As long as he did not abuse the power in the Cloak, she did not see any need to protest. People often came for his advice, now, leaving the terrible ones alone in their reeking darkness. The advice he gave was sound and the source to her of much prestige. It was not understood how he knew so many things better than the rest of the clan. It could only have come from spirits he held in his control, but the people felt the less they knew about such a source the better. Their intuition was correct, as some of his knowledge had come from the wood-demon. The rest was the wisdom he had acquired over the years which had never been acceptable without some magic to back it. Before this they had relied exclusively on their ancestors.

The secret the two shared about the presence in the forest made a bond between them which no other men and women in their tribe enjoyed. In silence she would lead him off into the forest, and none dared to question them about their comings and goings. Once they were clear of the village they would talk about important matters but when they came to the clearing the grandfather was the only one to speak. She did not complain about this, for even after her ordeal she was still afraid of the spirit and was happy to leave the old man to carry the burden of talk. If the truth were told she was not experienced enough to have anything to say worth hearing. She only accompanied the old man to ensure that she got her share of the prestige.

Then the old man had to die. Like his father before him he was killed by the leader of their greatest enemy. She had always known that one day she would put him in his coffin, yet now the time had come, devastating loneliness settled on her shoulders. Who would she talk to? Who would talk to the wood spirit for her and the clan? Most important of all, who would lead the clan in battle?

Her eye fell on the leader of the strangers who had come from the High King. He was very young, as young as herself, yet he carried a lot of prestige as his men deferred to him. With his broad shoulders and muscular legs he was a most promising figure for a battle leader. He had been doing grandfather the courtesy of getting drunk for his wake and was now sagging against the door of the guest-house. The old women were the drunkest of all that night and there was no time to go and ask the wood-demon for his advice. She tried to think carefully about the consequences of her actions as she had been taught to do, but her decision was made almost before she started. In the light summer rain she walked down to the guest-house and sat down in front of the youth.

Along with the clan and the High King's vassal she travelled down the mountain to find a home away from the lands of their enemy. On the third night out they found a wonderful place. A natural clearing in the forest, with plenty of grazing and as much water as they could ever use. There was a level area for building houses and plenty of big timber already fallen to make huts for the clansmen. They had all settled down and made plans to start building when, on their second night there, she had dreamed a power dream. In it she stood in the forest washed with moonlight. A voice she knew almost as well as her grandfather's had spoken to her; the wood-demon. Trembling with joy, she waited to hear her lord's first words to her since the days of her ordeal.

He said, "I do not want you to stay in this place. It may seem to you to be a good place now, but if you stay I will visit awful punishments on you. Your sheep will sicken and die with their bellies swollen. Your children will be covered with sores. Your women will fail to conceive and you yourself will be driven from the clan."

"Why will you do this to us?" she asked him, aghast. "Our presence here will not harm you."

"Not now, perhaps, but in the years to come, when the children alive now have children of their own, there will be too many living here. My hall is not far away and, as your tribe spreads out over the land, I will be invaded. I wish to stop this now, before it begins."

"We would respect your boundaries," she protested.

"You say so, but who else in your tribe do you speak for? You are not your grandfather and it will be many years, if ever, before your voice has his weight."

"Already men listen when I speak. I am still the only representative of my family here."

The answer was a laugh like a gale blowing through the forest. Angry, she said,

"I tell you, if I forbid them to go near your halls they will obey. I might be young, but I speak with the authority of my family."

"As long as you stayed high on the moorland where life was hard and the forest a dark mystery you would be obeyed. The clan believed that only your mother's kin could walk the forest safe from the spirits that lived there. Now you have brought them far away into the lower lands. Soon the smallest child will walk through the thickets with his head up where before he would stride boldly only on the naked crag. Your voice will mean nothing."

"How can you be so sure?" she protested. "You do not know how deep the customs run in our tribe. It is like the bones in our flesh."

"Some things cannot be avoided, and men's memories are short. I tell you I have seen much, much more of life than you.

As the leaves fall in autumn and the snow melts in spring, the life you led has passed away. With it have gone the customs that sustained it. Your duty now is to follow the hard young man you have joined with your body."

"Where will he take me?"

"To his father's fortress on the coast. There you and your clan will be treated as nothing much better than slaves, but you will be together. And you will wait for your time to come again."

Desperate to keep within the circle of his power she asked,

"What about the service I owe you?"

"What service can a poor creature like you offer?"

His answer was a knife in her heart and she replied tearfully,

"You helped my grandfather when poverty laid us as low as our rain-flattened barley. I must repay that debt."

"I have no demands to make of you. That debt died with your grandfather. All I ask of you is that you should not disturb my peace."

"Grandfather told me the debt was to have been paid by the whole tribe."

"Your grandfather had his pride, and offered the service of the tribe in exchange for the favours I did him. I accepted because he would not have taken my help otherwise. It is not good to make people grateful to you. Soon enough such gratitude turns to hate. I have lived long and I know it well. It is wiser to put a price on your generosity."

Appalled, she said,

"Are you not willing to accept our services?"

"Not I."

"Then why did you help me at my inauguration?"

"I know nothing about your savage notions."

"During my vigil there came a time when my strength failed me. I nearly died of horror on that night, but you were by me and walked with me through those dark hours. Do you not remember?"

"You have had a strange dream, child. I never meddle with the rituals of others. You owe me nothing."

"There is nothing you wish me to do for you?" she cried.

"Nothing except to return to your family and help them to work for their new master."

"I hate him, and I will have nothing to do with him!" she wept.

"Then you can do nothing for me," he answered, "for that is all I wish."

The sound of her sobbing woke her. Her husband had decided to spend that night with his men and she was grateful that he had done so. The grief was uncontrollable and it would have been too shaming for him to see her suffer like this.

She spent the rest of the night in thought and in the morning she summoned the old ones and told them of her decision to leave.

*

And she was betrayed again. He was planning to discard her — the fine young man with his hair blue and black like the raven's breast. To follow him she had told her people they must leave the forest clearing and abandon for ever all their hopes of a peaceful and independent life. They had come away, but resentfully, and only because she had used her last shred of authority to force them. She knew that from then on any control she may have over them would come from her husband's authority. Now even that was to be taken from her.

The evening she discovered this she had been lying waiting for her man. He was standing outside the tent door talking to one of his men and she could hear nearly everything he said. It was probable that he did not realize she could understand his language or he would not have given himself away so soon. He spoke of the wood-demon and boasted that he had got the better of him in a contest of guile. How he had done this she could not follow, but she was pleased that her husband had made the acquaintance of her master. It would give them equal status.

Then she heard the words,

"The woman I am to marry is young and healthy, and so am I. We will have plenty of children." She was puzzled. Were they not already married by the fact that he had taken her maidenhead? That night as he lay beside her she unsealed her mouth to ask.

"How do people marry in your land?"

"With a great feast," he answered ingenuously, "so that there are very many witnesses. Once the man and the woman have stood up in front of all these people and had their hands bound together everyone will know that they have a contract. Then they go to the bed together and make babies who will be the heirs."

"Does everybody do this?"

"Only the people who matter — who own cattle and land and forest and shore. When others decide to make children, they just do what is necessary."

"We are not married, then?"

"What an idea," he said, laughing uproariously. "I could not marry you. But do not be afraid. I have been well reared and I will not abandon my concubine. And at the end of the year you may go where you will and your people also."

When he had sated his lust and slept like an infant beside her, she slipped out of the tent. Beckoning the old one who was on watch they ran silently to the other women. When she told them the shameful truth their eyes glittered in the firelight.

"In his eyes I am nothing," she said, too wretched to weep, "and when he marries this other woman I will lose all face before my people. What shall I do? You must advise me."

"How shall I advise you?" said one, licking her lips, "I hardly know who you are. You have never found the need to seek our advice before, why do you need us now?"

"Always before you have asked your grandfather for his advice and left us to ourselves," said another. "Why do you not ask him now? Go back up the mountain and seek him in his coffin where we left him."

"We have nothing to say that you would wish to hear," said the third. The queen was angry at this presumption.

"I never sought advice from my grandfather," she said. "Many others did, but not I. I did not need it. I did not need the advice of any of my inferiors, until now. I have every right to ask you for your opinion at any time and I will do what I please with your answer."

The old ones dropped their gaze. After a pause one of them said,

"You did not ask our advice when you coupled with that youth. Why should we believe you need it now?"

"I do not have to listen to insolence," she snapped. "Since you will not give me your words on the matter I will tell you what we will do. I am probably with child by now, and I will not bear the brat in the man's own hall. Therefore we will leave and go back to the forest we know. The rest of the tribe will be under the man's protection, so they will not suffer any more than if I had stayed."

She paused, seeing that one of them had something to say.

"You will not be revenged on himself?" she said slyly.

"I will not," she replied warmly.

"The insult to your face must be paid for," said another.

"True, but it need not be now. My children need the man so I will spare him."

"There must be a blood payment now, or the spirits will be restless. With a child in the womb it is no time to anger them."

"Very well," she sighed. "I suppose it must be so. Who is suitable?"

"There is one," said the oldest and again licked her lips. "His battle chief is a foreigner — one who sells his sword and has no loyalty to clan or king. He fought with Aethelstan against our men, and the blood of one of them could well be on his hands. Let it be him."

"Do you others agree?" she asked, reluctantly, for the man had not harmed her.

The hooded heads nodded vigorously. She shrugged,

"As you wish," she said, "but as soon as it is done we leave this place."

They were gone as soon as the words left her. Before she might think better of it, they were back, their knives smoking in their hands.

"Now we go," they said.

*

In the misty dawn they returned along the track they had travelled. They had taken one horse and the goods they owned of right, nothing more, for they would not steal from the clan, however great the need. As they travelled the old ones talked as eagerly as children about how it would be when they got back to their home. She had to put an end to their hopes.

"How can we go home?" she asked them. "You forget, our enemies have taken the moorland we worked. We shall have to find other camping grounds."

"But the caves — our ancestors — everything is there." They were bemused.

"And everything is in the hands of the Fir Falbh," she repeated. "There is no return for us to that place. Do not be unhappy. The Fir Falbh at least will respect our holy places, not like the dogs who led us away from them. They would only have desecrated the shrines and torn the grave-mounds open for the sake of the treasure they would find there. Treasure! As if any as poor as we could find gold to put with our ancestors.

"We must move on. I only wish I knew where."

They struggled on in silence along the stony track. The trees on either side leaned down and hung over them without sheltering. The rain had come again — the fine, soaking rain of the hills — and, saturated, they slowed down and finally stopped. The track was proving to be a stream-bed.

"We cannot go on like this," said the queen through her dripping hair. "I know the forest is dark and treacherous — paths there twist and turn like adders in the grass — but it would be better to take a chance on losing sight of the road than on everything we own being soaked."

"True," said the oldest one promptly, "and if one of us walks backwards to see that the path we have travelled does not shift as we leave it we should be able to return."

"Good," said another, "over there is a place where the trees part and the ground between them is firm."

Hand in hand they left the track and made their way up through the trees. As she was the strongest person, Kigva led the horse. The creature seemed uneasy and as there was little underbrush she began to wonder if they had made a mistake. If the way was so clear there might well be people around to clear it, and people in the forest were even more secretive than the moorland tribes. She was opening her mouth to speak when the horse's bridle was snatched from her hand. It whinnied and reared, but whoever held it was strong and determined. She glimpsed a dark-clad form on the other side of the beast, then it was mounted and ridden off into the trees at a speed she would not have thought possible. In its panniers was their tent, their loom and their grind-stones, along with most of their food.

Too shocked to move the four women stared into the forest.

"What shall we do now?" whimpered one of the old ones.

"We must follow them." said the queen. "We have no shelter and no food if we do not."

"Easy to say," said the old one. "The wretched creature is nowhere to be seen. Will you risk us all in that wilderness?"

"The horse is gone but its trace is still on the ground. Look!"

"Oh, we know all about your tracking skills," jeered the old one, "but what happens when the horse crosses ground that does not take a hoof-print. What shall we do then?"

"If that should happen — and I do not think it likely — we shall turn round and re-trace our footsteps to the road. But let us not run ahead to seek out troubles. We need that horse and what it carried very badly. It is worth risking something to regain it."

Without waiting for more arguments she made off through the trees and, grumbling, the old women followed her. The horse's tracks were easy enough to follow as long as the rider took it over the soft ground between the trees. They followed on for a long time while the clouds above the tree-tops broke apart to reveal the blue of the sky. It grew hot in the shelter of the trees and the women began to look for water. They came to a fast, clear river and drank their fill, then found the prediction of the oldest was true. The river banks, uphill of them and down, were great slabs of stone. On them no trace of the horse could be seen.

Kigva told her women to rest and wait for her. They moaned and obeyed, gratefully sinking to the ground. She set off downhill with more assurance in her step than she felt. The higher slopes were familiar and she knew the ground was so rough that horses and horse-thieves were less likely. Fortunately she soon saw a hair of the horse's tail tangled in a low branch. She checked that the tracks were indeed visible beyond there and paused to look around. The sun had dried the rocks and the forest was brimming with the sound of birds and insects. She straightened up and threw back her hair with a sigh. The forest was a good place to be, and she would be nearer to her Lord here than if she had gone down to the coast with the youth. Cheerfully she scampered back to her women.

They had fallen asleep on the warm rocks. The pale flesh of their wrinkled faces slumped and pulled their mouths open so that they drooled and snored.

"These were the mighty ones of my tribe," she thought. "When they passed everyone looked at the ground and trembled in case they might look at them."

In that moment she came to a decision. Perhaps the way of life she had grown up in was truly finished — that could be a good thing for her. She was not her mother's daughter nor could she hope to be. Whatever happened, she was sure of one thing. She would not spend her days the way the old ones had done. If she must grow old like them and sag and make nasty noises, she must first see more than a piece of moorland and a few damp caverns.

A noise behind her caught her attention. Turning, she saw four or five men clad in dark, greasy skins. Each held a short, iron-headed spear and a strung bow. The quivers at their waist held small, bone-tipped arrows and the knives at their belts were long and made of blue metal. There would be no escape from such assailants.

"You will come with us," they said.

*

They were taken downslope for many miles till they came to a vast level space. There huge beech trees closed out the sky as far as the eye could see. The undergrowth between the trees had been cleared away for miles and in the open space many, many fine pigs were grazing. There were strong wooden houses in the shelter of the trees and yet smoke rose to the high, green canopy of leaves from only a few. This scarcity made Kigva wonder.

"Perhaps it is too warm to build cooking fires," she thought.

They were ushered silently into one of the houses and found it clean and dry. Good bedding was laid out for them. Food was handed in by one of the men and they ate well. In their clan they valued a full stomach as a means to clear thought and they had had a long fast since morning. After food they began to discuss their situation.

"Do you know these people?" Kigva asked.

"They are strangers to us."

"They have not offered us harm."

"There is no reason why they should do us good."

"Are they the ones who stole the horse?"

"We have no way of knowing, but we have seen no sign of any other people in this country."

"Many of the houses have no fire."

"Perhaps none live there."

"Such fine houses! They must have owners."

"I have seen no children."

"I have seen no women."

"They will be kept apart."

Their ramblings were interrupted by the arrival of one of the stranger men. On top of his head he had placed a boar's skull so that the fangs jutted forward from his head like horns. A whole boar's skin hung down his back in a cloak except for the pizzle which he held as a staff of office.

"You will all come with me," he said, quietly.

They allowed him to lead them between the trees towards a great wooden house that stood in the thicket. Kigva noted that the pigs in the clearing were all tethered to the trees by long plaited ropes of pigskin so that they could graze without wandering off. The mast they rooted in was two hands deep and the animals seemed contented. She wondered if the ropes were strong enough to hold them if they were not.

The man led them through the door of the house into darkness. As their eyes got used to the gloom they found themselves confronted by a crowd of men. Their gear lay at their feet and it was obvious that it had been thoroughly examined, for the tent was spread out on the floor and everything else lay on top of it. They heard a whinny from outside the house and were confirmed in their notion that these were also the horse-thieves. The man with the boar's head spoke.

"We are the boar people, now known as the Old Men. No one who comes to this part of the forest may pass without paying us tribute."

"How may we pay tribute," said Kigva, bravely, "when you have stolen everything we own?" She nodded towards their unpacked gear.

"That is ours by right of conquest," said the man.

"Then so, for that matter, are we," she replied.

"I like a woman who does not waste time," said the chief, "and because I like that I will explain our situation to you.

"For many generations our people worked for a great spirit who lived in the mountains ..."

A murmur of assent ran through the assembly. Kigva felt her body tingle at the words. The chief continued,

"His wisdom was our guide and his strength was our shield against dangers. But three generations ago we disobeyed him, and then his wrath was terrible. Since then the fertility of our women has been falling every year. Some cannot conceive, some cannot bring a child into the world alive. Many have died in the attempt."

A sigh ran through the crowd of men.

"What did you do to bring this punishment on you?" asked Kigva.

"We are not sure. Perhaps it was that we trespassed, unknowing, on his hunting land, or perhaps it was because we killed one of his servants with an arrow. He turned his face from us at the time and would not tell us what our sins were. All we can be sure of is that we are suffering for it."

"Why are you telling us about it now?"

"You are young and there are many years of child-bearing in you. We will keep you until you have borne us many children. If you do well, at that time we will let you go where you will. If you do not we will kill you because you know our shame."

Beside her Kigva felt the old ones stiffen with fear. They were long past child-bearing, if they had ever done so. If they had it was never spoken of — nothing they did was ever spoken of.

"What about my women?" she demanded.

"They are no use. We do not need any more mouths to feed which will not do their share of work."

"We are still strong," said the oldest, "we can do our share."

"I do not think so," said the chief with a shrug. "The raising and feeding of pigs takes many years to learn. That is why we want children."

"We know many things," said the old woman, "and we can make potions and charms to help restore your women to fertility. You may well need us more than you think."

"Do you all know these things?" the chief asked them.

The three nodded eagerly.

"Then we only need one of you," said the chief and beckoned two of his men to remove the two oldest. The old women began to wail, and the chief looked at them in disgust.

"What is the matter with you?" he said. "You are old and near to death. Why should you want to clutter the forest floor any longer?"

"Wait," said Kigva, "I have something to say."

"What can you have to say? Be quick, for we are eager to begin."

"The oldest is a very wise woman. Her charms are potent and she is very powerful in herself."

The chief rubbed his face and looked at his men.

"What do you think?" he said. "Shall we keep her for a while longer?"

"It is not good to offend powerful people," said one voice. "We know that too well already."

"She may truly know something useful to us," said another.

"Old women eat very little. Give her time to prove her worth."

"Very well," said the chief, "let the oldest stay." The old woman fell at Kigva's feet with a whimper. The soldier started for the door with her junior.

"A moment more, great chief," said Kigva hastily.

"Do you wish us to spare the other one also? I am afraid this is not possible."

"You want a fertile woman," Kigva blurted out. "Well, here you have one, but I am already with child."

"You do not look as if you are," said the chief looking at her flat stomach.

"It is early. A short while ago I was ravished by the son of the High King and I will show my state soon enough."

"How can you be sure?"

"I told you, my women are very wise. They have certain ways of knowing the truth of these things and they have told me. The second one especially is a very great midwife. Her hands have magic in them and many children of our clan owe their lives to her."

The chief pulled at his chin for an age while Kigva and the others stood like strung bows waiting for his decision.

"I suppose it will do no harm to believe you. If what you say is true, it would be terrible to destroy such a valuable person."

"Thank you, oh, thank you, great chief," said Kigva. "I am happier than I can say to think that she will be with me in my travail. You will see — her skills are great — I promise you."

They were restored to the house they had first entered and there they were to live till the child was born. The oldest was taken away daily to show the boar-people's chief all her secrets. Kigva had saved her life for a time, but her heart was broken by her trials and soon the second had to take her place. The youngest of the three was Kigva's personal attendant. This was necessary, for Kigva could not move abroad herself. Like the pigs she was tethered to the house by her ankle and like the pigs also she was contented to stay that way till her delivery. As the days passed and her belly became swollen she knew that her Lord knew of her fate. In time, she was sure, he would come and save her.

Lapis ex caelis

by Anne Cameron

> ... by the power of that stone the phoenix burns to ashes but the ashes give life again ... looks will not fade ... appearance will stay the same as on the day she saw the stone ... the same as when the best years of life began, save that the hair might turn grey ... such power does the stone hold and give that flesh and blood are at once made young again.

> *The stone is also called The Grail.*
> *Stone from heaven — It fell from the heavens*
> *a stone fallen from the heavens.*

The great egg hung in the void for ages untold, and then the force of life within began to surge and pulse. The shell of the egg cracked, and through the crack came the water of life, pouring out in a torrent that became a giant river which fell from on high and touched the waiting globe. Seeds were borne on the river, and from the seeds came grass and flower, tree and bush, reed and tuber, until the once barren orb was beautiful and green. Fish and birds, then, animals and bugs, all manner of creature came from the river of life, and when the world was ready, First Woman was created. Within her body she carried the seeds of life and her children were many.

When it was Time, the river of life divided itself into four rivers, and spread off in four directions. The children followed the rivers to find their own homelands, to fill the earth with the children of the Mother, to keep alive the dream and the promise, and Old Woman wove the fabric of destiny.

The ice of the earth began to spread, and the children of the Mother moved ahead of it, following rivers and streams, crossing the inland sea, moving south, ever southward, leaving behind them great carved stones so their grandchildren many-times-removed would be able to find their way back to the original homeland, and by the time the ice began to recede, these children were scattered far and wide over the earth, and still the dream of home called them.

Some of the children made their way back again, and found the inland sea was gone, in its place an ocean of grass in which grazed more animals than anyone would believe. They found valleys where the ice had not seized hold, valleys where the First Tribe had managed to survive throughout the long cold. They settled in, living together as friends, guarding the dream and protecting the promise.

Others of the children found themselves pulled by a desire they could not understand, and they searched, moving out from Persia, moving out from Libya, moving out from Africa, following the instinct they no longer recognized as the voice of the Mother. They moved through Russia and the Ukraine, and as they moved, they changed physically until they no longer resembled who they had once been.

Banba left the encampment and went to the thicket by the stream which drained from the small sweet-water pool. She sat smoothing the sand, removing the pebbles and the rocks, preparing the place and making it as comfortable as she could, then she lay curled on her side, hugging her knees, her swollen belly heaving with contractions.

The infant girl came easily, but the afterbirth refused to follow. Time and again, Banba's body convulsed in vain, then the placenta ruptured under the pressure and blood seeped from her body, soaking into the dry desert earth beneath her. She held her daughter and spoke softly to her, believing her drowsiness was natural after the effort of labour and birth. The newborn nuzzled close, her eyelids fluttering, one fist jammed into her mouth.

When the brilliant light flashed across the heavens the young mother, Banba, little more than a girl herself, was almost dead, her body exsanguinating, her mind drifting. She had no idea what the light was or what it meant, and it was only coincidence that out of all the seconds of eternity, her fluttering eyelids were open at precisely that pinpoint in the ocean of time, only coincidence that her dying eyes focused, however briefly, on the light.

Although there are many people, most of them clever, who deny the existence of that which is referred to as coincidence.

The light flared against the purple-black of the velvet night sky, and Banba's body trembled, each and every fibre of her being altered, made different, made more than merely human, made both ordinary and extraordinary, become what we all are, but something else, too.

The stone fell to earth, flaming with something hotter than mere fire, consumed as it plummeted, so that what might have been a mountain when it was first catapulted into the heavens was but the size of a small hen's egg when it came to rest in the sand beside the child-mother.

Banba's chest heaved, her lungs expanded, she took the deepest and most important breath of her life, and the air she drew into her lungs was scented with the perfume of lilies and roses, mayflower and apple blossoms. The torn placenta slipped from her body, the haemorrhaging stopped, the cells of her body stopped deteriorating and the encroaching chill faded. She slept briefly then, her skin pallid and clammy, her mind floating in some land she had never seen. The infant, lying on her mother's body, stirred and wiggled closer, seeking warmth, comfort, nourishment.

It was the child's wail awakened Banba. She rolled onto her side and moved the infant so she could suckle. Then, looking past the child's small head, Banba saw the stone. It was blue streaked with green, it was pink streaked with black, it lay in the sand gleaming, still hot, pulsing white and blue, giving warmth, giving life, giving comfort, giving strength.

Banba reached out with one hand but did not touch the hissing stone. She closed her eyes, not really sleeping, not entirely awake.

The infant nuzzled, her mouth closing demandingly on the nipple, and sucked strongly. Banba's body was practically desiccated. There was barely enough fluid left to keep her heart pumping, but something — something — pulsed from the stone, along her outstretched fingers, through her hand, along her arm. The child drank, then slept.

The sky was light and the first sounds were celebrating the day, the song of birds, the bleating of sheep and goats. Banba saw the hide tents of the nomadic people but she could not remember what they were. She saw animals but was ignorant of their use, she saw people moving toward her but had no reason to know they were her husband and two of her sisters. Nothing meant anything to her, nothing had reason or importance to her. She was actually younger than her own newborn daughter, for the child had been hours old when the stone fell from heaven and gave Banba rebirth.

The young husband and the two sisters saw Banba lying in a wide dark stain of blood-soaked sand. They did not see the stone, they did not smell the fragrance, they did not think the pulsing lights and colours were anything more than the false-water mirages they had learned to ignore. What they did see was the wide-open unblinking eyes, the sand stained black with blood, the child lying without moving. They were so used to death, so used to infant mortality, so conditioned to equating blood with fatality, that they believed immediately the evidence of their own eyes.

They wailed and screamed, they grieved and mourned, they rolled on the sand and howled. Banba tried to speak to them, not because she wanted to comfort them, not because she recognized them, but only to try to stop the dreadful noise. She made a sound deep in her throat, she even managed to lift her hand, but the three who had once loved her misinterpreted and thought the dead body had been taken over by a daemon. They shrieked in terror, whirled, and fled, stumbling and screeching.

Banba did not care if they left or stayed as long as the terrible noise stopped. She sighed, closed her eyes, and slept.

It was the uproar of the hysterical trio moved the young black bitch from the nest she had made and in which she had given birth to her first litter of puppies. The screaming and hollering, the wailing and roaring reminded her that her bladder was distended, her bowels rumbling. She stood, nuzzled her puppies, sniffed them, pushed them closer together to keep each other warm, then she moved away from the noisy encampment to stretch her cramped muscles and relieve herself.

The nomadic people needed only to hear that Banba had died and her body been taken over by a daemon, and they were racing in panic, stuffing their few possessions in carry-packs, hauling down their skimpy hide tents, gathering up their waterskins and cooking pots. The black bitch had not yet reached the camp when the hysterical people chased their herds of tough goats and stringy sheep away from the cursed place. She raced faster than she had ever moved in her life, but she did not get back in time to divert the herds or die with her helpless puppies. By the time she got there, they had been so trampled into the dirt there wasn't even a damp spot.

The young bitch lay grieving, glaring at the cloud of dust left in the path of the ones who had caused this to happen. She nursed her pain and her grief, madness threatening to engulf her spirit.

Banba wakened, blinked her eyes, and saw at once that the stone was cool, the tents and animals gone, the shadows lengthening as the hot desert sun moved toward the distant horizon. She reached for the stone and curled her fingers around it, and in that split second she knew what she needed to know. She knew that the child suckling was her daughter, she knew her daughter had come from her very own body, she knew how the child had come to grow inside her. She even knew her own name, Banba. She did not know from whose body she herself had come. She supposed, forever after, that she was the child of the stone that had fallen from the heavens, and since her own child was suckling and nuzzling at her body, Banba picked up the stone and put it to her mouth, her lips pressed against it, her tongue licking it, her entire body throbbing and pulsing with something stronger than life itself.

She did not sleep. She sucked on the stone until her daughter's belly was full, then Banba rose and began to walk to the stream. She did not wonder how she knew there was water there, or how she knew she needed to drink, she accepted that she knew, accepted even that she knew water was precious, and vital.

She knelt by the stream, bent forward, put her face in the water and drank deeply. When she lifted her face she realized, with no feeling of shock at all, that her hair was white, the whitest white she had ever seen. She smiled and the reflection in the pool smiled back at her.

Banba put her daughter Macha in the pool, and washed the dried blood from the infant's body. The baby squirmed protest, opened her mouth, and wailed with fury, flailing her tiny hands and feet. Banba's smile turned to laughter, and she was filled with love for this wonder which had come from her own body. When the child was clean, Banba wrapped her in the cloth she usually wore over her head and shoulders, then put the child on the ground and stepped into the water herself, washing her own body and the stained tunic that hung from her shoulders to just below her knees.

She came from the pool cleansed and refreshed, the wondrous stone clutched in her hand, an egg-sized sweet-scented marvel she knew the rest of the world would kill to get. The stone pulsed and Banba's body responded; her hand lifted the stone to her mouth, her mouth opened, she swallowed. If it had been any ordinary stone or if she had tried to swallow it before the magic had changed her forever, Banba would have choked to death, but now the perfumed stone slid easily down her throat and settled comfortably in her stomach. Banba picked up Macha and headed off across the desert, her steps firm and bold.

She walked all night, holding her daughter tenderly, feeling stronger with each passing minute, nourished by the lapis ex caelis in her belly. During the night the stone taught her to take the cloth she had once worn over her shoulders and head and fashion a sling to hold Macha safely and comfortably, leaving Banba's arms and hands free. The stone taught her other things, many other things, and by the time the sun leaped from its place of rest, Banba knew more than she had known before she was reborn. And all night as she walked, she knew she was being followed by a grief-crazed bitch who was waiting for a chance to do to Macha what the terrified idiots had done to her puppies.

In the morning the dog moved forward, hate burning, eyes glaring, but then the scent of the stone came to her on Banba's breath. Scent of lily, scent of roses, scent of cinnamon, scent of something without name on this earth, and the dog moved forward, heart healed, brain strong, tail wagging. "Chu," said Banba, and it was Chu who leaned against the woman's leg, it was Chu who thrilled to have her head scratched. "Good Chu," Banba crooned.

That night they slept together, the woman, the infant, and the dog, and only they knew whether it was Banba or Chu provided the milk the child Macha suckled.

When they wakened, the child was sitting upright, playing with her own toes, laughing and happy. Banba knew no ordinary newborn could sit so strongly or laugh so loudly; she also knew no ordinary newborn would have grown so much hair overnight, and every bit of it as white as her own.

Banba was thirsty and so was the bitch Chu, so Banba stamped her foot and the earth spewed water for them. When they had drunk their fill the water returned to the earth, leaving several large fish flopping in the sand. Banba gathered dry sticks, knocked them together, and there was a fire. She cooked the fish, sharing them with Chu, and then they moved on again, woman, child, and dog. And when next they stopped to rest the child had teeth, and could eat the same food as the woman and the dog.

They moved on, staying away from the nomadic people, staying away from those who thought Banba evil, staying away from those who had caused the death of Chu's babies and might well cause the death of her own dear daughter, and who knows how long they lived like that? And does it even matter? They walked and they fished, they gathered berries and wild food, they saw everything there was to see, and in the seeing, they learned.

At some point, it doesn't matter when, Chu began to whine, then to bark.

"Show me," Banba urged, and the dog moved forward.

"Wait here," Banba said, but her daughter shook her head stubbornly.

The trap had been set in a tree above the animals' path to the water, and the mare was caught in it, trapped so that she could barely move. Banba knew the horse was destined to be supper if the hunters found it.

"Hush," she said, but the horse still struggled. "You have to be still," she said, "or we won't get you out and the next ones to come will kill you." But still the horse struggled.

Then Banba's daughter was pushing past her, moving unafraid to the horse's head, patting the animal and whispering to it. The mare stopped her thrashing, bent her head as the child leaned forward to speak in her ear, and was calmed.

They had only their fingers and teeth, their wits and their determination, but they got the mare free of the net, and led her to where she could drink safely.

"If the hunters have set their traps here we mustn't stay," Macha said firmly.

"The child gives advice to the mother," Banba teased.

"I," the little girl replied confidently, "am older than you are, you told me yourself!"

"I should have told you nothing," her mother answered. "I should have left you in the dirt and gone off by myself." But neither of them believed her words.

Banba patted the animal and then suddenly she was up on the mare's back and the world was changed forever. Her child stared up at her and Banba laughed softly, then reached down her hand. "Come," she invited, "sit in front of me." Macha reached up her own hand, Banba took it, and as easily as that, they were both riding away from the place of danger, Chu loping alongside.

"What was it you whispered to the horse?" Banba asked.

"A secret," the girl teased, "and if I told you, it wouldn't be a secret any more."

"Listen to this," Banba marvelled, "the one who almost caused my death is talking to me in such a manner," and they laughed softly, knowing it was not the birth of the child had nearly caused Banba's death, for the child had slid easily into the world. Macha pulled gently at Banba's white hair, Banba lowered her head, and her daughter whispered to her the secret she had whispered to the horse.

"Oh," Banba marvelled, "how wonderful!"

Together they moved through the days and nights of their lives, Banba, her daughter Macha, the mare, and the bitch. The dog taught them there was food to be found in the nests of birds and in the bodies of small animals, the horse made travel easier than it had ever been, and the woman learned from the girl who learned from the woman, and life was more than merely tolerable.

Sometimes they found sheep or goats that had strayed from the herds of the nomadic people, and sometimes the animals were not strays at all, but taken at night by stealth. Sometimes they needed clothing, so they went at night and stole it. Sometimes it was a knife they took, or a bowl, or a warm cloak, or a blanket. Remembering how the wandering people had deserted them, cursed them, left them to die, they took what they needed when they needed it.

The tribesmen had no idea who it was would come in silence and make off with sheep or goats or other things. They had long ago forgotten the woman and child they had left to die. They invented wild tales of magic and mystery, and they spoke of beasts that could attack and devour an entire herd, then change form and move unsuspected as a man among men. They talked of giants and dwarfs, of phantoms and shades, and they scared each other half silly with each retelling of old lies.

Sometimes, and only when the free ones wanted, the tribespeople would see Banba and her daughter riding the horse. Instead of taking it as a lesson and learning to ride themselves, they spoke of an animal part human, part beast — and the human half two-headed at that. They told each other if ever they could find where this magical creature lived they would never need work again, or fight again, or do without again, for, they convinced each other, enormous treasure awaited the one who found the lair of this dreaded beast.

Banba and Macha did not know the people were inventing stories about them. They heard scraps and bits of the stories at night when they crept unseen close to the campfires of the nomads, but they never dreamed the fierce people were talking about them. They believed there really was a land of marvel, believed the tribespeople knew where the hybrid creature lived and were going there. They believed they were following the tribespeople when in fact the nomads were trying to follow Banba and Macha. In this way, they moved over land and over sea, over desert and over mountain, and though generation after generation of humans was born, lived, and died, Banba and Macha did not significantly change. The story of the damned woman and cursed infant did change, evolving gradually into the story of the blessed woman and holy daughter, and each version was as true as the version that came later and was even more changed.

One day Banba looked at her daughter and realized that the young woman not only looked as old as Banba did, she actually looked just a bit older.

"When I was younger than you," she remembered, "I was married and had a child."

"Yes," said her daughter. "Yes, and you were not lonely."

"Are you lonely?"

"Yes," Macha admitted, "I have watched other people dance, and listened to other people sing, and observed their lives for so long now, and in all that time the only person I have talked with is you."

"Well, then," Banba sighed, "I suppose we must do something about it."

Banba and Macha moved steadily toward the settlements of the herding people, living nearer and nearer to them. Bit by bit the people of the tribes grew to know the women, and began even to think of them as part of their own. When they no longer glared suspiciously at the two women, Banba moved closer, then even closer and soon she and her daughter were living among the travelling people, and Macha had all the company and all the friends she could want.

*

The truth of it was, Jehovah God was angry. More than just angry, Jehovah God was in a full-scale tooth-grinding hair-tearing rage.

First off, there was the matter of His Holy Name, Yhwh or Jhwh. Someone, somehow, somewhere along the line had lost the vowels, leaving only consonants, and the human tongue just isn't fashioned to talk nothing but consonants. Without the precious vowels, sound becomes noise and language becomes jargon, with nothing communicated and less understood. In the beginning was the word, but if the word is unpronounceable, people tend not to pay much attention to it. Lip service cannot be paid if the lips cannot twist themselves around the words.

Human lips could, however, twist easily around the many-vowelled Baalat, and were doing it with increasing frequency, even extending the name and the joy they took in saying it, extending it to Belit, Belit-ili, even to Beltis and Bilitis. They went to the temple and, ignoring Yhwh, they prayed to Baalat, sang to her, and took offerings to her. Calves, mostly, and Jhwh was very touchy around calves, cows, and even goats — unless, of course, they were sacrificed to him. Unfortunately, if your name is unpronounceable, people aren't inclined to direct prayers in your direction, and if they aren't calling on you to fulfil their desires, they don't have any reason to want to get on your good side, so the number of golden calves, burnished ewes, and silver-horned goats sent Yhwh's way was small and getting smaller.

And the people were living riotous lives, having parties in the name of Baalat, having other parties in the name of Belit-ili and

Bilitis and Ashtarte, having parties in the name of and to the glory of Epona the mare-headed goddess, but who was celebrating in the name of a name nobody could pronounce?

Noah.

Of all of them, only Noah was worshipping and honouring Jhwh or Yhwh, and Noah wasn't one for giving or having fun parties. Oh, he observed the observances and prayed the prayers, he disciplined his sons and let not his heart refrain from their grieving, he dutifully and with grim piety did what Yhwh told him to do, but not for Noah the loaf of bread, jug of wine, and happy song on the lips. Still, humourless or not, imaginative or not, fun or not, he was obedient and if you can't have love and affection, obedience will do.

Yhwh announced his coming. He rolled the thunder and cast the lightning bolts, he caused the winds to howl and the seas to churn. Instead of cowering and trembling, instead of repenting and smartening up, the people shrugged and said, "Oh, it's that guy with the weird name having another tantrum." They continued to honour the mother figures who, of course, put their warm and loving hands over the heads of the people and kept the worst of Jhwh's wrath from coming down on them.

Noah, however, looked at the signs and portents and knew something was about to happen. And it did. Jhwh descended from on high and showed himself to Noah and said unto him, "I'm going to wash this riffraff off the face of the earth. I'm going to cause it to rain as it hasn't rained since I don't know when, and the waters will rise until the entire earth is covered, then the waters will rise some more, and one way or the other, sooner or later, at whatever cost to whomever, things around here are going to change and be the way I want them to be."

"As Thou sayest, oh Lord God Most High," Noah answered.

"Build yourself an ark," Himself commanded, "and here are the measurements."

Noah took the blueprint in his hands and stared, uncomprehending. Yhwh reached out, turned the blueprint right side up, sighed, and mustered what little patience he possessed.

"When this boat is built," he said, slowly enough for even Noah to understand, "you will fill it with animals. Two of every kind of animal. One male animal and one female animal." He tried to cover all the bases because Noah was not what anyone would have called a quick-witted patriarch.

"And," Yhwh said sternly, "the only people who are to go in are you, your wife, your sons, and your sons' wives. All others, regardless of anything they might say, are doomed and damned. Understand?"

"As Thou sayest, oh Lord God Most High," Noah repeated.

"Noah, his wife, his sons, his sons' wives. Nobody else. Is that clear?"

It was clear. And as soon as Yhwh went back to that place from whence he had come, Noah set about having the ark built.

You can imagine the size of the thing. Never mind the cubits high or the cubits wide, pay no attention to the cubits long or the cubits deep, think of the load the thing was supposed to take. Think of the animals. Elephants and giraffes, rhinoceros and zebra, horses and cows, dogs and cats, jaguars and tigers, lions, buffalo, elk and moose, bears and raccoons, marmots and kangaroos, the list goes on and on and on; and Noah had been told to take two of each kind. How huge a space would you need for two grey whales? How much room do you need for a pair of musk ox? Camels and pigs, llamas and donkeys, chickens, turkeys, geese, ducks, cougars, wolves, and each of them needing food, each of them needing space, each of them needing shovelled out and cleaned up, each of them needing water to drink and air to breathe. Noah could have thrown up his hands and said it was impossible, but he didn't have the imagination for that. Jhwh had told him to do something, and Noah would do it. Helped by his wife, his sons, and his sons' wives.

Messengers went out with order forms, so many timbers of such-and-such a length, so many girders, so many thisses and so many thatses. Struts and ribs and crosspieces and mangers and stalls and shovel handles. Armies of workers were issued hundreds of thousands of axes and sent out to hack down entire forests. Hordes of haulers and pullers, scads of lifters and toters, phalanxes of bookkeepers and auditors, legions of assistants and apprentices.

"Crazy old coot," said some.

"Won't he look a fool," said others.

"Where's he getting the money?" asked many.

"What if he's right?" asked a young woman.

"Oh, Cessair," they laughed, "you've got to stop asking questions like that! There is no way at all he can be right! Flood the earth? Be reasonable."

"What if he's right?" Cessair repeated.

"It isn't possible to flood the earth. How could it possibly rain so much?"

"Why not?" she asked, but everybody laughed at her, and she walked off, sulky, angry, and more than ever convinced there were others besides Noah and his family who were short some of the basic necessities.

"I don't think he's crazy as a coot," she muttered. "A crazy coot couldn't get himself so organized in his fixation. He knows exactly how many nails he's going to need. He knows exactly how many hammers will wear out pounding all those nails. I think maybe he's on to something."

"Oh, I'm sure he is," Banba agreed quietly. "After all, Noah said Yhwh was in a foul mood, and sure enough, he shows up in a cloud of lightning, filling the air with the scent of brimstone."

"You don't think Noah is crazy?" Cessair asked.

"I don't think YOU are crazy," Banba corrected. "I've never been sure of Noah's mental stability. The man can't even throw a decent party!"

"What are you going to do if it rains?" Cessair asked.

"Me?" Banba shrugged. "Oh, I think I'll be ready for it." She waved casually in the direction of the docks where the Phoenician traders were arriving by ship at increasingly frequent intervals. "There are a lot of boats down there and sooner or later one of them ought to come up for sale."

"Boat?" Cessair frowned. "You mean ... ride 'er out?"

"He said," Banba lectured, "that it was going to RAIN. He

didn't say it was going to blow a hurricane, or storm for ten years. Rain. Drizzle drizzle drizzle."

"Float 'er out," Cessair agreed.

"That's it," Banba smiled. "Me, my daughter, my dog, our horses, maybe a canary or two just in case dim-bulb down there overlooks them ... and, of course, my daughter's kids."

"Would you like some company?" Cessair asked. "Some help with all the kids, perhaps?"

"That would be lovely," Banba agreed.

They went to the docks and spoke with the Phoenicians, they listened to the talk and hearkened the gossip, then Banba went into the hills with only her dog and her horse. She told a bit of a lie at that point: she told her daughter and Cessair and all the kids that she was going to pray, but that wasn't what she did at all. She went beyond the walls of the town, past the fields and meadows, into the rugged regions of the country, and sat with one hand on her belly, over the place where the heavenly stone was still lodged, and she thought about ships, and price, and how to pay. Then, when the stone knew what it was she needed, Banba stood up, stamped her foot as she had once stamped for water, and the earth split open for her.

She returned to the docks and before much time had passed she was the owner of not one but three fine tall ships. The Phoenicians smiled at each other and talked contentedly of fair exchange being no robbery, all of them dreaming sweet dreams of how they would enjoy the wealth of jewels Banba had paid for the boats. It beat the hell out of shipping mountains of timbers for that old fool's animal craft, said one.

Over at Noah's place the work was proceeding apace. Day after day, from dawn to dark, the hammering went unabated. Measuring and remeasuring, fashioning and shaping, taking possession of material and using it so more had to be ordered and shipped. Wagonloads of material were brought and off-loaded, the wagons returning empty to be refilled and another load of material brought. Saw saw, plane plane, sand sand, nail nail, hammer hammer, until the neighbours were ready to go right out of their gourds with the seemingly endless noise and uproar.

With all the coming and going, to-ing and fro-ing happening over where Noah toiled, nobody noticed at first that Banba and Cessair were gathering supplies and preparing for their own little project.

"Hey, Noah," shouted Bith, "if you're right and Jhwh sends the flood and the world is submerged ... what about me?"

"It is not permitted that you enter my ark," Noah said firmly. "The enormity of your sins is such that you too will be submerged."

Bith thought that was funny, and so did Fintan and Ladra, but their laughter weakened as the work progressed. Their eyes began to shift uneasily, and then Bith noticed that his daughter Cessair was spending a lot of time with old Banba the outlander and her daughter, who was mother of all those children.

"Hey, what are you doing?" he called. "And why aren't you at home getting my supper ready for me?"

"I have my work cut out for me right here," Cessair said firmly. "You might be willing to just stand around and drown, but some of us plan to help ourselves."

"Oh yeah?" laughed Fintan. "You and who else?"

So Cessair named the women who had joined Banba and her, and they were fifty of the most adventurous, fifty of the bravest, fifty of the most intelligent, fifty of the strongest, healthiest women on the face of the earth.

"Well," Fintan flirted, "why not let me help? I've done a bit of navigating in my time and I'm sure I'd be good company."

Banba laughed to herself, but made no objections, and the three men made arrangements to join the women.

"The one condition," Cessair said firmly, "is that from now until forever, I am the head of this expedition."

"Why you?" asked Ladra.

"Because Banba said she didn't want to be bothered and her daughter has her hands full with all those kids," Cessair answered easily.

"Don't be foolish!" Bith exploded. "I am your father! I am not going to take orders from you."

"Fine," Cessair shrugged, "off-load yourself and find some other way to survive the flood."

"Oh yeah?" Bith challenged. "And what if I just find some nice quick way to off-load YOU?"

"Oh, I don't think so," Banba said quietly. "After all, I am the owner of these boats, and if you try to off-load her, you'll have me to deal with. Try to off-load me and my dog will rip out your throat, try to touch the dog and the horse will trample you, look sideways at the horse and my daughter and her children will be all over you like hives."

"Oh," Bith nodded, as if convinced of something logical. "Oh. Well, right, then. For the time we're on the boat, you're the boss. After we get off the boat — "

"Right," Cessair laughed, "after we get off the boat you can piss off!"

Noah was still working on the very beginning of the skeleton of his ark and hadn't even started the monumental task of collecting animals, but Cessair, Banba, and the rest weren't of a mind to just sit around getting fat and watching him hammer, nor were they interested in waiting and letting Jhwh make the first move. They had food, they had fresh water, they had everything they needed thanks to the glittering jewels the earth had offered when she split herself open for Banba. They had, in short, everything a woman could want, and so on a Tuesday, the fifteenth of the moon, the little fleet sailed from the Isles of Meroe to the Nile in Egypt. In Egypt they were joined by Egyptus, a woman of the ruling house, and by Scota, who was the daughter of a wealthy family.

They were ten years in Egypt, touring and visiting, oohing and aahing, seeing wonders and marvels of which they had previously only heard. Then they sailed for twenty days to reach the Caspian Sea and twelve days on the sea itself to reach the Cimmerian Sea. One day from Asia Minor to the Torrian Sea, then a sailing of twenty days to the Alpine mountains. From the Alps it was nine days to Spain and another nine days from Spain to Dun Na mBarc, and in Corco Duibne they took the harbour on the fifth unit of the moon, a Saturday.

Two of the ships were wrecked on the rocks, but the women were saved for they could all swim. They salvaged what they could from the wrecked ships and they reached the rocky shore with all their goods and necessities. Banba was especially careful to moor the surviving boat safely for, as she told her daughter, a woman never knows what the future holds.

The men, however, had been deprived for many years of what they considered to be an absolute necessity. They clamoured amongst themselves, flirting competitively, arguing in jealousy, so Banba went to Cessair and whispered to her, and Cessair laughed heartily and whispered to the other women. Then, with all the women laughing, the division took place.

Cessair and sixteen other women took Fintan, Barrfhind and sixteen other women took Bith, Banba and fifteen other women took Ladra, who complained bitterly that he had less than the other two men.

"Oh, shut up!" Banba laughed. "Most men would consider themselves lucky to have one woman and you've got sixteen!"

"But they have SEVENteen each!" Ladra screeched. "It isn't fair!"

"We'll work overtime," Banba promised, and she must have kept her promise for within a very short time, Ladra was dead of an excess of women and was the first man to be buried in the new country.

The women who had granted Ladra's wishes went back to Cessair and told her that he who had complained he didn't have enough women had actually died of having too many, and when they had all finally quit laughing they contacted the women who had taken Bith and told them the great joke, too. The women re-divided themselves. Twenty-five of them took Bith and twenty-five of them took Fintan, and the others decided not to bother with the men at all for some were already pregnant and others were not interested in either of the two men who remained.

Fintan, who had always considered himself a great lover and a charming flirt, found twenty-five women more than he could even begin to imagine himself handling and he escaped, fleeing across Ben Suainme, across the Suir, over Sluib Cua in the headland of Febra, to the Shannon eastward, to Tul Tuinda over Loch Dergdeirc. Bith, the father of Cessair and not a young man before the beginning of the voyage, was soon dead himself. Only Fintan was left hiding in the hills, terrified of the women, who sometimes saw him half-naked with his hair hanging to his shoulders, his eyes so wide the whites showed, his mouth moving constantly as he recited the names of the women and trembled with the knowledge of his own limitations.

The flood predicted by Noah finally arrived and the women were ready for it. They had salvaged planks and beams from the wrecked ships and gathered fallen trees that had washed onto the beaches. They made a raft big enough to hold them and their herds and, in the middle of the raft, built a house where they could stay warm and dry. The animals lived on the deck of the raft and the falling rain washed away what a host of people with a ton of shovels would have taken most of the day to pitch over the side.

Fintan, of course, refused to get onto the raft with all those women. He detested the idea of drowning and didn't think much of the idea of getting wet, so he changed himself into an eagle and flew from crag to crag, hiding in caves, squalling to himself and nagging ceaselessly. To this day you can often see Fintan sitting hunched in a tree mumbling to himself and from time to time giving vent to a queer, wavering cry.

When the water finally began to recede, the women debarked from the huge raft and went into the hills and beyond the hills into the fertile valleys, to plant crops from the seeds they had saved, and to live life the way they wanted to live it, with singing and dancing, with laughing and loving.

The learned men of the Chronicles would have us believe the women were trapped when the waters of the flood covered the face of the earth, and it may be that they would have us believe it because then we would not wonder what happened when the next wave of takers arrived from Greece. They were led by

Partholon, who was followed by the Fir Bolg and Fir Failian, then the Tuatha de Danaan and the sons of Mil from Spain. The learned men tell us that each of these takings was pure and without women, but the men who came with each successive taking spoke of Macha, the queen of the phantoms, spoke of Macha Alla the Mother of Life, spoke of the Morrigaine who haunted the battlefields, spoke of the faery queen Mab and of Erinya the mother of Eirenn itself, so obviously there were women there when the takers arrived to take.

Women who sighted the first ships knew to stay out of their way, to slip quietly from their presence, until the men began to talk of magical women who could appear and disappear at will, women who could vanish into the very earth, women who could do magic which would make any man forget whatever it was the women wanted him to forget. In time the men spoke of a magical land where time had no meaning. Those fortunate enough to chance upon it would be fed delicious food, given wondrous wine, and pampered in every possible way by the most beautiful of women, each of them enchanting and proud.

Banba, however, was not among them. After the flood and before the first takers, she got busy cleaning and preparing the last of the three boats she had obtained from the Phoenicians.

"But why?" Macha asked repeatedly. "This is a lovely green land, there is music all day long and laughter half the night."

"You have what you wanted," Banba told her daughter, "but this is not what I seek. You were lonely, and now you have company, you felt alone and now you have family, but the soles of my feet itch and my eyes turn always to the horizon. Some of us are born to settle and some of us are born to travel."

"But you're my mother!" Macha protested.

"For as long as you live," Banba agreed, "and more to the point, for as long as I live. That does not mean," she smiled, "that we must live in each other's pockets. You have children, you will have grandchildren, great-grandchildren, and you wish to stay. I have no wish to stay, so I'm off to see what I can see."

There was, if you remember, one of the Phoenician boats which had not been destroyed when the women arrived in the harbour. It was this Banba took for her journey. The boat ordinarily required two or three dozen men to keep the sails in place, the decks clean, and the repairs done, but Banba had no trouble doing it alone. This should surprise nobody — there are scores of other examples in the lifetimes of each of us would provide similar examples.

Banba travelled on the ship for years, stopping regularly for fresh water, food, and whatever else she required, and feasting her eyes on everything she saw. She bought cargo in one place, delivered it to another, she took freight from here and transported it to there, she accepted passengers in one place and took them safely to another.

There was the tribe of Sarah, people who had lived following the rules and the religion of their great-grandmother, minding their business, keeping their customs, growing up, falling in love, getting married, having children who grew up to mind their business and repeat the cycle.

But forces were at work, and laws were passed, and soon the children of the tribe of Sarah were not allowed to move freely, for no other reason than that they called themselves the children of Sarah. So they changed their name to the children of Dan and they were allowed to move as they had always moved, following their flocks and minding their business.

But there were those who for reasons of their own turned things upside down and inside out, who brought in more rules and enforced them with weapons of war and hearts hardened to stone. The children of Dan, who had once been the children of Sarah, were denied the right to marry within their own tribe. Girls raised by the ancient customs were married to men who had been raised scorning the soft and honouring the stern, and year by year there were fewer and fewer of the children of Dan, who had been the children of Sarah. Other enforcers passed other laws, and more laws, until merely moving from one place to another with any of the children of Dan became in itself a criminal act.

Three times did the followers of the grim and stern one pass laws evicting the children of Dan from the land many now called the holy land, or the land of righteousness. The children of Dan were expelled once for continuing to worship the great-grandmother in her image of calf; once for not agreeing that there was only one manner of sexual congress; once for insulting what the grim ones said was an angel of their god come to the cities in search of even one righteous man.

And each time, in defiance of the laws, it was Banba who transported those who preferred challenging the unknown to staying in a familiar place and having the known visited upon them.

And where would she take them but to that place where the women who had survived the flood were living safe from the stern and cold ones, keeping themselves out of sight in the gentle valleys and hiding, not from fear but from prudence, in the hearts of the hills any time the outlanders came to explore or attempt to claim the soft green land.

The children of Dan, sometimes called the children of the goddess Danu, sometimes called the Danites, sometimes called the Danaanites, were welcomed by the women and their descendants, and in time they became as one people, often called the magic ones, the enchanted ones, the children of gods, or the Tuatha de Danaan.

And it was Banba who transported Fergus the Red to a new land. Fergus the Red was called so because of the colour of his hair, and he was a child in whom the urge to wander was strong. From the moment he could tuck his legs under him and stand upright on them, he explored, and when he was a young man, he informed the people he was not satisfied to stay where he had been born, but was moving on to a place he knew existed elsewhere, a place where he could rise in the morning and head off to see what he could see in a place he had not yet visited.

"Everything here," he said sadly, "I have visited two or even three times, and there is not one inch of this lovely place is not familiar to me."

Not a soul tried to discourage him for they wanted him to be happy, so why discourage him from travelling when it would only ensure his grief?

Scota, who had gone with Banba during her travels on the sea and who was the mother of Fergus, hugged him tightly and gave him food for his journey. "Do not forget us," she said, "and teach your children that we are all one people."

Fergus left with the most adventurous of the young people, and their adventures were many. The ship on which they travelled belonged to Banba, but Banba took her ship where Fergus asked, for it was his great adventure and not hers.

And when they arrived at the place Fergus had known all along was there, he remembered how Scota had believed in his vision, and had given him comfort and food, and he named the place after her. He and his people headed off in one direction to fulfil their version of their destiny, and Banba set off in another direction to do what she had so enjoyed doing for so many years. At her side was a black bitch, the many many times great-granddaughter of that first loyal creature.

She visited the women of the North, with their thirteen massive pillars of stone. Thirteen menstrual cycles in a full year, and to not notice, not count, not honour these pillars meant instant death, for it signified an unbeliever without the ability to honour the creative life power. The northern women marked themselves with the sign of the crescent moon, tattooed on the brow above the nose, to tell all they honoured and served the Crone. They studied the known arts and sciences, and with each successful completion of a course of study they had new designs tattooed on their bodies. Those who were fully qualified were covered with tattoos, the spiral of eternity, the circle of life, the stylized representations of the animals whose ways and wisdom they had learned. And these tattooed women knew the secrets of knots and ropes, the secret of the strangulation cords, the secrets of using the human body as a weapon of defence, and nobody who aspired to leadership in the defence armies of the people could achieve their goal without studying with these women. They could change shape, could vanish from human sight, could walk through walls and even stay alive while submerged in deep water.

Year after year, decade after decade, Banba travelled from the coasts to the mountains, along the rivers, and through the valleys. She saw the great forests, each tree so big it would take a dozen people with arms outstretched to encircle it, and she saw the waters teeming with fish, their bodies so closely packed a person could walk across the stream on them, which Banba and her dog often did. She met and had conversations with all the magic people, she met and had conversations with the goddesses, she discussed things we could not begin to imagine, and things as everyday as recipes and the best way to grow certain crops. And she watched as the people who had gone with Fergus moved out into their new land, marrying, having children, living their lives and passing into the arms of Ceridwen, the Crone, the collector, the grandmother, the old hag, the one who gathers the faithful to her. Ceridwen takes them where she can put their poor dead bodies into her huge cauldron, then make a soup, and the souls of the faithful are released to rise with the steam, freed and healed, with neither blemish nor fault. The soup is fed to the pack of black bitches, the red-eyed black bitches who swarm at Ceridwen's feet and who race across the night skies doing her business, seeking the fallen faithful, sniffing out injustice, taking news of any evil done to women and children, then moving on Ceridwen's orders to avenge the harm done to the helpless or the vulnerable. The bones are lifted from the cauldron, rubbed dry, cleaned and polished, then given to Arianrhod, who uses them to enlarge the great loom on which she weaves the lives and destinies of mortals.

Banba learned to recognize the baying of the hounds of Ceridwen and to give them any message she had for the Crone, she learned to look to the Milky Way when addressing Arianrhod, she learned to dance the Maypole in honour of Creiddylad, she learned that when she looked to the sky and saw the rainbow she was seeing the cobweb robe of Kelle, which also shows in the night skies of winter and promises peace in paradise. She learned that it was the salmon, returning from uncharted seas to spawn in the rivers and streams, that first taught Boann the secrets of navigation, and that in the salmon is wisdom, and the power to see the future. She learned that Ceridwen, who is the great white sow, disguises herself often as the raven, in which guide she is the transformer, the one who brings or causes change. She learned that Ceridwen and the raven are protectors of bards, of poets, of musicians, and of seers, and that those who have studied certain skills and arts for half a long lifetime become not only raven but salmon.

Banba watched as the ones who had gone with Fergus began to identify themselves properly, began to realize that we all are equal in the tapestry of creation, with no thread more important than the other, and we are all knotted into our places equally. She watched as the ones who had brought with them seeds of madness tried to subdue and control the earth's creatures. She watched as the one who would steal the power of the eagle was tricked and defeated by the magic of a sister, and she approved when the eagle accepted as cousins those who would honour that crest. She watched when the one who would have cut off the tail of the great red mare was stopped by magic and song, and she smiled when the horse, in honour and gratitude, accepted the friendship of humans and allowed them to claim her as cousin.

She watched it unfold, and saw every person claim a clan, until there were the people of the otter, the people of the bear, the people of the seal, the people of the wolf, the people of the hawk, the people of the wild boar, the people of even the small field mouse. And for each taking and naming there is a story, or even many stories, and if they are hidden, they are not forbidden, and can be found and reclaimed, can be again known and honoured. Banba herself was of the people of the horse, and of the people of the dog, she was of the people of the raven because of her knowledge of songs and stories, and, because of her long years of navigation, she was of the people of the salmon.

The four colours are red for the blood, white for the bone, yellow for the sun, and black for the night sky.

Banba laid stones in a circle, then laid other stones on top of those stones, then more stones and more until she had a conical hut made of stones and earth. Over this stone hut she piled more earth, and more earth, except for one place where she left a hole.

In this hut she built a fire. The smoke went up through the hole in the roof, the heat stayed in the stone walls, in the earth covering. Banba would go there and pray, would meditate and ponder, and would purify her body and her thoughts. The people watched, and learned, and soon they too built round sweat-houses of rock and earth, and with prayer and ritual they cleansed heart, soul, body, and mind.

*

Banba was visiting with the women of the North when the news came that ships had arrived and an army had invaded. Banba was no fool. She knew that any time there is an army on the loose, the best thing for ordinary people to do is assume a pacifism which is not passivity. And so she stayed out of the way of these legions.

For many years all she knew of them was that they seemed determined to cut down every tree in the land. The people tried to resist and were cut down, the people tried to fight and were slaughtered, and still the men came with the tools to destroy the forests and take the murdered trees back to their own country.

There were people in the land then who were dowsers, who knew the secrets of the earth, who could stand barefoot on the breast of the mother and determine what would best grow there, or whether it was land more suited to grazing or hunting than to crops. It was the dowsers who settled boundary disputes and found water, and it was the dowsers who walked the ley lines and knew their mysteries. The people believed the dowsers when they said that we are tied to the earth, connected to it as surely as is a tree, or the grass itself. With this knowledge, the people knew they had to defend the forests and keep the invaders from destroying the trees which were part of the earth herself.

And so the invaders moved against the dowsers. They gouged out their eyes so they could not see the beauty of the earth, they deafened their ears so they could not hear the song of creation, they slashed the tendons in their heels so they could not walk proud and strong upon the face of the earth, and then they cut out their tongues so they could not speak of what they knew; and when all that had been done, they took the children of the dowsers, slaughtered them, and hung their bleeding bodies around the shoulders and necks of their own parents.

Driven half mad by pain and more than mad by the anguish of knowing that their gift and treasure had caused the slaughter of their children, the dowsers were shoved and pushed along the ley lines they had once walked with such joy. Their agony was such that the earth herself roiled in protest and, to protect herself, withdrew from the crippled feet of the ones drenched in blood and shaking with pain. Our connection with the earth was severed, we began to lose the knowledge that we are part of, not apart from, all creation. And the great trees were cut and shipped off to be made into masts and decks for ships taking other legions to other lands to subjugate other people.

And Banba walked humbly among the people listening to their songs of sorrow. She grieved when the harpists were seized and their fingers smashed to stop the songs of protest, she wept when the fiddlers were taken and their elbows broken to silence the music that honoured Ceridwen, and she howled protest when the bards and poets were made mute that the stories of pride and tolerance be silenced. She watched as the people took the notes of the songs and hid them in the knots they twisted, in the patterns they wove and knit, and she prayed that one day the secrets would be uncovered, the knots and patterns would again become music.

Year after year horror and misery, and Banba kept herself out of it as much as she could. There were others who did as she did, and it does not matter whether they imitated her or she them, but some of the settled people, the Scaldie people, began to notice that the travelling Cairds managed never to be in one place long enough to be oppressed by the legions. If the legions marched to the north, the Cairds headed west; if the legions went west, the Cairds headed east or north. If Rome sent many groups out looking for the Cairds, they simply turned their herds of horses and cattle loose to forage for themselves on the moors, got into their small boats, and went visiting in Norway or Spain or Italy or wherever it was they could go and not encounter the mercenaries.

"Have you no pride?" some asked, "never to stand your ground and resist?"

"Pride," the Cairds laughed, "is cold comfort if you wind up buried in the ground, for there is no resisting the worms which will feast on your flesh."

"Only a coward," some said, "flees."

"Oh, fleas," the Cairds laughed, "great fleas have lesser fleas upon their backs to bite 'em, and lesser fleas have minor fleas and so on ad infinitum."

"And while you're being foolish and making jokes, the legions own your land!"

"Own? Own the land? And who can own a mountain and make the mountain believe in that ownership? Own? The land?" and the Cairds laughed happily.

*

Prasatagus was the consort of the queen of the Iceni people, the people of the horse, and to the legions this was interpreted as meaning he was king. Of course he was no such thing, only the one chosen to provide seed, but he too began to believe he was king, because the conqueror, Paulinus Suetonius, said so. Prasatagus made a pact with Paulinus Suetonius, to share with him the wealth of the Iceni in return for protection from the legions.

The queen of the Iceni was a tall woman with strong legs from the years of riding horses, and strong arms from the years of practising with the weapons of defence. She had spent time with the northern women, and had even sent her youngest daughter to study with them. The queen had copper-coloured hair, and eyes that were sometimes blue, sometimes green, sometimes grey, changing as the sea itself changes, depending on her mood, depending on the weather, depending, even, on what colour clothes she wore. And she had a voice that was as harsh as the voice of a raven, as loud as the call of an angered sow, as rough as the bark on the trees the legions were cutting and hauling away, and Boadicea was not pleased with the bargain her consort had made. And so, after Prasatagus died, the queen of the Iceni went to Paulinus Suetonius under a banner of truce, to discuss with him the pact she had never made.

The legions did not honour the banner of truce. Instead, they took the queen and her two daughters captive. They took them to the top of a hill, where all the people could watch, and then tied the queen to a post and whipped her until the bones of her ribs showed through the great gashes in her skin, and she stood in a pool of her own blood. The legion stood ringed around the hill, and the people, on orders of their own bleeding queen, made no move to storm the hill, knowing that to defy her would mean their own deaths and the deaths of the queen and her daughters. So they were forced to watch and to mourn, singing their grief to give courage to their queen.

Then the legions staked out the two young girls and ravished them, repeatedly, man after man, ten after ten, hundred after hundred until the young princesses were incurably mad and more dead than alive.

Boadicea was forced to watch this, forced to hear this, forced to endure this, and her rage grew until her body glowed pink. When darkness fell she used her strong white teeth to gnaw through the lashings holding her to the splintered and blood-drenched post. She freed herself, throttled one of the guards, then used his knife to kill another guard. With a knife in each hand, she crept to where the legions were still raping her daughters, and with her heart breaking she threw the knives to stop the horror visited upon her children. Straight into each suffering heart a thrown knife, and their pain was finished, their horror over, their collection by Ceridwen assured.

The legions searched for Boadicea, but found no trace. She was gone as if she had never been in their hands.

And months later she reappeared, riding her wonderful horse Vindicator, her body scarred by the whip but as strong as ever it had been, and her voice made harsher than ever by the sobs grief had wrenched from her throat.

"I do not command you to fight," she told the people, "and it is for you to decide what you will do. But for myself, as a queen, as a woman, and as a mother, I will fight."

They rallied from every corner of the land. Not just the Iceni, not just the people of the horse, but the people of the dog, of the seal, of the otter, of the owl, of the hawk, of the wolf, of the bear, of the eagle, of even the small field mouse, and when they were ready, they attacked.

For the first time known in history, one entire legion was slaughtered and killed. Still the army of the people moved out, chasing the legions in front of them. They took back cities which had capitulated, and people who had co-operated with or aided the invaders were taken prisoner. Then, because it was a sin to spill the blood of a family member, they strangled them, leaving the blood unspilled but ensuring there would be no further betrayals. And the Cairds watched, and shook their heads, for they knew Rome would never allow such a thing to pass unavenged, or every conquered people would do the same and the might and power would be gone.

From every corner of the known world the legions were recalled and sent after the queen. Ship after ship, each of them unloading soldiers and mercenaries of every colour from every known land, all of them armed to the very teeth. And in one day of battle sixty thousand of the men, women, and children of the land were killed.

Suetonius claimed the queen herself had fallen and that her body had been hidden by the survivors to keep the legions from parading it as proof of their might. But Banba saw Boadicea arguing with her own people. Banba heard her say she would rather die in battle than flee, and she heard the people order their queen to mount Vindicator and ride away, and prepare for the day she would return and lead them again to victory. Banba watched as the queen struggled with her own will and then, as a true monarch should, allowed the wishes of her people to command her.

*

Paulinus Suetonius was in such a fury over the audacity of the Celtic people who had resisted, rebelled, and slaughtered his legion, that he went out into the land he called Gaul and laid waste to three quarters of it.

Every Celt who bore a scar was assumed to have received it in battle and was taken prisoner, then shipped in chains to Rome, to be tossed into the Coliseum to be a gladiator for the amusement of the crowds. Man or woman, young or old, each was handed a short sword and told to fight or die. And since it was unthinkable that sister should kill sister or brother kill brother or cousin kill cousin or anyone kill anyone with blood tie, they refused to fight against each other. Prisoners who did not know they were all children of the one great egg, those who did not know that the skin outside is no measure of difference, fought each other and died for no good reason at all.

And still Paulinus Suetonius was not content. He sent his madmen from one end of the country to the other and anything that was Celtic was taken. Infant children were stolen and given to Roman families to be taught Roman language, Roman customs, and Roman religion — to become, in short, Romans. Children too old to adapt fully to Roman ways were made slaves, taught to be stewards and servants, taught to administer for Rome but denied citizenship. The Celtic language was forbidden, Celtic religion was forbidden, Celtic music was forbidden, and the great stone carvings were smashed or taken on barges to the middle of the Channel and dumped into the sea. So much was destroyed that even the written language invented by Ogma, the Sun Faced One, the consort of the Mother, the father of Her children, was thought to be lost. It was not lost, however; it was given to the cranes and herons to protect and guard. Watch them as they fly, study the way their legs cross behind them, study the motion of their wings as they move against the line of the horizon, and you will see where the secrets of the sign language are hidden.

So violent and so bloody was the vengeance of Paulinus Suetonius that the Emperor could not tolerate the horror and had his Governor-General recalled. When the turmoil and lunacy had abated slightly, the Cairdic people were still travelling quietly from one end of the country to the other, training and trading horses, training and selling dogs, doing magic, playing music, juggling, and practising the healing arts.

"Bend as a willow," they advised, "or as the grass itself. Whoever tries to stand upright against a storm is apt to be broken."

The coming of the Roman legions and the destruction of the forests, the slaughter of the dowsers and the shattering of our connection to the earth, the violation of the waters and springs which were holy places, were accompanied by the arrival of the new religion. Thou Shalt Not Suffer A Witch To Live, they said, and if there was suffering, it was not they who did it but those they deemed to be witches.

Those with red hair were taken and torched, those with freckles were taken and burned, those who were different in any way, or who owned something another coveted, all were taken and burned. Women who owned their own property were accused and convicted. There was no rhyme or reason to it. Those who were guilty and those who were innocent, those who were thin and those who were fat, those who were and those who weren't were denounced, convicted, and set on fire.

Banba saw the beginning of it all and saved her skin by simply tucking her feet under her and slipping away on the boat she had disguised as fog.

She went to the Culdees and transported them to safety, she returned for the tattooed women and took them out of danger, and the brighter the witch-fires burned, the easier she could find her way back to take yet another load of those who would have become ash and carry them three months or more over the heaving sea.

Banba had learned from the Cairds and the Cairds had learned from her that to the north and west lies freedom, and the grass grows everywhere.

*

It was a wonder that changed the course of history. It was progress and the proof of human intelligence, it has been honoured and continued; we know it as the Industrial Revolution.

Work once done at home by women became mechanized, huge machines were built and the people were sent to factories to work long hours for little pay. The machines gave and the machines demanded, and the cities were emptied of first the orphans, then the unwanted, then the children of the poor, and when there were no more orphans and the captains of industry needed a fresh supply, the people put their children to work before they were old enough to understand there was any other form of life.

But not the Cairds. They refused to allow their children into the factories, they refused to allow their children to be taken into the army or the navy, and if all else failed, they would slit the throats of their own children rather than have them slowly starved or mangled by machines.

They refused to pay taxes for, they said, we own nothing on which to pay any tax. They refused to join the army for, they said, generals are not part of our way of life. They refused to learn English or any language but their own, they refused to put their children in school to be educated in Scaldie ways or taught Scaldie manners. And so the Scaldies, for the good of the Cairds of course, gathered them up and transported them away from the land they had known since the days of Fergus, away from the paths they had trod all that time, to a land of which very little was known.

Banba went with the Cairds. She, who had travelled with St Brendan the navigator, knew there was more to this new land than a few miles of farmland ruled by the authorities.

"No need to mourn," she encouraged them, "for we are the travelling people and in this new land we can travel our lifetimes and never see the same rock twice. If we start now and put one foot in front of the other for ten years we will not reach the other side!"

Live this way, do this, obey that, the Scaldie overseers said, and the Cairds agreed, nodded their heads, smiled, and at night they vanished.

Banba took her fog-mist boat and went back to see what she might see. Each time there were dispossessions she was there, a small white-haired woman, giving comfort, giving encouragement, whispering promises that were kept. And the Cairds who share a secret with the horses listened, the Cairds who can look at a dog and be its trusted friend looked at Banba and knew her as a woman of the people of the dog.

And still the displacements continued. The people were taken from their land and the land turned over for sheep, the people were marched at gunpoint by their own clan lords and put on ships to be taken across the sea to starve.

But there were those already in the new land who knew how to live there, and at night, while the guards and the authorities slept, others heard the beating of the drums and were gone before the sun showed her face again.

It might be they saw Boadicea on Vindicator, calling to them with her harsh raven's-caw voice, or it might be that a small-bodied woman with white hair came to them and whispered a promise they knew she would keep. They moved ahead of authority, away from authority, in spite of authority, and at times into authority, and they took their songs, their laughter, their wit, their irreverence, their ever-evolving tales and stories.

And you must beware. They move among us and sing of subversion, they move among us looking like us and telling tales of disrespect. They joke about things decent people consider serious, they have no respect for what proper people consider important, and they are the people about whom you have been warned.

They move among you and tell you to honour the earth, they move among you and tell you to respect the forests, they move among you and speak of clean rivers and streams, they move among you and remind you of how it once was and can be again. They tell enormous tales of shape-shifters and form-changers, they sing songs that mock the laws of the land, they are in your churches and in your schools and they are the people about whom you have been warned.

Their men are dangerous and not to be trusted. They respect their wives and daughters, their mothers and sisters. They think fighting is foolish and armies insane. They will do no work that damages or injures the fullness of creation, and they have been known to openly express their feelings. Their women are abominations who think for themselves, who earn their own money and claim their own children, who refuse to be docile and who dress as they please and they are the people about whom you have been warned.

And, of course, none of this is true. There are few references in any respectable scholarly work of a people known as the Cairds. There is no dictionary in any recognized institution in which their language is laid out for anyone to study and understand. They never moved as they wished across the face of the land, they never told their stories only to those who understood Gaelic, they never resisted oppression by laughing and moving on, and that is why even today there are laws in Britain which restrict the right of the travelling people to park more than one caravan on any piece of land at one time.

None of it is true. You cannot stand on your front porch at night and stare up at the moon and see Banba's white hair wisping cloud-like across the dark sky. You will never see a woman with white hair who catches your eye and commands you with her gaze, then smiles as if you, like the horses, share a secret with her. You will never see a woman with white hair accompanied by a strong black bitch and you will never look at clean pure water and know in your heart why it is precious.

None of it is true. There are no people about whom you have been warned, and if there were, they would not be the Cairds. They have all died off and anyway they never existed. It is nothing but stories, and stories are lies, as are songs, and poems, and promises of truth.

PART II

The Tangled Dream

The Music from behind the Moon

EPITOME OF A POET

by James Branch Cabell

Judge thou the lips of those that rose up against me all the day. Behold their sitting down, and their rising up: I am their music.

PART ONE
OF MADOC IN HIS YOUTH

— De grâce, belle dame, si je puis vous demander ce que j'ai à coeur de savoir, dites-moi pourquoi vous êtes assise ici toute seule?
— Je vais te le dire, mon pauvre Madoc, avec franchise.

The Text From Genesis

To such as will listen I plan here to tell the story of Madoc and some little part of the story of Ettarre.

Now this is a regrettably familiar tale. It may possibly have begun with Lamech, in the Book of Genesis, — who was, in any event, the first well-thought-of citizen upon known record to remark, "I have slain a young man to my hurt!" And poets tell us that many poets whose bodies had survived to middle age have repeated this glum observation, although probably not ever since then, when Lamech spoke without tact, to their co-partners alike in the homicide and in married life.

Moreover, this is a regrettably inconclusive tale, without any assured ending. Nor is there any assured prophesying, either, that the next thousand years or so will remedy that defect in this tale, because the story of Ettarre is not lightly to be ended by the death of any woman's body which for a while Ettarre has been wearing.

And, lastly, this is a regrettably true tale such as no correct-thinking person ought to regard seriously.

1. Four Views of A Poet

Lean red-haired Madoc was the youngest and the least promising of the poets about the cultured court of Netan, the High King of Marr and Kett. When it was Madoc's turn to take out his bronze harp from its bag of otter-skin, and to play at a banquet, he assisted nobody's digestion. And, as the art-loving King would put it, twisting half-fretfully at his long white beard, what else was the lad there for?

The best-thought-of connoisseurs declared the songs of Madoc to be essentially hollow and deficient in, as they phrased it in their technical way, red blood: to which verdict the wives and the sweethearts of these connoisseurs were only too apt to reply that, anyhow, the boy was quite nice-looking. The unthinking women thus confirmed the connoisseurs in their disapproval.

But the strangest matter of all, in a world where poets warm themselves mainly by self-esteem, was that not even to young Madoc did his songs appear miraculous beyond any description.

To Madoc's hearing his songs ran confusedly; they strained toward a melody which stayed forever uncaptured; and they seemed to him to be thin parodies of an elvish music, not wholly of this earth, some part of which he had heard very long ago and had half forgotten, but the whole of which music remained unheard by any mortal ears.

2. *The Woman like a Mist*

Now, upon a May evening, when a plump amber-coloured moon stayed as yet low behind the willows in the east, this same young Madoc bathed with an old ceremony. Thereafter he sat beside the fountain meditatively disposing of his allotted portion of thin wine and of two cheese sandwiches. A woman came to him, white-limbed and like a living mist in that twilight.

"Hail, friend!" said Madoc.

She replied, with hushed and very lovely laughter, "I am not your friend."

He said, "Well, peace be with you, in any event!"

She answered, "There is for you, poor Madoc, no more peace, now that I have come to you all the long way from behind the moon."

And then that woman did a queer thing, for she laid to her young breasts her hands, and from the flesh of her body she took out her red heart, and upon her heartstrings she made a music.

It was a strange and troubling music she made there in the twilight, and after that slender mistlike woman had ended her music-making, and had vanished as a white wave falters and is gone, then Madoc could not recall the theme or even one cadence of her music-making, nor could he put the skirling of it out of his mind. Moreover, there was upon him a loneliness and a hungering for what he could not name.

3. *What Wisdom Advised*

Therefore Madoc comes to the dark and ivy-covered tower of Jonathas the Wise. And the lean and kindly man put forth his art. He burned, in a tall brazier, camphor and sulphur and white resin and incense and salt: he invoked the masters of the lightning and of volcanoes and of starlight; and he recited the prayer of the Salamanders.

Then Jonathas sighed, and he looked compassionately over his spectacles. "The person that troubles you, my poor Madoc, is Ettarre the witch-woman, whom Dom Manuel the Redeemer begot in Poictesme; and whom the Norns have ordained to live with Sargatanet, Lord of the Waste Beyond the Moon, until the 725 years of her poisonous music-making are ended."

Madoc said, "How may a struggling poet avoid the spells of this witch and of this wizard?"

Jonathas replied: "There is for a poet no defense against their malice, because their weapon is that song which is an all-consuming fire. Still, as one nail drives out the other, and as one fire consumes another fire, so something may be done against the destroying pair with this."

And thereupon, lean kindly Jonathas gave to young Madoc a very large quill pen fashioned out of a feather which had fallen from the black wings of Lucifer, the Father of All Lies.

4. One Patriot's Reward

With this pen Madoc began to write down his songs before he sang them: and the pen made for him a new kind of song.

Now the connoisseurs nodded approval. "The sentiment is wholesome, and, in these degenerate days, regrettably rare." King Netan clapped his hands, he laughed aloud, and he gave Madoc a greyhound, a white tunic worked with green embroidery, and seven chests of gold coin.

Thereafter Madoc lacked for no reward, and every week he had a lovelier lady for his love. At all the royal banquets he sang his new song, of how enviable were Netan's people in every heritage and in their sturdy racial qualities, and of how contemptible the other nations appeared in comparison: and everybody applauded his remarkable rightness.

But Madoc one day put aside his harp, he removed an amorous countess from about his neck, and he went alone out of Netan's shield-hung hall. All at that banquet were applauding Madoc; but through the shouting he could hear a skirling music which derided his patriotic perjuries: and Madoc knew that the fatherland he was praising showed as an unimportant pimple on the broad face of the world, and that its history, or the history of any other people, was but a very little parenthesis in Earth's history.

5. Some Very Ancient Games

So Madoc fled from the cultured court of Netan, where the superb emotions of patriotism were denied him by that music which a pallid and pestiferous witch was devising in the Waste Beyond the Moon. He fled southward, into the fertile land of Marna.

In a green field, beneath a flowering apple tree, a young woman was playing at chess against a veiled opponent. His face could not be seen, but the gray hand with which he now moved a bishop had four talons like the claw of a vulture. The woman was clothed in blue: about her yellow hair she wore a circlet of silver inset with many turquoises, and about her wrists also were bands of silver, and in her face was the bright pride of youth.

At the sight of Madoc this woman arose, she smiled, and in a clear sweet voice she cried out the magic word of the south, saying, "Berith!"

The veiled man was not any longer there, but beyond the apple tree you saw a thin gray wolf running away very swiftly.

The lovely girl then told young Madoc that she was Ainath, the queen over all this country, and he told her that he was a wandering minstrel. Ainath in reply said she did not know much about music, but she knew what she liked, and among the things that she especially liked was the appearance of Madoc.

6. Leads to a Coffin

Nor did Madoc dislike the appearance of Ainath. Nowhere in her appearance could he find any flaw: she was, indeed, so confident of her perfection that she hid from him no portion of her loveliness, and she refused to cheat him by leaving his knowledge superficial.

Her generosity and her fond loving ways led Madoc quite to overlook, if not entirely to condone, this queen's alliance with the Old Believers, when Madoc by-and-by had found out the nature of Ainath's veiled opponent and what game it was that Ainath played within reach of the fiend's talons.

Meanwhile with Madoc she played other games, night after night, inside the carved and intricately coloured sarcophagus in which, when the time came, Queen Ainath must be laid away under the dark and fertile land of Marna; for it was the intent of this far-seeing queen to make of her coffin a hospitable place, and to endear it with memories of countless frolics and of much loving friendship, so that (when the time came) she might lie down in her last home without any feeling of strangeness about her being there yet again, or any unwelcome association of ideas.

Now it was Madoc who, for the while, assisted Ainath in this poetic wise plan, and with all the vigour which was in him he set lovingly to work to keep that coffin dear to her.

7. Reward of the Optimist

Now also, for Queen Ainath, and for the shepherds who served Ainath, young Madoc wrote noble songs. It was not of any local patriotic prevarications that Madoc sang in the green fields of Marna, but of an optimism which was international and all-embracing.

"This is a fair world," sang Madoc, "very lovingly devised for human kind. Let us give praise for the excellence of this world, and — not exactly this morning, but tomorrow afternoon perhaps, or at any rate, next week — let us be doing exceedingly splendid things in this world wherein everything is ordered for the best when you come to consider matters properly."

The kindly shepherd people said, as they cuddled each other in pairs, "This Madoc is the king of poets, sweetheart, for he makes us see that, after all, this world is a pretty good sort of place."

But Madoc looked with dismay upon their smirking faces, which seemed to him, beneath their hawthorn garlands, as witless as were the faces of their sheep: and upon the face of Madoc there was no smirk. For all the while that he made his benevolent music he could hear another music, skirling: and this other music derided the wholesome optimism which was in the singing but not in the parched heart of Madoc, and this other music called him, resistlessly, toward his allotted doom.

PART TWO
OF MADOC IN THIS WORLD

Je t'ai secrètement accompagné partout, dans les luttes et dans les combats, sur les routes, dans les rues et partout: ma musique t'a préservé des atteintes et des agréments et des illusions du monde.

8. *"The Bravest Are the Tenderest"*

Madoc fled from the shepherd land and from the hospitable coffin of Queen Ainath, wherein optimism was denied him. Now he goes westerly, into the mountainous country of the Emperor Pandras, the third of that name.

There Madoc encountered a gleaming company of archers and spearmen with red lions blazoned upon their shields. Their Emperor rode before them, in red armour, mounted upon a roan stallion: and they went thus marching to make war against the people of Ethion, as was their annual custom.

"Our old traditions and our national honour must be preserved," declared the Emperor, "but, nevertheless, this year a war is rather inconvenient."

Then Madoc sang the newest song which he had made with

his black pen. He sang very movingly of how many young men would be killed in the impending war, and of how this fact would be a source of considerable distress to their mothers.

The spearmen and the archers dropped each a tear from each eye: the Emperor himself was heard to clear his throat. "I have a mother," said one warrior.

His neighbour replied, "I have not; but I formerly had one, and the principle is the same."

The entire army agreed that the principle was excellent; a retreat was sounded; and war was deferred.

9. Philanthropy Prospers

Then Madoc made yet other songs for the war-loving people of the Emperor Pandras. He made fine stirring songs about philanthropy, and many simple chanteys such as workmen use at their labours.

The warriors turned from their belligerent raids, to the building of schoolhouses and hospitals and public drinking-fountains and domed temples for their three national deities. Labouring, these warriors sang the songs which Madoc had made, and his songs put a new vigour in them: their philanthropic endeavours went forward the more nimbly because of Madoc's noble and inspiring songs.

"Build," Madoc sang, "for the welfare of those who come hereafter! Create for them a fairer and more enlightened world! Build, as befits the children of the great Builder!"

But in a while he heard another music: he reflected how stupid were these perspiring and large-muscled persons who toiled for the welfare of a problematic and, it well might be, an unmeritorious posterity, for people who had done nothing whatever to place anybody under any least obligations: and his songs, which brought benevolence and vigour into the living of all other persons appeared to Madoc rather silly now that again he had heard the skirling music of Ettarre the witch-woman.

10. Spoils of the Victor

But the people of Ethion, after they had waited a reasonable while for their annual war to begin, lost patience before this disrespect for tradition, and bestirred themselves. They invaded the country of the Emperor Pandras. They were driven back and were slaughtered cosily, in their own homes, which were then destroyed.

"Our triumph is gratifying," said Pandras, after he had attended divine worship and had sent for Madoc. "Only, now that we have won this war, it seems right we should pay for it; now that we have laid waste the cities of Ethion, to rebuild them is our manifest duty: and in consequence I shall have to redouble, or perhaps it would be more simple merely to multiply by five, the taxes which are now being paid by my people."

"Yes, Majesty," said Madoc, sighing somewhat.

"It follows, Madoc, that immediately after we have tried and hanged the surviving leaders of Ethion, we shall need a new song from you, as to the brotherhood of all mankind and as to the delight which a proper-minded person gets out of discomfort when it helps his enemies to live at ease, because otherwise my people may not enjoy paying five times as many taxes."

"I withdraw, sir, to complete this song," said Madoc, and after that, he withdrew, not merely from the presence of Pandras, but from out of the country of Pandras.

11. The Comfortable Music

Just so did it fare with Madoc in many kingdoms. He wandered everywhither, writing noble songs with his black pen. He sang these songs before great notabilities, before the Soldan of Ethiopia under a purple awning worked with silver crescents, and before the Pope of Rome in a white marble room quite empty of all furnishing, and before the Old Man of the Mountains beside a fire in a grove of fir trees at midnight. Everywhere people of every estate delighted in Madoc's songmaking, and they applauded the refining influence of his art.

Wheresoever Madoc sang, though it were in a thieves' kitchen or in the dark cell of a prison, his comforting music became a spur to the magnanimity of his hearers. They overflowed forthwith with altruism and kindliness and every manner of virtue which was not too immediately expensive: they loved their fellows, upon no provocation detectable by Madoc: and they exulted to be the favoured children and the masterworks of Whoever happened to be their tribal god, in a universe especially designed for them and their immediate relatives to occupy.

And Madoc envied the amiable notions which he provoked but might not share. For always, when his music soared at its most potent, he heard the skirling of another nature of music, which was all a doubtfulness and a discontent.

12. Puzzle of All Artists

Yet, as it seemed, no other person heard that skirling music. No other person willed to hear a music which doubtfulness and discontent made unexhilarating. They thronged, instead, to hear the sugared and the grandiose music which Madoc peddled, and which, like a drug, buoyed up its hearers with self-approval as concerned the present and with self-confidence as touched what was to come.

They listened, and they grinned complacently, who were — the kings and the archbishops and the barons and the plowmen alike, — each one of them already a skeleton and a grinning death's-head so very thinly veiled with flesh and hair. They grinned, while at the feet of each lay crouched the inescapable gloom of his shadow, to serve as an ever-present reminder of that darkness which would presently leap and devour him. Meanwhile they listened to the bedrugging music which Madoc peddled: and every heart made of red, moving dust, upon a brief vacation from the lawns and gutters of earth, was exulting.

It troubled Madoc whenever he heard any of his hearers talk exaltedly about the songs which Madoc made with his black quill, and it troubled Madoc that not any of the noble songs which he was making could ever wholly shut out from Madoc's ears the skirling music of Ettarre the witch-woman.

13. Leads to a Lizard

Therefore he went to Maya of the Fair Breasts, who controlled Wednesday. Before her at that instant stood an amber basin with green stones set about the rim of it. Inside this basin was the appearance of a shining lizard with very red, protuberant eyes which moved and glittered as the panting creature whispered to Dame Maya about that which was to come.

When Madoc came, the wise woman arose and put aside her cold, familiar counsellor. She went toward young Madoc with a light of wooing in her proud and sullen face. He found her exceedingly handsome, but he said nothing about this.

Instead, before her kindling gaze, he looked downward. Thus it was that he saw the lizard had put on the appearance of a tiny silver-coloured pig. As Madoc looked, this pig became a little horse, and then a sheep, and after that an ox, drifting out of one dwarfed bright shaping into another shaping just as a cloud changes. But Madoc said nothing about this, either.

He said only, "Do you, who are all-wise, show me that way in which I may win to the accursed witch Ettarre, who has made empty my life, who permits no magnanimities to flourish in my parched heart, and who turns to mockery the noble songs that I write with the quill pen made of a feather from the wing of the Father of All Lies!"

14. How Poets May Reform

Dame Maya led him to a peaceful place where every kind of domestic animal was dozing in her fine market-garden upon Mispec Moor. Sheep and asses and pigs and oxen and draught-horses all rested comfortably in this peaceful place. They had not any care in the world, and no desires save those which food and sleeping satisfied.

The wise woman said, "Through a magic well known to me, poor Madoc, you may become as one of these who have been my husbands."

He asked, "Were these once men?"

Maya of the Fair Breasts answered him, reassuringly, "Yes: all these quiet and useful creatures at one time were mere poets, troubled as you are now troubled, and all these have I saved from that music which is made by the witch-woman, as presently I will save you."

Madoc cried out, "I do not ask for salvation, but for vengeance!"

She said, "In vengeance there is neither ease nor wisdom; but upon Mispec Moor are both."

Madoc replied, "Nevertheless, I prefer that you tell me in what way I may come to the accursed witch, and may make an end of her music and of her also."

The sullen wise woman answered, standing now more near to him, "That way I will not ever tell you, because I like too much your appearance."

15. Right-thinking Remedied

Then Madoc sang yet another of the songs which he had written with the quill from the wing of the Father of All Lies. He sang of how much good there is in even the very worst of us, and of that priceless spark of divinity which glows in every human breast and needs but properly to be fostered.

The well-nourished beasts that once had been poets arose forthwith, and each lurched clumsily about upon his hind legs. "Let us be worthy, yet, even yet, of that heritage which we have denied! Let us abandon this wicked market-garden wherein are only ease and gluttony, let us discomfort the world's ease everywhere with right-thinking and with very other high-minded kind of intrepid morality!"

So they babbled and floundered about Madoc, who all the while sang on exaltedly and thought what silly creatures seemed these bemired and madly aspiring overfed animals.

But Dame Maya winced to see her fair name as a competent wife thus imperiled, now that all her transfigured husbands were in revolt. She hastily told Madoc the way to the Waste Beyond the Moon: he ended his singing: and the domestic animals fell back contentedly into the incurious sloth and the fat ease of the wise woman's market-garden, out of which Madoc passed toward his allotted doom.

PART THREE
OF MADOC IN THE MOON

Le chevalier Madoc lui dit: Vous voir est ce qui pouvait m'arriver de plus agréable, et je voudrais être avec vous jusqu'à la mort.

— Cela peut bien être, dit la jeune fille.

16. Leads to the Moon

All that which Maya of the Fair Breasts had commanded Madoc performed, with his sword and a forked rod and a cup and a five-pointed talisman. This magic brought to him a monster shaped like a feathered lion, but eight-and-one-half times as large, and having the head and wings of a fighting-cock. Upon the breast of the hippogriffin grew red plumage; its back was of a dark blue colour; and its wings were white.

Such was the gaily tinted steed upon which Madoc rode, along strange and unhealthy highways. The spirits of the air beset him: sylphs beckoned to this fine young fellow: Lilith, that very dreadful and delicious Bride of the Serpent, pursued him a great way, because she liked the appearance of Madoc. Nevertheless, he won unhurt to the pale mists and the naked desert space behind the moon.

Ettarre was at her accursed music: the gray place throbbed with it: it seemed the heartbeat of the universe, and the winds that moved between the stars were attuned to its doubtfulness and discontent.

"Turn, witch, and die!" cried Madoc furiously, as he came toward Ettarre with his sword drawn.

She made an end of her skirling music, she rose, and now for the first time he saw the face of Ettarre. Then Madoc knew it was not hatred which had drawn him to her.

17. More Lunar Happenings

He put her lips away from his lips. Madoc saw that the desert place was changed. About them now was a quiet-coloured paradise: lilies abounded everywhere, and many climbing white roses also were lighted by the clear and tempered radiancy of early dawn. White rabbits were frisking to every side. Instead of that music which was all a doubtfulness and a discontent, you could now hear doves calling to their mates very softly.

"Love has wrought this lovely miracle," Ettarre remarked, without any sign of disapproval.

Madoc replied: "Love has brought beauty into this place. Now also shall my ever-living love bring liberty to you, and loose you from all bonds excepting only my embraces."

Ettarre answered: "I like your appearance: your embrace is strong and comforting: but there can be no liberty for me until the 725 years of my post-lunar music-making are ended. No man may alter any word of the Norns' decree: and they have decreed that for 725 years my master Sargatanet shall retain me here as his scholar and his prisoner."

Madoc said, jealously: "What else has this Sargatanet taught you save music? No, do you not tell me that, but do you tell me instead the way to your music-master, whom I intend to discharge."

18. Truisms Come High

Thereafter hand in hand they passed toward Sargatanet where he sat under a vine which bore fruit of five different colours. Kneeling before the porphyry throne of Sargatanet at that instant were the five lords of hunger and fire and cold, of darkness and of madness. To each of these he was assigning the vexations to be completed during that week.

When his servants had departed earthward, to work the will of Sargatanet among mankind, and to stir up in human hearts the doubtfulness and the discontent which endlessly oppressed the heart of Sargatanet, then the gaunt master of the Waste Beyond the Moon bent down toward where Madoc and Ettarre stood at his ankle. He heard the plea of Madoc, and he heard the threats of Madoc, impartially; and Sargatanet shrugged his winged shoulders.

"That which is written by the Norns," said Sargatanet, "cannot be evaded. The Norns have written all Earth's history, they have recorded its Contents and its Colophon also. No man nor any god may alter any word of that which the Gray Three have written. For one, I would not grieve if such an evasion were possible, because Ettarre has now been my scholar and my prisoner for some 592 years. And you know what women are. That is why I do not bother to criticize seriously the writing of the three Norns."

19. The Nature of Women

Then Madoc said: "I am not certain that I do know what women are; but I know their ways are pleasant. Their lips have been dear to me. They have yet other possessions in which I have taken delight. A woman is a riddle without any answer; she is not mere bed-furnishing; she is a rapture very brightly coloured; she is a holiness which I am content to adore without understanding: and among all women who keep breath in them Ettarre has not her equal.

"And besides," Madoc continued, "Ettarre is more durable than are other women; for she is more than 592 years old; and never in the moon would you suspect it. Hers and hers only, it has been remarked by the diffident voice of understatement, is that perfect beauty of which all young poets have had their fitful glimpses. Her beauty is ageless. Her beauty has in it no flaw. And so, even if the completeness of the beauty of Ettarre may demolish common-sense, yet a generous-minded person will be ready to condone its excesses. A generous-minded person will concede, without any cowardly beating about the bushes of reticence, that among all women who keep breath in them Ettarre has not her equal."

Sargatanet replied: "Do you please stop talking. For we know what poets are; and all we immortals know what women are. But we cannot do anything whatever about it."

20. Love Scores a Point

Then Sargatanet lifted the two lovers 592 feet, and through as many dead years, to the stone table beside his throne; and now before them lay open a book of which the pages were as tall as Sargatanet. This was the book in which the Norns had written the history of our world and all that has been upon Earth and all that will ever be.

"As I was saying," Sargatanet continued, "we know what

women are. They very certainly do not excel as creative writers. Their imagination needs chastening; their bent is toward the excessively romantic. Thus the gray ladies have written a great deal of nonsense, and they have permitted entirely too much to hinge upon love affairs. Nevertheless, no man nor any god may alter any word of the Norns' out-of-date nonsense, of which all men and gods are a portion. So do these ladies keep the feminine privilege of the last word. And here it is written, plainly enough, that I shall retain Ettarre until the 725 years of her captivity are ended."

Madoc walked far up the page to inspect that entry in the giant book. "There is no need," said Madoc, "to alter any word."

With that, he took out the quill pen which had fallen from the wing of the Father of All Lies, he stooped, and with this pen Madoc inserted after the digit seven a decimal point.

21. The Pen of the Censor

And then of course — because whatsoever is written in the Book of the Norns must be fulfilled, and figures in particular cannot lie — then a changing followed of all that which had been since seven years and three months after the beginning of Ettarre's captivity in the Waste Beyond the Moon.

Everything which had existed upon Earth during the last 584 years passed very swiftly and confusedly before the eyes of Madoc, as these things swirled backward into oblivion, now that none of these things had ever happened.

Twenty generations of mankind and all their blusterings upon land and sea went by young Madoc in the appearance of a sandstorm. Each grain of sand was a town or, it might be, an opulent and famous city, just as that city had been builded laboriously and painfully by some twenty generations of a people's cluttered, flustered, humdrum, troubleful, lumped hubbub, ungrudged because of that people's high dreams.

All the toil and glory and folly and faith and irrational happiness of the many millions whom Madoc's pen had put out of living had now not ever existed, because that which is written in the Book of the Norns must be fulfilled. And it was now written in this book that the bondage of Ettarre should endure for only seven and a quarter years.

22. *Near Yggdrasill*

Not ever before had anybody essayed to cheat the Norns in quite this fashion: and so, from their quiet studio, by Yggdrasill, the Gray Three noticed this quaint expurgating of their work almost at once.

Verdandi, in fact, took off her reading glasses so as to observe just what was happening over yonder. "Oh, yes, I see!" she said comfortably. "It is only a poet altering the history of Earth."

Her sisters glanced up from their writing: and they all smiled. Urdhr remarked, "These poets! They are always trying to escape their allotted doom."

But Skuld looked rather pensively at each of the two other literary ladies before she said, "One almost pities them at times."

Then Urdhr laughed outright. "My darling, you waste sympathy in this sweet fashion because we also were poets when we wrote Earth's Epic. For myself, I grant we made a mistake to put any literary people in the book. Still, it is a mistake to which most beginners are prone: and that story, you must remember, was one of our first efforts. All inexperienced girls must necessarily write balderdash. So we put poets in that book, and death, and love, and common-sense, and I can hardly remember what other incredibilities."

With that, they all laughed again, to think of their art's crude beginnings.

23. *The Call of Earth*

"A poet is bold. There is no god in any current mythology who would have made bold to cheat the Norns," said Sargatanet, with odd quietness.

Madoc replied, "My pen is almighty; my pen is equally good at music-making and at arithmetic."

Sargatanet looked, for some while, with very pale blue eyes, at the two midgets down there beside his gold-sandaled feet. "Your pen makes music," Sargatanet then said, "such as all men delight in. Yet it cannot make my music. Your pen cannot write down nor may it cancel any line of the music which I eternally devise to be an eternal vexing to every poet, no matter what may be his boldness."

But, in the while that Sargatanet spoke such non-sense. Madoc had uplifted his Ettarre to the back of his hippogriffin. "I have done with all vexations!" Madoc cried out, as the glittering monster spread its huge white wings, and, flapping upward from behind the moon, plunged mightily toward Earth.

Thereafter the hippogriffin went as a comet goes, because its heart remembered that upon this Earth, among the dear hills of Noenhir, were its warm nest builded out of cedar trees and its loved mate brooding over her agate-coloured eggs. And upon the monster's back, exulting Madoc also passed with a high heart, toward his allotted doom.

PART FOUR
OF MADOC IN THE OLD TIME

Ils vécurent ainsi pendant quelque temps: et la plume noire lui donna de l'argent, du bien, tout ce qu'il faut pour vivre heureux dans le monde. Ensuite le chevalier Madoc partit encore pour voyager.

24. The Old Time Reiterates

Thus it was that Madoc and his Ettarre returned to an Earth rejuvenated by Madoc's pen, and lived in the old time which long and long ago had perished before the time of Madoc.

Now the Northmen ruled as lords of Noenhir, where the hippogriffin had left its riders. These Northmen were an unsophisticated and hardy people, exceedingly brave and chaste, whose favourite recreations were drunkenness and song-making and piracy.

They welcomed the singer who could make such comfortable and uplifting songs as Madoc wrote with the quill which had fallen from the wing of the Father of All Lies. Madoc sang to them about their own importance, about the excellence of their daily habits, and about the splendid and luxurious future which was in store for their noble Nordic race: he made for them that music which incites mankind toward magnanimity.

Under their winged helmets the ruddy faces of the attendant pirates were aglow with altruism and kindliness and every manner of virtue. In their thorps and homesteads they welcomed Madoc, and paid him well. So Madoc builded at Noenhir a fine wooden hall: he and his Ettarre began housekeeping: and Madoc had not anything to trouble him, and his fair wife's embraces were now as dear to him as once had been the embraces of Ainath.

25. Confectioner's Repose

Madoc had not anything to trouble him. For many years he made his songs, and these songs made his hearers better and more happy. The only difference was that Madoc, now, had invested some little faith in his optimistic and uplifting songs; and much of what they said appeared to Madoc to be, quite possibly, almost true, here and there.

Madoc lived statelily, with all manner of comfort, in his broad hall, with dragons handsomely painted upon each end of it, and with a stout palisade of oak logs enclosing everything. The most prominent thieves and cutthroats in the country delighted to hear and to reward the singing of Madoc; Druids had crowned Madoc with the sacred mistletoe, as the king of skalds; the fame of Madoc was spread everywhither about the world: and the renowned poet had not anything to trouble him, and no heavier task confronted Madoc than to make praiseworthy music.

But Ettarre made no more music. "How was it that little air of yours used to run, my darling?" her illustrious husband would ask, very carelessly.

And Ettarre would reply, with the common sense of a married woman: "How can I remember a music I never learned until centuries after this morning? And besides, what time have I for such fiddle-faddle with all these children on my hands?"

26. What Was Not Trouble

Madoc knew that he had not anything to trouble him. You were not really troubled by your vagrant notion that the face of Ainath or the face of Maya, or the more terrible strange pallor of Queen Lilith's face, seemed now and then to be regarding the well-thought-of poet that was Madoc, with a commingling — for so illogical are all daydreams — of derision and of pity.

Nor could you call it a trouble that, now and then, in such misleading reveries as were apt to visit idle persons when upon the plains and hills of Noenhir the frail tints of spring were resting lightly, and ever so briefly, the women whom tall, red-haired young Madoc had thrust aside, because of the magic laid upon the prime of his manhood, seemed to have been more dear and more desirable than anybody could expect a mere boy to appreciate.

Nor was it a trouble — rather, was it, when properly regarded, a blessing — that the one woman whom you had ever loved was endlessly wrangling nowadays over your meals and the validity of your underclothing, and over the faithlessness of all servants, and over the doings of her somewhat tedious children; and was endowed nowadays, with the chronic and the never wholly smothered dissatisfaction which is the mark of a competent housekeeper. Madoc very well knew that he had not anything to trouble him.

27. Too Much is Not Enough

Meanwhile love's graduates lived with large ease and splendour. About their rheumatic knees were now the flaxen heads of grandchildren: they had broad farmlands, and thralls to do their bidding, and many cattle lowed in their barns. Life had given them all the good things which life is able to give. And Madoc had no desires save those which food and sleeping satisfied, and lean red-haired Madoc now was lean and gray and pompous, and unaccountably peevish also.

He rarely wrote new songs. But everywhere his elder songs had been made familiar, in all quarters of the world, by the best-thought-of pirates and sea rovers, as the sort of thing of which the decadent younger generation was incapable. Everybody everywhere was charmed by their resonant beguilement. Even the most callow poets admitted that with a little more frankness about sexual matters and the unfairness of social conditions the old fellow would have been passable.

Madoc, in brief, had not any care or need, nor, it was plain, any contentment. He fell more and more often to asking Ettarre if she could not recollect, just for the fun of the thing, a strain or two of the music from behind the moon with which she used to keep him without any home and miserable. And the old lady would tell him more and more pettishly that she had no patience whatever with his nonsense.

28. The Respectable Gesture

Then his wife died. She died sedately, with the best medical and churchly aid, and after an appropriate leave-taking of her numerous family. There was a loneliness upon Madoc when he saw her white and shriveled old body, — so troublingly made strange by the forlorn aloofness of the dead, — lying upon the neat bed among four torches of pine wood. His loneliness closed over him like a cold flood.

He thought confusedly of the fierce loving which had been between them in their youth; and of their high adventuring because of a music which was not wholly of this earth; and of the ensuing so many years through which a sensible, unmoon-struck married couple had shared in all and in howsoever trivial matters loyally; and of how those fallen pale lips would not ever find fault with him any more. It was then that he fetched the black pen with which Madoc had written his world-famous songs; and he laid his pen in the cold hand of Ettarre.

"I call you all to witness," said Madoc, "that this day has robbed my living of its purpose and of every joy. I call you all to witness that I shall make no more songs now that I have lost my heart's arbiter and my art's arbitrary and most candid critic. Let my fame end with my happiness! Let the provokers of each perish in the one burning!"

29. "This Truly Does Not Die"

Thereafter Madoc stood beside the funeral pyre. About him were his children and his grandchildren. A company of white-robed boys, from the temple of the local goddess of fertility, were singing what many persons held to be the very noblest of Madoc's many superb songs, the poet's great hymn about human immortality and about the glorious heritage of man that is the ever-living and beloved heir of Heaven.

Four bondwomen were killed, and their bodies were arranged gracefully about the pyre, along with the furnishings of Ettarre's toilet table and her cooking utensils and her sewing implements. Then fire was laid to all. Ettarre's frail aged body was burned so, with the black pen that was in her hand.

The white-robed boys sang very movingly; and they enumerated sweetly and comfortably, and exultantly, the joys into which this noble and most virtuous lady had entered yesterday afternoon. But old Madoc heard another music, unheard through all the years in which he had held Ettarre away from her lunar witcheries to be his bedfellow upon Earth: and the bereaved widower shocked everybody by laughing aloud, now that he heard once more the skirling music from behind the moon which, whether it stayed heard or unheard, was decreed to be the vexing of him who had cheated the Norns.

30. Leads to Contentment

Such was the end of his prosperity and honour, and such was the beginning of his happiness. Old Madoc went now as a vagabond, a trifle crazed, a trifle ragged, but utterly satisfied to follow after that music which none other heard.

Its maker fled always a little before him, inaccessibly: she held before her that with which she made her music, upon no cumbersome bronze harp but upon her heartstrings: her averted face he could not see, nor did he any longer wonder if it were

Ettarre or some other who guided him. It was enough that Madoc followed after the music woven out of all doubtfulness and discontent which rang more true than any other music.

He followed its sweet skirling down the lanes and streets in which home-keeping persons chanted the famous songs of Madoc. Everywhere the smiling old wanderer could see his fellows living more happily and more worthily because of the contentedness and the exultant faith which was in these songs.

He was glad that he had made these songs, to be a cordial to guiltless men who had not cheated the Norns. Meanwhile — for him who had outwitted the Gray Three, — there stayed always yonder, always just ahead, another music, which was not wholly of this earth, and which a vagabond alone might be following after always, as was his allotted doom.

The Best Possible Postscript

Such is the story of Madoc: but of the story of Ettarre this is only a very little part. For her story is not lightly to be ended (so do the learned declare) by the death of any woman's body which for a while Ettarre has been wearing: nor is her music-making ended either (the young say), no matter to what ears time and conformity may have brought deafness.

I think we oldsters hardly need to debate the affair, with so many other matters to be discussed and put in order, now that all evenings draw in. If there be any music coming from behind the moon it echoes faintlier than does the crackling of the hearth fire; it is drowned by the piping voices of our children. We — being human — may pause to listen now and then, half wistfully, it may be, for an unrememberable cadence which only the young hear: yet we whom time has made deaf to this music are not really discontent; and common decency forbids one to disturb the home circle (as that blundering Lamech did, you may remember) by crying out, "I have slain a young man to my hurt!"

EXPLICIT

The Three Gwenhwyfars

A STORY ABOUT GUINEVERE

by Caitlín Matthews

The three great Queens of Arthur's court:
Gwenhwyfar, daughter of Cywrd Gwent;
and Gwenhwyfar, daughter of Gwythyr, son of
  Greidiawl:
and Gwenhwyfar, daughter of Gogfran the Giant.

(Triad 56, from *The White Book of Rhydderch)*

When they came for her, Gwenhwyfar was busily weaving the last leg of a warrior on horseback, determined to finish it. She had laboured long to get the just the right shade of blue for his mantle, experimenting with ill-smelling derivatives of woad and lavender, well-fixed with urine. She had spun and dyed the thread herself, but now the warrior in the woven picture she had framed from her solitary longing lacked but a pair of buckskin boots to complete his ensemble. Enid would have to finish him.

Gwenhwyfar had dwelt within her mother's bower so long, the long afternoons coloured only by embroidered people, that she now had to fight down a startled reluctance to discover what might lie outside these sheltered walls.

"Where is the girl?" she heard her father, Gwythyr ap Greidiawl, shouting from his seat in the hall, impatient to get the wedding party on its way. She took silent leave of the painted panels and woven hangings, reluctantly setting the shuttle down on the bench.

The tangle of women in the next room were fussing over her bundled possessions, squealing and hitting each other out of the way with exasperated taps of the hand. Enid alone stood, unmovingly despondent at the door, holding the comb and mirror — the rich and probably magical gifts which the King had sent his future bride, from out of the country of his battle-woman, Morrigan.

Neither Enid nor Gwenhwyfar quite liked to use these splendid articles, decorated as they were with otherworldly maidens and sea-nymphs. Whenever Enid had wielded the comb, her arm became heavy and resistant, and the inescapable impression of being upon a curragh tossed upon a stormy sea accompanied her. Whenever Gwenhwyfar looked in the mirror, she seemed to see the reflection of her lost mother, Creiddylad.

Gwenhwyfar felt ambiguous about her mother, whose beauty and virtues were said by poets to be mirrored in her daughter. For one thing, Creiddylad wasn't decently dead, like other people's mothers, but still alive and enjoying the embraces of Gwyn ap Nudd, by whom she had been, not unwillingly, abducted when Gwenhwyfar was a little girl. For another, Gwenhwyfar was as heartily sick of the bower-women's gossip as she was of their attempts to replace Creiddylad in his affections. Despite this, and with one notable exception, Gwythyr had been faithful to the memory of his lovely wife, assiduous in her pursuit and in his hatred of her abductor. None dared slander Creiddylad in the hearing of Gwythyr, but few were as careful around Gwenhwyfar herself. Thus, whenever she handled the otherworldly mirror, a sick feeling blent of shame and hurt gripped her heart.

She caught Enid's frightened stare, "Oh, put the wretched things in the comb-bag!" she called over the din. The men came to bear away the bundles and the bower-women turned their attention to their motherless young mistress with tender-hearted solicitude. She allowed them to swathe her in a hideous, hooded riding cloak of dismal hue. This garment had been made at Gwythyr's behest. It totally obliterated its wearer and her identity, making her appear no better than a fish-wife or stout sempstress. Having lost one woman through lack of caution, Gwythyr was not going to lose another.

Gwenhwyfar made no protest, well understanding her father's intention that she should be safely consigned and delivered to her future husband, but this did not stop the escort sent by the King from exclaiming at the sight she made as she was ushered into the hall for the last time. Through the complicated ties and fastenings of the hood, Gwenhwyfar was astounded to see the very same knight over whose image she had laboured so long. He was tall, dark, and blue-eyed with a blue mantle. He even had the boots of best cordovan leather that she had had no time to weave.

The knight's protests were polite and muted, and might have had no effect but for the fact that he bore the King's dragon ensign. "Very well, very well, let the Lord Yder look upon my daughter if he must. It's not as though we would send your sovereign lord a hen-wife after all!" Gwythyr growled testily.

Yder reached Gwenhwyfar before Enid could undo the hood. He came so close that Gwenhwyfar could feel his breath upon her face. For a heart-stopping moment he looked into her eyes while she drank him in. A handsome, intense face, full of secrets and hidden pain. He was older than she, but young enough to be the very image that her heart had dreamt of in the night. His mouth was thin, straight, yet sensual — a mouth made for skilful kisses. Under it, his beard curled ever so slightly and was flecked with red. All this, Gwenhwyfar was able to read before he dropped to one knee and kissed her hand, saying,

"I greet thee, sovereign lady of this land," in a voice which was both deep and intimate.

Charmed beyond measure, Gwenhwyfar took care to betray no emotion before her father, but acknowledged his salute with a womanly curve of the neck, docilely letting Enid do up the ridiculous hood.

Gwythyr embraced his daughter and blessed her in his own fashion, which was not that of Rome. "Do your duty to your ancestors, child, and never shame your kin!" He was reconciled to the fact that, in order to marry Arthur, Gwenhwyfar must become a Christian. The monk, Gildas, had been sent to instruct her in the rights of the matter, and stood ready to accompany her to Caerleon where she would be baptized by the archbishop the night before her marriage. It was good for a woman to share the beliefs of her husband, after all. For Gwenhwyfar, this instruction had been a novel interlude, a pleasant distraction from the formlessness of her existence, to be briefly enjoyed before she lapsed into an uncaring yet tolerant frame of mind. It was also some kind of defence against the awful fate of her mother for, to be a Christian wife was to enter another league of women.

Gwenhwyfar took polite and careful leave of Enid who had been her foster-sister and from whom she must now part since Enid's mother had been Gwythyr's only solace after Creiddylad's departure. In the opinion of Gildas, Gwenhwyfar's instructor, Enid could not therefore be a fit companion to one who was about to attain not only the heights of Christian membership but also the honour of queenship. Gwenhwyfar felt neither one way nor the other at this very moment since her eyes and thoughts were busy with Yder. Her whole life had been spent filling her idle hours profitably and harmlessly, her every desire gratified, her destined husband long predicted, that she had wasted little time wondering how others might feel. The distractions of her new life now crowded out any lingering consideration for her foster-sister and Gwenhwyfar brushed past her into the bright day.

A large company awaited her as Yder handed her out of the hall. The choice of a horse or a litter was offered her, and she permitted the first stirrings of warmth towards her future husband who had arranged such little matters as her comfort from the exalted heights of his throne. She flicked a glance at the company to see what was required of her, noting that the two ladies who were to attend her were both mounted. She saw too, with much loss of self-respect, that they wore their hair loosely braided and netted up beneath simple jewelled fillets, that their finely cut riding capes did not obscure *their* figures.

"I will ride," she declared finally, since, although she rode without flare due to her father's constraints, she did not wish to appear so dispirited as to travel in a litter like an old woman. She mounted the pale, proffered beast, expecting to be jolted into motion. She was agreeably surprised to discover that the beast was a palfrey, a walking horse, whose gait carried its rider evenly as though in a chair.

Gwythyr struggled with deep emotions as he waved her off. "Do not forget your kin when you are queen, daughter."

With Yder at her side and a contingent of her father's own household guard riding before and behind, Gwenhwyfar finally rode out of the valley she had never before left. When the last cow in the outermost pasture was out of sight, she fought her way out of the cloak and hood with swift fingers, letting her hair spill triumphantly in long dark coils over her shoulders. The laughter welled up in her like a song long suppressed.

Yder caught her mood; he grinned, "It is not far to ride, my sovereign lady. Keep tight hold of your reins." And with a whooping shout, he slapped her horse's rump into a canter.

What happened next was so unexpectedly sudden that Gwenhwyfar could not afterwards remember the order of events. The whole party shot ahead at a fine pace, leaving the foot-soldiers cursing and in disarray. With Yder at her side and the two woman following close, Gwenhwyfar was unable to rein in. At the same moment, from the cover of the surrounding trees, a great number of men in black and yellow livery fell upon the escort. Yder drew his sword, calling commands and urging on his steed. He seized the bridle of Gwenhwyfar's palfrey, forcing it into a gallop.

Frightened beyond measure, Gwenhwyfar wondered at his cowardice. How dare he ride off, leaving the embattled soldiers of her father's household to be cut to pieces in the assault! It was her last thought as an ash-branch whipped across her body and threw her to the ground.

*

Gwythyr's hall was in uproar. Brettawg, commander of the detachment that had accompanied Gwenhwyfar, knelt before his lord bleeding from ear and neck where a glancing sword had left him for dead. No woman dared touch his wounds until Gwythyr had heard the whole story.

Brettawg's tale was soon told. None of Yder's forces had countered the assault but had rather augmented it. The Lady Gwenhwyfar had been ... he had to say the word ... abducted. He showed the strip of yellow and black cloth which he had torn from one of his assailants. Everyone in the hall gasped.

"The colours of Gwyn ap Nudd," stammered the steward, unnecessarily.

Gwythyr groaned horribly. Was ever man so unfortunate as himself? That lightening had dared to strike twice in the same place!

"He said he came from Caerleon. He wore the livery of, bore the ensign of Arthur," shouted Gwythyr. "Who is he? Where did he spring from?"

The household poet was summoned, he who knew the genealogy of every family of significance from Arthur down to the latest by-blow of his pig-keeper. "Yder is a Frankish name, by lord. In the language of the Romans, it is Eternus, but in our own tongue, we would call this man Edern ..."

He stopped as Gwythyr clutched the arms of his carven chair in a contortion of agony.

"Taking into account the livery we have here, I would say that Edern, my lord, is the son of ..."

"... Gwyn ap Nudd!" Gwythyr spat the hated name through clenched teeth.

Ever since his wife had been abducted, Gwythyr had lived in hopes that he would die of shame before he was able to find and bring her back to his hall. She was the talk of the cantrefs, though he loved her still. His honour had been restored only when Arthur Wledig, the High King himself, had chosen his daughter for wife. That had silenced the gossips!

He focused upon the steward, cowering whey-faced before him. "Well, fellow?"

"My lord ... my lord, the guards report that the noble Cai is arrived from Caerleon and asks for the honour of accompanying your daughter to the High King."

Gwythyr covered his face with a fold of his cloak and wept.

*

Enid sat on the edge of the bed, overwhelmed by royal ceremony and very virgin apprehension. The welter of events had accelerated at such a pace, she was breathless.

Last night, she had been made a Christian. Today she had been married to the High King. Tonight — in a very few moments — the King's men would usher in their lord to her chamber and after the ribaldry and drinking would come the darkness and the descent into the unknown. But now, she was temporarily left alone by women and confessor to pray for her future felicity — a solitude that princes seldom enjoyed, though she did not yet know this.

In just a few short hours, so much had happened. Confronted with the immanent arrival of the wedding escort, Gwythyr had thought straight enough. Enid was like enough to his own daughter; she might indeed be his own blood, though her mother boasted of the night she'd spent with Lord Cwrwyd Gwent at the Lammas Night rites with some pride. Whatever the truth of the matter, she would pass for his daughter. By the time she had been baptized, she would indeed be called "Gwenhwyfar" in all earnestness.

They had detained Cai with some difficulty while the news of Gwythyr's plan was broken to Enid herself. Gwythyr had been clever enough to stress family honour and loyalty to Gwenhwyfar as the pretext for this monstrous deception.

"But I can't, my lord!"

"Why not? — Think of it! You will be Queen."

"But I know nothing about Arthur, about being a lady ..."

"What woman knows the least thing about her husband till he's bedded her?" Gwythyr had blustered, "Besides, you've been brought up with your foster-sister, you know how to embroider and make a caudle — what else does a woman need? You were with her when the monk came, so you'll know how to bow your head and pray when they do."

"But ... what will they do to me when they find out?" she had pleaded.

"Keep your mouth shut, and none will find out. I'll tell Cai that the monk went up country to convert the savages in the Forest of Darkness: no-one ever returns from there alive. — Use your wits, girl, and get your things ready."

She'd gathered up the old gowns that Gwenhwyfar had left her and a few childhood treasures. But as she'd picked up the work-box, she'd discovered the magical comb. Surely she'd packed it in the comb-bag — how had they come to be left behind? For the very first time, and greatly daring, she pulled the ornate comb through her own hair and closed her eyes, strongly imagining help. Again, a sense of seasickness struck her. She'd thrust the unchancy thing back into her work-box and let the women pack it with her meagre belongings.

When she'd come down shyly to accept the tall warrior, Cai's, blunt compliments, no-one had thought her behaviour unqueenly but merely modest. After all, it was well known how closely Gwythyr kept his daughter.

And so now, Enid sat alone in the bed-chamber of the High King at Caerleon, expected to make her orisons on some brocaded prayer-bench over the other side of an immense chamber. Her feet could not make it that far. The bed was altogether safer — so far.

Enid reviewed her situation. She had done well enough, though she knew that she had so far been shielded from disclosure by the trappings or ritual and ceremony, that when the formal walls were down, she would be hard put to it to keep up the pretence.

Arthur had been kind, attentive, but so unapproachable for a woman of her station that she had had to invent a story to help her sustain the role of queen. That was what she was — a concubine's daughter playing at queen. It was a game, one which she had told herself many times in the miserable darkness of her bed after Gwenhwyfar had perpetrated some petty and unthinking unkindness. But that game had involved some handsome minor lordling, not the High King himself.

She had no illusions that, when the news broke, as it surely would soon enough, she was for the fire or worse.

*

Gwenhwyfar woke for the second time, her limbs twined with those of Yder. An afternoon of exiting, frightening and informative passion had left them both deliciously tired. She traced the thin scar which snaked across Yder's shoulder and marvelled that men's flesh could be so different from women's. Yder stirred once more and kissed her left nipple like a horse taking an apple from an outstretched hand.

Gwenhwyfar giggled.

Later, when Creiddylad entered with the guest cup, Gwenhwyfar felt no guilt, no shame at the sight of her mother, only interest at how young she still looked, and speculation at the preservative power of love.

Creiddylad's smile was indulgent and astute. A smile which permitted Gwenhwyfar the first real freedom of her life: the freedom from what other people might think of her. She now understood the reflected radiance of her mother in the magic mirror: Creiddylad did not have one guilty bone in her body.

"Edern" Creiddylad called in a low, husky voice. "Go and see your father! Leave me and my daughter to talk in peace. — Fear not, daughter, he'll come back later! Abductor's privilege lasts at least as long as the lady desires here!" She gave a delighted laugh and flung herself down on the bed to have the conversation of a lifetime with her lost daughter.

*

Morning came very noisily in Caerleon. It was the royal stronghold and everyone was obliged to wake when the King did. Since it had been his wedding night the night before, everyone had been reasonably expecting a good lie-in and was most disappointed in not getting it, hence the extra noise. Arthur had called for his horse, in mighty good humour, counselling his wife's ladies to let their mistress sleep as long as she wanted. So although the cocks crew and pipers droned, despite armourers clanging and shrill-voiced hen-wives clacking their gossip, despite the whole panoply of cumulative din, Enid slept late.

Last night had been at all bad. She was her mother's daughter after all. She had pleased the King, that much was clear. He had clasped her to his massive, war-torn chest, and kissed her on the nose with much good humour. It was a shame that the game couldn't last, Enid mused. She wandered down to breakfast, expecting the leavings of the previous night's feast. Instead there were freshly coddled eggs and eighteen different little dishes for her to pick at, all served with the most delicious sweet wine. Enid had a bit of everything, determined to live well while she lived at all. She still had horrible premonitions about the outcome of the game, but the luxury of her surroundings were a considerable help in putting these to the back of her mind.

She asked after her husband's whereabouts. The King, she was informed, had gone hunting. If her highness wished to ride out and join him ... She wandered to the stables and asked for a mount, determined not to lose out on the fun. Her groom saddled up the strawberry roan and accompanied the queen and her ladies at a respectful distance. Enid had a better seat than Gwenhwyfar, since she had been allowed more often to ride abroad. She let the women do the talking, which she found advantageous in the circumstances, merely nodding and agreeing from time to time. This was exactly what Gwenhwyfar would have done in any case, ignoring the chatter and insisting upon her own opinion. Having lived with her foster-sister for so many years, Enid knew exactly how to behave. Gwenhwyfar would also have ridden out on the morning after her wedding night to surprise her husband's return home by loitering in some leafy arbour.

It was unfortunate then that they did not meet Arthur but a solitary lord instead. He was yawning uncontrollably, as though dragged untimely from bed, his horse meandering where it would. One of the ladies called out, cattily, "Who were you with last night, Gereint, that you set out so late after the King?"

Enid looked as severe as possible and the second lady nudged the catty one in the ribs.

Gereint immediately snapped into wakefulness and concerned attention. "My lady — my sovereign lady, I mean! You should not be riding unattended in these woods: they are dangerous. My lord King has gone hunting the White Hart and no-one can say what might befall a lady alone!"

Enid looked warmly upon Gereint. Although his air of lordly responsibility was endearing, he was scarcely much older than herself. He was, moreover, the epitome of every handsome lordling with whom she had ever solaced her unhappy hours. Now, as a married woman, she also divined exactly what she would most like to do with him.

She was framing a fittingly queenly response and disclaimer to his words when there shot into the clearing a silver, glistening animal whose speed and beauty took her breath away. Its antlers were wound with golden chains and its eyes looked to her with total understanding pity, so it seemed to her.

"Christ defend us!" breathed the groom at Enid's shoulder. "The White Hart — and none of us with a spear!"

Gereint forthrightly spurred his horse between Enid and beast. Before her mystic colloquy had ended, she realized that the stag had been transfixed by a cruel sword blow through the neck.

The tears leapt to her eyes with pity at its torment and loss for the communion which had been between them. It fell to its knees, a stream of blood cascading down the white neck, its lambent brown eyes turning up in the glaze of death. Beads of blood flecked Enid's skirts. She wept and shuddered still as Arthur crashed into the clearing. Enfolded in his embrace, Enid wept on: her tears accountable to the shock of the incident, but a great relief to her nonetheless.

Back at court, a solemn assembly of hunters was held. Enid sat quivering with the after-shock on her carved, royal chair next to Arthur's, the mud of the hunt still splashed upon him. The King's poet, Taliesin was speaking and everyone was very quiet, so as not to disturb the harmony and skill and depth of his eloquence.

"Whoever wins the White Hart shall kiss the sovereign lady

— the custom is clear. So it was in your father, Uther's, time and so it descends and falls upon you, O King, to take up the obligation of the custom of Uther. Bardic memory has no precedent but that the king himself should win the White Hart. However, the royal lady's life might well have been forfeit had the sword of Gereint not stayed the beast.

"My judgment is this ... Since the custom of Uther weighs heavily upon you, and since Gereint ap Erbin has saved her life, you should permit him to kiss the Queen. However, since the dishonour caused to your manhood is likewise great, let Gereint be banished from the Island of Britain for a space of seven years, and let him return to his father's kingdom in Armorica."

Taliesin had rendered his judgment and, as he laid aside his golden branch of office, everyone breathed again and dared to look at Arthur.

Though the King was dark with jealous anger, he bore the bardic judgment bravely, "Let the kiss be taken." He gestured roughly to Enid who found herself receiving the kiss she most desired in the circumstances least appropriate to lovers. Gereint's lips upon hers made the most perfect kiss a woman could have. They would never again make another, since, sundered on another shore, he would never know that Enid had been consigned to the pyre deserved by a woman who had dared impersonate a queen.

"And now, begone!" cried Arthur, and flung out of the hall.

Gwenhwyfar eventually emerged from her mother's secret bower a changed woman. For so long she had laboured under the misapprehension of Creiddylad's culpability that it was a relief to know the truth. She now stepped, vindicated, into the hall of Gwyn ap Nudd, warm with the love of Yder — whom she must now learn to call Edern — and triumph at her mother's solution to a loveless marriage.

"I never loved Gwythyr," Creiddylad had related frankly. "It was called a love-match, but that was just my inexperience and his persistence. It was Gwyn who really interested me. After you were born, he came for me, as I'd always know he would, and I never really looked back. — Of course, I couldn't have taken you with me; you were Gwythyr's true-born child. I had shorn him of his manhood, his self-respect. I had to leave him something."

Gwenhwyfar, revelling in the rediscovery of her mother, felt no pang of betrayal at having been left motherless. She rightly recognized the self-same brand of ruthlessness that ran through her own veins. Now she stood before her mother's lover without a shred of timidity. The ogre of her childhood, the rapist of her mother, was a charming, intent and slightly older version of Edern. It was now obvious to her that Gwyn and his son, were both of otherworldly stock and that the realm in which she stood was the enchanted and much-wished-for world where dreams came true.

As Gwyn received his step-daughter with joy, a swarm of multi-coloured faery inhabitants sang their welcome. The feeling of family reunion encompassed her. Gwenhwyfar was home at last.

Enid was not enjoying being Queen of Britain. The tedium of courtly affairs now hit her with full force. The interminable ceremonies, the long and often indigestible banquets, the ubiquity of her appearance at every function were all very irksome. She understood exactly why a queen had so many serving women and ladies attendant upon her: she would never have time to remember to sew torn hems, or pare her own nails or recall who was who among Arthur's battle-companions if it weren't for a troop of women surrounding her. Consequently, Enid was never private. Nor were her thoughts exposable. Though her women vied in becoming her confidant, trying to sound out their silent Queen, she dared not engage one in anything more dangerous than the time of day or the weather. She relied on them solely to inform her about complex familial relationships and state functionaries, of which she was totally ignorant. And if her women thought her singularly lacking in conversation, none were bold enough to say so, and put down her taciturnity to an access of piety.

Since there was no one else to talk to, Enid found herself dropping in to chat more and more often with her confessor. Not that she dared confess the thing that preyed most upon her soul, but she found the ceremonies of the Church most consoling, especially the licence to talk at length with the humble and discerning priest who had been allotted to her service, so different from the monk who had instructed Gwenhwyfar.

Father Beuno had been more than a little suspicious about Brother Gildas' sudden desire for martyrdom, but had said nothing out of deference for the modest piety of the Queen. Brother Gildas' zeal for conversation was somewhat fierce and it might well have irritated Gwythyr or one of his followers sufficiently for him to encounter "a little accident." Such things happened. He was sure that the Queen had had no part in it. Her inarticulate, rambling and inconsequential confessions, in his opinion, betokened a sensitive and retiring soul in search of the truth and not a little measure of loneliness.

Enid enjoyed their little chats but, much though she respected Father Beuno, she did not dare voice anything of her torment to another human being. She reserved her disclosures to the pleasant-faced Virgin in the basilica crypt. This rosy-cheeked and loose-bodied figure with its carven child perched on one knee had clearly had, earlier, non-Christian origins, and was not publicly venerated in any great ceremony. However, a good many common folk came here to offer flowers and tokens of propitiation, as well as to ask for help.

It was while in prayer — in actuality, a deep, urgent colloquy to the Virgin — that Enid encountered Arthur's battle-mistress, Morrigan. There were a great many rumours concerning Morrigan and Arthur: that she had been his foster-mother or lover. (No-one ever guessed that she had been both, as well as his teacher in arms.) She was out of Ireland: a warrior-woman of the old school, skilled in initiating youths into the passage of arms — in every sense. It was she who had gifted him with his great sword, Caledfwlch — a blade which many of the ancient kindred of the land recognized as the empowering, kingly weapon out of the otherworldly treasuries. Enid knew nothing of this.

Morrigan had been absent from the wedding, busy quelling a Pictish raid with her usual efficiency. Though she must have been at least fifty, the perpetual practice of her craft, or some deeper faery power, kept her lithe and beautiful. She was regarded with utmost superstition and dread about court, because she had the second sight and was said to have faery blood. Whatever she uttered in her tranced seership always came to pass. But Arthur relied on her abilities to keep the realm secure from invasion and so she was reluctantly tolerated.

Morrigan showed no qualms at entering a Christian basilica, contrary to popular expectation. She marched straight to the crypt to bring an offering to the image of Modron, the Mother, in thanks for her protection during the last campaign. So it was that she came upon the kneeling and suppliant Enid. With the aid of her sight, Morrigan saw immediately that, though the marks of sovereignty were upon the Queen, she was not Gwenhwyfar. She began to realize why she had felt such a strong compulsion to return to court across the seas.

"May your prayer be granted!" she said, her words booming resonantly about the crypt.

Enid started violently. She had been discussing with the Virgin the relative merits of confessing the deception to Arthur or of running away: her prayer had been that a solution be found — whatever and however. Morrigan's salutation had sounded like divine concurrence with her desire. She rose and looked upon the small, dark woman about whom so many stories circulated. She saw a broad-faced, determined warrior-woman, her hair bound tightly into hundreds of plaits which spilled like snakes from an ironbound cap onto strong shoulders. Her hands were gauntletted, a sword girdled her waist. From the state of her trews and boots, she had evidently ridden in recently. Her eyes, dark and opaque, were watchful and not unfriendly.

Enid was about to go into a studied semblance of Gwenhwyfar in confusion when she caught the shake of the other woman's head.

"No, it won't work forever, will it? What are you going to do?"

Enid's relief at being found out was immense. Through her tears she implored. "I really don't know. What *can* I do?"

"Well, I think we had better find some other, more private place for such avowals, don't you?" And Morrigan marched Enid up to the main basilica and out onto the steps. The Queen's ladies surged forward and made the necessary, but rather sketchy courtesies to Morrigan, before attending their mistress. They were all rather tired of her propensity for prayer.

Morrigan brushed them aside with a peremptory gesture, "We will ride a little."

"But Lord ... Lady Morrigan, the Queen must be attended ..." began Sibli.

Giving a great laugh, Morrigan cried, "Oh, by the raven, girl! The Queen will be safe enough with me!"

They rode to the shore of the estuary and let their horses nibble the salty grasses as Enid told all.

"And what is *your* desire in all this?" asked Morrigan, when the tale was done.

"To go to Gereint," Enid said simply, daring to voice her desire for the first time.

"Even though he hates you?"

"Does he?"

"Wouldn't you? I mean you *were* responsible for his banishment, albeit reluctantly. — He goes home in disgrace to his father's house, away from the favour and preferment of his kinsman."

"I would find a way," said Enid. "I love him ... I mean, well ... Arthur's very good to me, but it isn't right, is it?"

Morrigan sighed gustily, "No it isn't — but not in the way you mean." She had long ago looked into the waters and seen how things would be with her fosterling and had already made such provision as she knew how for the best government and peace of Britain. But such measures stood outside love and its vagaries: Arthur was not meant for Enid.

"Why are you listening to me?" Enid asked.

Morrigan turned her horse's head towards the sea, not looking at the Queen. "What passed between you and the White Hart, between you and Gereint ... that is how Arthur looks towards the land of Britain. If this had been any other time and you, Gereint and Arthur any other kind of people, none of this would matter to me. But I am a protector of the realm, and so I must help *you* and not the King now."

Enid didn't really understand, though she felt herself suddenly at the heart of a great thing, beyond her destiny to know. She no longer worried about what would be done to her, now that she was in the strangely reassuring presence of Morrigan.

She lifted her head and breathed in the sharp tang of the sea, saying, "For the sake of the White Hart, and for Gereint, and even for Arthur, I have to go."

"Exactly!" said Morrigan, and a wry smile creased her broad cheeks. "The question is — how?"

News came to the otherworldly realms, like everywhere else, on the lips of poets and wandering storytellers. The fact that Gwyn ap Nudd had his emissaries everywhere also helped. The very leaves and streams spoke to him and his kind, as well as the birds of the air and the beasts of the earth and the fish in the waters. There was always, gratifying, never a shortage of guests who brought their own news.

Creiddylad announced one morning at breakfast, "Giant Gogfran is coming with his family next week."

Gwyn and Edern made pleasurable noises through the business of munching. The pig's feet had been particularly well-spiced and everyone was very greasy as a result. Under cover of wiping her fingers, Gwenhwyfar cast an appalled glance at her mother, Creiddylad ignored her daughter and went on eating. Later, Gwenhwyfar seized her arm, urgently demanding, "Who on earth is Giant Gogfran?"

"Well, for one thing, dear, he's not *on* earth. He's like Gwyn and Edern — he comes and goes. It's only people like me and you who make do. Gogfran is a perfectly charming giant and his family are splendid company. You've never heard anything like the bitchy gossip I had to suffer when I first came here. All the other neighbouring mounds were insufferably rude to me — they were all hoping that Gwyn would marry one of their own daughters. Only Gogfran and his wife were kind enough to call ... Just be civil to them, dear — but do be careful not to leave anything delicate lying about — the whole family have *very* uncouth feet!"

Gwenhwyfar had been getting quite edgy of late. Her mother had put it down to an unnatural existence underground and indeed, Gwenhwyfar had found it very trying never to see the sun in the sky but to exist only by its fore and after glow. Not to feel the passing of the seasons, but to live in a perpetual summer haze was all very well. Her mother had explained that life in these circumstances prevented the very disagreeable mortal propensity to age.

There was a distinct dearth of the *ordinary* in Gwyn's realms. Gwenhwyfar wasn't entirely sure she wasn't pregnant and that made her feel disagreeable and distantly worried. Edern was a dutiful and skilful lover, never from her side, but she did begin to feel the need for placid Enid's company for once, though she dared not admit as much. She toyed with the idea of asking Edern to arrange Enid's abduction, just to keep her company, but the thought of what her foster-sister would make of Gwyn's kingdom stayed her tongue.

Preparations were well advanced for Gogfran's visit when another guest was announced.

"Morrigan! Here?" Creiddylad sounded appalled.

Gwyn wagged a finger at his mistress. "She is kin to me and you will welcome her politely."

"Of, of course," said Creiddylad, irritated beyond measure. "But she's Arthur's ..." She bit her lip, so that Gwenhwyfar never learned what Morrigan was to Arthur, but she remembered the mirror and comb, and shuddered. It was the first time that she had seen her mother less than self-assured. She silently slunk back to her room and fetched out the magical mirror — the comb had seemed to have been "borrowed" by some faery being. It reflected her pinched and miserable face. She thrust it back into the bag with loathing. The pleasant summer-land of Gwyn's world was warping around her into some misshapen and wintry place. She even saw Edern with other eyes, noting for the first time the narrow set of his eyes and the sharpness of his ears, the aged, world-weary air that sat strangely upon his seemingly few years. Peeved with the whole faery realm, she locked herself away and sulked for the rest of the day.

It wasn't until she heard gales of unmitigated hilarity issuing from the hall that she ventured out. She hailed a passing dwarf and asked her what was the matter. The diminutive wife skirled with mirth at sight of Gwenhwyfar and ran shrieking into the corridor. With her shawl clamped tightly about her, Gwenhwyfar strode into the hall.

It was thronged with Gwyn's subjects, all of whom immediately fell silent, but for a few snickers.

Gwenhwyfar glared at the dark woman dressed in red and black who sat with a sword across her knees, her feet hoisted on the table, then across to Gwyn and her mother, who had the most peculiarly expression on her face.

With twitching mouth, Gwyn summoned up his breath and said,

"You'll have to hear sooner or later, daughter ... Your handmaid, Enid, has apparently become Queen of Britain!"

*

The ignominy of her position hit Gwenhwyfar doubly hard. The ingratitude of the girl! After a lifetime spent in obedient service, she dared to usurp her mistress' place! Gwenhwyfar seethed with frustrated rage. *She* should have been Queen of Britain, not that plain, insignificant bastard of her father's concubine!

Edern found her ripping up the sheets and beat a hasty retreat to his father's den, where he took refuge in male counsel: "They invariably go like that, son. It's to be expected. Remember that she's totally human and hasn't the benefit of omniscience. Mortality is a strange thing ... If you get tired of her, remember that a little exposure to the world above will bring her down to size. When she starts to show her age, you'll have to find another mistress, you know you will!" With which piece of faery philosophy Edern could only dismally agree.

In the midst of Gwenhwyfar's outrage, Gogfran and family turned up. They were very nice about it, and kindly pretended not to notice Gwenhwyfar proud huffs and frequent tears. Being virtually immortal did bestow a certain amount of delicacy when dealing with such mortal performances as the erstwhile queen's. Gogfran's daughter was particularly sympathetic, listening patiently to Gwenhwyfar outpourings.

"I mean, it's me who should be queen," she protested to the large girl on the bed. Gwenhwyfar had completely overcome her timidity at social intercourse with giants and their ilk very early. Gogfran and family could accommodate themselves, at will, to the size of their surroundings — though it did still make moving about rather trying, since moments of expansiveness would come upon them and they would have to stretch suddenly, though mostly they did this discreetly in large spaces where servants and animals would not be inconveniently squashed.

Gogfran's daughter was a pleasant, blond girl who told everyone that she was studying to become a proficient shape-shifter. At any other time, Gwenhwyfar would have cut her dead, but she was starved of a confidant in this place. Her mother was busy avoiding the hated Morrigan who had brought the shameful news of Enid's elevation to the nobility, and even Edern had not been so attentive recently, so Gwenhwyfar took advantage of the nearest and certainly the largest shoulder.

"Well, I think it's a jolly shame. If it had been my dad did that I'd turn all his toes into pigs for a week. I'll tell you! What a rotten trick to substitute your old maid ... But what a laugh on Arthur! Mum always said he was pretty slow on the up-take! I bet he doesn't know how he's been tricked!"

Gwenhwyfar sincerely hoped not, though she secretly hungered for a thousand deaths to seize upon Enid. She squinted more closely at the young giantess. "What did you say your name was?"

The young giantess threw one plait over her shoulder, "Gwenhwyfach, after my aunty in Cornwall."

"Gwenhwyfach ... do you know any magic?"

Gwenhwyfach smiled broadly, "Course! What kind?"

A cunning expression swept over Gwenhwyfar's beautiful face and she dropped her voice to a whisper. "*Evil* magic."

Gwenhwyfach's bland and open face filled with puzzlement. It was her first encounter with a human at close range and, though her mother had told her countless tales about their switch-back cunning, she still did not understand their concept of evil at all. She decided to try the practical approach, "Well, what do you want to do?"

"Make Enid suffer!" breathed Gwenhwyfar

Before Gwenhwyfach could reply to this enormity, a voice cut between them, "Don't you think she's already doing that?"

It was the hateful Morrigan, as Gwenhwyfar already called her — she who had enjoyed rubbing in her shame before the whole court.

Gwenhwyfar retorted, "I imagine she's having a splendid time, queening it about Britain while I rot here."

Morrigan ignored her and addressed herself to the young giantess: "And how is your shape-changing coming on?"

"Oh, ever so well, aunty Mor. I can do eagles and serpents on good days. I even managed a dragon," babbled Gwenhwyfach, enthusiastically. Then, on a more modest note, "but it was only for a few seconds."

Looking straight at Gwenhwyfar, Morrigan said, "I should give dragons a miss until you're a bit older, dear; they don't really suit you."

Gwenhwyfar snorted and made for the door, "Well if it's going to be a *professional* conversation, I'll leave you two to it!"

Morrigan called after her, "Don't you want to be queen, then, Gwenhwyfar? It is your destiny after all ..."

Gwenhwyfar had never had her fortune told, though she yearned to know. This wretched, underground obscurity where everyone but she knew the in-jokes, was already too much for her nerves. She needed the stimulation of praise and flattery, the love of her people.

With a royal sweep of her train, she turned back and listened to what Morrigan proposed.

*

Enid knew at last, without doubt, that she was pregnant. She had no idea how long she could possibly hide the fact, but she knew well enough that she might start feeling sick soon, and so avoided breakfast altogether under the pretence of fasting. Her reputation for piety and virtue was growing daily, becoming a byword at court.

Arthur, who had asked after her absences from table, remarked to her one evening over the embroidery circle's excited chatter, "Do take it easy, my love. It's very gratifying that you should have taken to the faith so readily, but don't forget, we have other subjects who aren't Christian. It doesn't do for us to be *fanatics*, you know."

Enid dropped her corner of the altar cloth and smiled ashamedly to her husband, "Of course, my lord, whatever you say. I thought I should set an example, that's all."

Arthur gave her an encouraging pat, for his wife wasn't normally so talkative. "Well, that's the spirit, of course, but just take it easy." He coughed and lowered his voice, "I wish you'd call me Art, Gwen."

Enid pretended to examine her stitches more intently to hide her tell-tale face. She had taken Morrigan's advice and carried on as normal, but she couldn't see how anything would ever come right.

She embroidered Gwenhwyfar's face on the angel she was stitching and stuck her needle into it with exasperation.

*

The exchange wasn't going to be easy, Morrigan granted that. Gwenhwyfar was clearly pregnant, but ready to be queen. Enid was likewise with child and very willing to relinquish the queenship. May-Day seemed the best time to effect a switch, with as much mayhem and confusion as was possible to cover their tracks.

Gwenhwyfar was proving difficult about relinquishing Edern. "You can always come to some *arrangement,* dear," her mother said, reasonably. But as Gwenhwyfar had rightly reckoned that love might have to bow to honour in the new relationship, she was proving stubborn and sulky. She was also highly suspicious of Morrigan.

"Why are you doing this?"

Morrigan gave her a straight answer, "Because I believe in justice and destiny."

Gwenhwyfar's response was, "Well at least Arthur hasn't crowned her yet! There's some justice left!"

But she was still worried about what would happen when Arthur did notice the change.

Gwenhwyfach was most accommodating about lending her assistance. Morrigan encouraged the young giantess and would-be shape-shifter to act as a goad to Gwenhwyfar's desire to be queen. It was so that Gwenhwyfar had to envisage the face of her erstwhile maid and foster-sister for Gwenhwyfach's benefit.

It was surprisingly difficult, after so short a space of time.

"Now again!" commanded her youthful tutor, sternly. "Look in the mirror and see Enid's face."

Gwenhwyfar threw the magic mirror from her. "This is ridiculous. What woman ever wanted to be queen at the expense of looking like her maid?"

"One who wanted to queen more that anything else," Morrigan pointedly reminded her.

"Irish cow!" Gwenhwyfar muttered, but took the point nevertheless.

*

Enid was sick into the basin again. It was borne off triumphantly to the physicians to examine. The queen was proclaimed to be with child to universal rejoicing, for Enid was well-liked throughout the land.

She was actually feeling sicker than normal since that morning a messenger had returned from Armorica, bearing a reply to her urgent letter to Gereint. The message was pretty short and clear:

"I am already in exile because of you. Find someone else!"

Morrigan had said he hated her, and she had been right. She was about to lose a faithful husband, a friendly court and loving subjects in order to go into exile to a country whose language she didn't speak, to a man who didn't want her, bearing the King's child.

Morrigan counselled her, "Go to him anyway. I don't say it won't be hard, but your destiny is to follow him and win him round."

Enid, who knew the duty of following from birth onwards, resolved her heart.

The May blossom drifted from every bush and tree it seemed to Gwenhwyfar. Released from the underworld kingdom of Gwyn, she revelled in the wind and in the movement of the horse under her. She was a woman hundreds of years removed from the frightened girl who had ridden out of her father's court a couple of months ago. Gwenhwyfach rode at her side, beaming with excitement at being, quite literally, at large in the world of men.

Morrigan had pleaded with the girl's father to let her accompany Gwenhwyfar for, until Creiddylad's daughter grew more expert at assuming the shape of Enid, it was by far the best insurance against disaster.

Down in the valley below, Enid was riding out with her women to engage in the pleasant enactment of the abduction of Fflur. Every May-Day, the queen or one of her ladies, represented Lady Fflur, the ancestress who had been espoused or least promised to Caswallawn, but who had been abducted by Julius Caesar. The men of the court split into two parties, representing Britons and Romans. It was the duty of the Queen to ride out alone, and the duty of the two bodies of horsemen to try to capture her and bring her back to court. If she was captured by the Britons, she was restored to the King, since one of the King's champions might stand for the High King. But if she was won by the Roman faction, then Arthur had to pay a tribute of beer and saffron cakes to her captors before the Queen might be returned. It was a harmless game, anciently marking the beginning of summer, but more practically, indicating the seasonal commencement of campaign, quest and raid.

Enid had had some difficulty persuading Arthur, the doctors and her women that she was fit to represent Fflur. In fact, it was only when Morrigan agreed to ride with the Queen that Arthur assented to her participation at all.

Now, riding a good pace in advance of her women, Enid turned to Morrigan, "What do we do now?" she asked.

"Draw the comb through your hair. — You *have* brought it?"

Enid did as she was bidden, stifling her fear and loathing of the ivory thing. A sudden mist grew out of the ground behind them, creating confusion, hiding them entirely from sight.

Morrigan nodded with recollection, "A mist such as Caswallawn himself made to usurp Bran Fendigeid ... Now, into the grove!"

Enid found herself in a small clearing whose purpose was clearly not Christian, since severed heads perched in the lower branches, their eyes and cheeks pecked bare by carrion.

In contrast to these horrors, beside a delightful spring, sat Gwenhwyfar, bathing her feet, while, beside her, intently deciphering a votive tablet erected over the waters, crouched Gwenhwyfach. In moments of concentration she assumed a more titanic appearance, so that Enid was vastly startled by her size.

"Are you ready," demanded Morrigan.

Gwenhwyfar was aggrieved at having been discovered in such an undignified attitude by her maid. "Quite ready!" she cried, thrusting on her shoes and mounting up. She eyed the gold-clad Enid with ill-disguised distaste and fascination.

"You have the mirror?" Morrigan asked.

Gwenhwyfach brought it forth. "She'd got much better, aunty, though she needs a lot more practice," she said severely of her pupil.

"Well, she'll be getting plenty of that from today forward," remarked Morrigan. Then to Gwenhwyfar, "Hold it up to the Queen!"

Gwenhwyfar flushed scarlet, "Who do you mean?"

Morrigan pulled on a gauntlet and transfixed her with a glance. "Why, Enid, of course! Let you never forget that she is rightful Queen of this land. You but take her face, you but take her place, never forget it! ... Hold it up!"

With shaking hand, Gwenhwyfar turned the mirror to Enid.

Enid looked wonderingly into it for a long time, into the eyes of the White Hart that was figured there.

"Now!" cried Morrigan, "Look into it, yourself!"

Gwenhwyfar turned the mirror to herself and saw Enid's patient likeness looking back at her within it.

Gwenhwyfach breathed, "Why she looks just like her! Well done, Gwen!"

Gwenhwyfar's appearance was so like to Enid's that none could tell them apart. They swiftly changed clothes. But when Enid went to give the magical comb to Gwenhwyfar, Morrigan forbade her, 'Though this is one of Britain's treasures, it remains in your keeping. At your death, instruct that it be cast into the waters of the Fountain of Barenton; it will find its way home.

"How shall I know that place?" asked Enid, fearing to look on her erstwhile mistress.

"You will know it," insisted Morrigan, and called, "Accalon!"

A dark-browed warrior stepped from the trees and listened attentively to Morrigan's commands, "Take this lady to Armorica and do not leave her till she finds Gereint ap Erbin!"

"Is there any message for him, mistress?" he asked.

Morrigan turned her horse's head and smiled, "Yes! Say that you bring the scabbard of Arthur's sword. He will know what you mean."

And very gently for such a fierce warrior-woman, she kissed Enid, laying hands of healing upon her and blessing her for the journey. "Go, with the blessings of Britain at your back! Be strong and resolute. Death itself cannot over-set such love as yours!"

And Enid remembered the eyes of the White Hart whose message seemed to be for her alone, and her heart was gladdened. With pity and compassion she turned to her mistress, as to an equal, "Be kind to him, Gwenhwyfar. Let him never know how we have deceived him."

As she rode away with Accalon, Gwenhwyfar seethed, "We! The ungrateful, lying bitch!"

The frown of Morrigan seemed to obscure the very sunlight and the grove grew cold and dark, "Do you dare miscall the Sovereignty of the Island of Britain — here, in her very nemeton? ... May you know sorrow, lady! Sorrow, as *she* now bears!"

*

The sudden May morning mist had confused the mayers. Romans and Britons alike were unable to track the Queen. Her own ladies were alarmed but comforted each other with the thought of Morrigan's stout protection. It was Cai who first sighted the Lady Fflur in her unmistakable golden gown riding along the line of the hill. Setting up a whoop of triumph, he led his party of Britons to capture her. And so it was that Gwenhwyfar was at last brought home to Arthur, by Cai, as the rightful Queen of Britain.

And if in after years there was no love lost between Cai and Gwenhwyfar, nor between the Queen and Morrigan, there is, perhaps, little wonder. For Cai had marked well the Queen's face when he came to fetch her from Gwythyr's hall, and it was not the same woman whom he bore triumphantly back on May Day. Nor, very many years later, when he came upon the fearless son of Gwenhwyfar, Llacheu, asleep in the wood, did he fail to avenge the deception by thrusting the sleeping youth through with his sword, to the eternal sorrow of Gwenhwyfar.

They said that Gwenhwyfar's name signified "White Phantom" but they never knew the half of it, those poets who had never known what it was to stare into an otherworldly mirror and see there reflected the ghost of one's mother and one's serving maid.

They said that Arthur was never quite satisfied with his wife from then onwards. They said that he had three wives, all called by the same name. Well, that was true, though he was never wholly aware of the fact. The Gwenhwyfar who was Enid, the Gwenhwyfar who was herself, and the Gwenhwyfar who was really Gwenhwyfach and who occasionally filled in for the queen when her friend went week-ending in the underworld with Edern.

They said that the Battle of Camlan, that byword in futility, was caused by the blow which one woman, Gwenhwyfach, struck upon another, Gwenhwyfar. And that is partly true, for Gwenhwyfach never really learnt the subtleties of mortality. She was bad when little and worse when big, for that is the nature of giants — to meddle in the affairs of humans and cause them hurt. She had no means of knowing that, by inviting Medrawt to court, that it would be the undoing of Arthur. For Medrawt was half-mortal, half-faery and he had his mother's true sight. When he saw Gwenhwyfach sitting in the queen's chair, the great lolloping giantess that she was, he knew her to be false; he spilled wine in her lap, pulled her from the royal throne and cast her to the ground in full view of all. He spared telling none at court the true nature of Gwenhwyfar's relationship with other knights, both mortal and immortal, and so threw the kingdom into tumult and eventually war. For only when Arthur awoke to the traitorous relationships of his queen, did he attempt to punish her.

And if, in after years, the monk, Gildas, had little but insult to write of the High King, Arthur, in his chronicles, it is little wonder. His few months in faery-land with Gwenhwyfar had addled his wits, causing him to take a vow of silence, and to have a very low opinion of the marital affairs of kings and rulers in general.

As for Enid, she faced and overcame the fierce seas. Aboard the curragh bound for Armorica, she felt still the healing hands of Morrigan upon her. Her blessing sustained Enid even when

Gereint rejected her, making her pursue him through the trackless forest until at least he relented and married her. When her son was grown, she sent him to his father, but Amr was never destined to be king. He died at his father's hands: victim of mistaken identity in a passage of arms where game was subsumed in reality.

And at the last, when the final blow had been struck at Camlan, it was in Enid's lap that they lay Arthur's head. While, at his feet, it was Gwenhwyfar who wept and Gwenhwyfach who mourned. But when Enid raised her eyes to the woman in the stern who steered the crystal curragh to the blessed isle of Avalon, she met the eyes of the White Hart and knew Morrigan for what she was: the greatest of the Four Queens who bore Arthur to his final home and eternal healing.

Five Denials on Merlin's Grave

by Robin Williamson

myself, a brat who vaguely gazed
on the knee high nineteen forties
and the waist high nineteen fifties
and couldn't figure numbers worth a damn
was always a chancer
and given three lines to add I'd put the middle row
down as the answer
but I would read all day if I could get away with it
and all night too with a flashlight under covers
of that Green Man my namesake, or of Merlin
        of the borders
and in seeking out the stories of Britain's ancient lineage
I delved
on days subtracted from the blackboard's paltry tyrannies
among dog eared authorities, back shelved in libraries
who barked at point blank dogmatically
lacking their bell and candle
into my eyes at daydream from a skull.
among the glamoured fields of fine July I lazed
to read and revel through these pleadings
        in dead language
yardages of verbiage in the ravelled case
of the comings and the goings in the high and
        far off times
stacked and dried.
wherein it is recounted with clerkish severity
fish spearing, wizened, louts without modesty
displaying a crude cunning that might pass as perspicacity

beehived and coracled among our western isles
while Noah was still flattening his thumbs,
        and bending nails.
these people we so glibly call the Picts
whatever thoughts they voiced in hamitic vocables
whatever shades they prized, what light or dapple
refract; maligned with daubs of woad
        in patronizing words.
for they were clean as clams, witty and thick as thieves
gossiping maskers worthy of serious love,
        sticklers for detail
furred with wolf pity, honeyed as the claws of bears
tree truthful looters along time's inches
shooting a barefaced line, secretive as heather ale,
with leagues of breeding
brewing or brooding or brave enough in a pinch
charting and outstaring the vagaries of heaven
from winter's prick to the crack of summer
kept watch upon the Pleiades
calendaring from months of feathered dawns
just seasons for the eagle and the wren
owning red breasted lazarus laughter
no better or worse than we
as babes swim back in time, gilled and goggle eyed
evolving as now, intelligent as the green sea
that bloods to Egypt, India, and China
fathoming forgotten simplicities.
it is written bland as boiled cabbage
such savages were heaving out their oyster shells
all up and down the miles of Britain
since first the ice receded to the northern wastes
scouring our hills as round as breasts
until the time of Noah's brother, Partholon
whose children
haggling like gulls
mysteriously arose from Sicily
some say

herdsmen pipers quenching away through thirsty
        south Italy
and wending westward on
at the drone of cattle talk, fly hummed and bitten
by finger quick and cream fat moons
breaking new sod for barley seed
with wooden plows
and rooting for wild garlic
with spades of antler bone.
but let us sing the skill of the master builders
long ago
for it was no peasantry clodding after scrawny cows
who raised the hollow hills and henge stones
but calm and cunning wizards worked these wonders
continuing the snail line, dod flat at ring stand
ruling scribing and pegging out in granite
the windings of the dragon track
that writhes unhewn
in sward and marsh and moss and meadowland
that twines in stellar gravity among the eaves
        of the cubic sky
serpent bird of Hy Brassail
force of spring
wing sunk
bound free
as we perceive our dream at centrifugal spin
so green leaves grow
the rowan bears the crown
so they, upon the veins of Anu, blazed the eye of Bel
to print a spell of glory in our blinks of lives
rightness of the world self seen
the green
the garden
and poetry attests their artistry thus and otherwise
older yet and wiser far
and I will not forget.
it is recounted with an absence of drollery

next came copper workers with wheels and carpentry
from the land of the Greeks, drunken by starlight
north through the Daneland heroing and charioteering
and breaking bones like crockery
with their brown swords.
but let us sing these rovers homesick for sights unseen
and sounding for the sake of the silence between the stars
and garnering an elder lore within their druidry
for so bore Nuada of the Silver Hand,
master of the elements
into Alba
into Erin
the quest of the Seat Perilous
and of the White Bull's Spotted Hide
to make and unmake the demons of the mind to fly
honouring the unvisionable Dagda
and Mananan of the Letters in the Craneskin
and shining Lug of the Ways
of the world
the garden
and carrying always within, as is fitting
the shadowlit
whispering
marefaced
catfaced
owlfaced
ageless huntress and thrice queen
who musing in the blood whistles and whirls
her hounds and ravens, beyond all sacrifice
craven and unrhyming, nailed in a blackthorn tree
lest horned eyes be blinded by the tomb
          of the lightlessness
in the charm of the halcyon dark.
on this, our grave and Christian clerics in alarm
avert their pens
womenless men crooked in the cloister of their age
but poetry declares it differently

older yet and lovelier far, this mystery
and I will not forget.
the next wave brought the flaxen sons of Mil
as it is writ
by stuffy hermits with a bone to pick
blundering up the Danube and down the Rhine
the warrior forefathers of the Gael
who shipped and sailed deep waters
at wind beck
one arm
one hand
one finger
prowing west across to Spain
round France and through the Channel
plundering the coastlands as they came
till they too brought their reign into the glens
the horsemen of Muimnon of the Gold.
but let us chime in the heather blue
        of their two handed harpers
spiralling from red and silver wires
tones of the faces that speak from jurassic rock
with eyes like leaves
a winding music keening and exultant
through the green drum of the hills, the white briar rose
and the long dance of the horses cantering in threes
high and lonesome reel that galloped in the duple hoofbeat
sharp as the blade of January and soft as snow,
        their minstrelsy
that kissed
and parted
and found rest in journeying
they rode and billowed in the days of old
worshipping across the world a music
that nests in bird song, insinuates in river babble
sings in the soft south wind and burns
        in the burning flame
to lay a burden and a turn that catch still at the heart

and descant yet
to the echo of that oldest tune of all, that stirs the bold
and I will not forget.
and lastly it is told,
and quaveringly
by generals doddering in their second infancy
that in the days of Darius
before Christ's birth six hundred years
Labraid the Exile came pillaging and slaughtering
as if to prove Darwin right
with his darkbrowed Gauls
and their leaf shaped spears.
I hate the scribblers who only write of war
and leave the glory of the past unsung between the lines
but sadly and truly on the sinister left hand
the tale of Britain since the Flood is of crowing
        and croaking war
that gouged heart high
a fame that soaked away
that maimed all vision
spilt jewels both red and white
killed memory and might
turned amethyst to adamant
lamenting in the reed, the wound horn, the tolling bell
brother killers the salt sea it is salt with tears
a wave flooding without an ebb
toppling stone from story
before ever Caesar's lawful butchers came
or riddling Saxons setting flame to thatch
or rune wise Vikings whirling blood wet axes
or courtly Normans cutting off of hands
and the burning church jingling in pardoner's prate
of Hell, as pedants munched their roasted meat
dumped off a fear of Spirit on the heap
as if one life was all.
but long before we ever took the names
of English, Scottish, Welsh, or Irish

and long before the tower of Babel fell
        and language cracked
there was interchange and colloquy and
        conversation upon this world
and standing stones remain to bear it testimony
from China to the Americas, and from India
        to Ireland, patterning.
still sings the salmon louder in the wild deer's lung
above and below all weir the Green Man makes his play
and in a schoolboy's hands that cupped that water
Merlin of the borders turned in his river grave
where Powsail Burn meets Tweed
the wild bees hummed
a brown bull grazing in the meads
a seeming peace, a soft summer's day
where I first read, and reading, saw
        the paper dissolve away.
and I say now years later, well mindful
        of the risk of mockery
that nothingness I am was then set a wandering
upon the windings of the ways
of the world
the garden
restless in life and seeking no end in death
for breath of the ages in the face of the air
still ghosts to the vitality
of our most early and unwritten forebears
whose wizardry still makes a lie of history
whose presence hints in every human word
who somehow reared and loosed an impossible beauty
enduring yet
among the green islands of the grey north sea
and I will not forget.

Within the Brugh

by John Matthews

1. Élcmar

"And after that time did Boand, Cow Wealth, give birth."
— Ancient Irish Text

In the darkness of the mound he began to think. Reason where there was no reason. Who, after all, could find explanations for Their actions? Certainly not he. So after a time (but of course there was no longer time) he ceased from thinking and began instead to remember. Turn back the wheel. The stars flowing back. The clouds coiling backward across a slaty sky. The last glimmer of light vanishing as the stone rolled across ... he halted that train of thought, shifted himself to ease the throbbing in his right thigh, settled back, easing one hip into a hollow in the earth. Earth. He listened. Felt the slow, steady rhythm of breath. His own? Hers? Quietly he drew a breath of clear air — it would be many days, nights (meaningless terms) before he no longer needed breath. He allowed the images to rise, slowly at first, then quickly, until the hot torrent of memory overwhelmed him and he slipped away from the darkness and was himself again, in sunlight, under a pale, blue-washed sky ... running, laughter in his throat and wind tugging his hair. But hard though he ran, there was no overtaking her. Boand. The flash of her body, far ahead now, topping the rise, vanishing amid trees. He slowed, no longer racing, pulling air into his lungs in grateful gulps ... memory within memory, of Boand, in her green dress, smiling as she emerged from the door of her father's house ... Memory: the trees enclosing him, the path only a shadow in thick leaf-mould ... She must be far ahead now; unless she had waited? Was that a movement ahead, between the trees? The leaves shivered as though stirred by a breath of wind; but there was none. It was in his mind to call out to her, but knew this was not part of the pattern he had entered when he began ... saw for a moment the face of the priest, hand raised in blessing, and of the dark motion of Boand speeding away ... came into the place where the leaves had moved and found no-one. Softly now, he went forward. Somewhere near she was, for he could sense her presence. The trees ahead thinned suddenly and he found himself standing in a glade. On all sides great smooth trunks towered skyward — a brief flash of blue where they ended. Ahead, where the trees closed in again, he saw a long, low building, little more than a green mound. Momentarily, he was puzzled. He knew this place, knew the trees. Yet there was no clearing, no hut. Yet, they were here ... He went forward, unconsciously dropping into a hunting crouch. Closer too, the mound resolved itself into a bothy, roughly oval in shape, roofed with green turf, eves overhung so far that there was scarcely a handspan between them and the earth. At the end closest to him was an entrance, no more than a gap in the wall, black and somehow forbidding. He paused before it, ears stretched for sounds of movement from within. Thought he heard something. Moved closer. Stepped within ... In the mound that was now all his world he was again aware of the cold ground, the still sharp, though retreating, fire in his leg ... He closed his eyes, squeezing them tight until the coloured shapes danced beneath his lids. He laughed softly, a surprising sound in that place. What use to close the eyes when, open or shut, there was only darkness? He shifted again, moving softly until the space beneath the mound was replaced by the space within the bothy. (If indeed there was any difference.) He sensed movement, this time framed her name: *Boand*. No reply, but a definite sense of movement now, as though someone had moved away from him, retreating into the darkest recesses of the room. He glanced behind him; the door was outlined in dim tree-light, green and cool. He felt uneasy with the prickling of an unfamiliar place. Remembered it should not be there. He sniffed, breathing in the smells: earth mostly, and peat, his own sweat, and ... something else. A woman-smell. Gingerly, he took a step, hands before him like a blind man. There began to be born upon him an image, spreading in his mind as though someone had struck an actual light. This strange illumination revealed to him a shape ahead of him in the low-roofed hut. A woman-shape: dark hair, delicate limbs. Boand. Yet. Not. Not Boand. But. Then. Who? His senses swam, like inhaling smoke, the strong perfume of woman-flesh. His heart began to race and he felt rising heat suffuse his loins. Despite himself, he trembled. This could not be Boand; this was no girl. Yet it was she; he could, with what sight had been vouchsafed to him, "see" her: the pale, narrow face, framed in black hair; the slender body he had last glimpsed fleeing before him through the trees. He found it strangely hard to move; yet he knew he must. Advanced a step, and with that seemed to see more clearly. A gleam of pale flesh. Naked, then, she was naked. Lust stirred in him. But such lust! such a flood of hunger which, had it struck him in daylight, in his own place, could only have meant one thing. Here, he seemed held by the power as it mounted within him. His movements were as slow as a dreamer, as though he were suspended in liquid and could not impel himself forward any faster. He tried to focus his attention on the woman in front of him, at the provocatively tilted hips ... It seemed an age before he reached her, stumbling suddenly to his knees at her side, almost flung upon her by the sudden releasing of his body from whatever had held him. Now that she was near he felt suddenly afraid of touching her. Her face and body were Boand's, yet she was a stranger to him in a way that he could not comprehend. He felt her eyes upon him and with that a shock ran through his body that left him gasping. He felt life spilling from him like blood and he shuddered with the force of it — yet he was withdrawn, far away, detached, as though it were happening to another. Normally he would have felt shamed, but not now. And he saw that she-who-was-Boand was smiling at him. Had raised a hand to catch the seed that fell from him. She raised that hand, first to her lips, then to his brow, where she placed her fingers for a moment and immediately it was as though he had woken from a long sleep. He saw clearly. The face of the woman was close to him. He felt her breath on his cheek. In clarity of action he moved upon her, feeling excitement mount again within him. Never had he felt its like with any woman. And with it his perceptions grew clearer. As though from a great height he saw himself, far below, cover the woman's body with his own, her face, over his shoulder, blurred with ecstasy. He himself felt nothing: or if he did, felt it at such a remove that it was as though it were happening to someone else. He seemed a giant, standing hugely astride the land, and in some way that he could scarcely comprehend, the woman *was* the land: her rich limbs and mounded breasts the hills and valleys, combs and vales. Vast forms moved across his vision, and he was part of them, moving to their rhythm and their time — infinitely slower than his own. In ecstasy he spasmed, hot unquenchable fires in his belly and loins that seemed to come from far beneath him. For a moment he was both far above *and* present in his own body, and with that came the sense that he was driving deep into the earth ... with a shock of pain and a cry that echoed in his mind as it must have echoed across the land, he came fully awake, found himself standing with face and body pressed hard against a damp wall of earth — the wall of the mound. Rivulets of sweat burst from him and flowed over his breast and thighs. He tasted it salt on his lips and it stung his eyes. He felt that he was being pressed downward into the earth itself, compressed into a ball of clay. And with the feeling strangely came another. A sense of being expelled, of coming forth from sleep, or a dark place, or a long dream. In the silence which eternally filled the mound he felt the surge and flux of a great roaring sound, like a river which had burst its banks and then rushed away in a great flood, leaving its bed empty and dry. So he felt also, and the darkness which had been not-empty before, now seemed chill and barren ... For a timeless time he stood thus, trying to remember if this was the mound or the turf hut into which he had crawled long since (how long?). Or whether they were one and the same. Tried to remember the face of the woman. Of Boand ... The words of the priest came back to him, and with them the touch of her hand on his brow: *You shall know the wisdom of she who bore us and you shall have congress with her and of the twain shall be born the child who sanctifies the land.* Like an echo in his mind the thought ran, and he felt cold, alone, spent. Slowly he sank down in that lightless place, and eased himself into a position so that his back was against the wall. Sighing, he leant his head back and stared with sightless eyes towards where the roof must stretch. There, he saw what at first he thought was the illusion of lights: minute pinpricks piercing the darkness. He blinked his eyes, thinking these were lights he saw when he pressed his fingers upon his closed lids. But his eyes were open, and the darkness was less dark above him ... For a long time he sat still, until the pattern asserted itself into a dimly recognizable form. Stars. Sky. The roof of the world and the roof of the mound. Then a voice boomed out of the darkness, a voice so vast that it must come from beyond those tiny points of light. It was a single word, a name, repeated over and over, at first without meaning but gradually coming clearer. A name. ÉLCMAR. A name dimly familiar. His own name. With a cry he leapt up towards that voice, his own raised in feeble answer. The mound opened above him, breaking open like the membrane of an egg, and he burst upwards into light. Such light as he had never known or could have guessed at. And the great voice slid into silence, leaving him alone. He stood upon a great plain, stretching upon all sides, and above him the Sun glared like a golden beetle, and coming towards him ...

2. OENGUS

His name was Oengus but he was always trying to remember who had given it to him. In the distance, he remembered that he had once been called names like "Young" and "Son." In the distance, memory occluded, he was always trying to remember something. Images of a breaking flood, a great plain, the high round orb of the sun. And under it, within it, in the midst a face, seamed and wrinkled like the earth, with a wide lipless mouth opening to speak ... what words he could never tell, only that they were important to him, as important as a name, the most secret and powerful thing any one person could know about another. In his own name, he somehow knew, was a great mystery which would open doors, cause mounds to gape, turn rivers in their beds. But he knew nothing of its meaning, and did not dare to ask. Afraid of the answers and what they might mean. All quests began that way, he knew, and it was not long before he realized that he was already embarked upon just such a one ... The days dawned, indeed, when he found himself walking away from the place that had always been home, without a thought for where it would lead, where he was heading. He crossed the wide flat plain and came to the edge of the hills, and beyond them caught a glimpse of trees. He walked through the wood and drank in its scents and watched its changing patterns. All day he walked until the trees were left behind and he came to a place where the hills shouldered up from the earth, cracking it open and rising upward. Finally he came to an opening in the hillside: a cave-mouth opening into darkness. As he had been taught he entered without hesitation, raising his hand before him and speaking aloud the words he had learned long since but never, until that day, spoken. The darkness of the place ebbed before him and he stared about in the soft gleam of a light. The wall of the place told a story of habitation from the first palm-print to the last leaping stag. Here must be the secret, the thing he sought. He sat down in the centre of the strange rock world and set himself to remember all that he saw ... It took a while and when he was at last familiar with every mark on the walls of the cave he felt tired. Dousing the light he walked outside, drawing strength as always from the warmth of the sun's rays. Then he lay down upon the warm stones and closed his eyes in sleep ... Dreams came at once, and once again he saw the great face rising above him, speaking great words which filled his mind and fell like invisible fire around him. Then he was suddenly awake in a strange place filled with light that seemed to magnify everything upon which it fell: so that the earth was a map of cracks and crevices, each of which seemed to tell a story: what had once been there, who had come and who had passed, a chain of memories binding him to that place as though it had been his for all time ... Unbidden, then, came the memory, the scent of a white flower that made everything else seem like a wilderness — but it was not, stars shone, and grass grew here, under the high bright glow. And with the knowledge of the flower came another kind of knowing — that under the guise of stem and petals lay a form sleeping — a bright-stepping form in which the legend of Spring was reborn, moment to moment in the tears of Winter ... On his bed of stone the sleeper turned, restless as a bird before the onset of storms; and with his turning the dream turned, and from the images within the cave came further knowledge ... He stood at the entrance to a grove, deep-wooded, held in stillness like a breath of sunlight. In his hands was a harp, and though in the world from which he came, waking, he knew nothing of the art of music, here he drew from its strings such vibrations of sound that the very wind wept and the trees bowed before him their deep rustling valances. But she moved not, nor breathed but lightly, where she stood, white as swan's feathers at the distant end of the grove. Caught in arrested movement, like a deer in flight or a bird about to take wing, she turned an eye brighter than moonlight upon him, and the harp quaked and grew still in his hands ... With great sweeps of light, flashing like paddles in sunlit water, she grew feathered and beaked and swam in the air with great pinions of snow, so that he too must follow her as a brown hawk spinning in silver shadow. Driven by desire his raptor's cry rang out in the shadow of the sun, long and long their racing wings beat sparks from the anvil of air before her song broke free and all time stilled to hear it ... Restless again he turned on his pillow of polished stone, and stood again upon the bruised earth, which cried out for the passing of her love. Enraged, like a winter storm, he wept, and finding again the harp in his two hands, he fought the season to an end and brought the sun back from beneath the world as a gift for her ... Sailing on wings of spun silver the swan entered his dream and where her feet touched the earth sprang open and white flowers bloomed ... Waking, the dreamer sprang from his couch of stone and fled back down the hillsides and through the trees, on into the silence of the white lands until the green mound of his home swam into vision. Crying aloud — his words like a swan's silver singing or a harsh hawk's cry — he broke open the crusted wards of memory, saw again the retreating waters, the white hills opening and the blue-glass sky overhead. In his ears a cry rang forth and his name became to him a sword. Standing still on the top of the green mound he sought the strings of the harp and sang season through season until his joy was spent and the small flame of life burned steadily at his feet. Then he stepped down, sure now in the knowledge of himself, and took the hand that was stretched out to him and went into the green mound. And there he stayed long in the shadow of the sun and the purity of the rain and the blessing of the earth until their joy fruited into life.

An Adventure of the Grail

by David Spangler

"Out of my way, boy!" shouted Sir Kay, pushing Hodge roughly to one side as the knight strode quickly down the castle corridor. He was followed by two squires, young boys hardly older than Hodge himself. The smallest of the two was almost running to keep up with the knight's long stride. The larger paused by Hodge, looking at him with a smirk of superiority. "Yes," he said, imitating his master's tone, "out of our way, kitchen boy!" With that he gave Hodge another shove, and the younger boy stumbled against the damp wall of the corridor and fell down. The older squire laughed and ran to catch up with Sir Kay.

Hodge's face burned with embarrassment. Most of the squires were good-hearted lads who did not put on airs, but Sir Kay's squires were like their master, arrogant and rough. Once again, Hodge wondered how Sir Kay had ever become one of the Fellowship. If Kay had not been the King's foster brother, Hodge was sure he would never have qualified to sit at the Round Table.

Hodge picked himself up, only to flatten himself again against the wall as he saw another knight come running up the corridor towards him. It was Lancelot, he noted with awe, who, it was said, was the greatest of all the knights. (Other things were whispered in the kitchens about him and the Queen, but Hodge had felt it disloyal to listen to such tales and so paid them no attention.)

Running fast, the great knight passed Hodge with hardly a glance in his direction. Hodge sighed. That was his life. He was either in the way or invisible.

Looking down the corridor as the running figure disappeared around a corner, he failed to see another figure coming toward him. Turning, he walked right into a hard-muscled frame and once again, was knocked down, his cap falling over his eyes.

"Ho, there, little one," a firm voice said, "you must watch where you're going!" A hand was thrust down to him, and Hodge grabbed it. He was pulled to his feet, and a gentle hand rearranged his cap. He found himself looking into the laughing brown eyes and bearded face of Sir Bors, one of his favourite knights, a man of simple origins like Hodge himself who never put on airs and who was always kind to the castle help.

"Sor ... sorry, my lord," Hodge stammered, once more embarrassed. It was his secret hope to one day be accepted by Sir Bors as a squire, and he did not want this man to think he was clumsy and unaware of his surroundings.

"It's all right ... hmmn, Hodge, isn't it? ... but if I were you, I would not be wondering these corridors just now. There has been a most holy and miraculous event in the Great Hall, and it has stirred this place up like a bear's paw in a bee hive. Knights and squires are running all over the place, as you have seen, getting ready for a quest."

"A quest?" the boy blurted out.

"Aye, Hodge, a most holy quest. Only a short time ago, while we were at meat around the table, the cup of Christ appeared in the air above us. Like the disciples at Pentecost, we were all filled with a holy fire. We looked upon each other and saw things no mortal man should know about another. But rather than fear, we felt love and a great wonder. Then the grail disappeared, leaving us with a longing like nothing I have felt before, not even when I met my wife, comely as she was. We all sat stunned, when Sir Gawain jumped to his feet and pledged that he would go on quest to find the answer to the mystery we had seen. Then others joined him, pledging themselves to find the holy grail on behalf of Arthur and the realm. Even I, who, as you know, am not much given to quests, found myself on my feet, shouting with the rest. Then the King stood up and formally charged the Fellowship to find the cup of Christ, though if truth be told, he seemed sad as he did so. Indeed, Lancelot, who sits closer to Arthur than I, mentioned the King had leaned to him and said that this quest might be the end of the Fellowship itself."

Hodge listened to this story with amazement, not only at the story itself but at the fact that Sir Bors was taking the time to tell it to a mere kitchen boy. The knight obviously felt a need to talk about what had happened.

Perhaps, Hodge thought wildly for a moment, catching the knight's excitement, he has noticed me and wants me to accompany him on this quest! That hope, however, was dashed in the next moment, as Sir Bors patted him on the head and said, "I think, Hodge, this is not a good night to be roaming the corridors. If I were you, I would go to the kitchens and work there where you won't be run over by knights and squires rushing about to be the first to leave and find the holy grail. As for me, I go to spend some time with my family before I shall set off like the others." With that, the knight gave the disappointed boy a friendly squeeze on his shoulder and continued down the corridor himself.

Following Sir Bors' advice, Hodge made his way through the castle to the kitchens where he spent the rest of the evening washing dishes and listening to all the rumours that raced through the room faster than the knights were running about themselves. A new knight had arrived, it seemed, a youth in shining armour accompanied by an old man, who might have been the missing Merlin himself. Hodge listened astonished as one of the serving maids swore she had been told by one of the squires that this new knight, Sir Galahad by name, had actually sat in the Siege Perilous, the seat at the Table that no one ever sat in lest he be blasted by supernatural forces. Yet, the youth had sat there unharmed, much to everyone's amazement. Then the mystical cup had appeared in the air above them, and the old man had exclaimed, "There is the cup of Christ!"

It was very late that night when Hodge was finally released from his work to go to bed. There had been one demand after another as squires and knights prepared their gear and packed food for the journeys ahead. Yet, the excitement in the castle was so contagious that no one felt tired. Everyone talked about the wonders that had taken place or that would take place, and with each telling, with each new rumour, with each whispered "I have a friend who has a friend who says ..." the stories grew more wondrous indeed.

So it was that when Hodge was done, he was too excited to sleep. Instead, he found his feet carrying him to the great hall where the Round Table stood, the place where the Grail had appeared only hours before. He didn't know why he went there. He rarely came to this part of the castle, and he was sure that someone would stop him before he arrived. Commoners like him were rarely allowed in this hall unless they had business with the Fellowship or the King, and there were almost always guards at the door. But in the still early morning hours past midnight, the corridors were empty, and he saw no one. Strangely, even the guards were gone.

The great hall was lit only by the dim glow from a fire dying in the hearth. The Round Table was a huge presence in the room, and as always, Hodge felt a deep reverence and awe when he saw it. Like nearly every other servant boy in the castle, it was his dream to one day sit at this table, to be part of the Fellowship, to ride forth and do great deeds for God, King, and Realm. At the moment, the way such a dream might be fulfilled seemed as dark to him as the shadows that lay heavy everywhere within the room.

Hodge crept warily through those shadows and up to Table itself. Hesitantly, he put his hand out and touched it. Its rough wood had been carefully polished, and it was warm to the touch, as if deep within it, so faint fire burned, but as he rubbed his hand over its surface, he realized with a shock that it felt no different from the tables he cleaned in the kitchen or in the common dining rooms where the squires ate. In fact, as he looked more closely, he thought he saw a stain upon it.

Squinting in the dim light from the fire, Hodge saw that it was a stain. Someone had spilled gravy onto the table and it had never been cleaned up! He felt a wave of indignation at the thought. He knew the knights took their meat and drink at this table, as well as debating the affairs of state, but somehow, it had never occurred to him that some of them might spill their food like a common workman or that the Round Table might be stained like any common board upon which a poor man took his food.

Without thinking, Hodge took the edge of his sleeve and began rubbing fiercely at the stain. He thought he was cleaning it off, but the growing shadows as the fire sank deeper into its own ashes made it difficult for him to see. Yet, somehow, it seemed very important to him that this stain be removed. He rubbed even harder.

All at once, there was a light about him, as if a torch had been lit. Startled and frightened that someone had found him rubbing on the great Table and that punishment would surely now befall him, he jumped back. As he did so, his foot caught in the leg of one of the chairs drawn up to the table, and he fell backwards, landing unceremoniously upon his backside.

It was then that he saw the glowing object in the air above him. It was a simple cup, not all that different from one he might use himself in the kitchen, but it shone like molten steel from the blacksmith's forge. It gave off no heat, yet in its light Hodge felt a warmth like nothing he had ever known before. It was not as if his body were warm but as if something much deeper and somehow more real was being warmed and awakened within him.

He realized in an instant that this cup was what had appeared to the assembled knights, that it was what the old man had proclaimed the cup of Christ, the holy Grail. But that was all he knew. All other emotion, save awe and an overpowering sense of being loved, were swept from him in the light of this apparition. He did not even know that he had scrambled to his feet and was standing by the Table again, unable to take his gaze from the glory of the vessel hovering in the air above him.

Then, as suddenly as it had come, the cup disappeared, its light lingering for a moment in the room like the memory of a dawn. Then all was dark again. Hodge felt himself coming back as if from a very far place, and, shuddering, he drew a breath.

"So, you saw it, too, eh, lad?"

The deep voice coming from the shadows made him jump and whirl around in fright. Who had spoken?

From the shadows near one of the tall pillars that lined the great hall, a hooded figure stepped. Frightened, Hodge made ready to bolt from the room, sure that he would be punished severely for daring to look upon so holy an object as the Grail. However, the voice spoke again, and something in it held him rooted to the spot as if he had become a pillar himself.

"Don't be afraid, boy! I will not hurt you." The figure came closer, and Hodge saw it was an old man dressed in a monk's habit. The figure unceremoniously pulled out one of the chairs by the table and sat down. An old and weathered hand reached out from under the sleeve of the robe and took his arm. The touch, while firm, was nonetheless gentle, and Hodge felt all his fear drain away.

"You see, boy? I will not hurt you. How could I hurt one to whom the Grail has shown itself?" Now Hodge could see the man's face. It was in fact an old and wrinkled face, but the eyes were alive and fierce like those of a hawk on its first hunting flight.

"Tell me, boy, and hold nothing back. Who are you and what are you doing here?"

To his amazement, Hodge heard his voice pouring forth his life's story, how his father had been a farmer tending a landhold not far from Camelot, how the farm had been raided one day, how his father had fought the raiders but had been killed in the end, and how, when all had seemed lost and their house was burning, one of the knights of the Fellowship — Sir Gawain, it had been — had arrived on the scene and had killed the raiders and rescued him and his mother. He told how they had been brought to the castle, where he had become a kitchen boy, and how his mother had died the last winter from fever, leaving him alone. He told how his deepest longing was to be a knight himself, who could protect the weak and helpless, who would rescue people as he had been rescued him, and who would battle monsters and evil-doers in the name of the King and the Land. He told all these things and more, without emotion, like telling the story of a figure in a dream with whom he felt little connection. From time to time, the old man would interrupt and ask him a question, but for the most part he listened in silence.

Finally, Hodge had told all there was to tell, and his voice stopped, not as if he had willed it to do so, but as if it had simply come to the edge of a cliff and had stepped off into the silence below. The old man continued to hold onto his arm, and the fierce eyes continued their hawk's survey of his soul.

Then, like a soft wind from the farthest corners of the earth, the old man sighed and released him. For a moment those eyes closed, and Hodge felt like a mouse must feel who has finally reached the safety of his den. Then, the eyes snapped open once more, and he realized that that den was in fact no where around.

"Boy ... Hodge ... listen to me. It is given only to a few to see the Grail. No man can make it come or go, not the holiest saint nor the most powerful magician. It goes where and when it will, and no King or Queen can gainsay it. That it came to this company here tonight was an act of its own, not mine, not anyone's, and now we will see what results."

The old man sighed again. "The King, the Queen, the Fellowship, Camelot, all of us are called to a new undertaking, to a new vision, but whether that vision is one of questing or not, I cannot say. We are poised in time, and in this moment a new world could be born or an old world die. Perhaps it is both. I only know we will all never be the same. Our prayers must be that whatever emerges from this moment, from what occurred in this room will be for the good."

"But how could it be otherwise, if what we saw was the cup of Christ ...?" Hodge blurted out, and then was shocked at his impudence. What did the likes of him know of holy cups and heavenly visions? The old man smiled, and Hodge sensed it was not a smile of mirth. "Ah, that is a mystery, Hodge. The coming of the Grail does not foretell how men will receive it or interpret its presence. Its light is a flint that can set fire to wisdom or to folly. From it one can drink insight or madness. Which will you drink from it, boy?"

"I ... I ... don't understand ..." He was beginning to feel fear again beneath this stranger's penetrating gaze and hearing such strange words. Then, the eyes softened, and the fear blew away.

"I know you don't. I do not expect you to understand me, nor am I sure I understand all that has occurred. I only want you to listen to me as I have listened to you. For the Grail chose you, Hodge, as one of those to whom it would reveal itself. It was no accident you were here this night. There is a reason you were shown the same vision as those of the Fellowship."

At these words, Hodge's heart leapt and burned with an excitement as if a new grail had just appeared before him. "Does this mean I can be a knight and go on quest with the others, sir?"

The old man looked at him without answering, and Hodge now felt abashed and embarrassed by his outburst. Still, he *had* seen the Grail, and even this old man had said that was important and special.

"Hodge, knighthood and the quest are not yours, I am afraid. I can see that your life weaves a different thread. But I tell you this, knighthood comes in many forms and many ways, and not all knights wear armour and ride horses or are chosen by a king. Anyone who cherishes compassion in his heart and strives to do right for others and is a true servant can be a knight of a deeper order. There are many more fellowships than that created by Arthur."

At these words, Hodge's heart sank. He did not know of any other fellowships and could not understand this strange old man's words. How could a man be a knight if he were not invested by the king? What was a knight without his horse or armour? And why would he have seen the Grail if he was not to be a knight?

"I do not know why the Grail showed itself to you, Hodge," the old man said, as if reading his mind, "but I know it had a reason. You may not have a quest but you have a task to perform. Who knows, boy, it may be more important than all the quests put together. Only time will tell."

The old man stood up. "I must go now. There is still much to do, and time is short. And you, Hodge, should go to bed."

"Yes, sir," Hodge replied, but he felt unable to take a single step. The old man began to walk away, then turned. "By the way, boy," he asked. "I saw you rubbing on the Table as if you would set it on fire. What were you doing?"

Hodge felt all the indignation he had felt earlier rise up in him. "It was gravy, sir! A stain on the Table. Someone had spilled and had not cleaned up! I was trying to clean it"

The old man looked at him for a moment, then threw back his head and laughed, a rich, deep laugh. "Gravy! By the Gods!" Then, abruptly, the laughter cut off and the hawk eyes fixed themselves on Hodge so fiercely that the boy felt more like a trapped mouse than ever. "That is it, boy. That is what you must do! Clean the Table!"

Hodge felt a jolt pass through him. "Clean ... clean the Table?"

"CLEAN THE TABLE!" The old man did not raise his voice, but to Hodge, it sounded as if he had shouted at the top of his lungs. Then the hawk eyes flashed as if bolts of lightning were sparking from them, and the man pointed at Hodge. "And now, GO TO BED!"

Hodge flew from the room, down the corridors, down the stairs, down more corridors and more stairs and finally flung himself into his room far down in the bowels of the castle, onto the straw-filled mat he called his bed, and into a darkness of dreams in which cups glowing like molten gold floated over the land and a god-like voice said over and over, "CLEAN THE TABLE!"

*

It was late morning when Hodge awoke. He was astonished that no one had come to wake him, since usually his day began before the sun came up. With trepidation, he ran from his room and made his way to the kitchens. He hoped there was some food left and that he wouldn't have to begin work right away. His stomach felt as if a badger had burrowed a long hole in it and now lay growling at the bottom.

When he arrived at the kitchens, he was astonished to find it nearly empty except for the wise woman who supervized the collection and drying of herbs. He was glad to see her, for after his mother had died, she had taken a liking to him and had begun to teach him a little of her herbal lore.

As he ran into the room, the woman said without looking up from what she was doing, "You are late, Hodge."

"I'm sorry, Marta. I overslept. But why did no one fetch me? And where is everyone?"

"Everyone is off at the church watching all the Fellowship receive the blessing of the King and Queen and Bishop before they go off to find the cup of Christ. I did not think they would welcome someone who practices the old religion. Besides," she spat onto the floor, "we have our own cup already, and need not go traveling the land and leaving King and kingdom behind like some addle-headed swain in pursuit of the latest comely wench he sees."

Hodge knew she was speaking of those like her who followed the old ways. His mother had been a Christian, but she had not lived to give him much instruction, and now he found himself intrigued and drawn to what Marta had to say about the land and its powers. On the whole, though, he had little time or energy to think about religious things and generally did not bother himself with them. At least not until last night.

"There's some porridge in a bowl by the window for you and some bread there as well."

"Thank you, Marta!" Hodge said gratefully and ran over to the window to fetch his breakfast.

After he had eaten, he found he had little to do, a rare occasion in his life. Marta seemed occupied and unwilling to be bothered, so he wandered outside and climbed up a tree that grew by the wall of the keep. From there he could see down into the village square, where throngs of people were gathered outside the church. The sound of voices singing drifted up from down below and mixed in a pleasant way with the bird song he heard around him. The sun's warmth worked its way into his bones, and his eyelids drooped.

He slept without knowing it, and in his dreams, he was part of a brilliant company, each of whose members were garbed in armour that seemed struck from the colours of the rainbow. He could recognize Gawain, Bors, Lancelot, and all the others. Even Sir Kay looked different, resplendent in a new way, his harsh and arrogant face softened. Around them a great light gleamed as the sun dashed itself upon their shiningness and sprayed out as golden foam. Looking down he saw, his own body encased in a shining white armour which seemed to weigh nothing at all, sitting astride a great warhorse. Ahead of them stood three figures. One he knew to be Arthur, his great sword Excalibur raised above his head. The other was the old man he had met in the Great Hall the night before, and the third was unknown to him, a man of middle age with a trim black beard and hair, a brightly colored feathered cloak around his shoulders, and a harp in his hand.

Beyond them still stood another figure, this one wrapped in pure light. As Hodge watched, he raised his hands and held up a simple cup, but he might as well have been holding up the sun, for it rivaled in its splendour the fiery celestial orb high in the sky. As he did so, a great shout rang out from all the assembled company and ...

Hodge suddenly felt himself falling, and flailed wildly about him, grabbing hold of a branch just as he started to plunge towards the ground. He wrapped his legs around another branch and held on tightly. He had fallen asleep in the tree and had been dreaming. There had been a great shout ...

He realized that he was hearing such a shout that went on and on, and that it had not been in his dream. Settling himself back in the tree, he realized the shouting was coming from the village down below. Looking down, he saw that the knights were emerging from the church, their armour gleaming in many colours just as in his dream. As the people cheered, the knights made their way down the street, their warhorses cantering and prancing. Even Sir Bors was among them, not having spent as much time with his family as he had hoped. For a moment, he felt wholly disoriented. Had he not just been in that company? Where was his horse, his armour? Why was he not down there with them, heading forth on the quest of all quests?

Then he realized it had just been a dream. He was not a knight, not one of the Fellowship, not going forth on quest. He was just Hodge, a kitchen boy who would always be a kitchen boy. Yes, he had seen the Grail, but why? It seemed like a cruel joke by a cruel god. He felt a pain as keen as if a sword had twisted in his entrails. Tears swelled in his eyes as he watched the last of the knights ride out of the village towards the forest beyond, and a bitter taste rose in this throat. He was no knight. He was only Hodge, and the only quest he would ever know was to find enough soap to clean the pots and pans.

*

That evening, as things began to return to normal, Hodge was called before Gedron, the headman of the kitchen. He was a big, bluff man, given to petty tyranny at times over those who worked for him, but given to bursts of generosity as well. He had beaten Hodge in the past for minor infractions of rules or for jobs not done to his satisfaction, but he had also given him extra helpings of food and had even presented him with a new woollen blanket — a true luxury — the week after his mother had died. Hodge suspected that some of the man's favours came because he was afraid of Marta and knew that the wise woman had taken the boy under her protection.

"Hodge," Gedron said gruffly, "the King himself has just asked for you and wants you to see him by the Round Table in the Great Hall."

"The King? He wants to see me?" Hodge could not imagine why the King would want to see him.

"I have just now received the message." The headman looked at him suspiciously. "What have you been doing that I don't know about, Hodge?"

"I ... I don't know, sir. Nothing ... I have done nothing!"

"Hmmn," the man said, obviously not believing him. "Well, perhaps it is nothing, then, but you must get along. And wash your face and hands first! And mind your manners! I would not have you shame me before the King himself."

"I will, Sir! I won't Sir!" Hodge stammered, as he ran to a bucket of water and threw cold water over his face and hands. He dried himself off on his sleeve as he ran out of the kitchen and up the stairs and down corridors to the Great Hall. He had told Gedron he did not know why Arthur wanted to see him, but he was sure it was because of what had happened last night. Whoever the old man had been, he must have told the king that one of his kitchen help had seen the Grail. Hodge didn't know whether to feel excited or afraid, so he felt both.

He slowed to what he hoped was a dignified walk as he approached the great hall where the table was. Two men-at-arms stood at guard by the door.

"Well, look what we have here!" smirked one of the guards, towering over Hodge. "have you come to scrub the floors? Where is your bucket and mop, kitchen whelp?"

Hodge felt anger rising through his fear and excitement. He had done nothing to be mocked. These men had not seen the Grail, he was sure, so who were they to mock him?

"The King has sent for me," he said. "I am Hodge."

"'I am Hodge,'" the guard mimicked. "You sound like a knight. Who are you to put on such airs? You should feel the flat of my blade on your rump, kitchen whelp."

"Stop it, Pudge," the second guard said. "The boy is right. The King did send for him. Perhaps he wants his privy cleaned."

The two guards laughed while Hodge turned a bright red with anger and embarrassment. The first guard stood aside. "Go on in, Sir Hodge! The privy quest awaits you!"

Hodge darted past them as they laughed, then slowed again to a walk as he again entered the Great Hall. But he could feel his face still burning and his eyes were brimming with tears, which made him all the more angry and discomfited.

At first he thought he was alone in the hall again, which was unusual as there were almost always people in it who had business with the King. However, now it was as empty as it had been — or at least had seemed — last night. As he walked towards the Table, he cast his eyes about, expecting to see the monkish old man standing by one of the pillars. But the room was truly empty.

As he walked up to the table, he heard a door open somewhere. Then, from behind the King's chair stepped Arthur himself. He was no longer in his golden armour. He was dressed simply in a plain brown tunic and trousers, with a woollen robe about his shoulders. He wore no crown upon his head. His red hair was tousled, as if he had just been rubbing his hands through it. Blue eyes sparkled above a rugged face softened by his red beard.

Hodge immediately fell to his knees and bowed his head, gazing at the wooden floor below him. Two feet clothed in soft leather slippers appeared in his range of vision and a hand touched him on the shoulder.

"Arise, Hodge," Arthur said. Hodge was surprised to hear how soft Arthur's voice was, for he had always heard how the King could bellow like a bull. Hodge got to his feet, but still kept his head lowered and his eyes on the floor.

"Look at me, Hodge. Is your liege too ugly for you to look upon?"

"Oh no, my lord," Hodge stammered, looking up at the King. "You are the handsomest of all men!"

Arthur chuckled. "Well, I won't argue, but there are some who might disagree." A puzzled, wistful expression crossed the King's face so quickly that Hodge was not sure he had seen it at all. The King's eyes, blue like a summer sky, caught and held Hodge's own. "That is better, boy. Eyes that have seen the Grail have no reason not to see the world unafraid and with honour." Then Arthur look more closely. "You have been crying, Hodge. What is the matter?"

Hodge began to blush again, but the King's question had been so solicitous that his shame vanished. "It is nothing, my lord."

"Well, perhaps, but my guess is that my guards were teasing

you. They are not my regular guards, but two men called up from the barracks while my own men are attending to a matter elsewhere. With all the turmoil and changes around here today, I did not have time to be too choosy. Be assured they will not bother you again."

"My lord," said Hodge, aghast at the thought that something he had said or done might cause trouble for the guards, for though he had been angry at them, he still thought of them as something special for being the King's guards. "I would not cause any trouble for anyone."

"Nor have you. Yet, in my realm, the King is the servant of all the people. That is the basis of the Fellowship and of the Table Round, and I will not have any of my subjects, no matter how lowly, treated with anything but the utmost respect by those who represent me."

The King went over to his throne, beckoning Hodge to follow. He sat down and then indicated that Hodge should sit on the Queen's throne. "Gwenny won't mind," he said, "and besides, if the Father deems you worthy enough to be shown the holy cup that held the blood of his Son, then you are surely worthy to sit on one of these chairs!"

Hodge, head spinning with what was happening, gingerly sat on the edge of the Queen's throne, prepared to leap off in a minute should thunder roll or lightning flash in the sky.

Arthur leaned back, suggesting by his example that Hodge should feel relaxed as well. "Well, Hodge, Merlin told me all about you and your experience last night." So, thought Hodge wildly, the old man *was* the fabled magician after all. But where had he been for so long? "It must have been a shock for one so young. It was a shock for me and my knights when the Cup appeared. So naturally, I wanted to meet you. Merlin said you wished to become one of my knights."

Hodge sat up straight. "Oh yes, sire, more than anything!"

"Well, Hodge, perhaps one day I shall set you upon the path to knighthood, though you must understand that it is not the king who makes a knight."

"It isn't? But who, then? I mean, I thought ..."

"Oh, I formally proclaim a man a knight, but only when the man has already become a knight in his heart first. Do you understand what I mean?"

Hodge thought. Then he remembered Sir Bors telling him and other boys once about the trails and tests a man needed to go through before he could become a knight. "Yes, my lord, I believe so."

"Good. For it is important you understand there are many routes to knighthood, but they are all paths of service. A knight is simply another kind of servant, just like you."

"But not one who works in a kitchen, sire," Hodge blurted.

Arthur laughed. "That may be so, but imagine, Hodge, how useful a knight might be if he were always hungry because no one cooked his food or cleaned plates for him to use or kept the castle in good repair."

Hodge thought, then grinned back at the King. "I suppose we do all have our uses, Sire."

"Good, Hodge. Yes, that is what I want you to say, for a knight cannot always choose the kind of service required of him, nor where it will take him, nor what it may cost him. And a knight, pledged to service, may be called upon to do many things he does not like or would not choose otherwise. Do you understand?"

"Yes, Sire."

"Wonderful. Then, Hodge, you will not be disappointed if I say I wish you to serve me just as my knights do."

"Oh no, Sire!" Hodge's heart began to beat with excitement. He was going to become a knight, in spite of what Merlin had said.

"Fine, Hodge. Then here is what I want you to do. From henceforth, you will be one of my personal servants with one task and one task alone."

"And what is that, my lord?"

"You are to clean the Round Table. You are to keep it in good repair, in good polish, clean and shining. You will be the servant of the Round Table itself."

Hodge looked at the King blankly for a moment, for all he

could hear roaring in his ears was the voice of Merlin and the words "CLEAN THE TABLE!" Then he felt a wave of bitterness and disappointment, for obviously the old magician had put this idea into the King's head. For having seen the Grail, the King would have made him a knight if it hadn't been for that meddling old man.

Arthur looked at the boy. "Hodge, this is an honour I am offering you. It is a path of service, and perhaps it is the path that will take you to the knighthood you wish. You are not disappointed, are you? You would not refuse the King's gift, would you?"

Hodge shivered and threw off his feelings. "Oh, no, my lord. To serve you is my greatest wish, and if it is to be as the one who cleans your Table, then that is what I shall do!" And in that moment, Hodge knew he really meant it. He would clean that Round Table as it had never been cleaned before.

"I am glad, Hodge. Merlin told me it is the right task for you — your quest, if you wish — and I have never known Merlin to be wrong. However, I must correct one thing you said. It is not my table you clean and serve, but the Round Table which is its own thing in a way. No one owns it, you see, except perhaps the Land itself or the Son of God. I do not always understand it, but I know magic when I see it. It comes from being raised by Merlin." Arthur leaned forward and gave the Table an affectionate thump with his fist. "And this, Hodge, is magic!"

As if in response to his blow, a squire wearing the King's colours magically appeared from around the back of the throne. The King stood up, and Hodge did as well. "Hodge, you will now become one of my squires and wear my colours. I will have tutors teach you, for it is not meet that someone who has been graced with the vision of the Grail should not know his letters. You shall be one of my household, with all the honours there attending. And," his eyes flashed, reminding Hodge for a moment of Merlin, "everyday you shall clean this Table!"

*

And so it came to pass that Hodge became the servant of the Round Table. And while each day, somewhere in the Realm, a knight of the Fellowship would unlimber spear and sword to meet some adventures upon the quest for the Holy Grail, Hodge would each day come to the Table with bucket and sponge, soap and polish, and face the depredations of wine and gravy, oil and grease.

Of course, since all the knights were away, the Round Table was not used much. Now and then a knight or two would return briefly to tell of their adventures, only to leave soon thereafter. Sometimes after such a visit, Hodge had some real cleaning to do, but not always. Occasionally, the King and Queen would dine at the table, but they were not messy eaters. Mostly they ate in their chambers, though increasingly, Hodge noted, the King dined alone.

So, as it turned out, there actually wasn't all that much for Hodge to do. Somedays, a simple rinse with the sponge and a swipe with the polish was all it took. Then he was free to roam about the castle or the village or even the lands nearby (when he was not being tutored, of course). He still visited Marta, and she would take him into the woods and show him different herbs and plants. In time, she began teaching him the lore of the animals and even of stones, and the secret language that all things in nature know and to which they will respond. He was careful, though, not to mention these lessons to his tutor, who was a monk from a nearby monastery. Though the two religions of the old and new paths cohabited in Arthur's realm, it was not always a peaceful marriage.

In this way, Hodge's life settled into a pleasing, if sometimes boring, routine. Though he continued to dream of knights and far quests as he grew older, he realized that indeed he was very fortunate. And, deep in his heart, he treasured the vision he had had of the Grail. He had even come to appreciate his brief meeting with Merlin, who had once again disappeared, no one knew where.

*

One day, however, he returned to the castle from an outing with Marta to hear the news that Sir Mador, had died on the quest for the Grail. Saddened by the news, Hodge immediately went to the great hall, filled with an urgency to be with the Round Table, as if by doing so, he could come into communion with the slain knight and give his soul solace. Arriving at the Table, however, he was astonished and dismayed to discover a dark red stain upon it, right at the place where Sir Mador sat when the Fellowship was present. He had already cleaned and polished the Table once that morning, and he knew that the stain had not been there then. Puzzled, he went and asked the guards (who now were very respectful to him) if anyone had been at the table, but they both agreed no one had even been in the hall, not even the King.

So Hodge went to his room and got his bucket and sponge and soap and came back and rubbed the stain out. And it took a good deal of rubbing, as well, for it was like a bloodstain that has soaked into the wood. Eventually, though, he succeeded, and the Table gleamed as it had before.

There were no more stains for several days. Then word came to the castle that raiders, much like the ones who had killed his father and burned their farm, had attacked a couple of villages near the borders of the Realm. Normally, patrols of knights — plus the threat of the Fellowship itself — proved sufficient to prevent such depredations. Now, though, with the Fellowship dispersed throughout the land and into other lands as well, the Realm seemed more vulnerable. Gradually, those who took note of such things were growing more daring, venturing into the Realm in ways they hadn't before the Quest had begun.

The day this news arrived, Hodge discovered two new stains on the Table. These were black and red, like smoke and blood. Hodge got his implements and went to work. Three hours later, his back aching and his arms as sore as if he had been wielding as greatsword in battle for all that time. the stains were gone. As Hodge sat back to contemplate his work, he suddenly remembered Arthur's words: "I know magic when I see it, and this Table is magic!"

It was then that Hodge suspected that the Table in some way reflected the state of the Realm itself. When a knight died, the Table would bleed, When people suffered or the land was harmed, their pain would show up as a stain on the Table.

Hodge wasn't sure this was so. It was only a suspicion. He wanted to talk to Marta about it, but he felt shy in doing so. She had the knowledge of the old ways, but the Table seemed somehow different, not part of the old ways alone, nor part of the new, Christian ways. It seemed to be a place where both streams of spirit could come together and blend, just as it was a place where the different knights of the Fellowship could meet and blend their strengths, where otherwise there very differences might put them at each other's throats. Likewise, just as he couldn't bring himself to tell Marta, so he couldn't tell his tutor, either. So, Hodge kept his suspicions to himself.

The issue was proven a few days later when Hodge, arriving in the morning to perform his morning ritual of cleaning, discovered in the place assigned to Sir Ywain, a new stain. He immediately set about cleaning it, and by noon, the stain was gone. It was afternoon, though, before news reached the castle that in fact Sir Ywain had perished in pursuit of the Grail.

*

So it was that Hodge discovered the magic of the Table, that it reflected what went on in the Realm. This discovery renewed his dedication to serve the Table, but it also sorrowed him. When a new stain would appear, to be followed by news of another death or another village raided or lands pillaged before Arthur and his men-at-arms could arrive at the scene, he sorrowed that he could not do something to help. Once again all his dreams of knighthood arose to assail him. He desperately wanted to be out in the land, preventing the terrible things that were happening, not simply cleaning up after them, mopping up the stains of events where once he had only cleaned the stains of gravy and wine. More than once, his tears mixed with the water and polish as he worked to fulfill Merlin and the King's command: "Clean the Table!"

*

Then, one day there was a change. It began when Hodge discovered a new red stain on the Table and realized, to his horror and sorrow, that it was in front of the seat of Sir Bors, his favourite of all the knights. That day, the water with which he cleaned the Table was more from his eyes than from the well, and after the stain was gone, he retired to room which Arthur had given to him high in one of the castle towers. There he poured out his grief and anger and refused to see anyone for the rest of the day.

A week later, still mourning the death of Sir Bors, Hodge was resting in his room when he heard a great and glad shout from outside the keep. Rushing to a window, he looked out and down and saw a familiar figure riding into the castle, his once bright armour covered in dust. It was Sir Bors! Unable to believe his eyes, Hodge rushed out of the room and down to the courtyard, but the knight had already gone in to see the King, and Hodge could not intrude. Nevertheless, his heart was bursting with gladness, though he was puzzled at how the Table had been wrong.

That night, Arthur hosted a banquet in the great hall of the Round Table and Hodge was delighted to discover that he was invited, an almost unheard-of honour for a squire. It was, he knew, because of his connection with the Grail, but he didn't care. He was thrilled with a chance to see Sir Bors again.

After the banquet, where, under Hodge's watchful eye, everyone was more careful than usual to eat with decorum and grace, Sir Bors began to relate a harrowing tale. It seems that the previous week, he had been ambushed by a party of rogue knights. He had given a good account of himself, but they had outnumbered him. Finally, unhorsed, his shield broken and his arm wounded, he had lain back against a tree, exhausted, his sword in his good hand, waiting for the final rush of the three knights who were left. He knew without any doubt that the hour of his death had come.

Then, he said, as if from nowhere, a whirlwind had come up,

blowing dust and dirt. It slammed into the three knights knocking them back. Then a tree had been uprooted and had fallen upon two of them, killing them. The third knight had turned to run, but had been buffeted by the swirling wind, disappearing into its midst. The wind then vanished as quickly as it had come, taking the hapless knight with it.

"Whether it was magic or divine grace, I know now," Sir Bors concluded, "but that wind saved my life as sure as if the Fellowship itself had rallied to my side. Without it, I would not be supping with you this evening and seeing again my family whom I love."

As Hodge listened to Sir Bors story, he was struck with a thought. Suppose the magic of the Table now could warn him when something evil was to befall the Realm and give him the means to prevent it?

This theory was tested even before Sir Bors left again a few days later. Discovering a large black and red stain on the Table one morning, Hodge had worked furiously to clean it. He had only just finished when a messenger arrived at the castle, his horse exhausted. Raiders were attacking a nearby village, striking closer to Camelot than ever they had dared before. Immediately Sir Bors and King Arthur gathered a troop of soldiers and rode swiftly out of the castle.

When they returned two days later, it was with another strange story of magical intervention. The raiders had been seen marching towards the village, which was when the messenger had been dispatched, but as they had lined up on a hill overlooking the village preparatory to charging down upon the defenceless people, there had been an earthquake. It was a strange earthquake, for none of the village had been damaged, but the ground had opened beneath the raiders, killing most of them. The villagers had then either killed or captured the survivors.

That night, Hodge visited the Round Table by himself. He knelt beside it and gave thanks for this new power to serve that had been granted him. And then, before going to bed, he examined the Table closely for any new stains that might have appeared.

*

This began a new routine for Hodge. As the months went by, he would visit the Table several times a day, carefully scrutinizing it for new stains. At first, there were few, if any. And when one appeared, he would clean it off immediately. And during this time there would come to Camelot stories of miraculous events wherein knights were saved or whole villages and regions protected. One man came and told of a plague of insects that descended, biting and stinging, like a cloud upon a group of raiders that had threatened his village. Another told of a flash flood that wiped out a band of renegade knights. Knights of the Fellowship who were wounded or ill would experience wondrous recoveries. A protective spell seemed to hover about the land, and through it all, Hodge continued to wield his bucket and sponge.

From time to time, the King would appear as Hodge was cleaning or inspecting the Table. He would speak kindly to him, enquiring about his work or his tutoring, sometimes speaking about his dreams for the Realm. Though no words were ever said about it, Arthur seemed to know that through Hodge's work, the spirit of the Round Table and the Fellowship continued to watch over and serve his Realm. It was a magic that Hodge never spoke about, for fear that in voicing it, the power would somehow leave. Between him and the King it was like a precious secret that both knew but pretended that they did not. Only once, on an evening when he looked particularly worn with the cares of state, Arthur started to say, "Hodge, if it was not for you ...," but then he stopped and turned away, as if he had thought better of what he had been about to say. Still, Hodge was comforted and continued his work with renewed vigour.

But there were certain stains that he could not remove. They started small but grew in spite of everything he could do. They puzzled him, for they did not seem to correspond to anything happening in the Realm itself. No knight seemed to die, nor any village pillaged because of them. Yet, focused as he was on his work, his wanderings in the wood, his tutoring, and his times with Marta, he paid little attention to the gossip around the palace, or to the fact that one day the Queen left and never came back.

As the Quest for the Grail took its toll on the Fellowship, however, and there were fewer knights to defend the kingdom, the stains appeared more and more. Hodge cleaned and cleaned, sometimes never leaving the Table from early morning to late at night.

In fact, he worked so hard, that he became ill and had to be put to bed for several days with a fever. When he finally recovered enough to return to his duties, he discovered to his dismay that the Table was more stained than ever, and that some stains had even deepened into cracks in the wood. He worked as hard as he could, harder even than before, but now there were stains that could not come out. And every day he heard new stories of how the Realm was suffering.

As the months passed, he seldom saw Arthur, who rarely showed himself outside his chambers. When he did, Hodge was astonished to see how the King had aged, how his red hair and beard were now streaked with grey and white, and how his face had become lined with care. Arthur remained unfailingly gentle and respectful to Hodge, but he hardly ever came to see the Table, as if the very sight of it caused him too much pain.

Hodge knew that the castle was filled with intrigue, that stories swirled about Lancelot and Guenivere, that a new person had arrived at court, Mordred, who claimed to be a bastard son of the King, but he paid little attention to any of that. All his energy, all his being was focused on one thing, cleaning the Table. He no longer saw his tutor, and he even gave up his work with Marta. He took to sleeping in the great hall itself and eating at the foot of the table.

*

There came a day, though, when Hodge looked up from where he had fallen asleep on the floor near the Table and saw to his horror that while he slept, a great blood-red stain had streaked across the whole width of the Table, and in its middle, a crack had appeared that threatened to sunder the Table in two. With a cry, he leapt upon this stain, rubbing it, throwing water on it, weeping over it. He rubbed till he felt his hands crack and knew his own blood was now pouring forth over the precious, magical wood. Yet he kept on, hoping that somehow his blood would not stain but would clean and restore the Table to health. At first it seemed that his hope would be fulfilled, for where his blood rubbed into the table, the crack seemed to heal and new luster appear. However, even as he rubbed, he saw the evil stain spreading and new cracks appearing.

Then a strong hand seized his arm and drew him up and back, holding him up when he would have collapsed with exhaustion. He struggled to get back to the Table, but the grip would not release him. Turning, he found himself staring into fierce hawk's eyes.

"Merlin!" he gasped, knowing instantly who had him by the arms. "Merlin, let me go! I must clean the Table!"

Merlin's voice was soft but firm. "No, Hodge, it is too late. It is over. Arthur is dead, slain by Mordred. Even now his troops march on Camelot."

A groan burst forth from Hodge. "Oh, no, say it isn't so!" But he knew, from the state of the Table, that it was so. He sank to the floor, his body wracked with sobs.

"I have failed you, Merlin!" Hodge exclaimed between sobs. "I have failed the Table!"

The old magician gently lifted Hodge up, led him to a chair and sat him down. "Hodge, listen to me. You did not fail. To the contrary, if it had not been for you, the Realm would have collapsed long ago. You kept the magic going, kept Camelot and the Fellowship alive long after they might otherwise have died. You bought us time, time for the dream to sink deep into the minds of people. Now this place may die, but the real Camelot will live forever in the spirit of humanity. And because this is so, other Camelots, other Fellowships, will live again in the future and perhaps succeed where ours has failed."

"But the Quest? The Round Table?" Hodge's mind spun in

confusion. It was like the end of the world, and he knew neither what to do nor what to say.

"The Quest will always go on, but for now, it is over, save for a chosen few who found that for which they sought."

"The Grail? It was found?"

"Aye, and lost again. But the Grail can never be truly lost, Hodge. It is always closer than we may think."

Merlin sighed, and the sound, like an old wind whispering through dying leaves, brought back a memory to Hodge. "You knew, Merlin, didn't you? You knew it would end like this? You said the Grail was like a flint that could set fire to wisdom or to folly. Those were your very words, magician."

"Yes, I said that. No, I did not know. I feared. But there was a chance, Hodge, that the grail of the Fellowship could prove strong enough to hold the Grail of Love. But men need their quests. They want to be heros, to be knights, to do bold deeds, to fight enemies and emerge victorious. Tis much harder, and less desirable, to stay where you are, to be a cup yourself that can hold what is poured out to you. Listen, Hodge, if water is poured into your waiting hand, you will surely spill it if you run about, but if you stand still, some of it may reach your lips."

Merlin shivered. "It is cold in here, Hodge. The fire has gone out. I must be going. I have a long sleep ahead of me and more dreams. Perhaps another time we will understand the mystery of the Grail and the water will reach our lips."

The old man got up, but this time it was Hodge who gripped him from where he sat. "You said some found it. Some succeeded in the quest."

Merlin nodded. "Galahad, the one I brought here the day the Grail appeared. It was his destiny. And another, Perceval. And one more." Here Merlin smiled and looked down at Hodge. "Sir Bors."

"Bors found the Grail ...?"

"Yes, and he shall tell the world the story so it will not be forgotten."

Hodge sat silently. Then he, too, smiled. "Then in this most evil of all days since the world began, there is something of the good. I am glad. It does not surprise me that Bors succeeded."

Merlin pulled himself free from Hodge's grip. "I must go." The old magician walked across the room toward the door, and as he did so, Hodge thought he became fainter, somehow, even transparent. Before Merlin reached the door, though, he turned around and fixed Hodge with his gaze. "Hodge."

"Yes, Merlin?"

"There is one more."

"One more?" Hodge thought of the Fellowship. Who might it be. Lancelot, the greatest of the knights? Ector? Tristan? "Who, Merlin? Who is it?"

Merlin was silent, then his eyes flashed with inner lightning. "Hodge," he said.

"Yes, Merlin?"

"CLEAN THE TABLE!"

Hodge obediently got up. He did not see the old magician fade away like smoke before the wind. He saw nothing but the table, now riddled with cracks and covered with stains. He went to his bucket and picked up his sponge and soap. He dipped the sponge in the water, and spread soap on the table. With no more thought, he did as Merlin had bade him. He began to clean the Table.

As he did so, the Table began to sink in the middle. At first Hodge thought it was collapsing, so grievous were its wounds. But its sides were rising up, and Hodge was forced to stop rubbing the top and began rubbing the sides and bottom. The Table continued to slowly change shape, and Hodge continued to scrub it.

Then the Table began to shine, faintly at first, then more brightly. Hodge was forced to step back, as he was assailed by waves of light and heat. Shielding his eyes, his mind blank and unwondering at what was happening, but with a joy building in his heart, Hodge saw the Table finally fold in on itself. But where there had been a Round Table, there was now a Grail. The Grail.

Hodge looked down. Somehow he was not surprised to see

himself clad in a shining white armour. His bucket had become a shield and his sponge had hardened and lengthened until it was a gleaming sword.

From somewhere he heard Arthur's voice, speaking as once it had to him. "There are many paths to knighthood, but they are all paths of service." Another voice joined him, and it was Merlin's. "There are many paths to the Grail, but not all of them leave home."

Hodge looked about the empty room. No one was present, but it seemed as if the whole Fellowship were there, welcoming him. From far off, he heard the drums and shouts of approaching troops. Some part of him knew that Mordred's men were entering Camelot. But that did not matter now. He was not hearing them. Instead, he was hearing a harp playing softly from somewhere in the room, and a voice saying, "Welcome home, true knight of the Round Table."

With a glad shout, Hodge leapt forward to where the Grail floated in the air before him. It seemed to reach out and enfold him. For a moment it was impossible to tell the two apart. Then Grail and knight vanished, and the room was empty and silent in a way it had not been since the Round Table had been created.

My Lady of Hy-Brasil

by Peter Tremayne

Above the plaintive cries of the circling gulls, above the harsh whisper of the sibilant sea, and the angry smack of its white-foamed lips on the tall granite rocks, I can hear the soft sweetness of her voice gently urging me to return to the island: urging me to return to Hy-Brasil. Though seven years is a long time to wait, wait it I must. I must return for she, too, is waiting for me; waiting somewhere out there in the cold, black Atlantic swell; waiting for me with a patience that eternity cannot destroy.

*

The whistle of the steamship *Naomh Eanna* shrilled as it edged near the black mound of the island. "That's Inisheer," smiled a sailor, brown of skin, blue of eyes, with sandy red hair blowing in the sea breeze. Inisheer, the smallest of the Aran Isles! The islands from where my grandfather migrated to New York and which had been such a magical place in my mind ever since I sat at his knee as a young boy and heard his tales about his own childhood there. I could scarcely believe that the cluster of dark humps ahead of the steamship were the islands; could not believe that I had finally made the pilgrimage which every Irish-American dreams of — a visit to his ancestral homeland.

The *Naomh Eanna,* named after the patron saint of the islands — so I was told, had dropped its anchor off Inisheer and a flotilla of small curious shaped boats called curraghs — lathed ribbed, canvas covered and tar-painted canoes, propelled by long, narrow bladed oars — came crowding out to the steamer. Passengers and cargo for Inisheer had to be ferried to the island for its waters were too shallow for the steamer to approach it closely.

An animal, a cow, was hoisted from the for'ard hold of the ship in a sling; hauled limp and helpless over the ship's side and into the sea where it started to struggle fiercely in the water. Three men waited nearby in a curragh. One of them grasped a rope around the head of the beast, and while the other two began to stroke at the water with their oars, the beast was pulled along, its legs threshing in a strange underwater dance, towards the shoreline.

Soon, all was offloaded for the few hundreds who inhabited the tiny island, and then it was on to Inishmaan, the middle island, before we finally steamed into Killeany Bay on the biggest of the Aran Isles — Inishmore. On steamer days, the friendly sailor told me, most of the island's thousand inhabitants turned out to greet the *Naomh Eanna* as she tied up at the pier at Kilronan, the chief town of the island. Ponies and traps and jaunting cars were in profusion and here and there, surprising me, were a few automobiles. Around me, as I came ashore, there rose the lilting sounds of Irish and hardly anywhere did I hear a word of English. I stood perplexed.

"Are you the American for Bungowla?" a soft voice enquired at my elbow.

I turned to face a middle-aged, rawboned man, sandy of hair like so many of the islanders.

"Yes," I replied.

"I am Peadar Flaherty. I have the trap here to take you to Bungowla."

Without a further word he picked up my suitcase and led the way through the milling crowd to a pony cart and motioned me to climb aboard.

"So Father Connell wrote to you then?" I asked, stating the obvious since Flaherty had come to meet me. I had met Father Connell in Boston during the previous year and he had offered to find me accommodation on the island should I finally make the decision to visit it on the long promised trip.

"He did so," replied the taciturn Flaherty.

"If it's any bother putting me up, I could stay in a hotel." I went on desperately trying to make conversation.

Flaherty glanced at me almost pityingly.

"That you cannot do. There are no hotels on Inishmore. You are welcome to stay with us — indeed, where else should you stay if not in the cottage in which your grandfather was born? And are you not kin and cousin to me? Sure, I would be a poor sort of fellow to turn a cousin from my door."

He paused and frowned slightly.

"But it will be a simple place, I'm thinking, compared with what you are used to in America. There is no electricity in Bungowla ... only candlelight or gas lamp."

"Oh, that's okay," I said. "I'm used to roughing it."

I could have bitten my tongue for my unconscious discourtesy but Flaherty did not take offence.

"What I meant was that I'm a fisherman," I plunged on hurriedly. "I work on the trawlers out of Yarmouth; that's in the state of Maine."

"Is that so?"

I fell silent as Flaherty nudged the pony along the roadway; fell silent as I began to relax under the spell of the island, absorbing the scenery and sounds. The sea was everywhere; you heard it, smelt it, even tasted it from the brine that nestled on your lips. We trotted along the coastline of quiet coves and sandy beaches which would suddenly rise into sheer rock faces, cliffs as high as 250 feet, against which giant waves exploded with violence. Inshore the island was a maze of tiny fields, enclosed from the elements by low stone walls. Great slabs of limestone rock lay everywhere. I saw a few cattle or sheep. Now and again we drove by tall stone monuments set beside the roadway which exhorted travellers to pray for the souls of men lost in the grey froth seas around the islands.

Bungowla was exactly as I had imagined it from my grandfather's stories; a small collection of white-washed stone crofts shrouded in a pungent smell of burning peat and salt sea breezes. The cottage to which Flaherty conducted me was no different to the rest except in my romantic imagination for was it not the place in which my grandfather had been born? Flaherty's wife came to greet me with three children of varying ages, each topped with her own gold-red hair, clutching at her skirt and peering shyly at me. Maire was a tall, gentle woman with solemn eyes and rosey cheeks who never seemed to stop working but always found the time to make another pot of tea.

For several days I basked in the hospitality of the Flahertys and was introduced to the warm friendship of the local islanders, especially to Phelim Conor Donn, an ancient man who was the village storyteller or *seanchaí* — as they called him. He could recall stories of my grandfather's childhood on Inishmore. As a fisherman myself, I felt at home among these people and could sympathize with the hardy folk who wrested their scanty living from a harsh, unfriendly sea. If there was a lesson of courage to be learnt, it could be learnt from folk such as these. They rose early, baked their own bread, cut their own hair, built their own houses, constructed their own boats, worked, drank, prayed and — finally — made their own coffins. They were a determined and stoic people, who lived close to nature; a people who saw the realities and meanings in the fierce, ever-changing elements; a people who had not yet lost their psychic reality as have city dwellers; a people who could still read the future in the brooding tempests, and in whom nature and supernature met as one entity.

One morning, which dawned dark and ugly with rain sheeting across the island, I went into the kitchen having determined the previous evening to pay a trip to the Eeragh Lighthouse that day. Maire Flaherty looked up from stirring the porridge in a great iron pot.

"The day is angry with itself," she greeted, nodding to the grey skies beyond the tiny window.

"I wanted to go to the Eeragh Lighthouse," I said. "Is it still possible?"

"Eeragh, is it?" she frowned, as she ladelled my breakfast into an earthware bowl. "That's a strange place to be wanting to see."

"Is it still possible to go today?" I asked again. "Will the weather be too bad?"

"Not for a trip to Eeragh," she said. "But my man will not be able to take you today. He is off down to Kilmurvy to buy Concannon's goat."

"No matter," I said, smiling. "If I could borrow Peadar's boat, I'll not trouble him to take me. I bought a chart of the waters around the island while I was in Galway City."

She pouted at me as if I were a fool.

"You mean that you'd go alone? That is a crazy notion. The waters round here are contrary when a fierce wind and sea are running."

"I'm not afraid." I could not help but sound patronizing. After all, I was a trawler skipper of one of the best ships that ever sailed out of Yarmouth.

Maire Flaherty shook her head.

"A man who is not afraid of the sea will soon be drowned," she reflected, "for he will be going out on a day he shouldn't. But we islanders do be afraid of the sea, and we do only be drowned now and again."

Peadar Flaherty came in for his breakfast and I put forward my argument. His first reaction was similar to his wife's but I was adamant. It took all my persuasive powers, however, to convince Peadar to allow me to take his curragh, which was fitted with an outboard motor.

It was after lunch that I started the Yamaha outboard motor and nursed the curragh seaward. It was a light craft and easy to handle. In spite of the grey threatening day, the sea's long level — dim with rain — was fairly flat and the spray was like a gentle caress against my cheeks. Eeragh Island, on which the lighthouse was situated, was, according to my chart, one of a cluster of deserted islets called the Brannocks off western Inishmore. My grandfather had told me that there had been a light kept on Eeragh since 1857 in order to warn shipping putting into Galway City of the dangers of the rocks. It had been his first job to "keep the light" and hence my interest in it. A new lighthouse, manned by three keepers, rose tall and white on the rocks with a great 375000 candlepower lamp shining for fifteen miles in any direction. The trip there was pleasant enough.

There was no jetty on Eeragh and the place was merely a moonscape of rocks. I ran the curragh close inshore and jumped into the surf to push it beyond the reach of the waves.

"Dia dhuit?" a voice greeted me in Irish.

A moon-faced keeper stood near the jetty watching me curiously.

"Hello there?" I replied, finishing my task.

The man's face registered surprise.

"Is it American, you are?" he asked.

I nodded. "I wanted to see the lighthouse."

He gazed from me to the curragh and back again.

"Have you come over from Inishmore alone?"

I explained but he shook his head.

"The waters here are moody waters," he said as if addressing some wayward child. "It is easy to fall foul of them." Then he shrugged. "Still, come up and see the place if you've a mind to but you should catch the tide within the half hour or you'll not be getting off Eeragh this night."

It was four o'clock when I left the keepers, who kept shaking their heads and warning me of the changing moods of the waters. They watched me push off in the curragh to a chorus of *"Beannacht De leat!"* which I understood was an expression of farewell and good wishes. I pushed the curragh out into the surf and rowed a short distance before I started the outboard and began to ride the choppy swell towards the black hump of Inishmore.

I had not been out into the sea for more than a few minutes when the heavens suddenly ripped open, showing blinding white sky, and thunder growled menacingly overhead. The waves began to climb to incredible heights as the wind whipped up and the tiny curragh was tossed this way and that — sometimes the propeller of the outboard motor echoed the thunder with its shrill scream as a wave tossed it clear out of the sea.

Through the lashing spray I saw nearby a dark headland and beyond that the gentle slope of a beach. I thanked God as I turned the boat and made towards it. I had been thinking that I was still some way from Inishmore but I must have been mistaken. Strangely, as I wrested to get the curragh close inshore, the skies seemed to clear, the rain ceased and the wind died away to a soft whisper. I ran the boat into the shallows and then hauled it up on the soft grey sand of the beach and stood peering around in surprise. As if by magic the bad weather had suddenly swept away and the sun was shining high overhead, shining down with an intensity of warmth which made me feel hot and uncomfortable as I pulled off my waterproofs.

I climbed out of the rocky cove in which I had landed and walked to the clifftop and looked around me. I discovered, to my astonishment, that I was not on Inishmore. I was on an island which was almost a complete round shape — some three or four miles in diameter, containing a soft, undulating countryside, yet greener and more lush than the other islands. However, each field was marked out by the tell-tale stone walls and the place was as treeless as the other islands. Yet I could not help thinking that the vivid greens of the fields made it seem more like a painting than a true reflection of nature.

Dominating the landscape was a great grey stone house, almost castle-like in its structure and standing several stories high. It looked bleak and out of place among the low whitewashed stone crofts, with their yellowing thatched roofs, which stood in isolated groups around the house. It gave an impression of some strange and unreal picture postcard.

I was aware of a thunder of horse's hooves bearing down on me and turned to see a rider coming towards me like a maniac on a large white stallion. As he drew near, he hauled at the reins causing the great beast to rear on its hindquarters and lash at the air with its gigantic hooves, snorting in anger.

The rider, to my astonishment, was dressed in the brown habit of a monk. The sight of him, so incongruous astride his steed, brought a broad smile to my lips.

"Fág an áit! Fág an áit!" he cried, in a terrible voice that made me quiver with a sudden fear of him. *"ó mo chroí amach ..."*

I halted his tirade of Irish by telling him that I neither understood nor spoke the language for I was an American, a visitor to the country.

He stared at me for a moment, his lips trying to form unfamiliar words but then it seemed as if his eyes looked beyond me, over my shoulder, and widened a little. With one shaking thin hand he made the sign of the cross, suddenly kicked his steed and raced away.

A peal of merry, silvery laughter caused me to turn round.

A woman, no; a young girl, was sitting on a rock smiling at me. Never in all my years had I seen anyone so pretty as she. Her white heart-shaped face was surrounded by a tumble of golden red hair which shimmered in the bright rays of the sun and were tossed this way and that in the breeze. Deep sea-green eyes twinkled with a hint of mischief while her soft red lips carried a merry smile.

"You must forgive Brother Mairtín, stranger. He is a little demented but means no harm."

The voice carried a husky, rich seductive warmth.

My breath caught in my throat as I approached her.

"Good afternoon," I said. "Can you tell me where I am? I was running my boat before the storm and only just managed to beach her here."

The girl frowned, gazing at the sky.

"The storm?"

I grinned sheepishly, realizing there was now hardly a cloud in the sky, so quickly had the bad weather abated.

"The weather changes quickly here," I conceded. "I was making my way to Inishmore when the weather overtook me."

"Ah, Inishmore is it? Then you are only a little way from your course. Inishmore lies two miles to the east," she pointed with a slim brown arm. "You are on the island of Hy-Brasil."

It was my turn to frown.

"You'll forgive me, but I did not realize there was a fourth large island in the Arans. Inisheer, Inishmaan and Inishmore I know of, but, what did you say the name of this island was? I do not know it."

She pouted in mock displeasure.

"Hy-Brasil is the most beautiful island of them all."

It was a fact that I readily conceded for all its unreal quality.

"Hy-Brasil," continued the girl, climbing from her perch on the rocks, "is the last resting place of the O'Flahertys of Iar-Connacht."

"The last resting place?" I queried, smiling at her archaic phraseology.

"When we were forced from our ancestral lands on the mainland, in Iar-Connacht, we fled to Hy-Brasil to safety; we fled to our fortress there," she nodded towards the distant house. "In our tongue we call it *Dún na Sciath* — the fort of shields, for it was both refuge and shield to us in the days of terror."

She made it sound as if it had been only yesterday and as if she had been a part of it.

"I gather your name is O'Flaherty?" I ventured.

She startled me by the way she suddenly drew herself up and by the momentary blame in her eyes.

"I am *The* O'Flaherty now that my father is dead, *go ndéana Diabhal grásta!*" She crossed herself, at least I thought she did for it occurred to me afterwards that the genuflection had been performed in reverse to how I was taught at church. The girl was watching me with a smile. "My name is Aideen O'Flaherty — I am called the Lady Aideen. Let me offer you the hospitality of my home."

It was a generous gesture, most grandly made and I accepted.

We walked along the dirt track which led through the fields towards the great house. Here and there men and women working in the fields rose to watch us pass by. They seemed stiff and rather odd, almost like waxworks than real people, staring with unblinking hollow eyes.

"Do you get many strangers here?" I asked at last. "The people stare at me as if I had just dropped from outer space."

"From where?" laughed the girl.

"As if I just flew down from the moon," I amplified.

The girl gave a gleeful peal of laughter.

"What a strange saying but take no notice of these people," her voice hardened slightly. "They are but peasants and their curiosity borders on ill manners."

Watching her face suddenly set in grim lines I had a passing thought — that I would hate to displease this girl and win her enmity for I sensed a hardness that was neither charitable nor forgiving.

The interior of the house was more impressive than its stately exterior. Long tapestries and oil portraits bedecked the walls. Among them scowled a gallery of O'Flahertys from bygone ages, frowning down on the accoutrements of war — swords, battle-axes, spears and shields. The furniture, too, was straight out of an antique store. In one large hall a fire crackled welcomingly in a fireplace that was almost the size of an apartment room. A meal was laid out on a big table before this fireplace and, curiously, two places were laid yet there was no sign of other guests nor, indeed, of the person who had set the places.

The time seemed to fly by; I chatted happily with the girl ranging on many subjects, mainly about the Irish, their language, literature and folklore, on which she was more than well informed. I found myself growing strangely attracted to her — as if I were basking in the pangs of first love. Even her quaint archaic speech, which I attributed to her first language being Irish, held an attractive quality to it. Time sped like a strange dream, a pleasant blissful dream and only the darkening of the sky made me rise regretfully.

"I must be getting back to Inishmore."

"Oh no; no, please ... you must stay."

I was aware that there was something slightly different about her manner; perhaps it was the way she carried herself, the way she smiled at me. Her prettiness had gone; now she seemed more voluptuous, even seductive. Her lips were more red, more full than before, pouting in a lascivious grossness. A red tongue flickered nervously over small white teeth.

"I cannot," I replied. "The family with whom I am staying on Inishmore will be anxious if I do not return tonight."

She blinked her eyes and, to my consternation, I perceived they held tears in them.

"Please stay. It is so lonely, so utterly lonely here on this island and I do so like talking with you."

Automatically, I reached forward a hand to take hers in a reassuring gesture.

"I'll come back" I assured her. "I'll come back to explore the island tomorrow, if that is convenient."

She blinked and a tear dropped onto the back of my hand like a scalding hot raindrop.

The girl sniffed and forced a smile.

"Yes," she said. "Yes, I know you will come back now."

There was a curious intonation in her voice.

As the door of the great house shut behind me, after my brief farewell, it was as if I had entered another world entirely.

The sky had darkened into blackness, the wind was howling and sending sheets of rain across the island. I could hardly see my hand in front of me. I put my head down and began to propel myself through the wind and rain towards the cove where I had left the curragh. By the time I had gone a hundred yards I was beginning to regret that I had declined the girl's invitation to stay. The house had been so warm, so comfortable, a refuge against the elements — wasn't that what the girl had said it was — a refuge? Yet something inside of me, some curious anxiety, made me push on. It was a cold, wild night. I did not fancy the journey back across the roaring seas to Inishmore but that feeling of anxiety, of disquiet, could not be denied and forced my footsteps forward.

There was a loud crack of thunder and a white blinding flash as the sky split asunder. The rain intensified, beating down like a myriad of tiny pellets against my skin. I became aware of a strange smell, the smell of brine and ... I suddenly heaved, for it was an awful smell of rotting fish, a bitter sweet stench of corruption that made me almost choke on my own bile.

My perplexity gave way to a growing unease as I found myself slipping across seaweed strewn rocks with little dank pools of which I had no recollection of crossing a few hours previously when the hot sun was burning down on the summer island. Nowhere in the gloom could I perceive a landscape remotely like that which I had seen that afternoon. Instead I felt the awesome presence of the sea all around me, as if I was struggling over low lying rocks which its waves threatened to engulf at any moment. Apart from the howling of the wind and the surging roar of the sea I could not even hear the lament of a sea bird nor the friendly croaking of a frog. Grey-black slimy wilderness, from which granite and limestone rocks thrust themselves aggressively into the air, surrounded me. And that awful fetid stench of corruption ever assailing my nostrils.

I had lost all sense of direction. I no longer knew where the curragh was beached.

Then I heard it — a plaintive cry, a sadness filling the air with a doleful wailing which caused even the howling wind and splatter of rain to fall silent. It was a sobbing, a human cry of despair rung from the depths of a soul in torment.

I turned towards the sound.

A figure hunched in the darkness.

"Is there something the matter?" I cried.

The figure started. It was vaguely familiar. Around it flapped a robe.

"Go from here," a voice suddenly hissed. "Go away from here, stranger. Can you not see that this is a doomed spot? Shun this haunted solitude, shun this place of evil! Or you, too, will be reduced to such as I."

It was the demented monk — what had the girl called him? — Brother Mairtín.

"It's alright," I said, pacifying. "Perhaps I can be of some help?"

"Stranger, leave here or you will not be able to help yourself. I came to this island thinking I could help, I came here thinking I was protected being a man of God ... I was but a man full of the corruption of man, misled by the superficial beauties of this place, by the superficial beauties of the girl ... the Lady of Hy-Brasil ... It was all an evil facade. Now I am forsaken by my God!"

I sighed. The poor man was utterly demented.

It was then I suddenly felt the sea washing at my ankles and looked down in bewilderment.

The monk saw my glance and gave a deep wail of despair which froze my very blood.

"It is too late! Oh God protect you! Too late! We shall return to the depths of corruption from whence we came!"

A blinding flash of lightning abruptly lit the scene before me. It was as if the entire island were disappearing beneath the waves. Only a small out-crop of rock, seaweed strewn, rose above the waves. A fear came upon me such as I had never known.

Then I heard a voice echoing clearly in that nightmare gloom.

"You must stay now ... must stay. It will make me so happy ... I have been alone here far too long."

I looked up fully expecting to see the young Lady Aideen in the light of the flashing storm. Instead I saw an old woman hobbling through the rain towards me, skeletonal arms outstretched, claw-like hands towards me, a leering smile on a skull face whose teeth seemed oddly protruding and sharp white. It was a caricature of a woman and yet — yet her voice was an echo of my Lady Aideen's ...

"Stay with me ... stay with me ..."

Seawater suddenly swirled around my legs causing me to stagger and almost loose my balance. I felt a thud in the back of my legs, turned and saw the curragh floating by. With a cry I turned and hauled myself aboard, falling a-tumble into the bottom, gasping from the exertion.

"Oh God protect you!" came the wail of the monk which was over shadowed by a feminine scream of rage that seemed to end in a gurgle and kiss of the harsh sea.

I raised myself to stare around.

I was in the midst of a dark tempestuous sea with the dark shape of Inishmore not far away. I crawled to the stern and lowered the outboard motor and, after a couple of attempts, succeeded in starting it. The little boat smacked and bobbed its way over the waves towards the shoreline and, wet and exhausted, I rounded the headland into the tiny cove where the fisherfolk of Bungowla beached their curraghs. A tall man was standing on the foreshore holding aloft a storm lantern.

"Man, man," cried the voice of Peadar Flaherty, "is it yourself, safe and well?"

I hardly had the strength to beach the boat and he bent forward to help me. When we had beached the curragh, Flaherty gripped me by the hand and stared with concern into my face.

"Where have you been? We thought you were drowned for sure, and was I not cursing myself for the fool I was to let you go out in the curragh alone? Why, we have sent for the Kilronan lifeboat already. Och, man, where have you been?"

I gently tried to reassure him and apologize for the worry I had caused. My own fears had evaporated and I was beginning to rationalize the last few minutes of my leaving the island as a product of panic-strewn imagination.

"When the storm came up," I said, "I put in at one of the islands."

Flaherty frowned.

"Islands? You managed to get ashore on the Brannocks? Sure, but that was a dangerous thing to do."

"No, no," I smiled. "It was one of the most pleasant islands I have ever seen. The people were ..."

"People?" Flaherty was puzzled. "People? Oh, do you mean you stayed with the keepers on Eeragh?"

"No, this was a pleasant little island which was very green and fertile and had a great house and a village on it. I met a woman, a lady, who said she was The O'Flaherty. You must know it."

"Dia linn!" Flaherty started back and crossed himself. "What are you saying man?"

Again I felt a growing unease.

"Oh, come now," I insisted. "You must surely know who I mean. Why ..." I remembered abruptly. "She told me the island was called Hy-Brasil."

"Dia idir sinn agus anachain!" cried the islander, his face white. "God between us and all evil!"

"What ... what is it?" I cried, fearful of the expression on his face.

He was silent for a while, trying to overcome the emotions in him.

"Do you still carry a chart of these waters?" he eventually said, his voice trembling a little.

I felt in my pocket and nodded.

"Look, then, look for the island of Hy-Brasil," his voice rose a tone.

In the yellow glow of his storm lantern I spread the chart and looked vainly for my island.

"Why ... it's not marked at all," I said, desperately trying to fight back my fears.

"It will not be. It does not exist."

"Nonsense!" I forced a laugh. "I landed there, I talked with ..."

"Wherever you landed," Flaherty's voice was intense, "it was not Hy-Brasil! There is no such island. Speak no more of it."

And with that he turned and strode off towards the village.

The next morning, following a strange dream in which I heard my Lady Aideen calling me, calling me back to the island, I went down to the kitchen for breakfast. I had already booked with Flaherty to go fishing with him off the Brannocks but Maire Flaherty apologized for his absence. *"Tá stodam air ... tá taghdanna ann ...* He is in a bad mood ... he is subject to moods," she said by way of explanation. It turned out that Phelim Conor Donn, the old village storyteller, was going fishing that day and offered me a place in his curragh. We pulled for the Brannocks. I suppose I already knew what I would find. However, I took my sightings from the lighthouse of Eeragh to make sure. Where my island had stood on the afternoon before there was a large expanse of grey foaming sea above which the gulls wheeled and cried fretfully.

Phelim Conor Donn pulled a face.

"Do you hear them cry?" he asked, jerking his tousled grey head skywards. "Sure, you'd be thinking they were cries of souls in torment."

I peered into the black depths of the waters.

"Phelim," I said abruptly, "have you ever heard of an island called Hy-Brasil?"

The old man stared and then slowly crossed himself.

"Now that's a story barely told outside of Inishmore," he observed curiously. "How would you be hearing it?"

"Oh, just something my grandfather said once," I lied. "Tell me the story."

The old man heaved a sigh.

"Well, it was said that Hy-Brasil was once the most beautiful island of the Aran Isles — more green, more lush than any other. And that once its mistress was the equal of its beauty — my lady Aideen, chieftain of the O'Flahertys of Iar-Connacht. You will have noticed that many bear the name Flaherty in these parts for these were the clan lands of Flaherty."

He paused as I nodded and then went on: "It was said that my lady Aideen was so beautiful that she could charm the birds from the trees by the sweet sound of her own voice. Even a wolf would stop its baying when she began to sing. But her beauty hid a black soul. Aye, she was self-willed and skilled in the black arts and able to conjure demons to her bidding. Many a young man lost their hearts and their very souls to her. There was the tale of Angus óg Dara of Clanricade who left his wife and children to follow her to her accursed island and who was never seen again. Then another, Brother Mairtín of Loch Dearg who thought she was but a woman and he was a man of God; but it turned out that she was more than a woman and he was but a man.

"It was said that she consorted with the devil so that she might have earthly power and, in return, promised him a rich harvest of souls of young men who were enticed to her island. God have mercy on all the poor souls who followed her siren call to Hy-Brasil," he crossed himself again.

"Well, the story goes that my lady Aideen's evil reputation grew to the extent where even the Pope in Rome and his cardinals sent their emissaries to do battle with her in the name of God and to try to set free those souls she had enslaved. She defied them. Aye, she worked an awesome spell for her own protection which forced the entire island to sink beneath the waves of the cold Atlantic."

The old man shivered slightly.

"But, it is said, the spell was such that the island rises ... rises up, lush and green, once in every seven years; rises up with its fiendish inhabitants to prey on the blood and souls of the living."

I shuddered violently at the intensity in his voice and stared into the choppy swell.

Phelim Conor Donn smiled.

"Aye, aye ... I know the legend well. But have no fear, *a mhic.* Only if a man lands on the island at the time of its rising and is marked by the lady Aideen, can she eventually call him back to the island to become her vassal in the service of the dead for all eternity."

My mouth gaped in horror.

"Only if he is marked by her?" I echoed. "What mark?"

The old man smiled.

"It is said that if one of her tears falls on the skin of a man, he must become her slave for all time."

I felt the stinging tear, scalding on my hand and stared down at the blood red blotch which now lay there. Her mark! I could hear her voice, soft and mocking: "I know you will come back *now!"*

My cry was taken up by the circling gulls above, who cried like souls in torment above the black waters.

And above the plaintive cries of the circling gulls, above the harsh whisper of the sibilant sea, and the angry smack of its white-foamed lips on the tall granite rocks, I can hear her soft sweet voice gently urging me to return to the island: urging me to return to Hy-Brasil. Though seven years is a long time to wait, wait it I must. I must return for she, too, is waiting for me; waiting somewhere out there in the cold black Atlantic swell; my lady of Hy-Brasil is waiting for me with a patience that eternity cannot destroy.

Finvarra

by Ann Moray

Since Finvarra, whose pale and brooding beauty rouses even the Fairy Hosts themselves to wonder, was chosen to reign over them, according to earthly reckoning, in the fifth century, he has acted in a manner unfitting to a King, either Fairy or mortal, only once: when the cold rapture of his desire fell upon Ethna, bride to his friend, the young Lord Kerovan.

It was three days to May Eve, the Feast of Beltane, and young Kerovan was stroking the neck of his chestnut mare. The stables were sweet-smelling, and the horses whinnied welcome to him, and were gentle. He smiled as he patted each, in turn, and knew that during the night they had been Fairy-ridden, swift as light across his rich green farmlands, and high over the gathered peaks on the far shores of Lough Corrib, to return, skimming the water like swans, cool and refreshed. "High over Cap! High over Cap! The Fulparnee, and the Folpornee, and the Roolya-boolya, and high over Cap!" He reminded himself to say the Fairy words as he took off for the jumps in the race that was set for this afternoon. He lifted the mare's left forefoot, saw the fine-wrought silver shoe and smiled again. He knew that his horses would win above the others on the Currough this day, and he whispered to his friend, Finvarra, *"Go raibh mille maith agat,"* a thousand thanks. "Roolya-boolya, high over Cap!" And with a last stroke of the mare's nose and a pat on her arched neck, I'll send Finvarra the wine of Spain, he thought, and he left the stable and crossed the walled garden, and coming to the tower of the Castle, he called:

"Coll!" And he called again, "Coll!" His Chief Steward came running. "At dusk leave three casks of wine for Finvarra."

Coll bowed. "In the Cave of Calliagh, as usual, my lord?"

Kerovan nodded. "Yes, near to the thorn tree," and he thought, "To mix with the melilot flower, and the dew, for the Feast of Beltane," and he turned towards the Castle, musing and happy.

Young Kerovan was loved by his people. He spoke not mere words of might, and he was generous, and to women he spoke with soft voice, and because he was descended from the eldest of the twelve sons of the Queen of D'yerree in Dowan, the Well at the World's End, and from Cyart of Connaught, who climbed to the top of the golden rope-ladder, he had been since childhood the friend of Finvarra. He never transgressed the Fairy laws, and those who dwelt in his lands prospered. Each year, when the fruit ripened, his farmers would leave apples and pears, plums and cherries, for Finvarra's people, and berries unplucked and juicy whole on the trees, and all the year round a jill of fresh milk in the pail that stood nearest the door of the dairy. In winter the good wife would leave some potheen in a tiny basin beside the night fire, and a white bowl of fresh water, for the Fairy People take kindly to fire warmth in winter, and pleasure in the cool, fresh waters of earth. No child in Kerovan's part of the country would dare cut a branch from the hawthorn tree, nor would any lad touch a sod of the Hill of Knockma, where Finvarra held Court with an iron spade, and the Fairy Hosts, who delight in courtesy, showered gifts on their mortal friends. The gifts of learning and wisdom, of song and laughter, of light-dancing feet, and merry fiddle fingers, and everyone who lived in the land was content, in all, alas! but one thing. The young lord would not take a wife.

All the maidens of Ireland and Scotland, and the daughters of the Lords of the Isles desired to marry Kerovan, and live in his Castle of night-black marble from Anghlihan, and snow-white limestone from the rolling plains. Kerovan was courteous and gallant, but they all returned to their homes unwed, and when he was twenty-five, and he called his people to the yearly feast, to assess their tribute and taxes, there were meetings and gatherings in every place, and the Chieftains spoke, and Mayors of the towns, and the Head-men of the Villages, and among the people it was firmly agreed that no tribute, no tithing, nor taxes at all would be paid till their lord took a wife.

When they came to the Castle, the Chieftains, the Mayors of the towns and the Head-men, some were too shy, and some were too bold, and when the latter spoke freely, Kerovan threw back his head and he laughed.

"No tithing? No taxes? Is it starving me my people would be?"

They bowed, one and all. "Or making of me forever a prisoner?" They bowed again. "'Tis a fine choice that you leave me, to be sure." He bent his head, a mock frown on his face, and put his hand to his chin. After a silence Curoi, Chieftain of the Stone Circles, and the boldest there, bowing, said:

"'Tis the lesser of two evils, my lord."

"By Saint Brendan and the birds! You are right! So I'll starve."

"No! No!" Even the shy ones jumped forward, their hands raised in horror. "My lord! Oh! No! No!"

"We'll say no more," said Curoi.

"And will you not? It seems that the words flow with ease." Kerovan laughed again, then he turned to Curoi, and all who were there. "I thank you," he said. "My duty is clear, and this night, e'er we feast together, envoys on fleet horses shall be dispatched throughout the length and breadth of Ireland." And now Kerovan bowed. "For you and your weal, I will choose the greater evil," he said.

As the months passed, and the messengers returned, one by one, to the Castle, Kerovan listened, and he talked with Aillen, his Bard, and his Men of Wisdom, but he chose no bride, and his people were losing hope, till, late on an evening in early spring, he was alone in his room in the tower, when Coll came with a young messenger who had that moment returned. Kerovan bade him approach.

"How long have you searched?" he asked.

"For seven months, my lord."

Kerovan sighed and sat down in his chair. The young man, bare-headed, stood there and his eyes were shining. Kerovan smiled, giving him leave to speak.

"Thrice-fifty maidens have I seen, and one of them, O my lord, is the most beautiful in all Ireland. As lovely as Etain, she is. I watched her playing at ball, and her side is long and white and smooth, all russet-gold and snow she is, and her eyes green-gold like the mountain gems, but deep and warm, and her smile is the slow summer sunrise through the mountain mists ..."

As he listened Kerovan's breath came thin and slow, and his heart beat in his throat.

"From the sun-drenched misty lands of *Sid* Rodruban she is, and a King's one child."

"A King's one child." For the first time in his life Kerovan's blood was a fire in his veins.

"She is your equal in lineage, my lord, and by Fann, she is without peer among mortal maidens."

"Her name?"

"Ethna, my lord," the young messenger said, and from that moment there was joy in the land, and when the April mists entwined the sharpest winds, caressing them, and the birds called grace from the budding boughs, Ethna came.

Nine days she travelled, with her friends and followers, to the Castle where she would be bride to Kerovan, and when they looked at each other, the stars sang the noonday, and the sun and the moon, for a timeless moment, veiled their light. The wedding feast lasted for three days and three nights, and in the Great Hall of the Silver Corner Stones, there was unmeasured delight, and the music of fiddles, and reel tunes on silvery Irish pipes, and the Sons of Song sang their Lays, and the harps they played on were of white bronze, and planed oak, inlaid with gold and silver and hill gems, and the songs the Bards sang to Ethna and her young lord are recalled to this day:

"She is the white flower of the blackberry,
Her mouth is like strawberries,
She's the best herb for beauty, for the sight of the eyes.
The nut of his heart she is,
Tender of palm, long-footed, smooth-sided,
Slow-smiling, and sweetest of kiss ..."

A year passed as a day. The Castle rang with laughter, and the joyous voices of the young nobles of Ireland and their wives and sisters and sweethearts, and the people rejoiced. Every day the company took to the chase across the green meadows under a sky bright with small clouds, through the branching woods and up the slopes of the hills. They hunted the sly fox, and the hare, and the air was filled with their merry shouting, their calls and the sound of their horns.

Every night there was feasting, and as Ethna walked with her lord down the black marble staircase, sometimes her golden-brown hair would be long and loose-flowing, round her shoulders and down her back, and held from her brow with a fillet of yellow flowers; and sometimes she wore it in braids interlaced with jewel blossoms of rubies and emeralds and diamonds and pearls. Her robes were of velvet, berry-crimson, purple and apple-green, and of many-hued silks, but she was loved for the warm radiance of her eyes, her grace, and the joy and happiness she brought to her lord.

As the ice thawed and the flood tides filled the shoals of the Lough, there was hurling and stone-casting, and chess-playing, and the music of harps lured the birds from the trees; the seeds were sown in the waiting earth, and the voice of the swan was heard on the waters at dusk; through the bright days and soft nights Ethna and Kerovan held converse together, reading and making poetry, laughing and talking, and as day followed joyous day, Kerovan fell more into wonder and worship that Ethna was his, and he rose at the dawn with a singing heart. His crops burgeoned, and his herds flourished, and the cows moved slowly for the weight of their udders, and when the cuckoo began her early song and the soughing winds heralded May and the Feast of Beltane came round again, it was rife in the land to make this the greatest May Feast ever known.

At dawn of May Eve all the women and maidens rose with the cock's crow and ran to the high ground to dance the sun's rising, then the virgins among them tied a bunch of twelve primroses to the tail of every cow in their herds. The wives and mothers put half-spent embers under their churns and wreathed their pails with boughs of the mountain ash, and the men gathered white-thorn branches and fastened them over their doors, so that for the whole year to come, Finvarra's people, so strong on this night, and mischievous, could not work their magic; and yet, as the long spring dusk darkened the fresh green world to argent and shadows lengthened, every living soul in the lands of Kerovan stood till the moon rose, and listened, as their parents and grandparents had listened, for the music that is not sad through the ages, the music from the Hill of Knockma.

And as the night fell, the hearth fires in every house were put out, and the Beltane Fires flamed, wind-fanned and crackling from the tops of the hills. The men and the youths, with their rowan torches ready, and the maidens, with flowers in their hair, held hands and danced around the May bushes, and Kerovan's land was filled, every township and Village, with circles of dancers, lusty and lissom, with faces flushed and loosened hair, and the Beltane Fires on the mountain and hilltops threw long, tattered shadows aslant in the valleys and lit up Lough Corrib to watery fire.

On the stroke of midnight the dancers broke circles, and the men and the youths with their rowan torches climbed up the mountains in the flame-ripped darkness, to draw their hearth fire from the Fire of Beltane and rush swiftly down while the torches still flamed, to their homes.

In the Castle, in the Hall of the Silver Corner Stones, a thousand candles glowed in the crystal chandeliers of D'yerree in Dowan, five of them, hanging from the high-domed ceiling, and from the carved golden sconces between the tapestries on the walls, and the young Lord Kerovan led Ethna, his bride of one year, to the wild, merry sound of the fiddlers and pipers, down the marble staircase to lead the May Dancing. Ethna, her cheeks flushed and her eyes bright as stars when the moon is not shining, clasping her husband's hand, whirled in the dance, fleeting-light of foot, her hair streaming, flower-decked, till it seemed that her feet, like quicksilver, did not touch the ground. And all who were there watched and marvelled, and smiled at the beauty and grace of their young lady-lord. Then, suddenly she stood still as a stone, her eyes wide, dull and empty, and fell as one dead, to the floor.

The fiddling and the harping stopped on the instant, and the pipers, with a reedy moan, ceased their tune. Kerovan lifted his bride in his arms and carried her up the staircase, whispering over and over her name:

"Ethna, Ethna ... my love, and my treasure ..."

She looked frail and childlike on the huge canopied bed.

"Ethna ... my pulse and my heart's desire ..." He stroked her cheek, pale now, and cold, and kissed her closed eyes, and wept at the feather touch of her long, dark lashes on his fear-stiff lips. She lay as one dead, her white limbs as though they were carved in pearl. He stood up and looked at her for a long moment, then he turned to Aillen and Coll, who were waiting outside with the Chief Physician.

The man of medicine came to the bedside. He looked long, without speaking, at the bride of his lord, then he said:

"I have neither the knowledge nor the power to heal her." But he knew. She is Fairy-*taken,* he thought, and did not dare to speak, for Finvarra was the friend of Kerovan, his lord.

They sat down, one at each side of Ethna's bed, to watch over her. The Beltane Fires burned low, and died, and the hills were dark against the pale-rising moon, and from Finvarra's *sid,* inside the Hill of Knockma, the Fairy music came clear and faultless across the land.

The Physician fell asleep, but Kerovan did not move nor close his eyes, and when the first rays of the morning sun touched her pillow, Ethna wakened and looked around her. Kerovan stood up and took her hands, and anguish filled his heart, for her eyes were empty of knowing, and held no love for him.

"Alas ... Alas ..." she moaned, and her voice was cold, and seemed to come from a far place. "Alas ... that I am here. That I am not where I have been." And she looked about her as at a strange landscape, and did not see her love, her husband, nor feel the clasp of his hands. "Let me sleep. Let me sleep again. I would sleep," she was moaning and murmuring, "for in my dream is a man tall and slender. His hair is black as the raven's wing."

The Physician, awake now, knew that his thoughts were true.

"She must not be alone for a single moment," he said. "This I know." And he bowed his head in shame that he was helpless.

For seven days and seven nights Kerovan did not leave the bedside of his bride, but on the morning of the eighth day he was called to neglected duties, and trusting Ethna to her old and faithful nurse, he rode to the Rock of Doon, whence he had been called.

The old woman, crooning, sat close to her charge, coaxing and chiding, as she had when Ethna was a child, till as the hours passed, weary with the weight of her years, she fell asleep. When she wakened, Ethna had gone. The great bed was empty.

The Castle was wakened to frightened bustling life, and when Kerovan returned, search was made in every hall and chamber throughout the House, in the high-walled gardens, and the woods and parks around. Messengers rode away to the North and the South, and to the East and the West, but no one had seen the lovely Ethna, nor heard tell of her, and they returned, without solace to their master. Kerovan stayed alone in the high chamber he had shared with his love, and he took neither food nor drink till, on a day in late autumn, when keen winds stripped the last shrivelled leaves from the branches and the stags in the bare woods belled, searching for food, Aillen, his Bard, knocked on the door and asked leave to speak with him.

"My lord, our horses are saddled," he said. "Let us ride."

Kerovan rose from his chair, and without a word he went with his Bard. Without gentling his mare, he mounted, and away they rode, day and night, to Cahermorris, and Cahergal, and to Saint Brendan's monastery, to Incha Mor, where the great salmon leap, and to every village and hamlet that nestled on the shores of Lough Corrib, and everywhere they went in the land, they could see the Hill of Knockma, and at last Aillen said:

"Let us go to Knockma, my lord, for of a truth, I fear only Finvarra can help you now."

Kerovan looked at his Bard and nodded.

"He is your friend, master," said Aillen, "and he is your debtor."

"There is nothing of debt between us, Aillen, but most surely he is my friend." Kerovan turned in his saddle, a gleam of hope in his eyes. "And a powerful one. Yes! We will ride to the *sid* of Finvarra." And they put their horses heads towards the Hill of Knockma, and rode with all haste to speak with the King of the Fairy Hosts, and to ask his advice.

Kerovan, a visitor since childhood, left his mare with Aillen and climbed the slope near the Cave of Calliagh, past the thorn tree and up till he found the three circles of clearer green in the wet grass. He stood inside them, and called with strong, urgent voice. The door opened forthwith, and for a moment the whole of the wind-swept countryside was bathed in a jewel-bright light. Kerovan entered, and the door closed behind him.

"You are expected." A Fairy youth, one of Finvarra's seventeen sons, tall and solemn, bowed to him. "Follow me." He led the way along a passage lit by golden apples that hung along the ceiling on silver chains and reflected the light from a million gems that studded the walls. The passage widened as they went along. Kerovan thought of the times he had been here, and love for his Fairy friend filled his heart. "My father watches the Hosts in mock combat," the youth said as they came to a wide Fair Plain. Kerovan stood still for a moment, as he had always done, enchanted. Mountains, snow-capped and glowing with silvery light, were there, and crystal streams flowed down their sides to blue hollows in the valleys, lustrous with silver spray. He looked at the assembled Hosts. He recognized the Men of the Hill of Nephin, in green. They waited, their slim golden lances poised, to the left of Finvarra. They rode horses of dark midnight blue, with flowing green manes and tails, and their bridles were of emeralds, strong-threaded with silver wire, and in their helmets was a night-blue plume.

On the right of their High King his own company stood ready. They rode horses as white as the snow on the mountains, and their manes and tails were crimson-red. Their plumes were silver-white, and the fine-stitched ornament on their crimson cloaks was of silver and crystal stones, and the trappings of their horses were of silver filigree set with rubies.

Finvarra's horse, jet-black and shining like the back of a beetle, swifter than the wind from the North, and silver-hooved, was known through the length and breadth of Ireland. Kerovan looked at his master, astride him, and marvelled again at the beauty of his friend. Finvarra wore silver armour, clinging as the scales of a young salmon to his slender body. His face was broad above and narrow below, and his skin was white as the foam on the wave. He turned to face his visitor, and his eyes glistened, grey as the rain-washed crags when the moon is bright.

"You will see again the prowess of my Fairy Knights?" he asked. "Indeed, Kerovan, you are welcome."

But Kerovan was impatient to tell his sorrow, and begged his friend to help in the search for his lost bride.

"Messengers shall go forth from every *sid* in Ireland. Have no fear," Finvarra said, but he turned his face away from his friend as he spoke and towards the jousting companies. "If Ethna, your bride, treads upon the soil of Ireland, she shall be returned to you," Finvarra promised him, and Kerovan was comforted.

When the door in the Hill closed behind him, the young lord stood in the dark of the evening and breathed the air of earth. However beautiful the Fairy Realm, he thought, the feel of the damp turf under my feet and the sight of the first star above me, the love-longing in my heart, though it is pain, they hold a deeper beauty, and he walked towards the place where Aillen waited with the horses.

His mare was restive, and whinnied, afraid. Stroking her neck and murmuring to her, he prepared to mount, but suddenly, in the wind, yet close, they heard laughter, silver-sweet. Kerovan looked at his Bard, and they waited, holding the animals' heads.

> "Lapwings' eggs are yellow,
> And Finvarra is joyous ..."

A voice limpid-cool as the water in rock springs seemed to come from the thorn tree.

"Finvarra is joyful
Beneath the purple trees
And the chaffinch calls the rain.
Finvarra knows the kiss, honey-spice,
Of Ethna of the slow smile
And the water pippet is in full song."

They heard the words in their hearts while the frenzied whinnying of their horses filled their ears.

"Finvarra's dalliance is sweet
Beneath the purple trees
And the wren is the king of birds."

The young husband stood quietly, curbing his rising rage, to hear more.

"Dig deep! Dig deep!"

The voice held authority. The leaves of the thorn tree trembled.

"Dig deep!
In the heart of the Hill of Knockma.
Kerovan will find his bride."

In the stillness that fell about the place, the young lord spoke.

"May a mortal prevail against the powers of Finvarra?"

Suddenly, on the thorn tree's branches were a thousand birds, emerald and yellow, blue and green, and crested birds, and the evening air was filled with their full-throated song. The horses reared and shied aside. Then quiet fell once more. Not a leaf stirred. The thorn tree was dark, birdless and still against the grey hillside, and in the strange silence the pale moon rose.

"Finvarra and all his Fairy might shall not keep me from my heart's love." Kerovan's ringing voice, broke the stillness, and the wind's roared answer through the valleys and raged around the hills, and Kerovan and his Bard mounted their horses, and side by side rode with all speed to the Castle.

The young lord did not wait for the dawn, but sent every messenger in his household to the people who lived on his lands, to all who were guests in his Castle, and to all who lived in Caterhamen and on the far shores of the Lough, and called them to meet him and to bring iron spades, three days hence, at dawn, at the Hill of Knockma.

Not all of his countrymen would attack the *sid* of Finvarra. They, and their fathers before them, had been friends to the Fairy People, and they knew their laws, and their powers. They were afraid of being Fairy-struck, so that they withered away, or were blinded by the dust that is whirled in the Fairy blast. Kerovan well understood their reluctance, and gave them honourable leave to go home. But many more were stout of heart, and many had come to Galway with the daughter of their King, and they loved her and were loyal, and they set out, a whole army of them in the drizzling morning rain, farmers and fishermen, woodmen and carpenters, herdsmen and smiths, Chieftains and their sons, and Curoi of the Stone Circles brought his household regiment, who laughed to be carrying spades and not swords. Along beside the rushing bog-stream they went, past the ancient ring forts and the Pillar Stone, and the tunes of Kerovan's pipers filled the damp air with skirling sound as they came to the Hill of Knockma, looming high and desolate in the grey misty dawn.

All day long they dug, until there was a deep cave-trench down inside the Hill, but when the sun lowered, blood-red and clean-edged in the heavy sky, even the bravest of them ceased to dig, and not one gathered there would stay at the Hill of Finvarra after night fell. The young lord pleaded, his pipers played the music of valour, that stirs the blood, and the dusk was full of rousing sound, to no avail. Asking pardon of their lord, the people left the place, even Curoi and his soldiers, promising to return at sunrise.

For the first time since he had lost his bride, Kerovan, exhausted with digging and happy at the thought of the deep trench in the Hill of Knockma, slept for seven hours. But when they came to the Hill at dawn, his happiness turned to anguished rage. It was green and smooth, as though never a single spade had touched it.

"Finvarra is strong." The young lord looked up along the smooth green slope.

"He has power over earth, and air, and water," Aillen said, and the people nodded their heads and sighed.

Beside himself with grief, Kerovan went apart from them and threw himself on the ground. He buried his face in the dew-wet grass and wept with longing. After a while he sat up, and saw that he was near the thorn tree.

"You've made rare sport of me, whoever you are," he said, and every bough of the tree on the instant was loud with bird song.

"The wood peewee sings at dusk,
The work will prosper."

The voice was a cool thread of sound through the trilling.

"Sprinkle with salt.
With white salt sprinkle,
The earth that's upturned."

"Salt!" shouted Kerovan, "Salt!" And he bowed to the thorn and leapt in the air and ran down the slope. "Salt on the upturned earth! Salt on the upturned earth!" He was almost weeping again with joy and hope, and calling his people around him, he sent half of them with Aillen and Curoi to gather salt from all who could spare it, and he stayed with the others, to dig with renewed strength and a joyful heart. The pipers gathered their wind and played valiant tunes, and wielded by strong, willing hands, the spades dug deep and huge sods were flung up to the right and the left, and soon there was another trench, deeper than the first, far down towards the centre of the Hill of Knockma. Before night-fall, by seconds, Aillen returned with five carts of salt, and when it was all sprinkled, the upturned ridges of earth looked winter-white, as though the first snow had fallen.

On the morrow everyone rose before dawn, eager and full of excitement, and hurried to the *sid* of Finvarra. With unbounded joy they found the trench as deep as they'd left it at sunset. Strong now were their arms to dig deeper and deeper, and they sang as they worked, and the pipers played to echo around the shores of Lough Corrib. The spades gleamed in the light of the rising sun, and the sods flew higher and higher, and Kerovan knew he had won, and had power over Finvarra.

By midday they had come almost to the centre of the Hill. The Fairy music was all around them, and all who were there ceased their digging to listen. Into their veins it seeped, clear, cool and piercing-sweet.

"Listen to your pipers, men of Galway, and be not beguiled," Kerovan called to them with gusty energy, and they returned to their task. But suddenly, loud and clear, through the valleys and up and down the mountainsides, and echoing from the waters, and inside their ears, was a silver horn-sound. Then another long call, then another. Then, in a silence deeper than earthly silence, Finvarra spoke.

"Kerovan, my mortal friend, bid your stout men of Galway lay down their spades." All who were there stood spellbound.

"Ethna shall be returned to you. Wait alone at dusk, at the door in the Hill. I have spoken."

"How, Finvarra, shall I trust you again?" Kerovan stood tall, and called to the heart of the Hill. "How shall I know I am not twice deceived?"

The Fairy music was clear, and many voices answered:

> "At sunset Ethna will come.
> At sunset she will return ..."

And the sound was plaintive and matchless.

Filled with awe, but happy and tired, the people went to their homes, and that night they left out a little more wine for the Fairy People, and put flower petals in the bowls of fresh water they left by their doors.

Kerovan waited alone on the hillside, and at sunset he went

to the Place of the Circles, and in the moment between the light of day and night's darkness the door swung open. Ethna stood there, silent. Her eyes were closed. He took her in his arms and carried her to his horse. He kissed her eyelids, and took her up before him in the saddle.

When he lay her on their bed, though she was still and cold, a pulse beat in her throat.

"My treasure, my love ...," he murmured, and prayed as he watched by her side, but she did not move nor open her eyes, and there was no smile on her lips. She lay as one dead, and again there was sorrow in Kerovan's Castle, and throughout his lands.

And as they sowed the seed in the rains of spring, the farmers whispered:

"She has eaten of the Fairy food."

"She can never be free of the spell," the women said among themselves as they churned and they weaved. It seemed there was truth in their words, for after a year and a day had passed, Ethna had not moved nor given any sign of life, though her cheeks were red as the rowanberry and her heart beat in natural rhythm.

Kerovan was beside himself, and knew not where to turn for help, then, on the Eve of Beltane, he thought of the thorn tree, and the voice that came from its branches.

Angry that the thought was tardy, he called for his mare and rode in the twilight to the Hill of Knockma. He rode up the slope by the Cave of Calliagh and reined in his mare. He sat in the saddle, quietly soothing her and waiting. She was not restive. A nightingale sang early song from the thorn tree. Kerovan listened.

"Burn it with fire.
Golden, bejeweled.
Clasped by magic,
About her slim hips,
Loose the girdle.
Burn it with fire.
Burn it with fire."

The voice was clear as stream water in springtime, and the thorn leaves shivered, but Kerovan's mare did not whinny nor shy away. The young lord dismounted. He bowed to the tree, then in the light of the Beltane Fires, through townships and villages where no one was dancing, he returned with all speed to his Castle.

Ethna lay still and lifeless, and her young husband saw the finely wrought, gem-studded girdle she wore. Why have I not seen it before? he thought. I have been blind with grief. And he took his gold-hafted dagger and slit the fine mesh, and it fell away from her hips. Then he called for her nurse to watch over her, and with Aillen, and the Chief Physician and Coll. He took the girdle, put it into an iron cauldron, and in the Western corner of the walled garden, while they watched, he burned it and strewed the ashes of it under an aspen tree.

On the instant there was a great clamour, and when they returned to the Castle, friends and courtiers and loyal servants greeted their young lord, rejoicing, for Ethna had moved. Within a few minutes Aillen and Coll had found the musicians, the candles were all ablaze and messengers sent out through the land with the joyful news. Kerovan leapt three steps at a time up the stairs to their chamber.

"Ethna! Ethna, my heart's love ..."

She sat up and looked round her.

"My love ... Kerovan. .. why am I here? I'm not sick." She kissed him gently, and pulled his thick brown hair with her fingers. "Come, let us return to the May Dancing. How could I have fainted so? I am well. Let us dance ... O Kerovan, listen to the pipers ... and the fiddlers, the harps ..."

"Yes! Yes! Let us dance! Let the May Dancing circle the land." The great hall rang with music, and all who had followed their young lord into the chamber laughed with relief and were joyous. "Beltane is a feast again. Come, let us dance. Let us dance." With laughter and merry noise they went out of the room again, and down the wide staircase.

"Come, my love," Kerovan held out his arms, but suddenly, Ethna was still. She put her hand to her brow.

"It is strange," she whispered. "I had a dream."

And Finvarra, standing unseen, tall and pale by her bed, looked down at her.

"Forget your dream." He put his hand on her breast, and spoke to her heart. "Forget desire and delight in the Land that is beyond the stars, yet cool and fair in the space between each blood-beat." His eyes were stern and held an icy fire, "May you be the silver-white swan in full flight against storm clouds, and a fair silver stream in the darkling forest."

Ethna put her hand where Finvarra's had been.

"Ethna, my love," Kerovan's voice was deep and warm.

She smiled her slow smile, then she laughed and held out her arms to her husband. "Come, my lord! Why do you wait? Let us join the May Dancing."

PART III

The Opening Door

The Cold Well

by Margaret Elphinstone

She sat under the waterfall, letting the burn wash over her. The falls were white and full, churning the pool into a froth of air bubbles and brown water. Little waves lapped against the rocks, which were scoured into a smooth curve at the pool's edge, following the circling water. The water itself was soft with peat, bitter with acid, flowing over her with a touch like a northern breeze on a spring day, even while her shoulders ached under the weight of it.

It was snowing. The flakes were huge and wet, falling silently into the pool and melting instantly. The air was damp; she could smell it even over the spray from the falls. There was a gap between the black trees where she could look right over the valley. The landscape beyond the pool seemed curiously inverted. The sky was dark grey, heavy with the weight of unshed snow. The earth beneath was white in the daylight that seeped in under the clouds. Each tree was highlighted by blown snow which clung to its northern side like a shadow. Black trees, white shadows. Dark sky, bright earth. She chuckled, swallowed icy water, and choked.

The snow thickened. She could hear the wind rising behind it. The trees swayed and bent. The valley was blotted out: nothing to see but whirling whiteness. It was bright and dark all at once, like the pool and the waterfall, and herself. She laughed out loud, and stood up.

As soon as she came out of the water, the snow settled on her, and melted as fast as it came. She stuck her tongue out and tasted snow. She could feel the tang of it on her body, and stood still by the pool. When she moved she left two bare footprints on the rock. The snow pounced at once, obliterating them within seconds.

She climbed up the rock, careless of the fact that there was no trace of any foothold under the blanketing snow. She knew them all by heart anyway, and when she reached the top she followed the path between the rowans without hesitation, although there was no trace of it. Once she left the shelter of the pool the wind caught her, so that she was swept into an invisible world of wind and snow. She blinked snow out of her eyes, though even then she couldn't see more than a yard ahead. It didn't bother her. She twirled herself around on the path, naked under the north wind, letting the snow catch her all over, and melt in a stream of water drops that trickled over her skin. Her feet stung a little as they sank into the snow. She couldn't even feel the ground. She laughed again, and twirled faster, winding her way among the trees in an invisible dance. She couldn't see the trees but she could hear them groaning under the wind loaded with snow. She caught the last one by the trunk and spun round.

The path brought her into deeper snow. She could make out the outline of a mound of earth, a small hillock overlooking the burn, its contours as familiar to her as her own body. It looked alien now, a thin line of white beyond the flying snow. She circled it until she reached the entrance: a black rectangle of dark leading into the heart of the hill.

She was about to enter the tunnel when a different sound was blown down to her, neither wind nor water. It might have been a human voice crying across the mountains, but she knew better. She stopped at once, frowning a little, then raised her cupped hands to her mouth, and called back.

She was answered at once by a cry as high and wild as her own, wordless and inhuman. If other creatures were out on the hill in this blizzard they might think that it was the crying of birds, or some animal driven out of shelter, or, if over-imaginative, might think of ghosts. She didn't spare them a thought. If anyone were out on an evening like this they would be the more likely to die.

A shadow rose out of the storm just in front of her and

became substantial, a dark shape that loomed over her, bowed by the blizzard at its back. Snow swept between them, blinding her, but she could see as well as she needed to. She nodded as though satisfied, and turned back into the tunnel.

*

It was pitch dark inside. It didn't matter, because she knew exactly where everything was. It was calm, every small sound suddenly loud and precise after the undifferentiated roaring of the weather and water. There were faint sounds of movement, the scraping of wood on wood, and the clink of metal on stone. There were other sounds too, that of another body entering: the heavy tentative steps of one less familiar with the way; and quick breathing, as if the newcomer had been running hard.

A small flash, white and sudden, then a glow of orange, the crackle of flame on tinder, and a fitful light which grew and settled, until a soft glow filled the whole place.

The chamber under the mound was round and low, the walls built of corbelled stone, rising to a narrow roof of slabs with a black space between where the smoke escaped into the snow, and stray flakes drifted downwards to melt and vanish as they approached the fire. The room was already filled with peat reek, so that only near the floor was there any clarity. Kneeling by the fire she could see quite well but if she looked upward there was nothing substantial, only vague shapes through the smoke which appeared to move, though perhaps it was only the smoke and the falling snowflakes which changed and the rest was illusory. It didn't bother her: it was her own place and she knew what it contained. Down by the floor the room was bare, furnished only with a bedplace and a chest, with a spinning-wheel between close by the fire. There was a rough stone shelf holding rows of pots against the wall, and a few tools propped nearby. The floor was of trodden earth strewn with dried bracken away from the fire. As a dwelling it seemed poor at first sight, but curiously it never seemed to become plain by adjustment to the dimness and the smoke. On the contrary there was a hint of richness in the shadows, a glint of brighter colour, the suggestion of brilliance which could never quite be brought into focus. Gradually, as the fire grew in strength, the illusion of comfort became stronger, if illusion it were. But the woman by the fire was not attending to such everyday matters. She appeared to be concentrating entirely upon nursing the small flames into a blaze. If she were aware of her visitor she gave no sign of it, and the figure by the door waited with apparent patience.

At last she was satisfied with her fire, and looked up.

"I thought you might come down with the weather," she said. "I saw the deer had gone into the forest."

"None too soon," was all the answer she got, but the stranger came forward with the words, and crouched down on the opposite side of the fire.

If there had been any spy concealed in the shadows under the mound they might easily have given themselves away at this point. The stranger seemed to be a man, certainly, but not entirely so. He was man enough to be terrifying, in human terms, more so by his human-ness than by the lack of it. If he had been a ghostly, alien thing, it would be no more than anyone should expect if they dared to make their way into a hidden mound under the earth. But this was no ghost: on the contrary, he made every human thing seem a shadow by contrast, for he seemed all substance, a stronger presence than most human things expect to bear. He was big and dark, his face half hidden by the tangled hair that fell over it. There was snow caught in his hair, turning to bright drops which gleamed like diamonds in the firelight. There was driven snow across his shoulders, like the snow shadows beaten by the wind against the trees, which was also melting in small rivulets that streamed down his chest and back so that his skin shone fitfully in the firelight. He did not seem to be clothed; it was hard to take in details precisely. He was more animal than a man should be, and the eye does not readily absorb what the mind has learned to be impossible. But the antlers were clear enough, accentuated as they were by the shadow they cast on the curved wall behind him. As the fire flared they seemed to grow and vanish into the smoke like bare branches into twilight. The man leaned forward and laid another log upon the fire. Flames spurted up, green with the new wood, turning to red and orange. He looked up at the woman sitting opposite, and the gleam of light was reflected in his eyes, yellow and black, like a cat's.

"So you'll stay down till the storm passes?" The question was almost a statement, as if she didn't expect an answer.

He shrugged.

"Well, if you do that, remember what I said before. People come to the well even in winter. I don't want my folk frightened out of their wits. You'll have to lie low."

"Have I ever frightened them?" He sounded indignant. "Not once in a hundred years!"

"And that's not so long ago either. You can do what you like on the mountaintops, but this is my country."

"You don't need to remind me. Anyway," he sighed, "it makes no difference. They see what they expect to see, which means no one will see me. I don't know why you worry about it. There are some who'd give their left hand to be believed in. Does it make the people safe not to be frightened?"

"I'm not going to talk about that now. Do you want supper? I worry because I have to do with people, which is more than you do. Perhaps I see them too much. Sometimes I think the true part of myself is falling away, and I'm becoming only what the people make me. It's very dispiriting."

He laughed aloud. "Not you! Look at you now. You think I know nothing about it, but I see them in the mountains sometimes, even here. They don't look at all like you. They wear clothes for a start, usually a vast amount of clothing in ugly colours. Their hair is very dry, and so are their feet, and their minds are driest of all. You have nothing to worry about."

She shook her head, smiling. "No, no, that's just what you see. It's true they lack the influence of water, and so of course are impoverished. But underneath they're just like you or me, I assure you. Only they don't undress on mountaintops, that's all. If they did, you'd see the similarities."

"I knew all that several thousand years ago. They wore much

less then, if you remember. I'm speaking of essence, not substance."

"Well, if you could apply your mind to substance for one moment: I asked if you wanted any supper?"

"Essentially, yes."

She stood up. "Very well, but it was you that mentioned clothes, not I. I know what I look like, but I don't necessarily know what I'm becoming. I have my people and I can't afford to despise them. They are all the mirror we have, you know that."

He scowled. "Speak for yourself. Isn't the well mirror enough, and don't the deer know more of me than any man?"

"Water doesn't speak, and neither do the deer. We are what they say we are, and nothing in this world can change that. If you're not satisfied you can always seek another."

"I'm not even so sure of that now."

She had turned to the stone shelf to lift down a pot but she looked back at him, startled. "Not sure of what? There are more worlds open to us than anyone has dreamed of yet. If you cease to believe that, how can you live at all?"

He shook his head, his face hidden.

She put the pot down, then came and stood over him so that water dripped from her hair on to the top of his head. "There's something more, isn't there?" There was no trace of compassion in her voice but he had all her attention. "You didn't come down just because of the snow. You brought despair with you. I can feel it. You have no right to bring such a thing into my house."

He was silent at her feet, not looking up.

"There is no room for despair in this place. If you cannot twine yourself from it, you must go."

"Aren't you the guardian of the well?" he cried out. "Will you no longer give help to your own kind? Or do you keep all you have for those who destroy us?" He glared up at her and involuntarily she stepped back. "I never thought you would turn traitor, not in all the years upon this mountain. I would never have believed such a thing as that!"

She left him and went to open the chest. "Believe what you like. I'm not here to defend myself." She picked out a rough plaid of loosely woven wool, and wrapped it round herself. "If you came for help you should have gone to the well."

"I came to see you." He sounded sulky.

"To bring your trouble into my house?"

"To bring myself. You didn't always object to my company."

"I am always glad of your company, when you offer it. But your trouble is another thing, and I want none of it."

He stared at her with wide eyes. "So you refuse to help your own? If that is so, there really is no future in this world."

She sighed impatiently. "Understand me! I help any who come to the well, as far as I can, because I am the guardian. Any human, beast or spirit. But you did not come to the well."

He seemed puzzled. "No, I came to you. Because I know you."

"And I will have none of you, so you had better go."

He stood up slowly. "Very well. If that is all, and I'm no more to you than any passing stranger of any kind, I will go and take my trouble with me. Clearly it means nothing to you now."

"You talk like a man," she said with withering scorn. "But the water still rises from the earth, however low you fall. The burn still flows to the sea, whether I care for you, or you for me. What have you learned yet, if you don't seek the help you need where you know you can find it? I'm not here to listen to your troubles. So go."

She took a stick and began to trace patterns in the ash beside the fireplace. When he left she never raised her head but seemed absorbed in her task. She drew slowly and carefully, lines and curves and circles. By the time she had finished the sound of his footsteps in the tunnel had died away and there was no noise at all, except the muffled echo of the wind on the hill and the crackling of the fire. There was also the sound of falling water, but she never heard that; there was no more noise in that than in the blood flowing in her body. It was as much part of her and therefore imperceptible.

*

"The army?" she repeated. "In our hills? But the Covenanters have all gone. Religion is no longer important, I believe."

"No, no, Oddny, you have it wrong." The man standing outside the Post Office sighed. "It's not a religious army."

She frowned. "The English, you mean? But don't they have what they want already?"

"It would help if you tried to keep up with things between times," he answered with a touch of impatience. "Up there in the hills you just assume nothing changes, until the place is overrun with khaki. Then you expect a potted history of the last three hundred years as if it were a week. You'd better come in. It's freezing out here. The wife's not in. I'll put the kettle on for you."

"Freezing?" Oddny cast a puzzled look at the sun, which bravely flung its light across the snow-patched hills, although all its warmth was whisked away by the wind before it could touch them. It would have been pleasant to feel the light on her skin, instead of having to dress herself like a decent body in a long skirt and plaid. "No. It stopped freezing shortly after dawn."

"In a manner of speaking." The man shuddered and pulled his jacket round him. "I know you're not keen to come in, but I'm not speaking for long out here. I tell you, there's a wind you could cut with a knife, and that's a fact."

"All winds can be cut with a knife," remarked Oddny, but she followed him into the Post Office without further protest, just as she answered to the name by which he addressed her. These people had applied it to her for the last twelve hundred years. She had used many names: this one served its purpose as well as any.

The Post Office was also a small general store, crammed from floor to ceiling with shelves full of groceries, ironmongery, stationery and fishing tackle. The actual Post Office was a small desk behind a glass panel in a little booth. The door into the sitting-room was beside it. It felt cramped and strange indoors, with too many angles everywhere. She'd been here before in this man's grandfather's time, but the place had changed. The high wooden counter had gone, and the sacks on the floor, and the glass jars on the shelves. Everything was brightly coloured and covered with writing, like a jumble of unwholesome spells. Oddny tried to re-establish her bearings. "Don't you sell bootlaces any more?"

"Bootlaces? Of course. In those orange packets there."

"What's a packet?"

"Come in," he said firmly, holding the door open. "NATO is one thing, and that'll probably take all morning. Forget about packets."

She felt more at home in the sitting-room. The open range had gone, and so had the fat Empress cast-iron stove that had followed it. Now there was a sleek white Rayburn that took up the entire fireplace. The smell of peat was the same, only fainter. There was still a picture of deer on a hill over the mantelpiece, still china carthorses on the windowsill. The stone flags were covered now, as was the green linoleum. Instead, there was a brightly patterned carpet on the floor. Oddny regarded it with awe. The almanack by the kitchen door had changed, but that was only to be expected. No useful information this year, just a photograph of two kittens in a stocking, which seemed curious. The table had acquired a cloth, but the two upright chairs that flanked it were as they had always been. The resting chair by the fire had disappeared, and so had the rag rug. Oddny sat down cautiously on the edge of one of the matching armchairs, watching the man make tea. He did it as it had always been done. She sighed with relief.

"So," she said, "the army. I admit I was glad to find you safe, my friend. Aren't you afraid? And you with a wife and family? Grandchildren, it must be by now."

"Oddny, you'll have to take this in. It's not that kind of army."

"No?"

"They're doing an exercise."

She looked blank. "Tell me this, then. Are people no longer occupied with killing one another? They're now thinking of the good of their health? Is that it?"

"No, it's not," he said shortly. "Listen."

Oddny listened attentively, and consumed two cups of the revolting tea that people had never failed to produce for her for the last hundred and fifty years.

"They asked the Commander-in-Chief why he chose Galloway," her friend was telling her, "and he said because this was the only place they could think of in NATO where conditions approximated those of a Third World country. They're pretending to evacuate us, you see, after an invasion."

"Wait. You'll have to explain some of that more clearly."

"Oh God," he said. "Let's have a dram." He reached into the airing-cupboard next to the stove, and produced a bottle of whisky. "Let's get this clear. Did you know we had had a war in Europe?"

"Of course I know that. It began around the time the well was given a guardian, and has never ceased since. War came with the people, and when the people have gone, the well will no longer need me. How could I not know that?"

"It's no good," he said. "I have to tell you straight, my dear. I reckon your time is over. It's a different world now, and you can't expect to have any influence, not any more."

"The hills are still the same."

"Are you so sure of that?"

She hesitated. "No, I'm not," she said at last. "That's why I came. It's my own place that worries me, for what can I do about anywhere else? They say the gods have departed, gone away into the shadows, and that such as I survive only here and there, in small pockets of land that are too poor and barren for the people to bother themselves over. It's true enough, there are fewer folk that come, and the troubles they bring are smaller, as though they don't expect that water can heal anything great. But they are troubled, I know that. I tell you something, my friend, I feel like one besieged, and I think the assault will come soon. It's not the army. I thought there might be a connection but the soldiers have come before, and gone again, and the folk of the hills remain. But something else has happened which is beyond my understanding."

He looked at her with more attention, as though he had changed his mind, and now expected her to say something relevant. "What kind of things have happened?"

"The deer are sick," said Oddny.

"Sick?" There was a new sharpness in his tone.

"But there is nothing new. It's not the acid. We know about acid. We feel it in our skin and in our lungs. It's not the plantations. There is space enough still in the mountains and we understand the new trees better now, even the spruce, which I cannot learn to love. There is nothing new we can feel or hear or see, but there is a new danger in the mountains. There is one who knows the deer, who feels their sickness, but cannot sense the cause."

"One?"

"Not to do with you," said Oddny. "But so many have left already. If the deer are no longer in the mountains, then I will be alone here as I have never been before. I wouldn't be the last of my kind if I could help it. You tell me we are no longer necessary, so perhaps it doesn't matter to you if we are driven out at last?"

"I didn't say that," he said slowly. "I can't understand what effect it may have. I'm a practical man. Only I'm afraid it would mean the end of something more. That's all."

"Then if you care, you will explain to me what it is that you must know."

*

The snow was still thick on the ridge. It was a calm cold day, and standing on the summit it was possible to see for miles. To the west and north there were more mountains. There was a valley just below the ridge, high and bare, divided by the grey line of a burn. Further down there were trees, huddled in a dark mass against the white ground. To the east, the mountains fell away to rolling lowlands, a wild broken country touched with frost against the brown and grey of winter bracken on granite. Beyond the lowlands lay the sea, not so very far away, out of sight beyond the long line of hill that people called the Skreel.

Between the Skreel and Criffel, lying half hidden by rainclouds, there was a long gap and through it could be seen the mountains beyond the sea, white-capped, delicately etched against the sky, only a little more solid than a cloud.

Oddny stood on the ridge with her back to her own land, and stared at those other mountains as if there were something vital to be learned from them. She had known their names once but those names were maybe changed and, as far as she knew, the land was now deserted. There had been no message from any of her kind for so long that she had gradually begun to assume that they had gone. Now that she allowed herself to think about it, it was possible that there was no one out in the world at all, that there were none of her folk left upon the planet, except in these hills that had lain out of the way for long enough to be forgotten. Though she knew the world was large, she remembered what her friend at the Post Office had told her about the other countries so unlike her own. It was a curious thing, there were worlds upon worlds which had once been open one to another but the people now believed that there was only one, and that was dying fast enough. That frightened her. People had one power that other kinds did not, which was the power to dream things and make them happen, or the power to destroy, merely by the act of forgetting. Her mountains were only safe because they had been forgotten. She realized now that that was no security at all.

At last Oddny turned her back to the south-east and faced north-west into the heart of the hills. She was met by silence and the sun gleaming upon snow. She looked down into the valley, a long hard look that was presently rewarded.

The deer were below, grazing the thin winter grass through its frozen covering. There were only two or three of them, dull-coloured like the rocks around them, so that even the snow did not destroy their camouflage. The rest wouldn't be far away. Oddny cupped her hands to her mouth and called.

It was a long time before she was answered. She waited patiently, sitting cross-legged in the snow, gazing downwards. The sun rose to its highest, just topping the peak to the south of her, and lying in long gold rays across the hill, so that the snow was suddenly dazzling, the sky blue as the sea in summer. Then the sun dipped again, and the shadow of the mountain fell across her. A thin wind sprang out of the west, ruffling the plaid that wrapped her round and playing with the ends of her hair where it fell over her shoulders. Oddny never moved, except now and again to call across the silent hills. Two hawks wheeled in the still air below, then hovered motionless over the patch of woodland. She watched them for a little, then scanned the further peaks, while they drifted into a grey shadow. Presently she called again.

Twilight was in the air, an opaqueness settling over the horizon, bringing the frost down with it, when at last she had her reply. An answering call echoed faintly across the valley out of the white emptiness of the slopes beyond. Oddny stood up, alert as a dog after a sudden scent. She surveyed the hills one last time and was off, plunging down into the valley by a direct, precipitous route, leaping barefoot down the rocks and slithering through patches of snow. The floor of the valley was rough and rock-strewn; its smooth whiteness seen from the summit was entirely deceptive. Oddny bounded from rock to rock, forded the burn without hesitation, giving only a quick gesture of respect in acknowledgment of whatever might dwell amidst its waters, and was up again, climbing fast on to the mountain, scattering water drops as she ran. Burnwater froze on her hair and plaid, leaving her bedewed with brightness.

By the time she reached the next ridge it was almost dark and the wind was rising. She could feel it burn on her skin when she turned her face westward, a warning to any mortal folk that the hill this night would be deadly. Snow was winnowed thinly from the ridge top, fanned out into new drifts, and the ground where she trod was delicately patterned like sand after the retreating tide.

Oddny faced north and called again, half against the wind. The sound was blown away from her, driven upwards into the darkening air, where it was torn apart and vanished. Even so, she was still heard. The answer came clearly down the wind, closer than it had seemed before, just to the west of her. She faced the wind again and ran across the ridge, flitting like a small shadow across the face of the hill into the very teeth of the night.

The ridge ended in a cairn, the stones black against the snow on the eastern side, with a sharp drop below into a valley where the dark lay so thick already she couldn't see the foot of it. Oddny skidded down, bringing a slide of snow with her, and landed on her feet at the bottom. There was a big drift banked against the hill; if she had been any less lightfooted it would have swallowed her up. She ran lightly across the top of it, leaving a faint trail of bare footprints, and reached solid ground again in a mass of frozen heather which crackled like kindling under her feet.

She heard him call again very close by. Before she had finished answering him he was visible, a darker shape emerging from the gathering night. Then he stood in front of her, breathing hard. The night was falling so fast that everything visible had an unreal quality to it, as though she had only to blink and the whole world would vanish. For a moment she was disconcerted, as if she doubted herself so much that when she looked at her own folk with her own eyes, they gave her the lie. But if she was there, so was he. Oddny shook her head a little, and smiled with relief.

He had been watching her, a touch of anxiety in his face; clearly he had not forgotten the mood of their last meeting. When he saw her smile, he smiled back and his face was transformed, no longer harsh but alive with laughter. It revealed him suddenly for what he was, but she was undaunted, for she knew him of old. She saw no affection in him, nor concern for her, particularly, only a wild mirth, and an overwhelming liveliness that would be terrifying if she could not respond to it.

Oddny laughed in his face and ran past him, and he ran after her, their footprints weaving in a ragged pattern across the frozen slopes, one pair of bare footmarks running hard, interwoven with something even stranger, though perhaps more to be expected at this height and weather. Their tracks leapt another burn, then doubled back and recrossed it, running apart and together like an endless infinity sign spreading itself up and down the valley, crossing and recrossing the hill. The wind itself was caught between the hills and funnelled down the valley, with a high whistling that bore with it the thin echo of laughter.

She reached a flat marshy island in the burn and turned to face him amidst spiky hummocks of frosted grass that reached above her knees. He came up to her and was on her, rolling over and over among the grass tussocks. Oddny held on to him and turned her face to his. His hair was thick and cold and brushed her face with a touch like ice. She held him to her and felt the warmth of him against her, alive and damp and smelling of the deer. There was the coolness of snow under her back and over his shoulder she could see the stars, cold and piercing in a frozen sky.

*

"And now," said Oddny, her eyes on the cold pink glow in the east that presaged the dawn, "we have to talk."

He sat beside her, his feet, like hers, dabbling in the burn where it flowed brown and full between thin layers of ice that skimmed the water in the reeds. "If you wish." He spoke indifferently, as if everything important had already been said, although they had not exchanged two sentences in all the hours since they had met.

"No," said Oddny, "not by my wish. Do your deer sicken, or do they not?"

He turned to face her at that, his eyes bright and interested. "You know why? You did find out?"

"After you had gone," went on Oddny, as if he had not spoken, "I thought about your visit. Through all the years of decline and fearfulness I never saw you so touched before. You never listened or cared about what happened below the mountains. I knew none of our people had passed, or I would have heard of it. Your despair is nothing to do with me but if you had cause for it, it would be a cause that affects all. I can't help you because you haven't asked, but I do what I can to protect my own."

He didn't answer, but stared at the sky. The ridge above them was tinged with light, reflected from the brightening dawn.

Oddny waited a moment longer, and continued, "I have to do with the people as you do not. I went down to discover what I could. There is a reason for the sickness."

It was doubtful if he understood her explanation. The affairs of the people were of no interest to him and she was aware that he wasn't following very closely. Words had little power to move him, anyway, and words of alien matters, of which he could hardly begin to imagine, left him cold. Oddny told her story as if she were merely clarifying it for herself. Perhaps that is all, she thought, glancing at him sideways. He was still watching the dawn as if that were the only thing that life depended upon. It was growing fast; the sky had turned from pink to orange and the small clouds that scudded east were caught by the light and held fast, until they were tinged bright red, then swallowed up by the unseen sun.

She thought she had lost his attention altogether and was surprised when he looked at her again. His eyes were bright yellow in the daylight. He looked at her blankly, as though he had never seen her before. She was used to that too, so ignored it.

"Could you change it?" he asked at last.

She hadn't been expecting that, and it took her a while to answer. "I don't know."

"But if you were asked, you'd have to try, wouldn't you?"

He knew the answer to that, so she didn't bother to give it him.

"You would have to try until you had done what was asked."

"Or lost myself in the attempt," said Oddny lightly. He had her trapped, but she had no reason to protest. It was not in his nature to be considerate. Love, for him, was what he felt about the deer, and the mountain. He would always be true to that, and she would also be true to herself, until all things had their end.

"You would have no choice," he remarked, and bowed to the

sun, as it swung clear above the mountain and fell in golden rays around their feet.

*

"I would like you to make a telephone call for me," said Oddny, "and after that I shall leave you alone."

"I'm not bothered about that. But are you sure about doing this? You don't know what it's like. It's no place for your sort, I can tell you that."

"Have you ever been there?"

"No," said the man in the Post Office. "But I know enough. It's too different from what you're used to. And you can't change anything. I don't think you realize how powerful these people are."

"I have no choice," said Oddny. "I have some small powers of my own, and I have to do what I can. I have to go to this place and see it for myself."

"Why do you?"

"Because I am the guardian of the well, and if any request help from such powers as water has, I have no choice but to give it, except to cease to be what I am."

"And you have been asked?"

"No," said Oddny with a sigh, "but I shall be."

*

It was raining hard when she set off home. The burn was loud with meltwater. The rain was cold, hard heavy drops interspersed with splashes of sleet. The wind blew the rain into her clothes until they were soaked through, clammy and heavy on her back. The snow had melted off the moor, and the grass in her corrie was brown and withered as it emerged again. Oddny took off her boots as soon as she left the people's road and began to hurry. When she got home the burn was deserted, the rowan trees sighing mournfully against the gale. The well had been visited, she was quite aware of that without even needing to look for the prints that had churned the boggy ground below the pool. She stripped off her sodden clothes almost fiercely. She stood for a moment on the rock that overhung the pool below the waterfall. The pool had risen since she left it this morning and the water foamed whiter. She smiled down at it with something approaching her old insouciance. Then she straightened up and dived like an arrow into the whirlpool.

She came up under the fall and let it flow over her. Then she let it carry her down, and take her to the bottom of the pool where brown water churned over the rocky bed. She opened her eyes to water shot with light and air, white and black and brown roaring round her, sweeping her in a circle past the curve of rock and up into daylight, the rain splashing on her head, beating down on the water and being instantly swallowed. She lay on her back and saw the rowans circling slowly, black branches etched against a moving sky. She rolled and dived again, coming up at the foot of the pool. She climbed ashore reluctantly, knowing what she had to face.

He had left gifts, as she had known he would. Precious stones from the heart of the mountain, gleaming in their bed of plaited reeds, and a small horn carved from the antler of a deer, chased with gold. She took them from the hollow rock above the well in an automatic gesture. She had taken so many gifts from there, both rich and poor, more than she could count over so great a time, but never one had she accepted with a heavier heart. Oddny held the treasures of the mountain in her cupped hands, and regarded them with indifference. In the people's terms they were so precious as to be beyond price, but to her they were of no help. She could hear his appeal, echoed in the voice of the fall, just as he had stood here and made it only an hour or two ago. She was the guardian of the water and she had no choice. For the first time in all those years she knew terror, and was sickened by its sour taste.

*

The shore where she landed was familiar to her, and still recognizable. It was not the same as she remembered it; that would have been too much to expect, but the waves still beat in their old rhythm against a long sandy beach with dunes at the top. The crossing had been easy, though more years had passed than she could reckon since she had put to sea. The wind still served her, responding to her words as it had always done, and the tide still aided her, respecting her frail craft as it had never failed to do. Cheered by this evidence that the world had not changed beyond recall, Oddny beached her coracle in the right place and found a place to hide it in a hollow among the dunes.

So far she had tried to ignore all evidence of human presence on her journey, although it was ubiquitous and never pleasant. To travel in the old way, she needed to fix her mind upon more ancient things and not to allow people to impinge upon her thoughts. Her voyage was done, however, and it was time for her to adjust to this new human world. She sat at the top of the beach for many hours, watching the waves break and the tide rise and fall again, until she was ready to face the thing that loomed behind her.

No one saw her when she finally turned inland. She crossed the railway unheeded, picking her way over the metal tracks. The railway was not particularly strange to her. A similar track had once been laid across the foothills of her own country and, for a brief space of years, she had watched the trains chugging to and fro like clattering slugs crawling across the hills. She had seen them come and watched them go; had looked down from the hills at men taking up the line that other men had laid so short a time before. The railway held no terrors for her and neither did the fence, which was similar to the deer fences that men sometimes raised across the hills. It would have infuriated the one who sent her here. He only saw deer fences through a red mist of anger, for he could not climb them, and too often they separated him from his own. But they presented no problems to Oddny. She climbed briskly over, avoiding the barbs, and found herself confronting the danger she had come to find.

It was vast, greater than anything she had allowed herself to imagine. When she faced it she felt the force of it for the first time and her impulse was to flee, to get back over the sea to her own hills, as far from this menace as it was possible to be. She had encountered evil before, but never on such a scale as this.

The place emanated the distillation of all the horror that the people had brought into the world. She knew what people were capable of: the hills had seen suffering, betrayal, and bloodshed. Not even the people themselves could see what it was they were doing here. There was nothing to see at all except a vast ugliness. But it was possible for Oddny to feel, and she felt danger.

When she faced it, she felt reduced as if her bones had turned to liquid and her stomach churned. She turned her back; the sea was below her, glinting in the winter sun. She smelled salt. The waves broke against the sand in an erratic line of white. She watched them break nine times, and turned round.

She was better prepared this time. The thing loomed as huge as ever, but the fear of it could not pierce her as it had done before. She knew now she would not turn and flee. There was no going back, no safety in the hills anyway. She was here because the deer were sick. He thought they were sick from the short grass and lichen that they ate in winter. The hills were poisoned, and the man from the Post Office had explained to her that the source of the poison lay here. Seeing the place, she knew in the depths of her being that he was right. She could not go back.

She made herself study the place calmly, walking slowly round it. There were towers, high-curved like the fortresses the people once built around the coast when danger threatened them from over the sea. But these towers were not for defence. They were made of concrete and curtains of water fell in a circle round their feet. The water should have made her feel more secure, but there seemed to be no life in it. It originally had come from the burns and the lochs in the mountains to the east but it held no memory of them, not in this place. If such water still had its guardians in the hills, they could not have dared to make their way in here.

There were other towers, high and straight, one scarred by fire. Oddny distrusted towers. In her experience, people who built towers had dangerous thoughts. Among the towers were great rectangular buildings, all made with straight lines that made her eyes ache. But towers and straight lines she had seen before, and the hills remained unconquered. The buildings were pregnant with some hidden threat; the thing her friend had explained to her. She needed to get inside to do what she had come for.

The place was confusing, being full of roadways and buildings. To find her way through it she had to think another way. An image rose in her mind: dunes thick with marram grass, behind them a sandy plain thick with gorse and heather. In spring the place was bright with gorse and the thick strong smell of it mingled with the salt breeze off the sea. She saw herself standing on the dunes looking inland to the mountains, seeing rounded hills white with snow. She knew the names they had been called by, and maybe still were: Whin Rigg, Sca Fell, Yewbarrow.

There had been settlements along this shore; small patches of cultivated land behind the dunes. They had not been her people but they had respected water. There were many streams of water then, flowing from the hills to the sea. The waters had been clean and alive, knowing where they came from and whither they must go. Oddny remembered the waters and the place became clear in her mind, so that in spite of the strange angles and concrete monstrosities, she found her way through.

Presently she came out at the main gateway, flitting past the policeman in his glass hut. If he saw a shadow flicker on the road, he perhaps thought it was a cloud drifting over the pale face of the sun. Oddny ducked under the gate and felt the current which would have made the alarm bell ring. But no bells rang for her.

She had made an effort to look as modern and respectable as possible, and was rewarded when she gave her name at the Visitor Centre. They didn't glance at her twice but suggested that she walk around the Exhibition Centre until her tour was ready to begin.

The important thing to remember now was her task. It would be like following a thread into a maze. So long as she felt the thread under her finger, she would know her way and be safe. If she lost it, her whole being would be threatened, for she had never been anywhere so alien in her life. There was nothing in the entire place that would reflect back to her the truth of her own existence. Deliberately she conjured up images of streams flowing among the dunes and gorse, and imprinted them on her memory like a talisman.

Meanwhile she studied the exhibits obediently, pressing all the buttons and watching the film. It was a curious way of representing reality. It interested her that people now had a concept of what they were made. One would think it would have made them more aware of their relationship to other kinds, but that was manifestly not the case, seeing what they were doing. She was familiar with the idea, of course, though this language was new to her. Sometimes when people bored her it amused her to half-shut her eyes and to refocus, so that she could see them dissolve into their component parts, a mass of atoms whirling through space with a pleasant view of the sky through the gaps between. If she stared very hard at the atoms, it was intriguing to see the electrons circling round their nuclei, but hard to follow because they moved so fast. She had to speed up her mind, just as she had to slow it down to watch the stars doing the same thing. Interesting that people, who had such notoriously limited vision in every sense, should have followed these patterns in such detail; terrifying that they should know so much and emerge with less respect than ever. Oddny sat on the bench in front of the video screen, watching the infra-red rays and listening to the commentary. She felt alarmed and sobered by the implications of so much human knowledge.

She heard a name being called and recollected with a start that it was hers for the day. The tour was ready to begin. She picked up the thread of her mission. She was a spy, ready to subvert. The idea of it made her long for invisibility, but that would not be appropriate. A line of people, mostly keen young men, followed the guide into another room. Oddny hurried after them.

She didn't listen very hard to the talk that followed. It seemed to be a mixture of obvious facts and blatant lies. She watched the pupils of the guide's eyes contract and enlarge according to the accuracy of her statements. There was no direct evidence here of what she must do. No one mentioned the hills but some of them cared. There was more human emotion in the room than was comfortable for Oddny. She was glad when they all filed out, until she realized that they had to get into a bus. She had never yet ridden in a horseless carriage but today was unreal. She was penetrating another world because her own was threatened, and in pursuance of her ends she would have to endure whatever was required.

Twenty minutes later, still sick and dizzy, she stood on a metal platform five storeys up while the guide explained what lay beneath. Oddny needed no explanations: she could feel it. It was like standing on a battlefield, yet the people who stood beside her seemed neither to see nor to hear the signs. That gave the thing a deadly unreality. She could hear the matter of her world being torn apart, not just a little, as happens in the hills when the rocks fizz with strange energy, but hugely. The very stuff from which the earth was made was being torn apart only a few feet away from her and these people who, unlike her, were made of that same matter, ignored it as if their bodies felt nothing. Was it possible that they genuinely could not feel it? Oddny felt sick.

There was worse to come. She was shocked and dazed, so it was difficult to keep her bearings, but presently they entered a great white building and she made herself remember. She saw the plain, bright with gorse, yellow and orange, thick with butterflies, half of whom had left this land for ever, and the sun bringing out the scent of the heather which blew down from the hills and mixed with the pungent gorse. Oddny held that image before her like a shield and followed the guide.

There was neither air, nor light, nor silence, nothing real at all. A bleep like a heartbeat out of tune drowned out thought, obliterating the rhythm of her body so that the sun in the sky and the waves on the shore were truly hers only in memory. They had left the earth behind and all that dwelled within it. Life was no longer real, but only this dullness. White paint and endless staircases around huge sealed enclosures bombarded with the stuff of destruction.

She had never come so close to her own annihilation. Oddny was not matter. People might be destroyed in body, but if she were separated from the earth she would be nothing; she would be destroyed in essence.

I am nothing, thought Oddny, but the life that is born of living water; I am nothing but the sound of the burns that run for ever from the hills to the sea. I am nothing at all but the love of the people for their earth. I have no other name. If this is not the earth where I belong, I am nothing. I am becoming nothing.

Oddny leaned on a white metal railing, and felt herself grow insubstantial. If they had looked round at her then, they would have been shaken out of whatever world they inhabited, for they would have seen quite clearly the rail passing behind her body and the white treads of the staircase through the outline of her thin feet. There was a roaring in her ears which sounded like the sea, where all things have their end, but it was not the sea. It was like nothing on earth at all. Life was slipping away from her like a dream vanishing on waking.

She forced herself to remember what she had to do. There was still the thread to follow. She was here in answer to a supplicant who had come to the pool. She was an emissary with a task to perform. She remembered the gifts left beside the waterfall: precious stones from the mountain, the little horn encased in gold. She made herself imagine it as clearly as if it lay in the palm of her hand. She saw the chased pattern on the gold and remembered the coolness of horn and metal under her fingers. His deer were sick from eating the lichen that had been their winter food since the days when the hills were new to her. If there were no deer in the hills he would be gone, and the world would be drear and empty for the lack of him. She remembered what she had come to this place to do.

The people stood crowded around a screen. Through many thicknesses of material like glass she could see the poisonous stuff. This was the heart of the matter, the essence of the evil she had been sent here to confront. Metal arms guided it, stripped it of its covering, crushed it into a mass of concentrated death that would lie like a threat of doom in this place where the gorse should grow, until the sun grew cold and the world draw to its end. If it did not lie safe through all the centuries when the people would have gone as they had come, then life in the beauty she knew would have an end.

She clung to the image of the thread. They were in the heart of the maze now, and if she lost her track, she would be left to wander here like a disappointed ghost until the doom should fall. She had to keep her mission clear in her mind, clear as the yellow of the gorse in May, and seek for the moment when she should act. It must be very close now. A quiver ran through her, then, suddenly alert as she had not yet been amidst so much deadness, she followed the others.

Presently they all stood looking down on a great pool of blue water filled with metal containers that were lost in the depths. The hall was vast, edged with enormous pipes and walkways above the water. The water was sick and lifeless, not even aware of her presence. If death had power over water, it lay here. No such glimpse of death had ever touched Oddny before. She shuddered and drew back. The pool was making her weak and faint, a shadow of the thing she was. It was necessary to act at once, while some strength still lay in her.

It took all the power she had even to begin. But it was why she had come. She had never yet failed any who came to the well. He had come, not to her, but to the well, as a supplicant, in the proper form. She had to do what he demanded, and confront this thing, or renounce her place in the world. It was not fair of him to have demanded such strength from water, but the rules were inviolable. No supplicants who asked for what they had the right, had ever been refused.

She sat crosslegged on the metal floor. Far below, there was earth under her. She made her mind encompass it. There was water here on its way to the sea, diverted and imprisoned for an evil purpose. There was air trapped inside this place, forced down pipes and stripped of life, but still containing the vestiges of live air. There was fire, turned to an image of death. There was all matter, working in a way that belonged to the earth as much as the sun's rays upon her granite hills, magnified out of all proportion into a danger greater than any she had ever known.

Oddny summoned up the image of the land. She saw the gorse bent before the wind, westerly gales rolling in from the sea, the surf pounding on the shifting shore. She saw days and nights fading into eternity, the moon circling, the sun changing its pattern with the seasons. She saw the shore altering, dunes rising from the beach and being washed back to the sea; the mountains changing shape, worn by wind and rain, the burns turning to rivers, then back again to ice. She saw centuries of ice, water locked in the hills, the land sinking under the weight of it. She saw the same water flowing, the waves beating against the feet of the mountains, and the plain of gorse vanished for ever.

In the centre, where she sat, she saw the legacy of forgotten people, a danger that threatened the earth through a lifetime as long as hers, holding within it the possibility that consciousness should cease. She saw danger sealed here, while the land changed and the sea advanced and retreated, the rivers altered their courses in the slow washing of the hills to the sea. There was no guardian for such a power as that, nothing in life that could undertake the responsibility for such a thing; certainly not the people, for everyone but they knew they were as transitory as the summer's day. Her own powers were small in the face of such a thing, but what spells she had she would give to bind it, even if it left her without power for ever.

The danger was far stronger than she had realized. She was confronting it now. It loomed over her, aware of her. She experienced it as a series of images because that way she could make sense of it. It was the battle with the dragon, the serpent, the monster that dwells in the depths of the sea or below the waterfall. Yet it was not any of those, but they were the only symbols with which she could capture it. It shifted shape, and so did she, in a battle of energy that raged down all the centuries to come. A duel was fought that day across the plains of gorse, which left the place haunted throughout time, for those who had the power to feel. Again and again the new power threatened to overwhelm her, and each time she slipped out from under it and confronted it with new images: the snake, the bird, the tree, sometimes just words or notes, always elusive but never giving in.

But at last she felt her strength failing. The peril towered over her, about to sweep her down into oblivion. She would have fled, but the thread led straight into the heart of it. She followed, and held on.

It flinched. Then it struggled, changing its shape into further monstrous forms that terrified her, all armed and shielded against her. But she did not let go.

No power on earth prevails against water. In the face of direct attack she still yielded and gave way, but she never let go. Time had always been on her side, and she would not be hurried now.

She could not deflect it. Evil and danger lay there, and there they would remain. All she could hope to do was bind it, hoping it would be for long enough. She had the power to bind, but had never yet attempted to use it on a force so strong. She knew quite well it might turn and destroy her, which would mean that whatever she was, it would vanish for ever from the earth.

At last she gained the upper hand, and cast her spell. She almost felt it crack. She waited, quivering; to her joy it held. It was only partial, it only could be partial; but it held.

Oddny stood up and spoke to the gorse, the burns, and the waves that were still breaking on the shore.

"What was, will be," she told them. "All things change, but you will not die, nor cease to know yourselves. The people have betrayed their trust of consciousness. They may cease to be, but we will still know what we are, and they will never destroy us."

*

Oddny had taken very little time, of the sort measured by people, so no one had noticed her absence. The tour finished with a diagram of how the water was cleaned before being pumped into the sea. Oddny's head ached. She didn't use numbers in the same way that these people seemed to, so the explanation left her little the wiser. They left the last of the intrusive bleeping machines behind and were about to quit the building.

As they left they each had to step into a small booth, where a machine measured them for gross pollution. Oddny watched the procedure with a sinking heart. She was fairly sure of what would happen. Her turn came, and she stepped into the booth as instructed.

Nothing happened.

"Are you standing on the footrests?" called the guide.

"Yes."

"Put your hands right to the back of the slots."

Oddny obeyed, knowing it was useless. Her mind raced. She'd need to get out of here fast. She couldn't let them examine her. They'd learned too much in the last couple of centuries, and she didn't intend to upset the neat little system they'd constructed for themselves. She remembered the sickly blue water in that dreadful pool. The gods knew what they would do with her.

The guides were studying the machine. "It's very odd. It isn't registering that there's anyone in there at all."

"Shall we call the engineer?"

"Some sort of power failure, do you think?"

"Are you sure you're standing in the right place?"

"Yes," said Oddny wearily.

"Well, we'll have to wait until someone comes. I've never known this happen before. It isn't registering anything at all."

One of the waiting tour ventured a mild joke. "Perhaps it thinks you don't exist."

They all smiled perfunctorily.

There were footsteps in the corridor, and an engineer in white overalls appeared. "Now then, where's this lady who breaks our machines?" he remarked, looking over the tour, who stood like obedient sheep on the right side of the barrier.

"She's still in there, isn't she?"

"No."

"She must have gone back the other side."

"She's not round here."

"Look in the corridor, where the effluent diagram is."

"No, no, she didn't go back. I'd have seen her pass me."

"She must have gone through."

"She never came past me. We'd have seen her."

They looked at one another in consternation, while the engineer rolled his eyes upwards and muttered, "Women!"

Oddny scrambled lightly over the high, barbed fence, and ran for the beach. Her coracle was where she'd left it. She picked it up and hurried down to the waves. The coracle had left a small impression, round ribbed sides echoed in a pattern on the hollowed sand; then only faint bare footprints half running down to the breaking surf and the shifting surface of the sea, revealing nothing.

*

The snow had all melted now. She squatted on the rock above the pool. The moss was thick under her feet, soft between her toes. It rained steadily, drops of water trickling comfortably down her back and dripping off her. Her hair was wet and tangled. Water ran out of it, splashing into the moss which absorbed it silently. The daylight was almost gone, and the dark was comforting, blurring the shapes of things into the unseen unity of the night. A breeze came down off the hills. She could feel the nip of frost on her skin right down her left-hand side. The night was full of soft sounds, distinct over the falling water which she did not call a sound. Rain on grass, rain on rock, passing hooves muffled by turf, wind funnelling down into the corrie, bringing more rain.

"I thought I would never come back," said Oddny.

Her companion stirred. He had been sitting motionless on the other side of the pool, the outline of his antlers merging into the rowan branches. She felt him turn to look at her, though she could not see his eyes. "Even so," he said, as if following an earlier thought, "even if the thing is bound, it won't help the deer. Not now."

Something else had happened, then. She felt a flutter of panic, but said nothing. If he intended to tell her, she only had to wait.

It took him a while. He wasn't used to telling anybody anything, and the news he had was his own, not hers. "The people are driving the deer off the mountain," he said at last.

"I don't understand." She was alert now, straining to imagine what that meant. She had no concept of the mountain without the deer, or of the deer without the mountain, so that what he was saying seemed quite impossible. It would be harder for him. He had no imagination at all: imagination was not part of what he was. He must be searching for words to explain this impossible thing that he had witnessed. Oddny waited patiently.

"They have driven the deer down inside fences, where I cannot reach them. The people are concerned about the sickness." He paused again. "I am afraid of what they will do."

Afraid he might well be, but he could not imagine. Oddny could, and her heart gave a queer lurch, and seemed to rise into her throat. "And you cannot follow? What will you do, then?"

She sensed him shrug. "My own kind are lost to me," he said at last, with no perceptible emotion. "The deer are doomed and so, therefore, am I."

"You'd abandon them, then?" she said, too quickly.

"Abandon?" he questioned, not knowing the word. "I am the guardian of the deer upon the mountain. There was a time when I was not, when there were no deer. I always knew that such a time must come again, for the world does not stay still. It should not have been done by the people; they were not born for that. They take on too much and will perish for it. But that's no business of mine. If the deer are gone from the mountain, I cannot stay, for I shall be nothing."

"So you're going?" Desolation welled inside her, but there was nothing to say. As he said, it was always going to happen. That was the way time worked, and there was nothing to be said.

"Out of the world," he finished for her. "Yes."

She thought of her struggle among the fields of gorse, which seemed now to be all in vain. "I did my best," she told him.

"There was nothing else you could do." He seemed to be struggling for words, and when he spoke again she understood why. The concept was new to him, and it was very difficult for him to express anything new. "You did very well," he said. "If the thing is bound, then you have saved this world from a great danger. That is good, even if my own time has come. It is still good."

"Yes."

He was standing up now, and from where she crouched he seemed tall as the rowans themselves, a creature out of a dream etched against a dim starlit sky. A moment later he had turned and gone; only the faint thud of hoofbeats came down to her on the wind.

Oddny sat by the pool until the stars faded again and the dawn spread cold across the eastern sky. The world seemed empty. It was possible that she was the only one of her kind upon whom the sun still rose. She watched the water bubbling out of the earth, flowing towards the unseen sea. For the first time since the melting of the ice, when the spring burst out from the corrie floor, it gave her no solace. It was only water, and what was water? She would miss him, even if she stayed here until the end of time, and nothing that the earth brought forth would take his place for her.

A tear splashed down into the moss. She felt it hot on her cheek, and brushed her hand across her eyes. Then she crouched over the water, filling her cupped palms. The burn flowed over her hands and she realized for the first time that it was very cold.

Charliwill

A CAUTIONARY FAERY TALE

by R J Stewart

This story began as one for my daughter, while out walking. As sometimes happens, when I decided to write it down it suddenly took a strange turning and became one for adults. It contains many of the traditional themes and objects from Celtic faery tradition: the faery who guards a hoard of ancient gold, the path to grandmother's house through the forest, the curative blue bottle, and the theme of questions, answers, and temptations. But they turn into a mystery. This is a cautionary tale upon several interlinked levels, and I am reminded of the moralizing cautions written into faery tales by eighteenth and nineteenth century improvers. Not that there is any moralizing in this faery tale, for it is thoroughly immoral and corrupt. If there is a lesson in it, it is a complex and mysterious one, and I leave it to you, dear reader, to decide what it may be.

There was once a faery, a Leprechaun by nature, called Charliwill. This was not his real name of course, but he had taken it upon himself during the turbulent years of the seventeenth and eighteenth centuries, feeling that it combined both Jacobite and Hanoverian sentiments with a prophetic theme for the future of kingship in the twentieth. Faeries are very sensitive about their names, as their true names are keys to power, and their false names, which they change every few hundred years, are not to be taken lightly. This is a story in which even his false name is not discovered, so we will leave it alone and find out what happened instead.

Charliwill was the guardian of a large treasure, which had

been in his tribe since the youth of the world. It was a clay pot filled to the brim with wafer thin gold discs, and each disc was embossed with spirals and dots and swirls and zig-zags. Every morning he awoke at dawn, and began counting. He took the discs out of the pot with his right hand while he ate his frugal breakfast of raw mushrooms, the red spotted *amanita muscara* which grew in the northern corner of his house, with his left. Charliwill counted aloud, always, and the first few numbers of his daily task were often muffled. "Wud, doo, chree, hor, hive ..."

There were 3650 golden discs in the pot, and by sunset Charliwill was gasping "Three thousand three hundred and sixty, three thousand three hundred and sixty one ..." With the last coin put back into the pot, the sun set, and he drank some wormwood and broom-flower tea before falling exhausted into bed. Next day at dawn, he would begin again. He thought of it as a simple life but a good one.

One wet spring day Charliwill developed a cough. So every time he coughed he broke his rhythm and had to start counting again, which was distressing. The weather grew stormy and changeable, and in the middle of Charliwill's coughing fit, around number twenty seven, a girl called Rhiannon passed by. She was taking a short cut through the forest to visit her grandmother, and as she drew close to a large stone by the side of the path, she heard a voice issue out of it. "Twen — aaach — ooch-ooch oh shid argh — ty seven."

Rhiannon knew immediately that there was a leprechaun counting his treasure under that stone. She was, after all, sixteen years old, and had been to school, so was not totally ignorant of the world. She pressed her mouth against the cool rock and damp moss and whispered:

"If you give me a gold coin I will get you a bottle of my Granny's garlic, horehound and honey cough medicine and leave it on top of the stone when I come back this way tonight."

"Aarch ooch off" was the only reply she got, so she tossed her head primly and went to Granny's for the day. There she had a pleasant time learning how to make cakes for when she was married, and poisoned cakes for when she might want to be unmarried. Granny knew everything that a girl needed to set herself up in life, but Rhiannon did not tell her about Charliwill. Which is a pity, for if she had asked her old Granny's advice this story might have ended differently.

On the way back home she reached the stone in the woods at sunset, and heard a very hoarse voice whispering: "Three thousand three hundred and sixty four, three thousand three hundred and sixty five ..." In the gathering gloom, the exhausted Charliwill had a thought and said "If I give you a golden disc, then there will be only three thousand three hundred and sixty four, and that would be, well it would be ..." and a fit of coughing broke his concentration. Rhiannon smiled to herself in the dark, and said over the stone "I will come back in the morning." All night long she dreamed of gold smothered in cough syrup.

Early in the morning, with her little basket and clean white dress, Rhiannon came to the stone in the forest. This time she pulled a small round blue glass bottle out of the basket, and gently tapped it until the contents gurgled. Charliwill coughed and stopped counting to listen. Rhiannon took the cork slowly out of the bottle, and sniffed delicately at the delicious aroma of garlic, horehound and honey, dissolved in a base of Granny's neat one-hundred-proof rum.

"But if I give you a gold disc for the cough medicine," croaked Charliwill, "that would break my pattern."

"What pattern might that be?" asked Rhiannon innocently.

"The pattern of my counting the gold discs."

"But what do you have them for anyway?"

"To count them. It takes exactly one year."

"You mean one day, surely."

"Ach — ough, no, one year. Three thousand three hundred and sixty five discs is one year."

Rhiannon poured a tiny drop of medicine on to the stone and rubbed it in with the tip of her little finger. She waited for a few moments until Charliwill paused in his counting, and said sweetly.

"If you stopped coughing you could come to market with me."

"What for?" gasped Charliwill in astonishment.

"To buy some new clothes, of course."

"But I never go out."

"You would if you had a new velvet suit of green and yellow, with silver buttons. You'd really want to go out then."

"I'd need shoes."

"Yes, you would, with matching silver buckles."

"And a hat."

"With a broad brim and a feather."

"No ... I can't do it ..." and a fit of coughing and counting came upon him.

Rhiannon thought for a moment.

"No," she said softly, "I suppose that you give up all pleasures for duty. I suppose that you'll have to miss the best, the most pleasant pleasure there is, and just keep on counting."

"And what might that be?" whispered Charliwill, his jaw gaping open in suspense.

"Why, spending, of course."

"Spending! And is that the greatest most pleasant pleasure there is?"

"Oh yes," murmured Rhiannon softly smiling. "Spending and buying is the best combination of pleasures there is, especially when you buy things for yourself."

"And for others? Can you *spend* and *buy* for others too?"

"Well, you can, if you really want to, if you really like them and they can do something for you, but it's not as good as spending on yourself. Come with me to the market and try it out!"

"But I have a terrible bad cough, and I can't go out until I've counted all the gold, and then it will be winter."

"Don't you mean night-time?" asked Rhiannon, then before Charliwill could answer she had a brilliant scintillating idea. "I know, I will *give* you the medicine, and when you are better I'll come with you to market and help you spend your gold!"

So Charliwill had his cough cured and went to market.

Nobody saw him there except Rhiannon, but when she had chosen his suit, and shoes and hat, and he put them on, then everyone saw what a fine fellow he was. And he bought some brushes for his hair, and some shampoo, and a pair of dark glasses. Then he chose a fine black leather bag designed in Italy to put his gold in and threw the old clay pot away, and Rhiannon clapped her hands with glee. He bought her some presents, quite a few, the sort of things a girl cannot be without, and then he cut a proud figure in the main street when he poured gold into her little basket.

Charliwill realized that he had to have a tall mirror on a stand, for adjusting his hat in the morning and straightening the hang of his suit, and to carry this mirror and all the other packages that were accumulating, he bought a smart fast little horse and cart, the latest model with spring suspension. Then he went into the hotel, and bought food and drink for a crowd of new friends, and drank a huge amount of whiskey, which he had never tasted before. Rhiannon helped him into the cart when all the gold was gone, and merrily waved goodbye to him as he lurched away to the forest with packages and chests and boxes piled high and falling off the back.

When Charliwill reached home, it was winter. It was the longest winter anyone had ever known. The wind blew without ceasing, and the ice blanket crept down from the North until it covered the land. People froze and died.

Charliwill did not feel the cold, however, and kept happy by looking at himself in his new mirror. He set his hat and feather at a rakish angle and polished his chunky black shoes. He felt light and strong with his new found freedom, for the power of spending selfishly and using thoughtlessly was upon him, and it was good. He pirouetted before his very own mirror to show off his stylish velvet suit to himself, while outside, among the withered trees sticking up out of the ice, grey wolves howled and crunched on frozen bones. Rhiannon was nowhere to be seen. In the silence that followed the howling, Charliwill wondered if he could still obtain a credit card, now that the gold was all gone.

Two Stories

by Dwina Murphy-Gibb

THE RAINSLUG

"Those wains have to be kept away from thon bog, now, do t'see now, it's not the case of them fallin' into a boghole, naw, sure it's not the case of that at all. It's the horse that would drag them in that they have to have a care of."

The Uncle's face had a way of frowning when he said this that I mind well and old Henry who lived with them would give a wry smile. It was a smile that had no belief in it for anything that the Uncle said and so we would look to old Henry for our reassurances. If the wry smile appeared, we knew that the story the Uncle told was a tall one. And yet, when I cast my mind back, there was many a time when we found out that the stories he told were sane enough, like the time he wanted to save the hay and get it all gathered in before it would rain; there wasn't a cloud in the sky but he had seen a black slug and that to him, y'see, hailed the rain. He picked up this slug, sure it nearly sickened me to see it, and before our very eyes he stuck it on the blackthorn bush. He stuck it on a thorn, the thorn going right through it. I nearly fainted. My brother wasn't bothered but then I got to thinking about that y'know, why he shouldn't be bothered and I had the realization that he was used to sticking worms on hooks for fishing so a thorn was no different to him but I was mortified.

"There," the Uncle had said, "that will keep the rain at bay."

The clouds rolled over soon after, like big grey blankets blocking out the sun.

"Aw, no doubt Tommy is wrong this time." The Aunt had cast a cold eye at the sky. "It'll teem down before we get this hay all in."

The Uncle scythed the hay all day long.

Henry, the Aunt, my brother and myself lapped the hay, grabbing great armfuls and rolling it over in mounds. We didn't stop until suppertime and by then the grey blankets were turning into black ones which the Uncle said were only the night-clouds and old Henry had shaken his head but he hadn't smiled the wry smile then because he had not wanted to see the hay lost either.

That night the thunder we heard was atrocious, the rain that fell on the zinc roof over the scullery was deafening and not one of us slept except for the Uncle. My brother and myself were huddled together.

"So much for the black slug," hissed I to my brother.

The next day, we all traipsed to the field to see the extent of the damage.

The Uncle papped on the pipe and carried on with the work, pitching the laps with a fork into hayrucks and every straw of it was dry as a bone. The big grey blanket still loomed over it all but not one drop of water had touched that field and every patch of green beyond the four stone walls, sodden wet, sodden wet with the rain from the night before. In fact, I mind now that there was a fine drizzle about us but not on us.

We rucked the hay, my brother twisting ropes with a wire hook, ropes made of the hay itself, y'see, and myself bouncing on top of the rucks, trampling it all down.

All day long we worked it. We picked the black ticks off each other before we went in the house and all night long again we listened to the thunder and the pelting of the rain on the galvanized roof.

"The luck can't last two nights like this," I had whimpered between flashes of lightning, flashes that had lit up the room even with my eyes closed and my head under the pillow.

I can't quite mind how the hay was brought in but over the next few days there were a right few neighbours in the house,

Roman Catholics and Protestants alike and some of them moanin' about losing their hay and marvellin' at the Uncle's field being charmed. I mind the horses and carts and a tractor and trailer piled with the rucks taking the hay off to the hayshed and some of the greener stuff going to make silage.

The Uncle had taken us to the field after they'd all gone and y'know, he went straight to the blackthorn bush and in between the puffing on his pipe and an intake of breath, he slid the slug off the thorn and threw it aside. Myself, I could not watch it.

The dark clouds had remained above but now there was some movement that was not obvious, though there nevertheless, and we had to run like divils to get across that stretch of field. The cloudburst that shook itself upon us with a vengeance was like the blast of water y'd need to put out the fires of hell and all the while he was runnin', the Uncle was tittering, a wide smile gripping the pipe still, as the rain doused out the burning baccy, the thin funnel of smoke hissing to a standstill as we fled, fled for our lives, back to the dryness of every other bit of land beyond the stone walls.

That was the kind of man he was.

THE WATERHORSE

"It's the horse that would drag them in that they have to have a care of."

My brother used to dunch me with his elbow and snigger. The idea of a horse dragging us anywhere was so alien to us, never mind thinking of one pulling us into a boghole in a turf-field, we had to laugh.

The only horse on the farm was Bob and the only thing he had ever dragged was a plough, slowly round a field. The cat stretched out on Bob and he didn't even mind her claws. We hung on his neck and tried to play Bucking Bronco on him and he would stand still, shiver his skin and flick flies away with his tail.

My mother said that when she was younger, she had roped

a sledge to him and sent him off down hill. The sledge had gone faster than he and hit his back legs and he had bolted, tossing her into the river at the bottom but he had been a roan at the time. Now, he had slowed down and trudging round the field with the plough was almost too much for him. To say that we could be dragged through a bog and dumped in a boghole was an invention of an idea by the Uncle to keep us away from the bogholes. They were dangerous things, right enough, liable to suck a one under, with the bog-gas and the rancid water overcoming the senses. Dangerous especially for a child so we listened to the Uncle and the Aunt and we never ventured out there by ourselves.

Two summers passed when we stayed at the farm and on the third summer, old Henry arrived to live with them, old Henry with the wry smile who listened but didn't heed a word of the Uncle, old Henry who liked to sit and watch the butter being churned, and shuffled to help the Aunt with the pails of water from the well, the well that was on the other side of the bog.

"He's got a good strong arm on him, worth his weight in salt he is. He can put his hand to anything inside or outside the house. Declare to goodness, I haven't a notion how we managed without him before and y'know he even blacks the range for me, a filthy job if ever there was one."

It was this same year that my brother and myself heard about the waterhorse.

"Now, you two wains keep away from thon bog. It has been teemin' this last week and the lower land is awash with the water. Them bogholes are full and the waterhorse is about. Now, let me tell you, that waterhorse has mercy on no-one, no-one, do y'hear me? She'd drag you in as soon as look at you."

We both nodded. This was a new one. Could we have been mistaken all along and the horse he had been referring to in the past had been something other than Bob? For myself, I had a chill chase down my spine, a sudden quickening of heartbeat and by the look on my brother's face he too was startled.

Later that day, when the Aunt was rolling out dough, I broached the subject.

"Auntie May, what does a waterhorse look like?"

She pounded the dough and rolled it out again, taking her time over the answer.

"Y'don't want to be askin' me that, dear. It's not a thing I'd be inclined to talk about."

I persisted, "Have you ever seen one? Do they only live in bogholes?"

"Thank the One above that's the only place they abide and may he be fit to see that I never set eyes on one either. Tommy's mother was supposed to have seen one, aye, I believe she took to her bed for a week after it too, though y'know, she was inclined to a bit of dotage as she got older so y'wouldn't know whether to believe her half of the time. She had the doctor out to see her and he swore blind that she was in shock so something must have afrighted her. Now, you quit askin' me questions and let me get this batch of bread done before the men come back."

I bided my tongue until she got the bread in the oven. I waited until she got the chicken gruel made and I offered to pound it in the bucket for her. When she carried it out to feed the hens, I followed, then as she collected the eggs, I again brought up the subject.

"Auntie May, did she happen to say what the waterhorse looked like?"

"Are you still harpin' on about that waterhorse? And I suppose you're not going to let up till I give you an answer?" She raised her eyebrows and fluttered her eyelashes in only a way the Aunt could. I smiled and nodded, knowing I had caught her in the right mood.

"She said that when she passed the bog, on her way back from the well, there was the sound of splashing and flapping water, like a wave that would slap against a cliff-face and tumble back. She thought at first that it was the motion of the water in the pails and Tommy swears it was that to this day. Then, all of a sudden, didn't she hear this terrible squealing sound, like a horse whinnying in pain and, with that, the buckets flew out of her hand and sure didn't she see a big green and black serpent, snaky thing with the looks of a horse about its head and it tryin' to drag her into the hole. Aye, the way she described it, I'm surprised she didn't get heart failure. Mind you, there were a few dents in the buckets that we had no explanation for. One of them had a bend in it that a crowbar and three men couldn't have made, so Tommy said anyway. Now, you be a good wee cuttie and stay away from thon bog and keep wee Raymond away from it too."

Wee Raymond and myself had every intention of staying away from it. Now and again, we would go to the edge and peer over the stone wall, just to see if we could catch a glimpse of the thing. Something as fierce and glorious a monster as that warranted a look, if nothing else. Even if it was only a tall tale, there was a mystery about it and all our games from then on were spirited with its presence.

One day, the ducks flapping about in the duckpond made me jump nearly a mile high. Any bit of splashing water had that effect but, in a way, I was disappointed upon discovering that it was only ducks.

Everything went quiet until the end of the summer, just before we were due to return home to the parents in the village. There was one evening that was a very wet one. The Aunt had kept us in to help her churn the butter, a lovely yellow butter, the likes of which I have never seen since nor am I likely to see again. It was pelting down outside but by the time we had wound the handle until our arms were tired, there came a lull in the air. It was grey and quiet, not a titter of a bird to be heard. All of a sudden, in the midst of this stillness, we heard a terrible cry like the cry of a hare caught in a trap, y'know that half-human type of wail. The Aunt's face went as white as a sheet.

"Lord, save us all! What was that?"

We knew then it was something serious because the Aunt, y'see, was very religious and would never take the Lord's name in vain, not in front of us anyway.

With that, the door flew open, a hen in the scullery squawked with a great deal of flapping of wings and old Henry came tearing in. He had the look about him of having seen the devil himself. Hot on his heels was the Uncle, having heard the commotion from the byre and racing in to see what was wrong.

Old Henry could hardly speak but he motioned for the Aunt to get us out of the room. Reluctantly and with some fear we went into a room just off the kitchen and quietly kept the door open a crack. In the midst of all the kerfuffle, no-one noticed that the door was open ajar. We saw and heard all and wished that we hadn't.

Henry's jacket was shredded at the back and he was covered in a smelly greenish mossy looking slime, the stench of which was nauseating.

My knees were trembling and I knew what was coming but didn't want to hear. Nothing would have induced myself or the brother to close the door though.

The Aunt was peeling off the clothes from Henry's back whilst the Uncle went to get the methylated spirits. We knew then that there was an injury of sorts but Henry was emphatic about not getting the doctor.

"There'll be no doctor come to see this, do ye hear that? No doctor."

We craned our necks to see the affliction.

Henry's skin was as pale as a pig's back and we could see the join at the neck where the skin became a weathered brown. There was a definite line where the collar would be. The Aunt stood aside for a moment to reach for cotton wool and then we saw it. From one side of his back to the other, there were long deep scratches, like the marks of claws and something on one shoulder that looked like a massive bite. This was bleeding and the Aunt was slapping the methylated spirits on like there was no tomorrow. Henry was yelling at her and then it looked like she was rubbing butter in, or some such stuff. It was the exact shade of the butter we'd churned, whatever it was.

Old Henry was half-sobbing and I had a terrible soreness in my own throat trying to keep back my own tears of fright.

"Sure I'm lucky to have me life, aw, indeed, sure luck's not in it, lucks not in it at all," he said, his head in his hands.

"Did y'fall in then, trip up or somethin'?" The Aunt patted his hand.

"Not a bit of it, woman, sure wasn't I dragged in? Big as you, me, the lot of us put together! I didn't rightly see it as much as felt it ... sure what am I talkin' about? I'm a grown man ... not prone to madness either, you know that, Tommy?" he turned to the Uncle, who papped on the pipe and nodded. Old Henry sat up stiffly.

"I'll be rightly in a wee while. You were quick to get the wains out of the way, May. They'll have to be kept from them bogholes but I wouldn't want to put the fear in them either y'know, the wee cub and cuttie would be likely to get nightmares. I never believed in the waterhorse before now but I smelt her and felt her and that's the last time I'll cut across that field in a storm and I'd urge the two of yous to stay away from there too when the water is high. Now, we'll have a cup of char and not dwell on the matter anymore. Me nerves are a trifle frayed, aye, and me body is not far behind."

I heard the Uncle commenting on the weather and while the Aunt rattled the kettle, I carefully closed the door so that they never knew we had.

My brother and myself were shaking, shaking with the reality of it, the awe and the terror of it all, then catching each other's eye, we shook with giggles, laughter, strained hysterical laughter until our sides pinched and our pants were wet. It was the only release, the only sane thing we could have done at that time.

On Macha's Mound

by Diana Paxson

A cold wind was blowing up from the border, rippling across the grass that covered Emain Macha and swirling the crows like blown cinders out of the ash trees. Earlier it had been raining, but now the westering sun sent long rays beneath the retreating clouds. Mary Macrory stood on the crest of the mound, the white skirt of her uniform flapping around her knees. Hair blew across her face, and she yanked off the elastic that held it, turning so that the wind whipped out the long silky strands and kindled them to flame.

Eastward, the roofs of Armagh caught the sunset, the spires of the Catholic cathedral and the tower of the Protestant church glowing alike. She could just glimpse the hospital where she had spent the afternoon assisting the doctors to stitch up the leg of a little girl caught in cross-fire between the British soldiers and the Provisional IRA. Belfast was the centre of British power, but Armagh, the ancient capital, was known as the Catholic stronghold. Her work there seemed to belong to a different world when she stood on the mound. But even here the wind hissed and muttered in the trees. There was no peace in Ulster: not in the earth and not in the air and certainly not in the hearts of men.

"Aren't you cold up there?"

Mary turned, squinting into the wind. At first, with the sunset behind him, all she could tell was that the man who had hailed her was tall, with ruffled tawny-fair hair. He was wearing countryman's gear — an ancient jumper and corduroys jammed into muddy Wellingtons — but his voice was educated. A student, most likely, and hadn't she learned the look of them these past years, with the archaeologists from Belfast forever burrowing into the old mound?

"Not to me — " she said. "My grandfather minds yon kiosk and tells tales of the Red Branch heroes to the tourists when they come. I've played on this hill since I was five years old."

"You must be Mary, then — " said the stranger. "Your grandfather told me to look out for a lass proud as Macha herself watching over her mound."

Mary found herself grinning in reply, for she could hear the very lilt of her grandfather's voice softening the clipped English of his words.

"And who are you, to be making so free with my name?"

"Rob Morann at your service — " he smiled.

"From Queen's University?" she looked up at him. But on closer inspection, she could see that his hair was beginning to retreat from his high brow. He was not young, then, despite the hint of uncertainty in his eyes.

"As an undergraduate," he looked around him almost hungrily. "But I got my doctorate at Oxford, then a job in York." He took a deep breath. "Now that I'm here, I begin to think I've been too long away."

"Then you'll have come about the new Visitors' Centre — " she frowned towards the field on the other side of the road, where a framework of steel rods gleamed raw against the red soil.

"Don't you approve?" he asked. "Remember, the buildings will be covered up — by the time six months have passed green grass will be growing over the new mound and you'll hardly know it's there. Or are you objecting because they hired an English firm to set up the exhibits inside?"

Mary forced a smile. "Or that the new Centre will take from my grandfather the job he's loved so long? Oh, I understand all the reasons for building a great fancy place took out of the mound. They've got Newgrange down in the Republic, and we need an attraction of our own, something to tout in the papers that's not another bombing, so the tourists won't be afraid to spend their money here!"

"But you don't want to see more loud Americans crawling all over Macha's mound ..." he said softly. She glanced at him under her lashes, grateful for the understanding. "Well," he turned to survey the countryside, "it's better than cows. And the tourists will not be the only customers — it's the school groups they're hoping for, so the children can understand there's something here that belongs to us all ..."

"Navan Fort ... n'Emhain ... Isamonis ... the sacred hill. Its earth is red with the blood of heroes, and every stone's a treasure," said Mary. Through the soles of her feet she could feel the life in the land. If she were ever forced to leave, surely she would wither and die.

"And a story — " he added. Their eyes met, and she felt an odd pulse begin to beat in her throat.

He's one who can hear the old music, she thought then, *not like the dry sticks who sit about counting potsherds and worrying about their fellowships. But it has not made him happy.*

"You're working for those York people who are doing the exhibits, but you're Irish — " It was not quite a question.

"I am," his gaze had gone inward. "Though there've been times, these past years, when I wondered. The Heritage Trust brought me back as a consultant."

"And what are you knowing that those fine lettered folk up at Queen's University do not, that they had to drag you all the way back to your home?" she said softly. It was not so surprising that he had left Ulster — Catholic or Protestant, too many of their brightest children lost hope and moved away. What was unusual was that he had returned.

"Druids ...," he answered. "I study the People of Wisdom, to learn what they did, and sometimes why — "

She stared at him. To make such a claim was pride or foolishness, surely. "And do you know why they built the great henge of wood here, and filled it with stones, and then burned it all to ash before they covered it with the turf of the mound?" Mary asked then.

She had seen the photos they took of the excavations before they filled it back in, with the spoked patterns in the great heap of stones. And she had heard the men from Belfast talking about postholes and pollen counts and carbon-14 till she could mutter the figures like a litany. But what did it all have to do with the brightly-clad figures who walked sometimes in her dreams?

Dr. Morann was staring at the green turf of the mound as if his gaze could penetrate to the layers of rock below. Absently he pushed back the thinning hair at his brow.

"Perhaps — " he said softly.

"Well, I will take your word for it that you know whatever can be learned by reading in one old book what was said in another. But I do not see how you can be knowing men's hearts without walking the same earth as they did, and breathing the same air — "

"I thought I could," he said quietly, "I thought I could stay in England and read my books and escape all the pain. But since I began to work on this project I've had odd dreams. I had to come back and see."

"Poor lad!" She reached out to him in unexpected sympathy. He started, flushing as his attention snapped back to the here-and-now.

"Forgive me — " he shivered suddenly. "I don't usually run on so. By now even you must find the wind cold — why don't I walk you back to the kiosk, and then I'll be on my way."

Mary smiled to herself as they made their way down the slope of the mound. Despite his learning, there was a need in him that made him seem very young to her. She thought he would be back again.

*

"Honoured One, the first of the sledges is full of stones. Does the driver wait for the others, or start for the bruiden now?

Moranos squinted at the sky. The sun had slipped beneath the clouds and was sending its long rays to touch the stones of the old mound with gold. The ox-drawn sledges moved so slowly, the first would not reach the rath where they had erected the sacred hall before nightfall. The Druid turned back to the foreman, a man of the older race.

"Do you send off the first of them now, and turn the other teams out to graze." He spoke carefully, avoiding the convolutions of speech he had laboured so long to acquire. The man nodded and stumped across the muddy ground, round-headed, broad through the chest and bandy-legged next to the long-limbed warriors the king had sent with the Druid as a guard.

His grey gaze went back to the heap of boulders. Time had stripped the turf from the mound already, and the weathered limestone was jeweled with lichen. Somewhere in the centre they would find the tomb. For generations these rocks had covered it, absorbing the power buried within. Moranos had no doubt of their magic, only of their numbers. The light deepened. Three cranes winged towards the nearby marshes, curving necks part of a broken spiral, arched wings beating the air. Moranos rubbed his hand across his shaven brow in a gesture that had become habitual when he was thinking. Had he calculated correctly? Would the stones fill the bruiden? He frowned, his mind busy assessing space and volume. Then he realized that the men were staring past him and turned.

A woman was watching him; no, it was a queen that was standing there, with gold on her neck and arms. But it would not take a Druid's learning to know that, even without the ornaments. The royalty was in the woman herself, in that skin the colour of new milk, and the fires that burned in the dark waves of her hair.

"Lady — " he gave her the salute with which he would have honoured a wife of King Equos. "Your presence blesses us."

"Does it indeed? Is it not instead a curse I should be laying on you for disturbing the old ones' mound?"

She stepped closer and he realized that he must look down to meet her dark gaze — there was a force in the woman that had made her seem larger. Of the old race she might be, but in her, the strong ribcage was a fitting foundation for breasts that thrust against the pale wool of her gown. A verse shaped itself in his inner awareness — *White thou art as a swan in her swimming, red as the heights of the hills in the dawn ...*

He knew her now. She was Macha, like her mother and

grandmother before her, goddess to her tribe, the Royal Woman of the People of the Fire. Generations had passed since his people had first swept through the North with their swift chariots and iron swords, but the old race clung to their land, and in time the two peoples had settled to an uneasy co-existence in which the Gaels ruled but were never quite sure of their sovereignty.

"It is not a destruction I am performing here," he said softly, "but a transformation. With these stones we will make of the old royal dun a holy place where all our peoples can join. Is not that a deed worthy of your blessing?"

She crossed her arms beneath her breasts, pulling the fabric of her gown taut so that he could see the shape of her nipples through the thin cloth, and Moranos felt his own flesh quicken. He took a deep breath, calling on disciplines he had not needed since he was young to curb his response. It was natural to desire a woman like this one, but he was not used to being subject to the same lusts that drove other men.

"My foremother dwelt on that hill and fought for the right to rule; she made her nephews build the ramparts of her dun on the height beyond. Now your king rules there and the queen's house is no more. The time for a warrior-queen to claim sovereignty is over, and the high places are held by your kin. But I am still Macha; I am still responsible for this land. There are those among my people who cry out against you, who say that we were first here, and should rule. They call this thing you are doing a desecration and say that it is not the bruiden we should be burning."

Moranos stiffened, repressing the temptation to look around for his guard. He had been told that it was all arranged; that the king had paid many cattle to the chieftains of the Fir Bolg to recompense them for the stones. But did the chieftains speak for their young warriors? He was a Druid and had studied the old tales; the rage of those who felt themselves without power could be a powerful thing. But there was no hatred in the dark gaze that held his.

"I wish to make the hill sacred ...," he said hoarsely. "All my life I have studied how to make a new holy place that will belong equally to the Sons of Mil and to the Fir Bolg, and link both to the tribe of Danu in the Otherworld. Hard it was to bring the king around to my way of thinking, but Lugos himself put into my mind the pattern of the oak posts in the great henge, like the spokes of a wheel, for the great father to look down on."

"And the Goddess?" Macha asked softly.

"She shall enclose it all, when we turf over the mound ..."

"So — the stones that you take from here shall be repatterned, the substance within uniting old and new. I begin to understand."

Moranos' breath caught as the woman smiled. She reached out and placed her palm against his chest, and he realized that he had moved towards her. The warmth of her hand was kindling a fire beneath his ribcage that could set his flesh aflame.

"Not now, my tall one, my man of learning. There are those among my people who would slay you for touching me, as they already hate you for digging into this mound. Be patient — my heart tells me that a time for us to go into one bed together will come."

Moranos watched her stride away, the sway of her round hips shifting the folds of her mantle, but his pulse fluttered no less than its fringes as he thought about what she had promised him.

*

The Visitors' Centre at Navan had been long in the planning. But once building started, the structure rose quickly. Soon, the steel framing was hidden by massive pourings of concrete and the roof slabs covered the gap, muffling a little the perpetual clatter and whine of machines. Like the mound of Macha itself, the outer appearance of the new Centre would be vastly different from what lay within.

For Mary Macrory, there was a dream-like quality to the passing of that spring, especially in the evenings, when the din and dust of construction had faded and peace returned to the hill. Her grandfather complained about the noise, but by the time Mary got home from her shift at the hospital the site was always deserted. When her day had been especially wearing she would climb Macha's mound and sit there, listening to the wind in the trees. It was not until early summer, after the workers had mortared the great facing stones into the entryway, that she again encountered Rob Morann.

"It is warm enough this evening — " she called down to him. "Come and enjoy the view." For several days now the weather had held fair. Marching weather, the Protestants called it when they put on their bowler hats and orange sashes to celebrate the Battle of the Boyne on the twelfth of July. But from this vantage point, the illusion of peace enfolded the land.

For a moment he hesitated, his hand on the gate. Then he let it bang shut behind him and began to climb the hill. He was still in corduroys, but this time his jacket was slung over one shoulder. Underneath he wore a T-shirt bearing an interlaced design from the Book of Kells.

"I'll not ask how you have been," he looked at her for a moment with a puzzling intensity, then away. "You are clearly blooming."

Mary raised one eyebrow. She wished she could say the same of him, but despite the healthy tan he had gained from being so much outdoors, there were shadows beneath his eyes as if he were not sleeping well.

"I can see that the building is going well," she said pleasantly.

"Well enough — " he shrugged. "We should be ready to open at the beginning of August."

" — At Lughnasadh, when they held the games here for Macha and for Lugh." Mary laughed. "Did they think of that when they made the plan?"

"I don't know." A little colour came into his face. "Have you eaten?" he asked diffidently. "Will you come have dinner with me at the pub down the road?"

She stared at him, thinking of all the reasons why she should not go. But as he watched her she realized that the expression she had seen in his eyes was hunger — not the need of the body, despite his invitation — but a hunger of the soul.

*

The Red Branch inn was neither particularly old nor charming, though it had been newly tarted up with fake thatching and brightly coloured pictures of Cuchulain and the Ulster heroes to prepare for the influx of tourists the new Centre was expected to bring. The menu, though, was fried fish with the traditional thick Irish chips and mushy peas, the usual lavish assortment of bottles weighted the bar, and the men leaning against it were the lads Mary had grown up with, or their fathers and brothers, drinking up the week's pay. One or two lifted a hand in greeting as Morann escorted her past the bar to the dining room, eyeing him curiously.

Mary felt a betraying flush rise in her cheeks and turned her face away. They knew her well enough, but Rob Morann would be a stranger. The English voice might make them suspicious, but the T-shirt would confuse them. In Ulster, it was the Catholics who learned the traditional arts of the Gael. And it was not as if she were marrying the man, whatever he might be. They were going to have a civilized dinner, that was all.

"You said that the building was on schedule, but you were not sounding happy," Mary said when their food had come. "What's wrong?"

He shrugged, his grey gaze flicking to her face and then away. "I'm not quite sure. The narration for the exhibits is done, and I'm working on the script for the video. On academic grounds the work is well enough. Even Professor Mallory approves."

"But surely that should please you — " she began.

"There have been ... objections," he said carefully.

Mary raised one eyebrow. "Lad — this is Ulster. Whatever you do there'll be someone to say no. And hasn't it been that way from the beginning, with the archaeologists arguing over the ethics of disturbing the cowpats in the fields?"

Morann's lips curved briefly, then he shook his head.

"It's a little more serious than that. The word has got around finally about what the Centre is intended to be — "

"A celebration of our common heritage — " she quoted from the report, "'far back beyond the unhappy divisions of more recent history ...'"

"Yes. Well," he sighed, "there are some on the Protestant side who don't like the idea of celebrating the Gaelic heritage. And there are Catholics who think that only good Irishmen from the Republic should be telling the story. Neither side likes the idea that the project might actually be a force for unity!"

He cleared his throat, embarrassed by his own vehemence. In silence they finished eating. "It's late," he said finally. "I should be getting you home." He came around to pull out her chair.

"I understand what you are talking about," Mary said as they walked back to the car. The night had clouded over, hiding the stars. "That's why I agreed to have dinner with you. There are times I could weep for what's become of this poor country, with neither side willing to give an inch, seeing only their differences. Those lads in the bar — now they've seen me with you they'll be checking. I didn't ask you which foot you dig with before I accepted your invitation, but I grew up with these people, and they will want to know."

For a moment he stared at her in blank incomprehension. Then, clearly, he remembered the old reference to the different kinds of spades used by the Catholic Gaels and the Scotch-Irish Protestant farmers, and his gaze hardened.

"Do you know, I'd almost forgotten that question, living away. Tell them I'm an atheist — " Morann said bitterly, "or a pagan. That would be closer to the truth."

Mary shook her head. "You know very well that the Troubles have little to do with what you believe in. Catholics and Protestants are tribes, not religions. It's not faith that matters here, but power."

He sighed. "Strange, isn't it, how romantic it is to read about king Conchobar's wars with Maeve of Connaught, and how terrible it is when the Provos battle the UDA. Two thousand years have passed and we're still killing each other — only the weapons have changed."

"You're a Protestant, aren't you?" she said into the silence.

"My parents were," he said finally. "My older brother joined the Constabulary, and was shot one night coming home from taking a woman in labour to the hospital. The Provos apologized for that one — the woman was a Catholic, you see. But my father was never the same after. He and my mother emigrated to Canada ten years ago. In a way I left as well — I retreated into my books, got scholarships all the way to Oxford and thought I'd never come home again. And then they offered me this project, and I thought, maybe ... just maybe, I could help things to change ..."

Once more, Mary found herself wanting to reach out to him. But his voice had become very English and she knew he would not welcome it. And even in the carpark there might be Catholic eyes, watching for what they would consider her treachery. She saw only the shape of him, silhouetted against the light, but something in the way his head was bowed caught at her heart. *He is wounded ...* she thought then, *the power that should be in him is locked away.*

Morann leaned past her to open the car door. She pulled back, then glanced quickly to see if he had been hurt by her withdrawal. But as he went back around to his side he gave no sign of having noticed. She felt moisture on her cheek and wiped it away, but it was only rain.

*

With dawn the rest of the Druids would be coming to preside over the laying of the stones, resplendent in brightly chequered cloaks with golden fringes. But tonight, the fresh hide of a sacrificed bull was Moranos' covering. Tomorrow the air would be sweet with the mellow sweet tones of the harps, pulsing with the heartbeat of drums. Tonight, it was his own heart that was drumming, and the wind in the thatching that made music for his song.

Moranos sat cross-legged at the base of the oak centre-post with the wet hide wrapped around him, facing the door-way. Behind the trees at the foot of the slope the moon would soon be rising. Moment by moment the rectangular opening grew brighter, the darkness that enclosed him more profound. The Druid straightened, controlling his breathing by the disciplines his masters had taught him, willing his heartbeat to slow. Breathing in and out he lost himself in the beauty of Number.

Awareness of time receded, until suddenly a shaft of moonlight struck down through the doorway. Moranos opened his eyes. At first the brightness only intensified the shadows around him, but as the moon lifted fully over the treetops the lengthening beams penetrated inward, striking from post to post, silvering the scattering of stones that littered the roughly-leveled floor.

Moranos drew a deep breath, centering his awareness within his body, pulling up strength from the soil. His skin began to tingle as if some presence were flowing along with the moonlight into the mound. It was time to do the work he had come for.

"A noble hostel is the bruiden of Macha, perfect in proportion. Firm it is founded, strong shall it stand ..." he sang,

> "House fashioned of oak, fairest of dwellings —
> walls of the whitest, seven the spaces
> traced twixt them and the kingpole,
> aisles three in that hall ..."

More than two hundred oaken posts had gone into the building of the bruiden, arranged in five rings around the centrepost. Each and every one of them had a meaning carved in ogham down its edges. Moranos needed no light to see them — the plan of the bruiden existed in his mind in all its perfection. He had supervized the setting of each post; he knew them all by name. And so, as the moonlight flowed through the doorway like a mist of power, he chanted them into his song.

Dim in the gloaming, the stag in the deep dales,
Gales gust on the hilltops, from the heights soars the
eagle,
Regal his flight, overlooking the land."

Pattern and number and design flowed forth from the lips of the Druid as they had flowered first in his mind and then in physical form. The bruiden was more than a structure of wood and reed, it was a spell.

"In duns, din of warriors, spear on shield resounding,
In round raths, fair women weave the bright wool,
Full of kine are the meadows, their milk everflowing,
Growing and golden, full of grain are the fields ..."

Glimmering light filled the pillared spaces around him as he sang. Time lost meaning — he sang for moments, he sang for an age of the world. But at last there came a point beyond the reach even of this exaltation. The words made a single tone that reverberated through the charged air. And yet the incantation was not finished. He was holding the pattern in place by the power of his will, but despite the solidity of the building around him, it was not yet anchored in physical reality. What must he do to establish it so firmly that it could become a bridge between the worlds?

In that moment of awareness, when his soul hung suspended between need and reality, a shape appeared in the doorway, as if it had precipitated from the moonlight. Moranos' voice wavered. The figure moved forward and he heard, low and unmistakable, a woman's laugh.

"Man of Wisdom, I salute you. You have been making a mighty magic here." Her voice was only a breath, but it carried clearly in the charged air. He strained to make out her features but could see only the glitter of embroidery in her mantle and the gleam of the ornaments on her neck and wrists and brow.

"That is so, and yet not well enough," his voice cracked and he strove to control it. "This hall must endure throughout time and through all the worlds."

"I know it," she came closer. "That is why I am coming to you. To complete the work you must invoke an older magic — I am that magic." She turned, and he heard the soft slither of cloth as she unpinned her cloak and let it fall. It was all she wore. His breath caught. Her body was a white glimmer in the shadows, all shining curves and enchanting hollows.

"If you would root this bruiden in the land of the Ulaid," she said, "you must come through me ..."

Moranos recognized the Royal Woman of the People of the Fire. But the woman who stood before him was something more — she was Macha the great queen, incarnation of her foremothers' power, and beyond that, she was for him in this moment the living presence of the Lady who was the land. His head spun. Moranos had dreamed of her; he desired her above all things, but he could not move.

Once more Macha laughed, looking down at him. Then she knelt and took his face between the palms of her two hands and kissed his lips sweetly and long. Her fire flared through him then and the power to serve her rose up within him. He put his arms around her and they lay down together and their bed was the holy earth of Eriu.

*

It was a long time after, an age of the world it seemed, when Moranos became aware of his own separate being once more. Moonlight no longer flowed in through the door — the waxing moon would be near to seeing by now. But there was still light. The doorway had been a rectangle of silver; now the light it shaped was fire. Torchlight flared and darted outside, and where there had been silence, he could hear raised voices.

Macha stirred in his arms and lifted herself on one elbow, listening. "Are they folk of yours," she asked, "part of the ceremony?"

He shook his head. "The king assigned guards, but they were set to watch the outer edge of the hill." He felt a sudden tension in her body, and an answering flicker of alarm pebbled his skin.

The shouting sharpened, and Moranos heard weapons clash. He scrambled to his feet, but the woman was before him. Before he could stop her, Macha pushed through the doorway, naked as she had lain in his arms.

"Hold!" her voice rang across the clamor.

The confusion of light and movement before them stilled. Men's faces were contorted by fury, torchlight glanced from drawn swords. He recognized the lean grace of Equos' warriors, and the stockier figures of the men who opposed them. But they were all staring at white flesh turned golden by the firelight, at firm breasts and the sweet curve of hip and thigh.

"Put away your swords," Macha spoke more softly without losing the note of command. "This is sacred ground."

"That is it not," one of her own people found his voice at last. "It was sacred ground that yon priest destroyed. Why should we honour his magic?"

"Then honour mine!" Macha stared him down. "Why else do you think I came here but to hallow this hill so that we can join the new magic with the old, and both our peoples be remembered?" There was a little stir among the attackers as an older man pushed to the forefront to face her. The tattoos that covered his burly body were blurred by old scars.

"Lady — I think you came here to serve the oak priest's lust!" A low growl of agreement echoed him.

"And if I did, is it not my right to choose?" Macha challenged. "Have you forgotten who I am?"

"It is not I who have forgotten it," said the warrior. "I did not lift my tail like a mare in season to be mounted by my enemy. What did he buy you with, lies or gold?"

A wave of colour — not shame, he thought, but fury — pulsed through Macha's pale skin. "It was a sacred thing," she began.

"It was sacrilege!" he retorted. "You know the penalty. Stand aside." He lifted his spear. The Gaelic warriors recovered their wits and tried to thrust the men who opposed them aside.

"That I will not! It was my choice to come here — "

"Then you shall die first and the man after," the warrior said furiously. His arm swung back, but as he released the spear one of the Gaels rammed into him and the weapon went wide. It was one of the others, not so close to the enemy, whose cast pierced Macha's white breast and knocked her backward into Moranos' arms.

The force of it slammed them against the doorpost. Still holding her, he slid to the ground.

"Macha — " he bent over her, reaching for the spear. Her hand closed on his with surprising strength, stopping him. Her eyes were wide, and as she drew breath, blood bubbled from her lips. Moranos went cold all over; he had seen men struck through the lungs before.

"Bury me — " she whispered, "in the mound."

Unable to speak, he nodded. The Druids had been debating whether a sacrifice would be needed to complete the magic. Even in the first moments of his grief he knew that Macha's blood would indeed hallow the mound. She sighed a little and her gaze went inward. Moranos clutched at her shoulders.

"Wait for me! Wait for me in the Blessed Isles!"

Slowly, it seemed, she focused on his face. "We ... will meet ... again ..." He waited, but she could say no more. He was still watching when the spirit slid out of her body on a last, bubbling breath, and the meaning faded from her eyes.

*

"Mary, my dear, I am sorry — " Rob Morann looked down at the piece of paper she had handed him. The letter was such a small thing to carry so much hatred — only a single, badly-typed, page. It had not been signed, but it did not need to be. The threat was clear. "I never meant to cause you any grief. I wasn't thinking when I asked you to come out with me."

Mary took it back and crushed it in her hand, gazing at the shadowed walls of the atrium in the new Visitors' Centre so that she would not have to look at it again. The building was the only place she had been able to think of where they might talk safely when Morann had called. Even though it was she who had warned him that one side or the other might object to their friendship, she had not really believed that the Provos would order her not to see him, as if she were selling herself for English gold. It was not fear that brought the high colour to her cheeks, but fury.

"I knew the risk. It is not yourself that should be bearing the blame." Mary thrust the crumpled paper into her pocket. "But now that we are here, let us get some good of it. Will you show me what you have done? Already I am impressed," she said, changing the subject determinedly. "Just to come in here is like going into a mound!" Indeed, she had felt odd ever since she entered — there was a sense of pressure inside the building that was not unpleasant but strange, as if she were truly underground.

"This is only the outer circle — " Morann's voice became more English as he retreated into technicalities. "It includes offices and the coffee shop. The exhibits are farther in." They began to move towards the tall timber posts that flanked the second set of doors. "We have just finished installing the video. Would you like to see?"

The empty auditorium was a circle within a circle. Mary's nostrils flared at the scent of new cloth. She moved silently over the carpeting to the last row of seating and as the lights began to dim sat down. Softly at first, and then with a piercing intensity that brought tears to her eyes, the music of uillean pipes filled the air. In rounded Irish script the words "The Otherworld" appeared.

As the titles began to stream across the screen, Morann slipped into a seat beside her. "It will run automatically now."

But Mary was half-tranced already, and as the hero-tales of the Red Branch and the Táin flickered to life before her, she found herself drifting deeper and deeper into a world which seemed more real to her than her own.

"Well, that's all of it," said the man beside her. "You already know all about the archaeology, so I don't need to show you the exhibit, but you should see the display that illustrates the building of the mound."

What was he talking about? She understood the words but not their meaning. Blinking, she let him help her from the chair — so soft — and lead her from the hall. There was some wondrously smooth stuff on the floor. She looked down, a part of her mind providing the words "indoor/outdoor carpet" while the rest stared in amazement.

The man was still babbling. "Rob Morann," that other part of her mind supplied a name for him, but she knew him already, as Moranos. Why was he dressed so oddly? And what was this place, with its coloured floor and its walls so smooth. Had they come to the Otherworld?

"And you can see here," he pointed to one of the cases, "a model of the bruiden as it was just before they began to fill it with stones — "

"You did it, then? I remember only that the men of the Fire Clan came," she said slowly. "They did not want the magic to go forward. I tried to stop them and they turned on me. I remember ... now I remember the spear!" She turned to him, feeling once more that dreadful weight and the beginnings of pain.

The man was staring at her as if she were speaking a foreign language. She reached out to him, remembering how his body had felt against her own. He jerked as she touched him, and then she saw in his face a dawning wonder and his eyes became the eyes of the Moranos that she knew.

He gripped her arms, his face working. "You are Macha! But you died!" His fingers dug in painfully, as if he were trying to reassure himself of her reality. "He — I — dreamed of you!" He blinked, and she saw the uncertainties of the scholar giving way to the serenity of the Druid. "I did what you asked, beloved — I laid your body in the mound. And then we burned it — the flames licked the very stars and the posts glowed like pillars of gold. I saw the bruiden pass into the Otherworld."

He stared around him, and she saw her own confusion reflected in his eyes. But now she was beginning to get her bearings, the two sets of memories settling into place as the spirit accepted them.

"I am Macha ... and I am Mary ... and you are Moranos and

Morann, a man of wisdom then and now. Druids have always taught that the spirit is eternal. Why are you surprised?"

"It has been so long," he said ruefully. "It is not often given to men to remember ... Is it because I have found you again that we are able to do so now?"

Macha moved closer, and very gently he kissed her. She remembered the charged silence of the bruiden, and moonlight flowing through the door. *Does this place need to be consecrated,* she wondered, *as we blessed the other one*? There was a reason she should not do that, her modern self remembered, but the Macha who was here now was as scornful of any who might question her choices as she had been all those centuries ago.

She pulled back, looking up at him, but before she could speak, a sound from outside made her turn. Moranos' gaze sharpened, together they started towards the entry. A car door slammed; they heard a mutter of voices.

"Are they folk of yours?" The words died on her lips. She had asked this before.

"Stay behind me," he answered. "I will not let them hurt you again."

A voice came more clearly. "I don't like this, Johnnie — there's a light on inside — "

"Automatic, no doubt. These university types don't care how much bleedin' money they spend." The second voice had a nasal edge to it, as if the speaker were a Belfast man.

"But there might be someone inside. There was a car parked up the road — "

"Bad luck to them, then," a third man growled. "Get the tins out of the boot, we've not much time."

Her skin prickled with alarm as Moranos slid open the dark glass door. There were four men outside, arrested in mid-motion as yellow light spilled across the grass.

One of the men straightened, black-haired and burly, bad teeth showing as he grinned. "Well now, you might call it trash removal, or you might call it reclaiming the ground."

"That's petrol they've got there," whispered Macha as Mary's memories identified the tins.

"Do you still burn folk in their houses then?" Moranos frowned. "But you have no enemies here — "

"This building is an enemy!" the dark man spat on the ground. "An abomination where poor bloody sods can worship the dead. Old gods or old saints, it's all idolatry!"

"This project is funded by the government," Morann's voice had become very English. "It has been approved at the highest levels — "

"The more fools they. Can't they see it's fair subversive?" said the one called Johnnie. "Get the kiddies all mooning after old legends — old *Irish* legends — and they'll be voting to join the Republic first thing you know."

Mary's eyes widened. She had assumed these men were IRA, but it was clear now that they were on the other side.

"That is not true. If you had ever read anything but football scores, you would know that Ulster, God help her, has been at war with the other provinces of Ireland more often than not. In any case, it's not for you to decide!" snapped Morann. "Go now, and I will not bring charges against you."

The dark-haired man shook his head.

"A lot of nerve you've got, making threats when we can burn you, too, you and your Catholic whore. You promise to keep your mouth shut, fancy-boy, and maybe we'll let you go."

"If we die here it will be murder — " Morann began. Johnnie began to laugh.

"What's one death more or less after the past twenty years?"

"That's not so," Mary cried. "Ulster is more than a battle-ground. Are you all so afraid of life that destruction is all you can think of to do?"

The dark man glared at her. "It is now, bitch, it is now — " He screwed the top off the gas tin and started forward.

Morann thrust Mary backward and grabbed for the doors. They shuddered as the UDA men tried to slide them back open, but the lock was a good one and the glass reinforced.

"Never mind," came a shout from beyond. "We can burn you from outside as well as from within!"

"Call the Constabulary!" Morann pushed Mary in the direction of the phones. "I'm going to turn on the watering system they embedded in the roof to keep the grass green — " He disappeared through one of the office doors.

When he came back, Mary was staring towards the entry, where orange light flickered dimly through the doors. In another moment light began to flare through the glass dome above them as well.

"I think the dome is reinforced too well for them to break it," said Morann. "I hope so — " In his face she saw the old uncertainty returning, reached out and grasped his arm.

"Moranos ..." she spoke in the old tongue, "Remember who you are, and what you know. Was it not you yourself that set the first bruiden aflame?"

A shudder ran through him and he straightened. "I remember," he whispered, "and though I die for it, I will complete the magic."

"The power of this land is yours, through me," she answered him. She closed her eyes and reached out to the earth below and around them. At first she felt nothing, then came a quiver as if something long asleep were stirring at last. Mary's memories began to fade. She was Macha once more, and the connection made between them in that other life still strong enough to link them now.

"A noble hostel is the Brugh of Learning," said Moranos, "perfect in proportion, strong shall it stand! In earth it is cradled, by water protected, by air consecrated, by fire transformed!"

His voice deepened in incantation, reverberating through the room. Macha was raising and extended it into the building around her. Just so the magic had cycled between them when they lay together; desperation made it greater now.

"Palace of learning and lore of ancient days,
Praise of the poets, protection of warriors,
Flower of fertile fields, craftworkers' skill,
Will and wisdom in this brugh are welded."

Above the sound of his chanting rose a wilder music, not warpipes but the shrilling of sirens. Outside wheels screeched as their enemies sped away. But Moranos continued to sing.

"A place of peace, this palace, and of understanding,
Hands clasped in friendship, honour upholding,
Old tales and new tribes together finding healing,
Sealed by song, thus do I set the spell!"

Moranos' voice faltered. As his song faded, Macha felt the power that had sustained her ebbing into the earth and remembered that her name was also Mary. She swayed, and Morann took a step forward and caught her in his arms.

Queen and Druid they had been, but as the sirens grew louder, those identities were fading. Already what they had done was becoming like something remembered from a dream, or from the video they had seen inside. And yet she still retained an awareness that had not been there before.

"The fire is going out, I think, but something is different," she said.

"Yes." With wondering eyes he looked around him. "They meant destruction but they worked magic. This place is truly a *sidbrugh* now. I have studied it for so long, but I am just beginning to understand ...

"The Gaels made the forty metre structure — the bruiden — to honour their own gods, then filled it with the power of the neolithic culture whose descendants they had conquered. They burned it to send it to the gods, but they turfed over the mound with native soil. Ulster was as divided then as it is now. That is why they built the mound. The druids of Ard Macha were trying to make their two peoples into one!" He grasped her arms.

"Do you understand what I am trying to say? At Emain Macha the old and the new were bound together in one great act of magic. And now there is this Centre, filled with old magic and consecrated by fire. It is a new link between Ulster and the Otherworld!"

Above then the glow of the flames had faded. Someone was banging on the door. Morann straightened, all uncertainty gone. Then he turned to Mary and smiled, and she saw that something of the Druid still looked out of his eyes.

"Well, my Queen," he said, "shall we let them in?"

She reached up and slipped her arm through his, and together they went forward.

HISTORICAL NOTE

This story was inspired by the creation of the Educational and Visitors' Centre at Navan Fort in Armagh whose building began in 1992. The design is as described in the story, as are the archaeological findings at Emain Macha. However Mary Macrory, Rob Morann, and the dramatic events accompanying the construction of the Centre are fiction.

The stated intent of the Centre is to "provide a focus for the community's diverse cultural traditions" and "an opportunity to explore a common heritage far back beyond the unhappy divisions of more recent history." May it indeed be so.

For more information on Emain Macha and the Centre, see Emania (Bulletin of the Navan Research Group, c/o School of Geosciences, Queen's University, Belfast BT7 1NN*), especially C.J. Lynn's article, "The Iron Age Mound in Navan Fort," in number 10, and the discussion of the Navan Centre project in number 11.*

Notes on the Contributors

JAMES BRANCH CABELL was born in Richmond, Virginia and published his first novel when he was twenty-five. This book *The Eagle's Shadow* was the first of many successful works in which Cabell pursued a fascination with medieval literature and mythology. In a marvellous sequence of eighteen books, which included poetry, essays, and fiction, he told "The Biography of Manuel," a multi-dimensional character who reflected Cabell's own concerns whilst enabling him to relate a kind of mythical inner history of the Western world. He attained notoriety in 1919 when his novel *Jurgen* was labelled "vicious and indecent" and banned. In time it was re-instated and Cabell's fame was established. He died in 1958.

ANNE CAMERON's novels include *Stubby Amberchuck and the Holy Grail, The Journey* and *The Dreamspeaker,* which won the 1979 Gibson Award for Literature and whose film version received seven Canadian film awards. Two collections of North-West Coast native myths, *Daughters of Copper Woman* and *Dzelerhons* have become best sellers all over North America, along with her six children's books. She is also an accomplished poet, with several volumes in print. *Tales of the Cairds* from which the story included here is taken, was published in 1989. Anne Cameron lives in Powell River, British Columbia.

MARGARET ELPHINSTONE has worked as a writer and gardener in various parts of Scotland. She is the author of two novels, *The Incomer* (1987) and *A Sparrow's Flight* (1989), as well as two gardening books. She has published poetry and short stories, including *Outside Eden* (1990). She is currently working on a new novel while teaching English Studies at Strathclyde University.

SIAN HAYTON was born in Liverpool in 1944. She was educated in Paisley and at the RSAMD in Glasgow. Her brilliantly realized trilogy of novels *Cells of Knowledge* (which won The Scotsman's first Book of the Year award in 1989), *Hidden Daughters* (1990), and *The Last Flight* (1994), exemplify the very best of historical Celtic writing.

CAITLIN MATTHEWS is a singer, musician and the author of twenty-one books on mythology, spirituality and Celtic Tradition. Her best known works are *The Celtic Book of the Dead,* a card system for exploring the inner worlds of the Celts, *Sophia, Goddess of Wisdom,* and *the Arthurian Tarot* which she co-wrote with her husband, John Matthews. She has a shamanic counselling practice in Oxford.

JOHN MATTHEWS is the author of thirty books, including several collections of essays and a volume of poetry, *Merlin in Calydon,* published in 1981. He has published numerous short stories, including the collection *Song of Taliesin* (1993). Widely in demand as a teacher and speaker, he has recently begun to turn to the art of storytelling, and has in production *The Story-Tellers Pack* a method of creating stories by with and for listeners of all ages. He lives in Oxford with his wife, the writer Caitlín Matthews, their son, Emrys, and two ginger cats.

ANN MORAY is the author of the celebrated novel *The Rising of the Lark* (1978) and of a glittering collection of Celtic love stories *A Fair Stream of Silver* (1966) from which the story printed here is taken.

DWINA MURPHY-GIBB is an Irish-born writer and artist, an award winning poet and playwright, and the patroness of the Order of Bards Ovates and Druids. She is the author of *Cormac: the Seers* (1993), and *The King Making* (1994), the first parts of a trilogy of novels about Cormac Mac Airt, a third century Irish Peace-King. She lives in Oxfordshire and Miami Beach, Florida, with her husband Robin Gibb and son Robin-John.

DIANA PAXSON is the author of many short stories and novels, including the popular "Wystria" series. In recent years she has begun to produce a series of powerful novels about the Celtic peoples, beginning with *The White Raven* in 1988. Since then she has written *The Serpent's Tooth* and *Master of Earth and Water* written with Adrienne Martine-Barnes. She also writes bardic poetry and composes for the Celtic harp. She lives in Berkeley, California with her husband, the writer Jon DeCles.

DAVID SPANGLER was born in Columbus, Ohio in 1945. In 1951, he and his parents moved to Morocco, North Africa, where they lived for six years. During that time David began having intense mystical experiences that brought him into contact with the spiritual dimension of reality. He was a co-ordinator of the Findhorn Foundation from 1970 to 1973, and is a Lindisfarne Fellow. Since his return to America in 1973 he has lectured widely on the idea of a New Age, designed and taught classes at the University of Wisconsin and Milwaukee, and worked as a consultant and games designer for Lucasfilm games. His books include *Revelation: Birth of a New Age, Emergence: The Rebirth of the Sacred* and *Reimagination of the World* (with William Irwin Thompson). His latest work, *Manifestation: The Inner Art* will be published in 1995.

R.J. STEWART is a Scots author, composer, and musician. His career spans twenty three years of touring, recording, writing, and composing. He has thirty-one books in publication world-wide, of both fiction and non-fiction, and his work has been translated into French, Dutch, German, Spanish, Portuguese, Italian, and Japanese. As a composer and musician he has written, directed and recorded five LP records, a series of cassettes, and written music and songs for feature films, television, radio and the theatre. He lives in England.

ROSEMARY SUTCLIFF is one of the premier historical novelists of our time. Her brilliant evocation of the Arthurian world, *Sword at Sunset* won her great acclaim, and her numerous children's novels (including *The Lantern Bearers* which won the Carnegie Medal in 1959) have made her among the most popular and best loved children's authors in the world. She died in 1992.

HENRY TREECE is best known as an historical novelist and writer of children's books, but he was also a fine poet, and in his youth was a founding member of the New Apocalypse movement, a group of young poets dedicated to bringing to their work a deeper understanding of myth and its relationship to everyday life. This is born out in all of Treece's work, though he soon left the movement behind. His best works are his Celtic and Dark Age novels, including *Red Queen, White Queen* (1958), *The Great Captains* (1956), and *The Green Man* (1966). He died in 1966.

PETER TREMAYNE is the pseudonym of a well-known Celtic scholar, who as well as writing several fine historical studies, has also produced a number of fast-paced Celtic novels, including the trilogy *Fires of Lan-Kern* (1980), *Destroyers of Lan-Kern* (1981) and *Buccaneers of Lan-Kern* (1982) and the powerful story of the druidess and warrior woman Scathach in *Island of Shadows* (1991), in which scholarship and Celtic magic go hand in hand.

PETER VANSITTART read history at Oxford University, taught and lectured on History and English and is a regular reviewer in various leading newspapers and periodicals. He is the author of more than twenty-one novels, three books for children and has written and compiled seven books of non-fiction, including *Voices from the Great War,* a narrative anthology which was adapted for the stage. In 1969 he won the Society of Authors Travelling Scholarship, and in 1981 he was one of six recipients of the first Writers' Bursaries awarded by the Arts Council.

ROBIN WILLIAMSON first sprang to fame in the sixties as the lead singer, virtuoso instrumentalist and founder of The Incredible String Band. He influenced a generation of musicians as diverse as John Lennon, Bob Dylan, Robert Plant and the Eurythmics. After 1974, Williamson developed a contemporary song-writing style based on Celtic instrumentation and tradition and has become increasingly known throughout the world as a story-teller. His first book of stories *The Craneskin Bag* was published by Canongate in 1989. He lives in Wales and California.

Further reading

Most of the works listed here are either by the contributors or constitute what, in the opinion of the editor, constitutes the very best of modern Celtic writing. Not all of the books listed are by Celts, but every one of them reflects the vision and power of that people.

All titles were published in London, unless otherwise stated.

Bradley, Marion Zimmer. *The Mists of Avalon,* Michael Joseph, London 1989.

Cabell, James Branch. *Jurgen,* McBride, New York,, 1919.

——, *Figures of Earth,* McBride, New York,, 1921.

——, *The Cream of the Jest,* MacBride, New York 1923.

Cameron, Ann. *Daughters of Copper Woman,* Press Gang, Vancouver 1981.

——, *Stubby Amberchuck and the Holy Grail,* Harbour Publishing, Madeira Park BC, 1987.

——, *Tales of the Cairds,* Harbour Publishing, Madeira Park BC, 1989.

——, *Dreamspeaker,* Harbour Publishing, Madeira Park BC, 1990.

——, *The Journey,* Harbour Publishing, Madeira Park BC, 1992.

Crowley, John. *Little, Big,* Methuen, 1983.

De Lint, Charles. *Riddle of the Wren,* Ace Books, New York 1984.

——, *Greenmantle,* Ace Books, New York 1988.

——, *Moonheart,* Pan Books, 1989.

——, *Jack, the Giant Killer,* Ace Books, New York 1990.

Elphinstone, Margaret. *A Sparrow's Flight,* Polygon, Edinburgh 1989.

——, *An Apple from a Tree,* The Women's Press, 1991.

Fairfax, John. *Adrift on the Starbrow of Taliesin,* Phoenix, Newbery, 1974.

Flynn, Casey. *Most Ancient Song,* Bantam, New York 1991.

——, *The Enchanted Isles,* Bantam, New York 1991.

Godwin, Parke. *Firelord,* Bantam, New York 1982.

——, *Beloved Exile,* Bantam, New York 1986.

——, *The Last Rainbow,* Bantam, New York 1986.

Haldeman, Linda. *The Last Born of Elvenwood,* Souvenir Press, 1978.

Hayton, Sian. *Cells of Knowledge,* Polygon, Edinburgh 1989.

——, *Hidden Daughters,* Polygon, Edinburgh 1992.

——, *The Last Flight,* Polygon, Edinburgh 1994.

Holdstock, Robert. *Mythago Wood,* Gollancz, London 1984.

——, *Lavondyss,* Gollancz, London 1988.

——, *The Hollowing,* HarperCollins, London 1993.

James, John. *Votan*, Cassell, London 1966.
——, *Not for all the Gold in Ireland*, Cassell, London 1968.
——, *Men Went to Cattraeth*, Cassell, London 1969.
——, *The Bridge of Sand*, Hutchinson, London 1976.
Kennealy, Patricia. *The Copper Crown*, New American Library, New York 1986.
——, *The Throne of Scone*, New American Library, New York 1986.
——, *The Silver Branch*, New American Library, New York 1988.
Macavoy, R.A. *The Book of Kells*, Bantam, New York 1985.
Matthews, John. *The Song of Taliesin*, Aquarian, London 1992.
——, (Ed) *From the Isles of Dream*, Floris Books, Edinburgh; Lindisfarne Press, New York 1993.
Moray, Ann. *A Fair Stream of Silver*, Longmans, London 1966.
——, *The Rising of the Lark*, Longmans, London 1978.
Murphy-gibb, Dwina. *Cormac: The Seers*, Pan Books, London 1992.
Paxson, Diana. *The White Raven*, William Morrow, New York 1988.
——, *The Serpent's Tooth*, William Morrow, New York 1992.
Roberts, Keith. *The Boat of Fate*, Hutchinson, London 1971.
Stewart, R.J. *Magical Tales*, Thorsons, London 1990.
Sutcliff, Rosemary. *The Lantern Bearers*, Oxford University Press, 1959.
——, *Sword at Sunset*, Hodder & Stoughton, London 1963.
——, *Mark of the Horse Lord*, Oxford University Press, 1963.
——, *Sun Horse, Moon Horse*, Bodley Head, London 1975.
Treece, Henry. *The Dark Island*, Bodley Head, London 1952.
——, *The Golden Strangers*, Bodley Head, London 1956.
——, *The Great Captains*, Bodley Head, London 1956.
——, *The Green Man*, Bodley Head, London 1956.
——, *Red Queen, White Queen*, Bodley Head, 1958.
Tremayne, Peter. *The Fires of Lan-Kern*, Bailey Bros & Swinfen, Kent 1980.
——, *Destroyers of Lan-Kern*, Bailey Bros & Swinfen, Kent 1981.
——, *The Buccaneers of Lan-Kern*, Bailey Bros & Swinfen, Kent 1982.
——, *My Lady of Hy-Brasil & Other Stories*, Donald L. Grant, Rhode Island, 1987.
——, *Ravenmoon*, Mandarin Books, London 1988.
——, *Raven of Destiny*, Mandarin Books, London 1989.
——, *Island of Shadows*, Mandarin Books, London 1991.
Vansittart, Peter. *Lancelot*, Peter Owen, London 1988.
——, *Parsifal*, Peter Owen, London 1989.
——, *The Death of Robin Hood*, Peter Owen, London 1991.
Williamson, Robin. *The Craneskin Bag*, Canongate, Edinburgh 1989.